THE TROJAN PLAGUE

THE
TROJAN PLAGUE

COUNTDOWN TO ARMAGEDDON

PIERCE ROBERTS

March 2020 Second Edition

ISBN: 9781686134265

ACKNOWLEDGEMENTS

I would like to give thanks to my lifelong friend Marty who is an ency-clopedia of all thing humorous, ironic and things nonsensically political. He is the Good Humor Man.

My wife Kathy puts up with my writing habit and looks on with curios-ity as I hunt and peck my way through one chapter to the next. Literally these stories take life from one index finger working overtime. Thank you my love for putting up with me for all these years.

I also must recognize that my story lines revolve around the profes-sion of Veterinary Medicine which has provided me with many adventures and a lifetime of enjoyment. Please note the veterinarians are almost always the good guys.

Last I want to thank Mike Valentino for the fine editing job he per-formed .

Our familiar characters are already started on a new adventure, The Atlantis Gene, which will be released later this year.

DEDICATION

This book is dedicated to my late son Christopher who enjoyed tales where Good defeated Evil whether it be a galaxy away or in our backyard. Love you and miss you!

Deuteronomy 33:27
The eternal God is a dwelling place, and underneath are the everlasting arms; And He drove out the enemy from before you, And said "Destroy".

1 John NIV 5:19
We know we are children of God, and that the whole world is under control of the evil one.

CONTENTS

CHAPTER 1

East of Point Hope, Alaska

The Far North
19 March

It had been a long, unusually bitter winter which had relegated the postal and provision delivery services, who made regular quarterly deliveries to remote Inuit villages, to treacherous emergency overland routes. The unrelenting extreme winds, frigid sub-zero temperatures and blinding snows had kept even hardened brush pilots firmly grounded for safety. As the long weeks passed, a decision was made to revert to the old-fashioned way to transport critical supplies and medicines like insulin to 'the People', as the Inuit preferred to be identified. Emergency overland Snow Cats and dog sled teams were enlisted. Lives were at stake.

Rich McKnight was brought in as close as mechanically possible to his first two villages by Snow Cats, which could only come in so far. His yapping dog team was unloaded along with a double tandem rigged sled that would be pulled by his ten dog team of mixed hound huskies. Two more dogs would follow with him behind the pulling team to provide relief from any injuries acquired on the hazardous icy trek. Rich had figured a three day inbound trip depending on their final route and trail conditions, followed by two more days to the second village as he looped back to his pick-up point. A hardy third generation Alaskan commercial fisherman and trapper, McKnight sported a heavy brush beard peppered with red, black and gray that framed his ruddy wind-blown complexion. He was tall, six three, a forty-two year old father of six children. The considerable fee he commanded to take on this risky job seemed a no- brainer; he could feed all those hungry mouths till ice out in May, then he would sell his winter fur catch into a depressed market. This year, he figured, every penny would have to be pinched.

He rested and refreshed the dogs every two to three miles during the short daylight hours, starting early in the predawn moonlight and ending as evening twilight gave away to the star studded black of night. Not much time to travel but that was winter in the far North. With temperatures dipping multiple tens of degrees below zero each evening, the dogs buried themselves in the snow, content to be covered in the warmer than air blanket of frozen water. Rich set up a small one man heat reflective pop up tent and wormed himself into an Everest rated sleeping sack. He ate dried Ptarmigan and apricots, peanuts and hard biscuits, forcing it down with hot chocolate prepared from snow melted into a steaming pot of liquid heat, using a small propane hot plate. Spartan, but he was looking forward to soon feasting on seal, walrus and possibly polar bear after he reached the small village.

Only one more day, Rich thought as he drifted asleep on that second evening.

The next morning seemed to begin brighter as the team broke trail for the last leg of the journey. By noon McKnight should have been able to spot the tell-tale smoke from the cook stoves, but as he double checked his GPS navigator, he sensed something was amiss. He was within one mile under clear crisp conditions and the typical visual signs of village life were not yet apparent on the low horizon.

Something is wrong.

"Mush –move on!" he commanded firmly and the dogs sensing the urgency in his voice pulled hard, generating ice grinding momentum. Soon the tiny village was clearly visible, compact buildings of plywood and tin, layered in drifted snow. Rich pulled up the team, brushed the ice off of his frozen beard and dropped his polarized snow goggles down to his chest to look through a compact spotting scope.

No smoke, no dogs carrying on. This is not good.

He took the team forward, the sleds fish tailing on the thick crust of ice covering the compacted snow. No one had traveled this major trail for many weeks, not man nor beast.

Suddenly his lead dog, Hank Williams, Jr., pulled up, the hair on his neck bristling. His instinctive alert put the rest of the team instantly on defense, frozen in position, staring intently toward the village, sniffing the air. They sensed something and despite his urging and firm commands, they were not moving forward, something they had never refused to do before.

McKnight's heart was pounding as he hand checked his holstered .45 caliber Smith and Wesson revolver —something he carried as an emergency survival weapon under his seal skin parka. It was a heavy gun that could handle most any problem on these dangerous trails, his extra insurance.

Rich then grabbed the 35 Remington sled rifle from its moose hide scabbard and checked its action.

He put out the sled anchors, pulled up his goggles and moved on snow-shoes for that last quarter mile. The village was only about a dozen small residences plus a multipurpose community center that served as a church, post office and gathering place. That multipurpose building was well built but was small, less than one thousand square feet, just enough room for the village's thirty-one residents.

Horror waited just around the corner as McKnight entered from the south into the Eskimo village.

CHAPTER 2

The small houses he passed were abandoned, doors wide open with wind-blown snow filling their entrances. Rich methodically checked each, calling out for signs of life. Igloo style kennels had chained dead dogs which appeared to have either starved or froze to death. The dogs in the primitively fenced kennel yards were still intact, but those housed traditionally, in the open, had mostly been ravished by foxes and other protein starved scavengers. Every home was open and abandoned as he checked and worked deeper into the town center. This village lived off the sea and the winter ice was backed up in stacked sheets behind the community center. Kayaks and old wooden work boats were laying upside down on cradles where they had been relegated for the winter to the right of the community center. As he came around to the left, horror hung from the village game dressing hooks.

Two men, two women and one teen boy were hanging frozen from skinning gambrels, upside down, hung through the Achilles of their heels, hides partially ripped from their bodies. This was the place where seals, polar bears, walrus and caribou normally hung to be skinned and processed. Now it was an altar of murder.

McKnight who had seen the horrors of war in Iraq, felt the bitter bile of nausea rise to his throat.

My God, who could do this?

He turned away, doubled over to control his gag reflex, suddenly aware of the possible danger he was facing. He gasped several icy breaths, holding them to settle his stomach and then made his way carefully over to the community center. Its front door was covered with blood and hair, streaked in long trails. A bloodied small hand axe was buried firmly into the doorframe by the doorknob. There was no lock, and McKnight pushed hard but could only barely move the door. It was blocked somehow.

He loosened the small axe and moved around to the rear of the building where he knew the mail was stored in a locked room, as required by US Postal regulations. He found a heavy iron harpoon leaning against the side of the building and jammed it between the door and the frame and forced the door open, breaking the dead silence with a deafening CRACK! of the splintering wood. McKnight pushed past equipment and parcels of dried pelts that had been piled inside against the door and then slid around the small service counter into the main room.

"Jesus Christ Almighty!" he swore as he found what looked like the remaining villagers huddled into two groups, frozen to death. The women, children and the Ancients were pasted together, layered in fur blankets, frozen it appeared as they slept. Six men faced the barricaded front door with shotguns and rifles on their laps, sitting defensively. All were blue gray with frosted ice crystals coating their exposed flesh. Twenty-six souls frozen in time on the gray painted wooden floor, scared enough to hide and succumb to slow death rather than face whatever forced them out of the warmth of their homes and into the unheated shelter of the community center.

McKnight was petrified. What or who could manifest this demise of a tough, self-sufficient people? Was their mortal enemy still out there waiting for a new victim—possibly him? He peered out the back door using all his well-tuned senses. He then made a mad, panicked dash, nearly falling many times as he ran breathlessly back to the sleds and the security of the dogs. He dug deep into his personal duffle bag and found his SAT phone. His hands fumbled as he yanked off his mittens with his teeth and powered up the device. He pushed the emergency service icon, hands trembling. It took almost a minute to connect through a series of satellites. The US Coast Guard picked up the distress signaling call.

"This is Rich McNight and I'm at Tennita Village on an official mail and provision run. They are all dead-everyone-I mean everyone and everything. Get the hell up here right now and bring a lot of body bags! I am scared shitless and need immediate help here. *God help us all!"*

CHAPTER 3

Western Border

Fort Peck Indian Reservation
6 April

The small pack of Timber Wolves were just past their late winter breeding season and the two young females in the group would soon give birth to litters of pups. These two and their mates were led by an old barren alpha female and her mate. The male had been severely injured two winters before but still was able to help her maintain control over the pack. The two younger pairs were likely to either split from them or take control once their spring pups matured into hunters; either scenario would likely mean the senior canines barely surviving as carrion scavengers and ultimately starving to death. This was nature's way. The strongest survive, the weak perish.

The pack was now surrounding a yearling white bison, a coveted rarity for the Plains Indians, which had been intentionally shot with a 30.06 through a rear leg to become live bait. That left rear leg dangled from the smashed bone, a compound tibial fracture, useless. The wolves had immediately sensed the animal's handicap and attacked her right rear hamstring while the bison twirled wildly as the ravenous predators tore at her flesh. Unable to lift the good leg to defend herself with slashing hooves without falling, the bison was doomed. Once that leg's support was severed the animal would go down with only the hope of a rapid death before being consumed.

After eight to ten expert passes, the weakened animal went down with an exhausted 'huff,' powerful jaws tearing and crushing her carotids and trachea. Merciful death came in a shower of crimson blood over the snow-colored animal.

The alpha was rightfully the first to tear at the quivering warm belly, opening up the abdomen with a tympanic release of gases. She pulled and pushed moving the steaming belly fat and intestines until she had expertly located the nutritious liver. She fed deliberately, the others pacing to and fro, salivating in anticipation. Finally she backed away, her face bloody from feeding. Next her mate, the handicapped male was in line and he also went straight to the liver. That was the signal for the others to feed, so growling and jockeying, they satiated their week-long hunger. The old male moved, blocking their way to the liver because it was the easiest for him to consume. Two years before during a similar early spring hunt, a cow elk protecting a new-born calf had swung around and squarely hit him in the head with a powerful rear leg kick. The blow had sent him flying through the air with a ruptured right eye, fractured eye socket and a crushed right mandible. Had it been in the fall, he would have never survived the approaching long winter. Blinded in the right eye, with a jaw that only opened halfway, he was forced to spend his entire summer eating insects, grubs and small vertebrates for which he painstakingly foraged. Thin and weakened, he should have died but the ensuing winter was a bounty of food and mild. Slowly he was able to work the fractured, fibrous jaw with some strength but with only about half of his normal mouth biting power. He could not kill a large animal and really only functioned as a decoy, distracting prey while the others took the beasts down. He was simply an accessory to the pack, only included because of his Alpha mate. When the pregnant pairs finally split off to raise their families, they would become a pack of two and likely not survive another winter.

They fed, nervously looking up often to survey their surroundings for others that might try to poach their kill—especially the cougars that seemed to appear out of nowhere.

The Alpha suddenly sensed a sound that they had heard often over the last two weeks. It was the whirling buzz of a small remote drone which had passed back and forth above them several times before. At first they scattered, but then they were simply curious and with bellies full, laid and watched as it passed lower and lower, each pass slower, making less noise.

A tiny red beam of light projected from the drone and danced from one wolf to another. Then another beam projected out. The drone hovered steadily above and with a quick pneumatic 'pop' spat two mini-darts of powerful sedation at the old male and the Alpha. They howled in protest, biting at their flanks, while the other wolves scattered in panic. Soon the old wolf couple was lying unconscious and their attackers moved in to claim their prizes.

The countdown to Armageddon stood at 10.

CHAPTER 4

Tristar Veterinary

Biologics Office of the CEO
Leipzig, Germany
17 April

"It is my pleasure to welcome our executive leadership to this progress meeting updating the status of our critical field experiment. I'm happy to report all our goals have been met and we will launch our preliminary bio-attack next week as planned. All specimens are acquired in the United States and have been infected with the new virus. They will be released in four major metropolitan areas to maximize their impact on the general population. I estimate within ten days of their discovery and elimination, the CDC will have identified this new, unique, unknown strain of Rabies. Sometime after that, they will realize that they have no firewall against it, our secret novel pathogen, and ultimately will turn to us to produce a new vaccine against the disease. We have strategically positioned ourselves to be THE only company in the world with the physical capacity to develop and produce their emergency vaccination with the speed and in the volume they will require.

"Little do they know, it's our virus and we already have that vaccine in production. Millions of doses will be needed and we will do our duty and ship a two dose version. In that second or booster dose, will be a unique surprise—our recently tested human specific add-on, that will be shed by those second dosed animals in their saliva, urine, fecal matter or if the animal coughs or sneezes, airborne. It is a neurotrophic viron, viral RNA hybridized with the BSE or Mad Cow prion, and it will turn loose a proverbial zombie apocalypse on the Americans."

As Hans Vogel concluded, he scanned for a reaction from the three others sitting at the large black walnut conference table. There was none.

"So, Hans, how did those three field tests with our product conclude?" Frederic Wiltz asked.

"All the test subjects became clinical. The homeless Dutchman was intoxicated when the effects of the viron peaked and unfortunately he was too close to a street canal and went in. Our field observers said he was crazed but hit the water and drowned before they could establish any aggression toward the 'normal population'. The second subject was a college student in Toronto that walked right into the path of a TTC bus after her incubation time. The best result was the Alaskan trial where a single man was infected in the same way as the others had been, with what they had thought was an asthma inhaler. The viron, TVB1975, was immediately absorbed into his bloodstream and was inoculated into the brain tissue within a minute. Our 'Missionary' observer had to run for his life as the man was severely clinical in eight hours, much faster than our primate trials suggested. He butchered five people and hung them from meat hooks and the report from the US Coast Guard indicated the balance of the citizens of this village barricaded themselves in a building and chose to freeze to death rather than face that crazed individual. Probably felt he was a demon. Three weeks had passed before they were discovered and unfortunately we have no idea where our infected man ended up as the observer also disappeared after his last report, a day before we could extract him. It is unlikely either will be found in that God forsaken wasteland."

"Was there anything on our employee that could tie him back to us if he would be discovered?" asked the third man, Yeager Martin.

"No, he carried only fake documents and his SAT phone had a 72 hour non-use self-destruct function, which had been activated so basically the guts of the phone burn out, like an electrical short. There also was no memory function or recall function on that phone," Vogel replied.

The fourth man, with a tall, muscular, thick build pushed himself up slowly from his black leather executive chair and walked to the head of the table. He was older, his face deeply lined, nearly pure white hair, pale blue eyes and a trimmed short white mustache. He was the only participant not wearing a designer business suit. Instead he sported a navy blue crew neck sweater and white linen slacks. Vogel sat down submissively as the man silently displaced him.

"Well my friends," he started, "we appear to be on our verge of our revenge, our new final solution which will allow our followers to celebrate victory after all these years over our enemy, the United States and the Jewish Financial Complex. Over seven decades have passed since my father's escape from the collapse of Berlin. He would be proud of our efforts to revenge the destruction of our fatherland and our eventual culling of the modern weaklings that now call themselves Germanic. Yes, they are Germanic but not of pure blood, Aryan blood!

"We are now unconventional warriors in this fight to restore the glories of the Third Reich. We will topple the most powerful nation on earth and restore the greatest race to its rightful dominance over the weak, inferior ones. We will select, breed and produce our Pure Culture. All others will submit or be destroyed. No Slavs, Jews or non Aryans will be included and eventually will become extinct. In my blood are the genes of the greatest world leader of all time. That is why we will succeed."

Caesar H. Mendoza nodded to the others and turned, moving deliberately in exiting the room.

The H in his name represented his father's surname ---Hitler.

The unknown son from the demonic Nazi dictator.

CHAPTER 5

Mall of America

Bloomington, Minnesota
May 5

The automatic doors slid open silently and the Alpha female staggered back and forth causing the glass sliders to shutter open and close. Several people attempting to exit to the outside, seeing the wolf, turned screaming as the animal found its way into the retail area. She saw the motion and smelled the fear of the shoppers as she surged in a disease-fueled rage, heavily salivating, foaming streams of liquid. The bright mall lighting burned her eyes and the canine darted forward into the panicked crowd, slashing at any movement, bouncing to and fro off the scattering crowd. A senior woman was pushed down by the surge and screamed as the wolf slashed at her thigh, easily severing her femoral artery. A twenty something woman, who felt she could talk down a simply frightened beast, approached it, arms out, speaking soft platitudes.

"Calm down my beautiful creature, listen only to my voice and I will get you out of here. Calm and peace, calm and peace."

The sick animal only saw the flames of hell as her brain burned with pain and swiftly leapt forward, tearing three fingers from the woman's out-stretched right hand while moving past her.

Two unarmed mall security guards rushed to the scene but pan-icked at the site of so much blood and the animal's aggression. A pair of ex- Marines and a man in a ranch hat grabbed nearby benches and corralled the animal forcing her, pushing her away from them toward a marbled corner. As they did, an armed policewoman ran up and shot the wolf twice, ending the crisis. A second level crowd observing the drama unfold, cheered as the shots echoed loudly through the mall levels. The wolf expired, free of her insane torture.

Five people had been bit, two seriously. The old woman had gone into shock from her massive blood loss and died before paramedics arrived.

The TriStar Nazi's first new rabies virus field test had been a great success. It had been captured on dozens of cell phones and mall secu-rity cameras. Fear and panic would seize most who watched what the news media would call the 'Weird Wolf' attack unfold. Once the virus was typed, the CDC would understand the magnitude of the crisis they faced.

Six days later, the handicapped mate of the Alpha would wander outside the Denver Airport in a short-term parking lot. He however would not directly infect anyone as a parking shuttle bus hit and killed him as he darted out from between the rows of automobiles. Because of his emaciated condition, he was mistaken for a coyote and placed by the Asian bus driver, who was wearing gloves and surgery mask because he was undergoing chemo treatment for leukemia, into a nearby dumpster.

The next day, reports of sick, odd acting raccoons were reported around Arlington, Virginia and the local animal control shot several and submitted them for rabies testing. One day later a crazed tomcat at-tacked a parish priest who regularly fed feral cats in the alleys around his South Boston Church, shredding his face. He was hospitalized and the cat destroyed.

The seeds of the Apocalypse had been planted.

CHAPTER 6

Westerville, Wisconsin

June 6

Dr. Tom O'Dell had just arrived home after a hectic day of farm calls, his busy dairy practice keeping both him and his partner running from farm to farm. He loved his work but unlike two years before as a single man, relished coming home to his new family.

His black lab Jed had grayed a little around his muzzle but as always was the first to greet him with his usual canine enthusiasm. Right behind him was his wife, Dr. Kate Vensky, who was the true love of his life and the mother of their almost one year old son, Robert Nelson O'Dell. They had settled into a familiar routine now; Tom in his practice and Kate, a working mother who still was a USDA Supervisor in charge of a region hundreds of miles away in the Southeast. Computers and a devoted husband allowed her to work from home and travel the twenty percent of time her job required. Highly respected for her problem solving intellect, the Government was willing to relax their normal employment requirements just to have her expertise.

Kate and Tom had met over two years before on a USDA project where they and others were trained and commissioned to find the source of worldwide mass animal die offs. During that investigation, they fell in love and survived the murder attempts of a war criminal physician who had fled Nazi Germany at the end of World War Two and settled into a life in the jungles of Argentina. There he experimented for decades, developing an anti-aging formula and a DNA based weapon of mass destruction. He was duly labeled 'The Destroyer' by a Lakota Sioux Shaman, Nelson Blackfeather, who had been haunted for decades with premonitions and dreams of this man's plague upon the earth. In the end, the evil Dr. Wilheim Berhetzel was killed by two of their team as they pursued the Nazi during his attempt to overthrow the government of the United States on a blizzard plagued Inauguration Day.

Kate gave Tom a kiss and hug as he entered the kitchen and pointed over to their son who smiled and waved to his dad as he swung back and forth in his Swing and Bounce. Tom stopped its action and picked his one year old son up.

The boy had thick jet black hair like his dad, hazel eyes like his mom, and started laughing as Tom gently tossed him up in the air.

"Check his diaper please," Kate asked, "I don't know if it's him or you, but one of the men in my life is pretty stinky."

"Must be me," Tom said peeking in the diaper, "I'm so used to it. I'm surprised you didn't pick up on it when I came in."

"I guess I was overwhelmed by your Irish good looks," she chided.

Tom was the classic tall, dark and handsome, with now a little gray in his black hair and carrying a few extra pounds due to Kate's good cooking.

"Thanks for that, there is no man in the county as lucky as me," Tom offered.

"Wow, in a county of 3,000, you're the luckiest. I'm overwhelmed."

"Wait a minute, I meant the country," Tom chuckled.

"That's nice, but I think you could do better."

"Ok, let me give this a little careful thought...There is no other woman in the universe that could make me happier, be a better mother or is more beautiful."

"Awwh, I love you too, honey. And you're the most handsome veterinarian in the county."

"Gee thanks. I'm honored, especially since there are only two veterinarians in the county." Tom laughed as Bobbie tried pushing his fist into his father's mouth.

"Looks like junior has had enough of this conversion," Kate added, "he wants your undivided attention, Daddy!"

"Between him and Jed, I'm going to be real busy!"

"By the way, Brad joining us for dinner and he should be here fairly soon.

"I asked him to come over because I received an alert from the CDC about those presumed rabies cases around the country and it looks like we are going to be recalled to Atlanta for an emergency meeting of our original 'die-offs' group. Only for a couple days. I already checked with your mom and dad and they are thrilled to take Bobbie and Jed for several days," Kate explained.

There was a brief knock at the screened porch door and Jed ran over barking aggressively.

"Lock up your mangy animal!" Brad Upton shouted through the door.

"Whatever you are selling, we already have one," Tom tossed back at the big man.

"Kate, talk some sense into these two flea bitten varmints. Start with the dog, he understands English better than that Irishman!"

"Jed, you know Brad's shiny head. Let him in," Tom yelled to the excited dog.

Immediately, the black lab backed off as Brad entered the kitchen and then jumped up licking at a laughing Brad.

"You old faker," Brad said rubbing the slobber from his face. Jed jumped down and lazily plopped down by Bobbie's playpen.

"Kate, you are as beautiful as ever," he said giving the woman he had once dated a light kiss on her cheek.

And Brad was right, Kate was fit, a dedicated runner and sported long darker auburn hair which she normally wore in a runner's ponytail. She looked much younger than her thirty-nine years. To top that all off, she was super intelligent, spoke five languages but was humble about her intellectual gifts. As Tom regretfully once said after a night of partying,

'You would never guess she is so smart by looking at her.' Boy, did that get him in trouble for a couple days.

"I got a text this morning from my supervisor in Chicago about pulling together the members of the original investigation group from two years ago and get everyone to Atlanta next week for a Thursday and Friday conference and because they are still on government payroll, they have to be there. I have two exceptions; Sally Rogers is due within a week with her fourth child so she will teleconference the meeting and Frank Grant is too sick with his cancer chemo for any of it. This must be pretty serious to have to have us there in person," Brad reasoned.

"Here is what I got from Atlanta this morning," Kate started, handing both the men a cold bottle of PBR, "those rabid animals that surfaced in the last few weeks were infected with a new strain of rabies. The CDC couldn't get a positive FA test on the brain tissues but still suspected it was rabies and took the testing all the way to the RNA level and confirmed it is a Rhabdoform virus with a structural variation from all the other known strains like raccoon and bat. It's so different it might be eventually classified separately. Here is the real problem. In the people that were actually bitten and who started the standard infiltration of the wound with the rabies serum and the follow-up vaccine series, it appears the therapy is not working. All are becoming clinical. To make matters worse it looks like the virus either persists on surfaces outside the body or may be infective without an actual bite."

"Why do they think that?" Tom asked.

"Because a total of five were bitten but now thirty-seven are infected. None of those not bitten had direct contact with the animals or their salvia. All the healthcare workers like the techs that removed the heads for submission wore gloves, gowns and eye protection. None wore respirator or antimicrobial masks. The current feeling is this is a likely highly lethal, highly infected, easily transmitted, potentially airborne mutation of the rabies virus. A true public health crisis."

"One of those four letter cluster things," Brad said somberly.

"Yes, one of the worst kind."

CHAPTER 7

Center for Disease Control

Atlanta, Georgia
June 12

"Thank you all for coming on such short notice. We would appreciate your cooperation, so please take your seats so we can get the program started.

"Again please be seated."

"I'm Dr. Ted Johnson, Head of Emerging Diseases here at the CDC and I am pleased to welcome you back. Unfortunately, the circumstances that brought you here are extremely serious. Last time we were together, we were searching a way to find answers, now we have answers framing some very serious questions. We will first go over some background information and then I will turn the podium over to Dr. Kate Vensky of the USDA, followed by Dr. Jules LeClerc from the Pasteur Institute and then Dr. Hans Vogel from Tristar Veterinary Biologics.

"You all received the CDC email alert last week with its general information. Be assured this health threat we are facing is a real and immediate danger to the nation and the world.

"Humans have dealt with the threat of rabies since probably the dawn of mankind, certainly since dogs were domesticated and Dr. LeClerc will give us an overview on the virus from the Institute named after the man who found a way to beat a disease that terrorized the world. Dr. Vogel will then review the process that will hopefully develop an effective vaccination. Rarely does the CDC subcontract out new vaccination development, but in this case only Tristar has the infrastructure in place to develop, test and produce with the speed, quantity and quality that will be necessary to neutralize this zoonotic threat.

"So. First we will review what has happened so far. The most publicized event was the wolf in the Mall of America. The biggest problem we are facing is the virus isolated from these attacks is the result of an unknown strain of rabies which looks to be spread conventionally through saliva and bites but also is infective when airborne. It appears to have high morbidity and a probable 100% mortality. Thirty-seven people from that single event are clinical now, undergoing coma therapy and none at this point are expected to survive. As you understand, it is a horrible way to die.

"I know most of you saw the social media posted cellphone videos that were also broadcast after the attack, but the actual security camera footage was not made public. We have put together an unedited real-time version for you to watch."

The lights in the large modern auditorium dimmed softly and the multiple Jumbo E or Exceptional High Def computer screens morphed from the CDC logo to the wolf staggering into the mall entrance and quickly showed the events leading to the wolf being shot. The room was buzzing with comments as the screens reverted back to the logo and the lights came up.

"Pretty graphic, I hope that doesn't give any of you nightmares. Again, that was the total real time video. In less than three minutes, our world as we know it was changed forever.

"The wolf was shipped here immediately by the Minnesota Public Health Service after they had a negative dFA test so we had her on the table within eighteen hours of the attack. We repeated the initial standard rabies protocol which was a true negative and completed a comprehensive necropsy including radiography, tissue cultures and advance virology testing using immunology, histopath and electron microscopy. We suspected rabies and confirmed a Rhabdoform virus that was unique in its appearance. Ninety-five percent is considered classic and five percent is novel. Here is an example of the classic bullet shape of a Rhabdoform and here is what looks like a rocket ship in the variant test virus. It is that small percentage that confused the standard dFA test reaction.

"The wolf was female, had not birthed a litter last year or was pregnant this year. She was nine years old, normal in all ways for her age with osteoarthritis, broken and worn teeth, normal blood chemistries and blood counts. Unlike most in the Minnesota wolf population, she was negative for heartworm and all the usual tick borne diseases. One strange thing, she had been microchipped by the University of Montana Wildlife Club as a two-week old pup in a population survey done to determine how far they move within their range and this one must have hitched a ride east as she was approximately one thousand miles as the crow flies from her birth den when she died. No one I've talked to can explain that.

"Now we are going to have Dr. Vensky go over the general field strategy which once we refine a consensus approach in our smaller work groups, will become your protocol to bring to all healthcare workers in your regions. I'm sorry but you are going to be fairly busy for a month or so bringing everyone under your supervision up to speed. *YOU* will be the authority, the direct line to Atlanta for your region. *ALL* press releases and critical information will come directly through us to you. You are not authorized to talk to any news outlets independently. You are only to be the conduit from us to the local public health and general healthcare employees. We don't want mass hysteria or a bunch of animals being euthanized for no reason. Nothing scares people like a non-treatable, one hundred percent lethal disease.

"On that happy note, I'm going to turn this over to Kate."

Kate came up to the stage dressed in gray slacks and a conservative white blouse. She was radiant, smiling and obviously enjoying taking on another major mystery. She was a problem solver–this was what she was born to do.

"Good morning everyone. I'm pleased so many of you could be here on such short notice. Let's hope we can expedite a solution that does not have us on the menu for some South American Army ants."

There was laughing and murmurs from the crowd as they remembered Kate's and Tom's, along with Joseph Blackfeather's, close encounter with the tiny hungry foragers, courtesy of the Nazi Berhetzel.

"Unfortunately, this new virus will keep all of us from any kind of normal life until we defeat it. There are a lot of questions to answer like where did it come from? Is it natural or perhaps the unintentional result of man's constant meddling with nature? We may never know but here are the numbers on potential animal vectors that live in close association with humans.

"There are about seventy-five million canines and ninety millions felines living in approximately forty percent of American households. Feral cat populations number in the tens of millions. Wild animals vectors that live in close proximity to population centers include raccoon, skunk, possum, fox, coyote, and bat. The small mammals that were generally excluded from being rabies carriers because they would not survive the bite attack of a vector, now must be included as potential threats because this disease may be airborne or persist in the environment. So, countless millions of mice, chipmunks, groundhogs, gophers and squirrels could bring the disease to your backyard.

"Currently, the only region where it is taking hold is Northern Virginia and Maryland. There the raccoon population seems highly susceptible and there is an effort to trap and destroy large numbers of the animals and about two hundred nuisance control trappers are setting box traps in a hundred mile radius of DC, euthanizing their catch and submitting the animals for testing. They are being made to wear biohazard suits and place the dead raccoons and the traps in trailered dumpsters filled with sealed ice packs, which are shipped overnight to Atlanta. In the last seven days, the CDC has processed over two thousand animals of which seven carried traditional rabies and one hundred thirteen that tested positive for the new strain. That is a huge number of infected animals when you take into account that in the Northern Virginia -Washington -Baltimore region there is estimated one raccoon for every twenty-five people.

"I was asked the question about placing poisons out but that simply is not safe with so many pets and humans in densely populated centers, plus it would be inhumane so if the virus really persists in the environment for any length of time, it would not solve the problem anyway.

"So our initial plan is isolate, vaccinate and eliminate. The details of which will be developed in our small groups. Brainstorm ideas with your colleagues this afternoon, then submit your plans, we are placing no time limit on you. You can work all night if you need. We will feed you and provide whatever help you require.

"Let's break for twenty minutes and I see Dr LeClerc has just arrived from Paris, so when we reconvene we will get some history on rabies from Jules. Be back in your seats at ten."

There was scattered applause, then the room quickly emptied as the assembly of scientists, split into coffee seekers and rest room rushers. Several sat in their seats talking on their cellphones while Brad, Tom and Kate gravitated to Jules.

"Bonjour, Mes Amies!" he greeted.

"Bonjour, Jules!" they announced in near unison.

Kate was awarded a true friendship hug and kisses on both cheeks; Tom and Brad, firm, warm handshakes.

This was the first time the four had reunited since Kate and Tom's wedding at the home of another friend, Jean DuBois, in his Paris court-yard garden two summers before. They had celebrated the wedding but also their successful mission to find and eliminate 'The Destroyer,' Wilheim Berhetzel. They had survived a deadly task where four of their friends died during the pursuit of the demonic Nazi. Their bond of friendship was cemented in their defeat of this evil.

"I am so happy to see you all again but wish it was while relaxing in my beautiful Paris and not under these circumstances. I'm afraid the scientific community in Europe will be in a total panic once the full details on this zoonosis is presented to them, something unfortunately I will be tasked to do at Le Pasteur after this conference. We better come up with a good solution, but unfortunately, either way, I am sure the EU will over-react with travel restrictions, and agricultural trade restrictions and such. Liberal politicians always overreact just to get votes," LeClerc explained.

LeClerc was in his mid-fifties, trim and fit with his dark hair now styled neatly, wearing tailored off white slacks and a black lightweight cotton crew neck pullover. A small silver monogram that identified a designer had been stitched on the left cuff that was pulled up just above his expensive Rolex. He was French and with that came a bit of sophisticated flare that intrigued women.

"To get you up to date, we have yet to duplicate Berhetzel's anti-aging formula in the laboratory but keep working on it. There is some missing factor or agent that we haven't hit upon. We even harvested three cubic yards of soil from his original mushroom garden and brought it to Paris and gathered ten thousand liters of water from the small crystalline river that they used for everything from drinking, cooking, bathing and feeding the stock to watering the crops. Our current thought is we are totally missing an element like an unknown or some rare extinct fungus or perhaps those people were just at the right place at the right time.

"As far as his DNA weapon is concerned, we are continuing to re-purpose it to kill at the cellular level cancer cells, bacteria, and parasites. So, whereas the gamma knife is a precise targeting tool, this would necessarily be exact in determining the target but would not have to be delivered in a precise way. Hopefully one pulse would kill all the defined targets. Our big concern is making sure there is no spillover into non targeted cells and also how much cancer cell death load the body can tolerate without adverse reactions. If all the cancer dies instantly what happens to all the cellular debris? We still have a long way to go but this has the potential for changing medicine as we know it!"

"Sounds great! How is Jean doing?" Brad asked.

"He is physically well but his memory is not quite as sharp and he has flashbacks to that night when Berhetzel shot and killed Robert, and nearly killed him. I suspect that the episodes he suffers just drag him down a little more each time. Thank God for Susan and the grandchildren —she makes sure he is rarely alone and that seems to help.

"So, my friends, this looks to be a real interesting problem that I hope, and I mean no offense, stays on your side of the Atlantic. I'll have some real good historical information on Rabies to go over and perhaps the virus has done this before and hopefully this new pathogen eventually can be limited and contained to those three regions where the positive animals surfaced. Vaccination will be essential and if what I am hearing about it possibly being airborne, then a human vaccine will also be essential. That will be difficult to accomplish because there will be a real phobia about mass immunizations; all those conspiracy theorists will have a field day!" Jules offered.

"Social media is already blowing this up. People are dumping pets in record numbers at shelters and the Greater DC Veterinary Association reports large numbers of requests for non-medical euthanasia. Most communities are posting large fines and have a zero tolerance policy on stray pets and feeding any wildlife. The Metro Parks and other public outdoor venues are nearly deserted and businesses that rely on good summer sales for outdoor activities are already suffering. The impact of fear just keeps trickling down, creating more problems," Kate said.

Tom, who had been really quiet, also had a fear.

"Professionally, I'm afraid it will result in owners not taking pets in for treatment of routine illness or surgery until there is a vaccine. That could result in many clinics going under, veterinarians losing their livelihood."

"I think," Brad said, "that this makes the 'Destroyer' stuff seem like small potatoes.

"And like I said before, probably is those damn Aliens, ET's and Leprechauns messing with us again!"

Jules smiled and added, "And remember what I said last time, who better than us to save the world?"

CHAPTER 8

"I am pleased to see so many familiar faces from our last scientific gathering. I know most of you have not had to use any of your advanced training but I suspect in the near future we all will be tested on our ability to stop possibly the greatest pandemic since the early twentieth century Spanish Influenza outbreak. Millions, possibly billions of lives may be at stake if we lose control of this new illness."

Jules scanned the audience which was somber, some staring blankly down at their computers. The seriousness of their responsibility had seemed to have hit them hard.

"So, I am an administrator and research coordinator at Le Institute Pasteur which is not only a French entity but an international scientific community that tackles a grand range of issues from preventive medicine to solving social issues rising from poverty, such as malnutrition and lack of clean water. All this resulted from one man's efforts to rid the world of an infectious disease of which he is remembered most for —his work on rabies. But also remember all the food-borne diseases that have been controlled by Pasteurization. Louis Pasteur was a medical giant, a man who was often ridiculed and a man who opened the door for many of the advances we now take for granted. He certainly also advanced veterinary medicine into the realm of legitimate science.

"I have prepared for you some historical illustrations from the archives of the Pasteur.

"Many of you may belief that Pasteur was the father of modern vaccination but Edward Jenner, shown here, no relation to your Caitlyn Jenner, really developed the first significant protection against Smallpox by discovering that persons working with cattle rarely contracted the disease. Smallpox had a thirty percent mortality rate in many outbreaks and was responsible for not only devastating populations in the developed nations but wiped out native, immune populations during colonization of the world by European empires. Here are some modern examples of survivors of the disease. Jenner's discovery spurred Pasteur, a man that had lost two daughters to Typhoid Fever, to focus on disease prevention by vaccination. Pasteur discovered that the bacteria that caused Chicken Cholera could be 'aged' or essentially attenuated and could then be used to protect the chickens against fresh active infection. Here is an illustration of him working in his long lab coat, taken from an early medical journal that released his scientific thesis and results. You would have thought he would have been revered at the time, but as you see from this news journal headline from the time 'PASTEUR EST UN FOU!,'l Pasteur is a Madman! He was not. This was a common response from the established scientific community who at the time stood solidly against new discoveries. Pasteur eventually developed how to chemically attenuate Anthrax and facing vigorous scientific doubt, demonstrated in a public test that his discovery really did protect livestock. Here is an illustration of the penned sheep that survived the exposure and the adjacent pen with the dead unvaccinated animals. Now look at how Pasteur is represented--- with reverence, almost 'holy' features and respect. This was the signature moment in Pasteur's legacy.

"Rabies now became his focus and he started to work with M.J. Bourrel, a veterinarian, retired army, who had postulated that Rabies was transmitted in the saliva of an infected animal when someone was bitten. At that time Bourrel recommended filing down teeth of all dogs, especially those that roamed or hunted, to prevent bite penetration. Here is an illustration of a 'mad dog,' salivating, terrorizing a small French village around eighteen eighty two. I would suspect a veterinarian's worst nightmare. At the time, immediate wound cauterization at the local blacksmith or bite area excising, amputation and silver nitrate chemical cautery was recognized therapy. Primitive and non-specific. If you were bitten and didn't seek these treatments, you lived in fear for up to a year post bite. Death by rabies has always been a horrible passing. Here you see a bite victim being held down as a blacksmith applies a white hot iron poker to the —wound-- note the heavy leather mouth gag so the victim wouldn't bite off his tongue.

"Pasteur was the first to call rabies a virus, although that was not confirmed until nineteen-o- three. His first treatment occurred in eighteen eighty five using a series of injections of spinal cord tissue from a rabbit that died of rabies, saving a young boy's life.

"As more bite victims from around the world were treated, Pasteur became an international celebrity and donations flowed to fund his work. In eighteen eighty seven, Le Institute Pasteur was established to further his work on Rabies and other infectious diseases. To this day, Le Pasteur is not a non-profit entity but engages in money making projects and research. In eighteen ninety five, Louis Pasteur died in his home after suffering strokes and heart failure. His remains rest with those of his wife, Marie, in a crypt beneath the Institute. I work in his shadow, the father of modern Preventative Medicine."

LeClerc stepped away as the audience heartily applauded his presentation. Kate returned to the podium.

"Merci, Dr. LeClerc. We look forward to working with Le Pasteur. Now before we break for lunch and split into our small groups we will hear from Dr Hans Vogel of Tristar Veterinary Biologics, the world's largest and premiere producer of veterinary vaccines for agricultural and companion animals. Dr Vogel---"

Hans Vogel stood and walked to the podium. He was silver blonde, intense pale blue eyes, hair cut close in a military fashion, sported a short precisely trimmed goatee, was average build and wore dress jeans, white dress shirt and navy blazer. He moved fast and precisely.

"Danke, Dr. Vensky," he started brightly with an distinct German accent, "I accept this challenge with little trepidation. My company, if you were unaware, is the world's largest and now with EU consolidation acceptance, the fastest growing producer of Veterinary Biologics in the world. In an effort to standardize quality and expand, my company has acquired every major player in the vaccine business from around the world during the last five years at a cost of over five hundred billion euros. The only other primary producer left is Jei Ping International in Shanghai, China. They however focus more on human than veterinary immunologic discovery. We are truly a company devoted to animals and by extension, Public Health. My company has the developmental capacity and intellectual capital to produce a vaccine solution to this zoonosis."

He turned to the large monitors.

"Here is our research and production facility in Leipzig, Germany. The modern mirrored glass building has four levels and is as advanced as your CDC. In fact, several of our department heads came to our company from the CDC. It seems we pay much better. This aerial view demonstrates the size of the plant property which covers eight hundred hectares. We currently produce and ship four hundred thousand doses of veterinary biologics daily and to the left side of your screen you see our new plant expansion with a thirty thousand square meter state of the art production facility which will be able to go on line in two months. This will bring our production level to 1.2 million per day assuming four work shifts a day. Yes, four because our workday is only six hours with breaks at three and five hours of which one is a meal break of forty minutes. It is a good thing we are going to be eighty per cent automated, otherwise our socialistic society might slow our ability to produce life-saving products. So much for German work ethic!

"We already have the virus in tissue culture in our Level 4 biohazard research area growing in chicken and duck embryos, rabbits, mice, and sheep. If we are lucky we may be able to produce a sub unit vaccine where we will only have the immunologic fraction of the virus in the vaccine product. That means whether we produce a killed virus product, modified live or a sub unit product, there will be no way for this virus vaccine to revert to its lethal origins. We also may be looking to clone antibodies from vaccinated and challenged horses and cattle to effect a cure.

"What we need is time and hopefully this is a virus that can be diluted in the field by trapping the vectors, but I think your country has too many ways, too many animal sources for this disease to vector from.

"That is all I have. We at Tristar look forward to our important collaboration. Danke."

Vogel sat as Kate returned to the podium. She was solemn.

"Dr. Johnson has just informed me that despite intensive treatment, seventeen of the thirty-seven Minnesota victims have passed away overnight, the rest, they feel will likely not survive the day. The priest in Boston has died and they have two more human cases. Also, two raccoons that tested positive in Northern Virginia actually came from Washington, trapped near the Capitol Mall. You are the first to receive this information, it is strictly confidential and you are to speak to no one outside this group about it. The CDC will produce a press release as soon as the media starts inquiring.

"We are now breaking for lunch. Please return here promptly at one and we will divide up into regional groups by state and then brainstorm this dilemma.

"I for one believe in the power of prayer. This seems the appropriate time to ask for guidance, strength and intervention. Lord, hear our prayers!"

CHAPTER 9

Bariloche, Argentina

19 May 1949

The man paced back and forth in short but precise lines, his left foot dragging slightly. He held his hands tightly together behind his back to quell the tremors of his advancing Parkinson's disease and moved with his head slightly bowed as if contemplating some great thought. This place was his refuge and his prison, a place waiting for him to die at or rise from again to great power.

His second wife was in labor with his first child. The baby had been conceived by artificial insemination, his chronic heavy metal poisoning from his personal 'physicians' attempt to control his nervous chorea, had rendered him impotent.

His mind however was consumed with what ifs and revolving psychotic plans to return his Reich to power.

His had been the face of evil from the last World War. Responsible for millions of deaths on the battlefield and in concentration camps, he would be barely recognizable now. His thick black dyed hair was now short and white, barely a fuzz on his head. The signature short mustache was gone. Plastic surgeons had remodeled his profile to match his new assumed Latin heritage. He was now August Mendoza, a retired Brazilian financier. Surgeons had scarred his vocal cords to change his voice and acid washes removed any traces of fingerprints. He was a different man than the one who had 'died' deep in his personal bunker on April 30, 1945 — a literal truth.

The Soviets had pulled the incinerated bodies of his beloved German Shepherd Blondi and the remains of his first wife, Eva Braun, from the destroyed bunker. The male corpse removed was assumed to be him but in reality was one of his doubles, Frederick Seimer. A well placed explosive-tipped bullet fired into his mouth had obliterated any dental identity. Finally, the intense petroleum fire had made sure nothing else from the body would confirm that identity. The Soviets suspected, but the world needed closure and the bodies ended in an anonymous grave in a remote forest. He was secreted out of the country in the false bottom of a livestock truck carrying pigs to be processed into Poland. It was the opposite direction any Nazi fugitive would have traveled to escape--deeper into the Soviet territory. From the processing facility he was transported to the coast where a U boat with ten crew secretly transported him slowly to Cuba while shipboard plastic surgeons modified his appearance. The boat took two months to reach Santiago de Cuba where he purchased his new identity as August Mendoza, wealthy investor. His crew left to return to Germany leaving only two trusted 'servants' to attend to his needs. The U boat sank trying to cross the North Atlantic after the hull split during a violent storm. Only a few people in the entire world now knew the man was alive and at large.

His stolen wealth had been hidden in South America for the last two years of the war after it was apparent the conflict could not be won. Billions in wealth had been transferred to various Brazilian and Argentinian banks under the name August Mendoza and a financial history and personal resume fabricated. It was an age when communication was slow, irregular and was trusted on face value because wartime verification was difficult. He was easily recreated.

He had paced for nearly three hours as his German Shepherd dog, Heidi watched lazily from the shadows. She jumped to her feet as he shouted with brief excitement at the birth cries of his newborn son. Fifteen minutes later, the screen door to the large compound's residence swung open as the midwife came out with the baby.

"You have a fine son, Señor Mendoza. Your wife is also doing well," the nurse announced as she handed the swaddled child to the former dictator.

He took a brief look and smiled broadly with satisfaction, his genes finally being replicated.

"His name will be Caesar, Middle initial H. Tell the doctor he is NOT to be circumcised. Tell my wife good work!"

He walked away, his dog Heidi close by his side.

He had more love for his dog than his young spouse, who had been waiting at the secluded compound when he arrived---her only purpose to be a vessel to birth an heir. She had been a Hitler Youth and 'assigned' the task to carry his child to which she readily agreed. She was a classic Aryan beauty with a good pedigree, stunning blond hair and vibrant blue eyes. She was innocent, the virgin he required.

Young Caesar grew up at his father's knee, learning political and military principles. His tutor taught him mathematics, science and the classics. He also studied German and English to supplement his Spanish. His father would test him, going from German to Spanish to English during a story and then quizzing him using all three. There were few distractions in the jungle, so the boy was a virtual sponge, absorbing everything presented to him.

He also was taught to hate. To be revengeful. To get even at all costs. To be powerful and how to crush the weak. By the time he was thirteen, he definitely reflected all his father's world views.

About this time his father revealed the truth of who he was and set forth his plans for the young man. He was to be strong, powerful and invincible but also to be patient for the right time to claim his worldly throne. Caesar had time but his father did not. The Parkinson's was progressing to where he aspirated his straw fed gruel nearly daily. He stayed on oxygen but could barely pull a breath. On Caesar's twenty-first birthday, he finally succumbed to the disease as a very old man, thus passing the torch to his only heir, a birthday gift to his son.

Caesar had loved and believed in his father and that his destiny was to restore power back to his family. It became his life's goal.

He knew what he had to do to secure his future. He arranged for everyone that was living at the compound to board a plane for the first leg of a vacation trip to Germany. It was a very short trip on a plane that exploded and burned on a mountainside on the way to an airport in Chile. Caesar's first evil violent act. His mother was a true loss but she could not be trusted to be silent. As his father taught, do what is necessary and don't look back. He never would.

In a modern world with nuclear weapons, his revenge would have to come in an indirect form. He was secretly worth billions and he started acquiring pharmaceutical businesses through corporate entities, which made him many more billions. He had years to prepare and finally formulated a plan to crush the Allied nations without firing one weapon.

His coup d'état was to be payback for the humiliation of total defeat at the hands of the Americans, Soviets and the other Allies.

He was indeed his father's son.

CHAPTER 10

CDC

Atlanta June 13 4 p.m.

"I am pleased that you all were so productive in your groups. We certainly have developed a basis for our initial approach to this massive problem," Kate announced.

"Some of you worked till midnight brainstorming. Others I understand were out drinking right after dinner. At any rate the team's leadership met this morning while the rest of you were sleeping in or out running and here is the consensus report.

"'L.I.V.E'. This will be the acronym *you* will live by, if you excuse the humor.

"Thank you, Ohio, for your group's idea to simplify our efforts to a four letter word!

"L stands for Learn. We need to know everything we can about the etiology, vector pools and how the virus can be treated.

"I is for investigate. *EVERY* suspect animal or incident must be investigated.

"V is for vaccinate. EVERY domesticated mammal in the zoonotic zone must have priority for immunization, then the secondary zones. Compliance must be mandatory with stiff fines and jail time for those who do not participate.

"Eradicate is letter E. The goal has to be to put this virus to bed. The transmission of this virus is too easy. Unvaccinated vector populations may have to be reduced dramatically in a humane way to dilute transmission. This will be the most difficult task as there are millions of mammals living in proximity of our population centers."

"I could add few more four letter words to describe what we are wading into," Brad said to Tom.

Kate looked around at the serious group.

"So now you are going to earn that paycheck that shows up in your checking account every month. We have verified all your contact numbers and will be emailing you daily situation reports. So please head home, have a great weekend and remember L-I-V-E."

The assembly started to disperse, the noise level rising dramatically. Vogel had already flown home but Jules was still there.

Kate, Tom and Brad gravitated to the Frenchman.

"Mes Amies, would you please join me this evening for dinner, my treat, before I leave tomorrow for Paris. We need to catch up and I have some concerns we should discuss."

"Thanks, we don't fly home till noon tomorrow so that will be perfect," Kate replied.

"D'accord, then I will meet you in the hotel lobby at 1900 hours and I have a surprise restaurant for you to enjoy. Gentlemen, please be so kind to wear a sports jacket."

"Not an Argentinian Steakhouse?" Brad asked. "Because Kate and Tom already have been on that menu!"

Jules laughed. "No. Something more civilized. I promise you will enjoy."

The friends parted anxious to see what LeClerc had up his sleeve.

CHAPTER 11

La Belle Fleur

Downtown Atlanta

"Here we are my friends," Jules said, holding open the door for his guests, "the best French restaurant on the East Coast, perhaps in your entire country. It is owned by the son of one of my dearest friends and he holds two Michelin stars for culinary excellence, and he has only been open for about five years! When I called to say hello, he insisted we come to dinner. So perhaps it may not be my treat after all."

A tall, trim thirty something man wearing a crisp white chef's jacket waved from the far side of the restaurant where he was greeting diners and hurried over to the group. He had short dark hair, a tan complexion and sported a three day stubble beard growth that was popular with hip young men.

"Oncle Jules! Comment ça va? It is so good to see you again and of all places here in Atlanta! Tell me who are your friends?" Richard Moreau asked.

"These are my very good American friends, Doctor Kate Vensky, her husband Doctor Tom O'Dell and our mutual friend Doctor Brad Upton."

"Enchanté," he said bowing down to give Kate a light kiss on her left hand and then shaking the men's hands confidently.

"I could use Dr Brad some nights here as a bouncer," Richard said, complimenting his large size and obvious strength, "I don't think anyone would test him. It is so sad when on occasion a client sometimes enjoys our fine French wines a little too much."

Tom sympathized, "Some people just can't control their liquor." "I had a dog once that couldn't control his licker," Brad joked. Only Kate got it and gave him a playful jab on his shoulder.

"I have for you the best table in the restaurant, so enjoy your evening. I will check in on you with each course. Maurice, please seat my friends."

"Merci beaucoup. Nous sommes impatients de profiter de votre excellente cuisine!" Kate said in French, one of five languages she spoke fluently. *We look forward to enjoying your fine food !*

"Je vous en prie! Docteur Kate!" the chef answered. *You are welcome!* The Maître D' guided them to a table in a private cut out, surrounded with wall to ceiling windows, overlooking a formal garden with a centered fountain. He pulled out Kate's chair as the men stood. The table gave them the ability to view the entire restaurant in relative privacy.

"Jules, this so very elegant," Kate said. "I bet the food will be unbelievable!"

"With two Michelin stars, how could it not?" he replied.

"I'm confused, what do tires have to do with good eats?" Brad asked.

"Honestly, you never heard of Michelin rated restaurants, the most difficult award of culinary excellence in the world?" Kate asked incredulously.

"Nope, my standard is the AAA ratings when we vacation. Although when you think about it though, AAA is about cars and fixing tires so I guess it makes sense!" the big man answered.

"You are so weird!" Kate laughed, understanding it was Brad trying to be funny again.

"I will proudly take that as a compliment," he replied, with a laugh of his own.

The wine and food flowed, each course an amazing example of culinary magic.

After the third course, Kate received a call from Ted Johnson from the CDC. She listened, affirmed something she was told and then said goodbye.

"Looks like we are going to stay through most of tomorrow. They just confirmed one more case in Denver. The victim is a forty-eight year old shuttle bus driver at Denver International Airport who is a chemo patient with chronic leukemia. About a month ago, the man killed a large coyote with his bus and not thinking, placed it in a trash dumpster in the parking area. At the time he was wearing a surgery mask and disposable nitrile gloves to protect him from infection since he had a lot of contact with riders and their personal bags. If the coyote was the carrier, then he must have punctured a glove or contaminated himself in some other way. Initially they thought he was having an atypical reaction to his chemo, possibly a brain lesion or encephalitis. He had a full regiment of tests but nothing really was found until they did a brain biopsy. The pathologist found negri bodies in the tissue and ordered an dFA which was negative. The electron microscope level testing found our virus and they contacted the CDC. His doctors have placed him in a drug-induced coma but he is in real trouble. So far no one else in the Denver area is suspected exposed."

"So why do we have to stay in town?" Tom asked.

"Evidently, Homeland Security wants to pick our brains about the virus and our plans to control the disease. Not to interfere I was told but Ted said if we don't give them what they want to hear they will pull the responsibility from us and take over," Kate explained. "Ted suspects they would institute a scorched earth policy."

"That would be fine with me. I have a real bad feeling about all of this. Deja Moo!" Brad said.

"Deja Moo?" Jules asked.

"He's trying to be funny again. It's that feeling you've heard this bullshit before," Kate replied.

"Bull Merde?"

"Oui," she laughed.

"Sorry, but we have gone down this rabbit hole once before and this time there is the real possibility we could die a horrible death," Brad lamented.

"And I think we should relax a little. This is not the Black Death or even a new lethal influenza. We understand, control, and can prevent the old parent virus so I think we will be fine once we get to an effective vaccine. With today's communication and social media we will know rapidly how our efforts are doing as well what's happening in the field. People will be hyper aware," Jules added as he picked up his wine glass.

"I wish to propose a toast."

They all picked up their crystal wine glasses.

"To our friendship, to our previous successes, and to our future efforts. Salut!"

"Salut!" they voiced in unison.

Kate then added, "Santé!!" *To Health!* "And God help us!" Brad voiced, "God help us!!"

They voiced their friendship, colleagues again, placed by God, The Creator, to stop this newest 'Destroyer'— a man who had designs on the world and would kill everyone that stood in his path.

CHAPTER 12

Fort Peck Indian Reservation

Poplar, Montana
June 17 5a.m.

Dawn was almost at full light as the days lengthened with the approach of the summer solstice. The far North had the longest summer days and the almost four thousand square miles of the Fort Peck Indian Territory was at Montana's eastern northern edge, just fifty miles from Canada. It was the final resting place for the heirs of the Sioux and others who had wiped out George Armstrong Custer and his command at the Little Bighorn. A massive property for its six thousand eight hundred residents, it was remote and wild, purely reflecting the spirit that once had been the beating heart of the Lakota.

Joseph Blackfeather had just finished loading his paint Indian pony, Wakinyan, which meant Thunderer, into a rarely used old horse trailer, something he needed only once or twice a year. This time it was a biannual event where a few tribal members were assigned designated survey zones to conduct a population census of their beloved Tatanka or Bison. Spring calves and yearlings were specifically counted in each herd personally by hand instead of aerial surveying which some tribes enlisted. Joseph knew the reservation lands as well as any man could and now felt greater respect for his ancient culture since the death of his great grandfather Nelson. He not only had inherited his grandfather's worldly possessions, but also the awareness his grandfather had in spiritual connection to the ancestors. As young as he was, just twenty-one, he now held those shaman powers, and was more a true Lakota than ever before. His grandfather's most important gift.

A couple years before, just before his great grandfather's death at nearly one hundred, he had met Kate, Tom and Brad when they arrived to investigate a sudden large cattle kill on the reservation. His grandfather had been plagued for decades with dreams and visions of a great 'Destroyer' which would be a plague on all the earth's living creatures. While working with the veterinarians on the cattle necropsies, he mentioned this to Tom and the USDA team met with the old man who explained the 'Creator and Destroyer' concept from his Lakota culture. Nelson Blackfeather had kept meticulous journals with detailed tribal history but also recorded those dreams and visions that often terrified him. Then in the next day's early morning hours after meeting with the three investigators, he died, leaving the responsibility to stop the 'Destroyer' with Joseph and the three veterinarians. Shortly after that, Joseph read all his grandfather's journals and found the drawn image of a man surrounded by swastikas. Nelson had unknowingly recorded an image of the man who would nearly decapitate the Government of the United States with his DNA programmable death 'ray' nearly seventy years in the future. Berhetzel, it turned out, was the 'Destroyer' of the old man's nightmares.

After he returned from near death in South America and had helped rid the world of the Nazi Berhetzel, the young man's life had been peaceful. Joseph enjoyed taking online writing classes and spent a majority of his time interviewing Lakota, Cheyenne and others who had knowledge or family stories of the proud peoples that had, by simply defending their sovereign rights, been emasculated and relegated to vast tracts of land with minimal support to survive as a culture. He had fortunately inherited his grandfather's cultural self-awareness. His goal now was to learn to write and luckily he had the time, the drive and now the income to do so because of the prize' money he received from the Pasteur Institute for recovering Berhetzel's instrument of death. Joseph hoped the weapon that once held such an evil purpose in the Nazis' hands could now be converted to an instrument of healing. He had not heard yet, but the money kept coming.

Thanks to that income, he now drove a new black Chevy Silverado heavy duty pickup. It was his one splurge from the money he collected. Joseph smiled with manly satisfaction each time the dashboard lit up with a multitude of data. The XM radio had been programmed to his favorite country station and for the first time in his life, he could listen without losing a weak signal every five minutes.

Slowly he drove the Chevy out, grinding the cinder driveway that had been crushed over time into a mixture of red dust and quarter sized clinkers. The bone jarring ride that his twenty-five year old rattle trap Ford provided, just making it to the road, had been replaced with smooth shock absorbing luxury. He carefully pulled out on the reservation road southwest and drove for twenty minutes till he saw a marker labeled N 17. It was a rough, rutted tractor path intended for hunters and off roaders to use to get deeper into the wilderness areas of the Reservation and as he pushed the truck forward, it grabbed the ground firmly as it transitioned to automatic four wheel drive.

Joseph was specifically tasked to do a population survey on two bison herds, 17A and 17B. One was relatively large, over one hundred eighty Tatanka. The other herd was smaller, only seventy or so animals but the herds mostly were close but separate, usually grazing away from each other. The exception was winter when the herds merged as protection from predators.

Wakinya bounced in the trailer until Joseph felt he was close enough to ride the horse out for the search. Normally he could find the bison because they left no doubt where they had been by short cropped grasses, trampled ground and a trail of scat chips. He could also smell them by staying downwind and then letting Wakinya locate the herd. The Indian pony was really just a slightly smaller horse but in his pure blood were the genes of his ancestors who had transported ancient hunters to the herds and then pushed the Tatanka around like a cattle cutting Quarter Horse.

49

Joseph tightly cinched up his comfortable old worn saddle, tying up saddle bags of food and water, both for him and the horse. He also secured a sleep blanket, his emergency supplies and the spotting scope he always carried. He had just purchased an adapter from Amazon so he could use his iPhone with the scope to take his survey photos from a distance before he approached the animals more closely for a critical specific assessment of their condition.

It only took forty-five minutes to find 17A, the larger herd. He took survey photos at about two hundred yards and slowly approached the animals in a non-threatening way and although several young bulls feinted charges, they seemed to accept his presence. Thirty-five spring calves and twenty-nine yearlings meant this herd was succeeding quite well despite the increasing pressure from predators.

Joseph figured the second herd would likely place themselves up-wind of the larger 17A. About two miles away in that general area, he located the smaller group and took a GPS reading and photographed the herd from a distance. It was getting very hot as the sun hung nearly directly overhead, so he pulled off his T-shirt and could feel the radiant energy on his skin as he drank from his old aluminum canteen, drying his mouth with the shirt.

He barely had to give Wakinya a nudge and he was off at a canter creating an instant cooling effect. Joseph felt the energy of the 'hunt' and gave the gelding a silent push and the instinct that lay dormant for a lifetime took over. Wakinya ran to and parallel to the herd which got their attention. Their instinct to flee as a prey animal was triggered, and what was to be a simple task to count, now became a game triggered by a generational relationship; the hunter to the horse, the horse to the pursuit, and the bison to his survival.

They rode parallel to the moving herd, the huffing and snorting ru-minants lumbering, pounding the ground under their hooves. Joseph's ponytail opened and his long black hair moved in the wind across his bronze shoulders. He dropped the reins, letting the horse have his head. The young fit Indian sat tall in the saddle and feinted a series of bow draws sending imaginary arrows flying into the largest of the herd. He was connected to the bison by his blood and could feel that heritage in his rapidly beating heart.

It was a good run but he pulled up the horse to prevent him from over-working muscles that were generally used on easy trail rides. A foam of sweat ran down Wakinya's neck, the energy of the race being dispersed.

Joseph was laughing at the spontaneous run and imaginary hunt and bent down over the horse's neck to whisper thanks to the animal. A familiar voice interrupted him.

"Enough fun, Joseph. You are needed again," came a resolute voice from nowhere.

It was his dead great grandfather Nelson.

Joseph was startled and jerked up to search around him. No one.

"Look to the North, away from the sun."

Used to doing what he was told, the young Indian searched with his eyes to the Northwest, spotting a small white form about three hundred yards from both the Tanaka and where they were resting.

He pulled up his spotting scope and focused in on a small white bison calf!

Joseph was excited but confused. A white bison was an extremely significant Holy animal for the Lakota, a sign of hope and good fortune. But why was the tiny animal so far from the herd? And where was it before the run?

"Go and see my son," came the old man's voice.

As if he also heard the old man, Wakinya moved on silently while Joseph fired a series of phone photos. Click, click, click, click in a burst. The calf was steady, standing quietly but staring directly at the horse and rider. Closer, then another burst. Joseph returned the phone to his rear jean's pocket twisting away to push it into the tight space. When he looked forward an instant later, the calf was gone, no sign of it in any direction. Panic gripped Joseph as he frantically swung around in the saddle searching.

Nothing.

The air was suddenly engulfed with the loud cries of unseen wolves, the howls sending shivers up and down Joseph's spine. Wakinya pricked his ears trying to locate the source, expressing an equine disapproval in snorts of hot air and nervous movements when he didn't find the wolves.

Joseph moved the horse forward in a slow trot as he searched with his spotting scope, not seeing any physical evidence of the predators. As he approached the site where the calf had stood, he saw the sun bleached bones and dried white hide scraps from the winter kill bison with the broken leg. The kill had been a white bison! *But what about the calf?*

He walked the kill zone in expanding circles picking up tufts of white hair and hide. Then he spotted a pair of bright orange feather fletched silver tubes. They were fitted with short hypodermic needles and a rubber syringe push rod with a pneumatic cuff, about the diameter of a penny pretzel. They were laying in the prairie grasses about ten yards apart. Confused, he photographed the entire area and placed the syringes and the gray fur entwined around the needle tips into one of his sandwich bags he had turned inside out.

Unsettled, he looked to the sky. He was meant to discover this, but why?

Grandfather, help me, give me wisdom!

Wakinya huffed and Joseph turned toward the horse. Looking past it, he saw the Tatanka, the entire herd, standing like they were at attention, staring at him; not a movement, not a blink, not a swish of a tail.

Joseph pulled himself up on the saddle and turned his equine friend around and slowly moved past the silent bison soldiers.

He was getting creeped out. Unusual because nothing that was natural, of nature, ever bothered him. He started to feel a rising tide of panic and put the horse into a fast canter to escape. Joseph took one last look over his shoulder and gasped.

There at the spot where the Tatanka had ran was a group of buckskin clad Lakota women, apparitions, skinning and quartering the bison he had shot with imaginary arrows. He quickly turned away, not believing his eyes.

I must be going nuts. Who can I bring all this to?

He decided to call Kate and Tom.

CHAPTER 13

Office of Hans Vogel Tristar Veterinary Biologics

Leipzig, Germany
The next morning

"I assure you, sir, everything is on schedule," Hans Vogel explained to the man sitting in his executive desk chair, Caesar H. Mendoza.

"And exactly what does that mean?" questioned the second generation Nazi.

"We have the production of all the initial dose vaccines on site and in storage. Fifty percent of those will be set aside as a booster dose for those fortunate enough to receive the real item. That will support our challenge trial data on efficacy and not raise suspicions from the CDC about our vaccine being in any way related to the new plague infecting millions until it is too late. We will end up depopulating about sixty percent of the general population with our focus being on urban population centers and government centers where the less desirable citizens, socially or genetically, gravitate. Rural communities will be uninfected."

"How do we assure that?" Mendoza asked.

"We will direct ship the vaccines. No middle man or storage of the product will be allowed. Demand should assure that not one vial ever is held in storage---anywhere. We ship just enough to create the illusion that we can barely keep up.

"After that we turn loose Armageddon by shipping our modified version booster to the targeted areas. Two to twelve days after that dose is administered, the vaccinated animals, which will show no outward illness, will shed the virus in urine, feces, saliva and blood. Within three days of that, all exposed primates or humans will become morbidly ill, aggressive and very very violent. They will become the walking dead, zombies if you will, attacking all life they contact. From that will come chaos, and cultural collapse. At that time, we can choose to continue to let Hell rain down upon them or we can become saviors, and rescue the nation by assuming control. As you know, there are over sixty-two thousand loyal party members leading normal quiet lives, ready to be activated when the time is right. Each one and their families have received oral vaccines and daily preventive against both the new rabies and the secondary human viron. We have enough for those oral combo vaccines stockpiled to protect approximately sixty million and eventually we will have another thirty million. Our actuaries estimate there will be 100 million killed directly from the disease or persons affected by the viron. The logistics of that many dead in a three to four week period will be the factor initiating the government's collapse. The only other thing that could do what we will accomplish would be an EMP-- Electro Magnetic Pulse. Too bad we couldn't give them that kind of an one, two punch!"

"I looked into that, but the post EMP depopulation would take 12-18 months with the undesirables as likely to survive as the ones we want to propagate. As long as we control the degree of infection and vaccine protection we wish to provide, and can do it undetected, we will be able decide that in real time. The first thing I want to accomplish is to depopulate the CDC scientific community. That will be a difficult task but our imbedded people will be sure the 'terrorists' who attack will destroy critical computer and research areas as well as the leadership. First Atlanta, then the Pasteur in Paris, Moscow and London a few hours later. We then will be the scientific community and will control all the outcomes," Mendoza asserted.

"I am headed back to Argentina to organize the shipment plan of the contaminate doses. I am the only person to order its release and I want your target lists encrypted along with the actuary data in Argentina exactly seven days after I return there. Email nothing. understand?"

"Ja, Mein Führer!" Vogel replied. *Yes, my leader!*

"Gut! Gott hilf uns vorherrschene!" *Good, God help us prevail!*

CHAPTER 14

Home of Kate and Tom

June 18

"Joseph! How good to hear your voice! Tom will be so sad he missed your call, he's out on a milk fever call. Bobbi, it's your Uncle Joseph," Kate said with a big smile. "How are you?"

"I'm feeling a little guilty for not calling sooner. I don't think we've talked since I came down for Bobbi's baptism. That's my fault, I have been taking a lot of classes and organizing my interviews for the book. Hard to believe I could lose track of time when I have so much of it. Tom and Brad ok?"

"Tom is working hard but loving being a dad. Brad is Brad, a combination of gentle goofball and sarcastic nitwit. I know he misses you, he told me so when we were in Atlanta for an emergency meeting of our original die-off investigators," Kate explained.

"Wait a minute, is something up again? Another die-off?" Joseph asked in a surprised voice.

"No, nothing like that but potentially as serious. You probably know about the rabid wolf at the Mall of America, right? Well there's more. Rabid feral cats in Boston and raccoons in Northern Virginia. The problem is this is no ordinary rabies. It is unique, virulent and highly contagious. There have been forty-two deaths so far."

"I had no idea. I haven't watched the news or listened to regular radio in a couple months. So this is bad?" he asked.

"This is horrible, because we have no protective vaccine, although there is one in preliminary field trials and controlled laboratory challenges," Kate answered.

"If I can help, please let me know. I called also because I had something really weird happen to me yesterday and I wanted to run it past you, Tom and Brad.

"I was out yesterday on a solo population survey on the Tatanka, you know our Bison.

"It was a beautiful day and I was feeling real cocky riding Wakinya in the hot sun counting animals and feeling like a real Lakota. Just me and the horse in the middle of God's Country. Anyway, we made a run at the animals pretending to be old time hunters and when we rested, Grandfather spoke to me for the first time since we wrapped up Berhetzel.

"He told me I was needed again and then directed me to look to the Northwest.

"I automatically did what I was told, just like he was standing right next to me.

"When I looked over, there was a rare white Bison calf standing alone about a football field length away. I moved Wakinya forward and used my iPhone to fire bursts of photos. I moved closer but took my eye of the calf for a split second and poof, it disappeared.

"I couldn't believe it and rode to the exact spot and found the bones of probably a yearling white bison that had been killed last winter, likely by wolves which by the way were howling and carrying on the entire time after the calf vaporized. It just freaked me out!

"I saved some hide and fur from the Tatanka so people wouldn't think I was nuts, but there was one more strange thing."

"What was that ?" Kate asked.

"I found two syringe darts, I think like the ones we used to sedate the steer when we had to sacrifice him for our control animal at the cattle die-off. These are just smaller and look more aerodynamic."

"Send me some pics of the syringes but treat them like evidence in a murder trial. Don't contaminate them if possible," Kate asked.

"I remembered from our work and did just that. There also is some fur on the syringes and needles and it is not the bison's. I would bet it's wolf or coyote but I'm leaning toward wolf because it's softer, not as coarse as the coyotes around here and also it's more gray black than brown. One more thing."

"What's that?" she asked.

"I looked at my photo stream and I captured the white calf on all but the last two frames. It literally was like he vaporized. Between that and Grandfather contacting me, I'm not sure what to think or feel."

"Brad calls that Deja Moo. The feeling you've experienced this bullshit before," Kate explained.

"Yeh, that's it. Just like in Argentina. That's why I called. Something big is up and I think that we may be sucked into that vortex again. Grandfather wouldn't waste my time on something trivial."

"Then I think we are in serious trouble again!" Kate offered.

"I'll send the photos, but if you don't mind, I can drive down tomorrow and bring that evidence with me, if that is alright with you?"

"We would love to have you come down and also to stay with us. Lord knows we have plenty of room in this old farmhouse. I'll invite Brad and Ellen over for dinner. I've been wanting to try a Beef Bourguignon recipe from Julia Child, so this would be a good time to cook something special. We ate at a great French restaurant with Jules in Atlanta last week and now I am having serious craving for more French Food," Kate said.

"Cravings, eh?" Joseph teased.

"No, nothing like that. It's just I miss the elegance of my Paris and the food!"

"Ok, I'll see you tomorrow. Don't tell Walking Bald I'm coming. I want to surprise him!"

CHAPTER 15

O'Dell Farm, June 19

"When are you expecting Dr. Tom home from his calls?" Joseph asked Kate.

"I never really know, but Brad should be here in the next twenty minutes. He called just as he was leaving his office. Ellen can't make it, their oldest daughter Ruthie is in a softball tournament. The good news is my yummy French meal will be ready anytime they are."

Joseph picked Bobbi up and gently tossed him up in the air. Giggles turned to laughs as the toddler relished the play time. As Joseph slowed the toss game, Bobbi started babbling a story to his new friend.

"He sounds like his Uncle Brad, lots of words that don't make any sense!" Joseph laughed.

"We had a great time last week with Jules in Atlanta even though the reason we were recalled to the CDC was very, very serious. I know you hadn't heard of the new Rabies strain but this is as bad as it could be and believe me this has the potential to kill a lot of people and animals. The brains in Atlanta who estimate morbidity and mortality, you know how many get exposed and how many die, estimate between now and the time we have an effective vaccine program up and running, there could be two hundred fifty to six hundred thousand exposed with a near one hundred percent chance of those being dead within two weeks. The vaccine time line is estimated to be four to six months and over a year to get all the companion and farm animals protected. The real problem is the virus has multiple ways to infect, with airborne being our primary concern. Wildlife populations in urban areas will need to be decimated and that will make it a double tragedy. The hope is a human vaccine will be quickly developed and Jules at the Pasteur, along with the CDC and the Russians are currently working on that," Kate said.

"I better get an updated television and new satellite receiver. Sounds like this is not a great time to be out of the loop," Joseph replied.

"I will keep you up to date. This is probably a great time to be isolated way up north because so far the complete news of this hasn't hit the fan but when it does, there will be widespread panic and Lord knows what else. Remember the hysteria over just letting those few Ebola patients in the country for treatment a couple of years back? Well, just multiply that threat by thousands and put it in everyone's back yard. The economy will shut down and people will get very angry and violent. The Department of Homeland Security is looking at scenarios and none of them are good. They might cordon off urban areas, stop interstate travel and commerce and poison any living wild mammal within those zones. What got me is they have had these plans drawn up for years. What kind of crazy people do that?" she asked.

"You know, all the way down here, I played over and over in my head what happened yesterday and tried to figure out what Grandfather wants me to do. He said I was needed but that was it. It was as real as the two of us talking right now.

"It was kinda scary but in another way, because of what we went through with Berhetzel, strangely exciting."

Jed jumped up and ran to the back screen door, his tail wagging in happy anticipation.

"Tom must be home. Jed can hear that work truck coming halfway down the road. We had to put special tear resistant screen in that old door because he kept ripping it."

Jed barked a welcome as Tom pulled off his shoes and put them in a plastic covered bin on the porch and came into the kitchen.

"Joseph, great to see you!" Tom exclaimed as they shared a hand-shake and brief man hug.

"Man, that is some sweet truck. Wait till Brad sees it ! You are going to get harassed."

"I know, but that is something I am strangely looking forward to," Joseph said.

"Speaking of strangely, Brad just pulled in," Kate said, looking out the window.

Jed started barking fake aggression as Brad lumbered up the drive and onto the porch. Brad announced himself though the screen.

"Open up in the name of the law. I am a federal agent, I have a war-rant for a fugitive renegade injun named Blackfeather," he declared with a laugh, having fun with this.

Kate went to the door and pleaded ignorance.

"I don't know what you're talking about, there's just my son and hus-band here and of course this poor dog. Please kind sir don't harm us as we have done nothing wrong!" Kate said in her best Southern belle voice.

"Let me in or I will huff and puff and huff and puff and blow your house down!" Brad roared, really setting off Jed.

Joseph jumped out from behind the door—"Not by the hair on your shiny, shiny head, kemosabe," and he laughed.

Brad pushed past the screen and gave his friend a great bear hug as Joseph groaned. They laughed, their friendship renewed.

"Kate," he said, giving her a hug and light kiss, "why didn't you tell me this smart ass Indian was coming. I would have picked up some road kill for dinner. You know you could cook it Southern style with a thick rich gravy and biscuits."

"I don't think road kill is a real good idea under the current circum-stances," Kate reminded him.

"Ouch, that's right. Sorry, son, I guess you'll just have to suffer through Kate's cookin'," he kidded as he dodged her jab.

Tom walked over and handed Bobbi to his godfather Brad. "Ok, Bobbie, let's play horsie."

Brad placed the giggling boy on his shoulders and did a slow hop around the room, the big man definitely in his element.

"I hope Bobbi doesn't try to hold on to that shiny dome," Joseph joked.

"Wise Aaa—-," as Brad remembered his young rider.

"Ok," Brad said, "now for your humor lesson. How about some knock knock jokes?"

Bobbi tried grabbing the big man's nose.

"When I say Knock Knock, you say who's there?

"Knock. knock."

"Glub bee bo," Bobbi drooled.

"Mayonnaise."

No response.

"Now you say mayonnaise who?"

"Glub, glut nat."

"Mayonnaise a real nice new truck out there!"

They laughed at the stupid joke and Brad strapped Bobbi into his Swing-n-Bounce.

"And that is how I knew Joseph was here when I pulled in. Those Montana license plates with the 'Lakota Nation' on them was kind of a giveaway."

"Nothing gets by you does it?" Joseph teased.

"I hope everyone is hungry. I tried a new recipe and hope everyone is famished!" Kate said.

They sat at the old oval farm table and Tom offered the Blessing. "Lord God, we thank you for the blessing of this day, for family and good friends. Please bless this meal and bless our future endeavors that we may do Your will. Amen."

Kate served the bowls of French Beef Stew, homemade French bread and a mixed greens salad with a light champagne vinegar dressing. The final course was a vanilla bean creme brûlée.

"That was a fantastic meal!" exclaimed Joseph. "It reminded me of our time in Paris, Thank you, Kate."

"Thanks, Kate," Brad affirmed.

Tom gave her a wink and smile and started clearing the dishes.

"It's getting a little late and after I get Bobbi to bed, Joseph has something he wants to show you two so we can try to figure it out," Kate said as she picked up Bobbi who was fast asleep in his swing.

Tom gave him a light kiss as she went to put him to bed. The men went out on the screened porch where the warmth of early summer had cooled comfortably and the pond and tree frogs were croaking and trilling a kind of amphibian symphony in their efforts to find mates.

Kate returned with three beers and an ice tea for Joseph, who refused any alcohol.

"This is nice! I do feel bad that we haven't gotten together before now," Kate said, "but with getting settled here and having Bobbi, it seems like the time roared by.

"Joseph, please feel free to visit or call -- no, I will make sure we do this on a regular basis. Now why don't you fill these two on what happened to you yesterday."

"Kate, I will stay in contact, I promise," Joseph started.

"Yesterday I was out on the reservation land doing a biannual Tatanka survey. This assures that the bison herds are in a good expanding population with healthy reproduction. With the increase in the top tier predators like the wolf and cougar, we have to adjust our pressure on both the bison and the predators to keep a good balance. I was assigned a zone with two nice herds and the first one I located by riding Wakinya into the summer grazing area and that herd was in great shape-- lots of yearlings and spring calves. I moved on to the second and was overcome by the urge to make a run at them while shooting imaginary arrows. It was exhilarating and when I pulled Wakinya up, and rested, I heard my grandfather Nelson's voice. He told me I was needed again and had me look to the northwest, and I saw this."

He pulled up his phone as they strained for a good look.

"He stood maybe a couple hundred or so yards away. Tiny, but no question a white calf. Very important in my culture and would have been the cause for great celebration. So I took this first burst and then when I was closer, shot this second one."

65

They watched as the calf suddenly disappeared in the final frames.

"What the Hell?" Brad gasped.

"Just like that, he was gone and some wolves started vocalizing in a crazy way. It was like they were right there but they weren't."

"Just like the Indian Museum in D.C.?" Tom asked.

"Exactly, so much it creeped me out. But here's the kicker. Where the calf stood was the carcass bones, hide and fur of another white bison that had been killed and consumed most likely in late winter or early spring. There wasn't much left but I picked up some hide and hair to verify it was a white Tatanka. I walked the area like you taught me, you know in expanding circles and found these hidden in the prairie grass."

He opened the beaded leather pouch he was carrying and pulled out the plastic bag with the two syringe darts.

"Son of a bitch," Brad said, "someone poached that animal!"

"No, I don't think so. See, the fur kinda stuck at the needle hub. That's not from that bison or probably any other. Looks like wolf to me," Joseph explained.

"So what do you think? The wolves were the targets?" Kate asked.

"If they were feeding on the carcass, whether they killed it or not, they would have spent quite a bit of time filling their bellies. I just haven't figured out how someone could get close enough to make an accurate shot in that open of an area, let alone plug two of them. They are extremely wary," Joseph explained.

"Possibly some sort of automatic booby trap set after the kill. Like something attached to a trail camera," Tom offered.

"I don't know, any human scent would've sent them running. And why would someone want two live wolves anyway? For a private collection or zoo?" Joseph questioned.

"Maybe," Kate speculated, "they wanted it to create panic in the Mall of America as a rabid animal. This could totally change the investigation into the new rabies outbreak. Maybe it is manmade --a bioweapon?

"I'm going to call Ted Johnson and see if they can match up the hair on one of those syringes with the DNA of the Mall wolf. If it does, that would easily explain why she was a thousand miles from where she was born. Someone captured and transported her there!" She went to get her iPhone. "Hi, Ted, yes we are fine. Listen, Ted, can you test some fur found up in Montana to see if it is a match with the Mall wolf?" she asked.

"It's only a hunch but if we are correct, it will change the scope of this rabies thing three hundred sixty degrees. Yes, I'll overnight it. No, I haven't seen the news. My God when? I gotta go and turn on the news."

"What was that about?" Tom asked.

"Paris is under a general terrorist attack, the Louvre, Metro, Notre Dame, and a huge explosion in the general area of the Pasteur. He said nearly two square blocks leveled and on fire. Get the news on please, I'm going to call Jules."

The phone rang and rang. No voicemail with Jules welcoming voice. Kate felt a rising panic.

Please, God, protect my friend Jules. And help the people of Paris!

Fox News Network was flashing 'News Alert!' with a four-way split screen showing the Louvre's famous I.M. Pei glass pyramid collapsed with flames shooting skyward. Long streams of water shot from firefighters; hoses and fell over the skyward flames creating plumes of smoke and steam. A second quadrant was filled with a similar fate suffered by Notre Dame, the Seine River facing south facade was collapsed and burning. Fire boats pumped huge streams of river water onto the burning Cathedral. The third screen was at the Metro major station, Étoile Charles De Gaulle. Smoke poured up from the street as rescue workers pushed into the subterranean tunnels. The final screen was a helicopter view of destroyed and burning buildings with fires and smoke pluming skyward. It was huge area of total destruction.

Kate stared in disbelief, tears streaming down her cheeks. She swallowed hard, trying not to start sobbing.

Brad started swearing solemnly, "Sons of Bitches, God Damn Sons of Bitches!"

"Kate, try Jules again," Tom asked.

She hit redial with the same result.

They were glued to the television as reports of mass casualties and Martial Law taking place with an immediate curfew shutting down the City of Light.

Kate's phone rang. It was a call from Paris! "It's from Paris!" she said with excitement.

"Hello, Kate Vensky-O'Dell speaking."

"Bonsoir Kate, it's Jean Dubois. I'm sure you know the disaster we are facing here in Paris. I wanted to let you know that I haven't been able to contact Jules yet. All local cell communication has failed so I am calling from my home land line. Call this number and I will keep you up to date. He must be ok because I feel it-- he is like a brother so I would know. Pray for us please, ask everyone to pray. I will call as soon as I know something. Courage, Mon Chéri."

"Merci Beaucoup, Jean. Nous allons tous prier." *We will all pray.*

She closed her phone and began a prayer of hope.

CHAPTER 16

Mendoza Compound

Bariloche, Argentina
June 20, 6 a.m.

Mendoza sat in front of his encrypted computer waiting for the security screening delay to complete. After thirty-five seconds the screen flashed 'Secure' and Vogel appeared on the screen.

"Good afternoon, Hans," Mendoza greeted.

"Good morning, Sir!" Vogel replied, noting their time difference. "It looks like our friends who hate us 'infidels' were very successful in their endeavor in Paris yesterday! It is amazing how much chaos they can create when given the right equipment. I think their choice of targets was excellent and they did their required job very effectively. I don't think the Pasteur will be doing any research on our pathogens, effecting any cures or sticking their big Gallic noses in our business," Mendoza said.

"I was also quite impressed that only a dozen so-called terrorists could pull off such a wonderful job. I can forward their bonus this morning and our American agents are waiting your order to move on the CDC," Vogel replied.

"No, I prefer the Paris operatives be taken out because I've decided to wait on the CDC until we get the diseases better established. That way any of their projects in the works will be destroyed along with the brains that might find a solution to our threat. I want to get them all in one place and take them all out at one time—German efficiency," Mendoza said.

"Paris should be shut down for quite a while thanks to our terrorist friends but I will order their termination. Unfortunately for them, our operatives in the Sûreté know all their rat holes and will become instant national heroes when they turn on them and eliminate them in dramatic raids. There will be no one left alive to be persuaded to talk or expose us, their benefactor and arms connection. The idiots have already announced through social media their responsibility and touted their shitty short-sighted cause," he added.

"So we are on schedule?" Vogel asked.

"If everything is ready at production, you will submit your trial data to the CDC in 21 days. They should approve production within 7-10 days. We have the human infective pathogen ready, secure here, to add to those booster dosages. We will 'spike' one in six of those second doses, like Russian roulette. We expect that every animal vaccinated with those doses will shed billions of infective units exposing dozens of people. Any non-primate animal will not be affected but will be a huge reservoir of transmission. A simple, highly lethal agent. In the meantime we are going to infect more cats and raccoons in major cities with TS1975 to assure the rabies panic will start to overwhelm the Federal Health Agencies."

"Which cities?" Vogel asked,

"Atlanta, that should keep the CDC busy, St Louis, Chicago and Nashville. Our so-called nuisance control trappers are already inoculating their catches with our contaminated bait we loaded in their live traps. They are being paid a premium thinking we are concerned tree huggers that don't want our furry friends destroyed. In the end when those animals explode the disease, the news media will have a field day. Then our company will be their very important savior and you will be under a lot of pressure to rush to solve the threat. They have no idea what is in store for them or that we are going to turn loose Armageddon in the process," Mendoza replied.

"This WILL be the ultimate final solution, something that technology has made possible, nothing like my father initiated in the

Old-fashioned, direct, in your face way. Our way will be a surprise, so much so, these governments, or what is left of them, will ask 'What the hell just happened?' Their own diseased citizens will be our soldiers waiting not just to be in someone's face, but to rip it off. Once the dust settles, we will be their masters, and masters of the universe!" he exclaimed.

The countdown to Armageddon was at 10, 9...

CHAPTER 17

Paris

15th Arrondissement, Six hours after the explosion
June 20

The devastation was complete. The venerable Institute was a pile of rubble, smoke and small pockets of fire. The majority of the flames had been suppressed by hundreds of Pompiers and citizens flooding the streets, trying to save their historic neighborhood.

Jules LeClerc was alive but buried in the sub-basement under tons of stone rubble. He had regained semi-consciousness several hours after the blast's concussion, which had sent him up and against the thick sandstone and oak timbered wall of the original animal housing sub-basement. The area was now storage for the nineteenth century faded experimental documentation on Rabies and other diseases from those early years, the majority which had not been summarized and then digitized. Jules had traveled down there to read these handwritten journals to see if perhaps there was something they had considered back in the nineteenth century that might be applicable to the current outbreak. His trip two floors below the ground level had put him in the damp, musty sub-basement next to the Pasteur's crypt just minutes before the massive explosion. Kneeling down over a waxed cardboard box, he had just pulled a handful of Louis Pasteur's original written notes when the three blasts had sent him bouncing around in the old animal stall like a pinball. He eventually regained consciousness in the total darkness, his head caked with clotted blood and a layer of fine dust and dirt covering him. His skull throbbed and his ears rang and he thought perhaps he had a fractured rib on the right side of his chest. It was dark, damp and clammy with water dripping down from the firefighting above. Jules could feel a cool subterranean breeze rushing by, being sucked upward to feed the above ground fires.

Jules removed his phone, dialed 112 - emergency, 117- police and 115 - medical emergency and the phone rang and rang with no acknowledgement.

What if all of Paris is gone? What if the attack was nuclear? Mon Dieu!

He held his breath to stem a rising panic and thought optimistically — *perhaps natural gas!*

Jules activated the flashlight function on his phone and searched for a way out. He was confused and noted his phone battery was almost dead.

This historic old area had been preserved much as it would have been in the 1880s and he found two oil lanterns hanging inside an adjacent stall, both holding old lamp oil in the fuel reservoir, but no mantles to light. He felt around and found a discarded burlap feed sack and cut pieces loose with a hoof knife he had located in a farrier's boot box. Old matches were in a desk drawer with a Molin Rouge advertisement cover lying next to a pre-World War Two pack of unopened Gauloise cigarettes.

He tightly wrapped the burlap in place of the missing mantle and pumped the old brass piston until he could see the burlap was wet with the paraffin oil. He struck several matches before one sparked and flared. The oil slowly took on the tiny flame until the makeshift mantle was burning. Not much light but enough for him to explore deeper into the underground animal housing area. Jules reasoned that there had to be at one time a way to receive large animals and remove those that died. He walked deeper down the long hallway past stacks of old equipment, cans of paint and maintenance equipment. He passed many boxes filled with yellowed records as rats scurried past him, squeaking disapproval at his one man invasion.

As he moved down slightly, he could smell the stronger odor of raw sewage gas as the air was sucked past him. Eventually he reached the far wall which was newer brick, evidently the old entrance closed up after the animal housing was no longer used. The floor was covered in cast iron grates that looked to cover an open sewer pit. Most likely that was where they washed the urine and manure.

Jules figured if he could find a way into the Paris sewer main, he could eventually find a way to get back to the surface. He strained to lift up the heavy grate but was unable because shooting pain from his right side nearly took him to his knees. Frustrated after several attempts, he started searching for something to give him a mechanical advantage and slowly felt wall to wall in the faint lantern glow. Finally, located on the far right wall, he found a rusted heavy chain and hook pulley system, something likely used to move large carcasses onto waiting rendering wagons. The device hung from the wall on a massive swinging steel arm that creaked and groaned in protest as he moved it away from the wall for the first time in decades.

Jules pumped more fuel onto the lantern mantle and it flared slightly in a black smoke cloud. Using the extra light, he pulled down on the hook till the chain lay flat on the floor and then secured the hook to one of the iron grate's bars and slowly pulled on the pulley's tail chain. The grate lifted, sliding away from the sewer opening. After the few minutes' struggle, he was able to push the heavy suspended metal away from the sewer opening. Then he collapsed to the ground from pain and exhaustion and silently prayed for deliverance.

Almighty Father God, have mercy on me, your servant. Guide me and deliver me from this evil. Use me to find who did this! Your will be done. Amen.

The lantern wouldn't project enough light to see more than a meter. Jules leaned over the pit's edge and extended his left arm down into the opening holding the brass lantern. To his left were hand-hold steps extending downward and at full arm's length he could see a reflection off a good stream of flowing waste water about 2-3 meters down, flowing to his left.

Thank God, I should be able to stand and walk!

He rolled over to his back and laid there exhausted from the painful effort.

The water moves to the left. This sewer must flow to the Seine, North.

He pulled himself up to his knees and wiped around his face and eyes to remove more of the clotted blood that had formed over his right eye. He pushed the monogrammed handkerchief in his back pocket and then pulled off one of his brown alligator loafers that he had just worn today for the first time. Jules felt the smooth leather sole and heel and started to rough them up over the stone floor's rough surface. He wouldn't risk slipping in the wetness below -- he wouldn't die here and become dinner for a pack of hungry rats. No way!

Jules thought about how to get down those narrow rails that served as steps. His right arm, his dominant strong arm was essentially useless and even hanging on to the two kilo lantern was very painful. He switched the lantern wire handle to his mouth and started down the steps one at a time, hooking his left elbow around the vertical rail and sliding down from step bar to step bar. He was placing abnormal stress on the verticals and suddenly rivets snapped and threw him down to the sewer floor, onto his left side crushing his elbow under his weight and the iron rail. He screamed in pain.

"Mon Dieu, Mon Dieu! Merde! Merde!" *My God, My God! Crap, Crap!*

There he lay for several minutes, his arm throbbing, his side burning. He tried moving his fingers. They worked. He then tried moving his forearm and was able to flex and extend it a little. Pulling carefully, he freed the arm from the iron bar and slid it against his side. Not broken he figured, maybe a nerve or solar plexus injury.

Jules sat up and then stood. The lantern lens had broken but the makeshift burlap mantle was still glowing. He pumped up more fuel. The mantle came to life again with a sooty flare.

The sewer was massive, built at a time when everything from human waste, to animal feces, when horses were the main transportation, flowed with storm water runoff into these tunnels and then dumped directly into the Seine. Now they were storm water only but did carry street trash, leaves and junkie's needles down to the screening filters before the water mixed with the Seine. Rats thrived and there always were rumors of gigantic crocodiles and demons living in the squalid darkness.

Determined, Jules followed the water flow, slipping as he walked the muck covered surface. Rats, some as big as tomcats stared and warned others with rodent chatter.

Eventually he passed street grates with light streaming down into the darkness with the frantic noise of a city under attack audible. He yelled for help, over and over but no one heard. He moved on hoping to find a way out.

Finally, exhausted, he saw a cut out in the wall with a small red arrow reading SORTIE, and pointing up. Jules nearly fell, rushing to his salvation. Fifteen stairs up and there was a door with a push handle emergency exit. He leaned into it and stumbled out onto the street. He was a sight and was soon surrounded by people trying to help.

He fell to his knees, sobbing with tears of joy. Here was life, his Paris had survived the attack. The street signs put him at Rue Bellart and Boulevard Garibaldi so he turned and squinting, looked behind him. The southern sky was black with massive clouds of pluming smoke. He focused his eyes again, straining, not believing the amount of destruction that must have occurred. Sirens filled the air and two paramedics made him lay on a mobile gurney.

They placed an IV and covered him with a warmed blanket. Jules' brain was wheeling.

Why? Why? And who?

He closed his eyes and remembered his prayer. *First redemption, now revenge!*

Lord, deliver me from this evil, use me to find who did this.

That prayer now became his promise.

CHAPTER 18

Air France 3412

On approach to Charles De Gaulle International Airport
22 June, 6 a.m. CET

Kate leaned forward to take in what had been one of her favorite scenes in the world-- Paris at dawn on approach to France's busiest airport. Today was different. She held her breath looking for signs of the trauma the city had endured just three days before and was relieved there were no obvious smoke plumes or anything else that identified the attacked areas.

She had watched the inflight news, both the French and the American broadcasts of the overnight raids that had resulted in the deaths of twelve suspected terrorists and three French police. Rocket launchers, automatic weapons and bomb making materials were captured in the largest operation in modern French history. Kate still didn't believe the amount of destruction and death those twelve had perpetrated on 'her' Paris. Over thirteen hundred killed, countless thousands injured and the near complete destruction of two square blocks in the Fifteenth. The city would never be the same again.

Jean had called with the news that Jules had survived, although injured, and was in the St. Lazare Emergency and Trauma Center. That was the same hospital that had saved his life after he had been shot by the Nazi Berhetzel. Kate decided, and Tom agreed reluctantly, that she would go to Paris to see her old friend. After their visit with Joseph and hearing his weird experience, followed by the attack on Paris, she had again gotten that same strange feeling that she had when they had originally searched for the 'Destroyer'. It was horribly unsettling.

She took a taxi to Hôtel Midi, showered and ate a light breakfast of juice, coffee and fruit. Then she took another taxi over to the hospital and after going through security, was personally escorted to Jules' room. Every room had two to four occupied beds and some patients with less threatening injuries lined the family lounges and cafeteria. Kate had never seen so many injured people in one place. Jules however was in a small VIP suite at the rear of the high security area. She quietly walked over to his bed while he slept and touched his hand.

"Mon Dieu! An angel has come to take me to heaven," he said laughing lightly while trying to silence a cough, "Mon Chérie, you are a vision!"

Kate always dressed fashionably, but when she was in Paris she seemed to glow with her love for the City of Light. She wore a pale blue silk blouse and tailored black slacks and very stylish black short heel shoes.

She leaned forward and placed at light kiss on his forehead as he smiled, now contented.

"Jules, I had to come to see you and what they did to our Paris. C'est horrible!" Kate said, holding back tears.

"I know how sad you are. Many, many very good people, including over two hundred eighty-six colleagues and patients at the Pasteur, died at the hands of these monsters but I am confident that they will be judged by our Lord God. I hear they already have been discovered and eliminated by the Sûreté. Too bad there is no one left to question. That will likely put us back to square one, which means we may never understand the true depth of it," Jules replied.

"I should be released tomorrow," he continued, "many bruises, one slightly cracked rib and rat bites on my ankles. Funny thing is, I never felt any of those furry bastards biting through my forty Euro bamboo fiber socks. I hope the little SOB's gagged on the stuff.

"The bottom line is, I was in the right place at the wrong time. Had I been at my desk, you would be attending a memorial service. Probably a very nice service though with many very sad, beautiful ladies crying their eyes out."

"You old goat, you haven't changed, have you? Wait, don't tell me, yes I know, you are French," Kate joked.

"Oui, c'est vrai." *Yes, that's true.*

"How about your office staff? Did Margot get out?" Kate asked.

"Yes, all my staff are ok because they went to her favorite brassiere to celebrate her fiftieth birthday. I was to join them later. Here is some bad news."

"Quoi?" she asked. *What?"*

"We lost all the research on Berhetzel's device and the entire team working on it. We, like idiots, archived all our data on site. I fear it is all is gone."

"Why wouldn't you store it off site?" she asked incredulously.

"There were plans but the board procrastinated just to save a few Euros. Bastards!" Jules replied angrily.

"When you get out of here I want to update you on what is going on in the States. Also, Joseph had a real strange thing happen to him in Montana. His grandfather spoke to him again and he strangely found two syringe darts next to the dried remains of white bison carcass. He thinks that the syringes have wolf fur wrapped on each. I don't know exactly how to approach this, but on the flight over, I had a lot of time to think. Remember when they said the Mall of America wolf was almost a thousand miles from her birth home? What if she was darted, infected and moved just for the purpose of a dramatic introduction of the virus?"

"You think this epidemic not naturally occurring? Manmade? Bio-Terrorism?" Jules questioned.

"I know it is far-fetched and crazy but if Joseph hadn't found those syringes, directed by his grandfather, nobody would even imagine it. Bigger powers are at work here, just like last time!"

"Is there a way of testing that fur?"

"It is already on the way to Fred Garrett at Ohio State where he will compare it to the Mall animal sample that Ted Johnson is overnighting from the CDC. If it matches, all hell will break loose!"

"I 'll bet my expensive socks it matches. Someone is behind this and if this is not natural, then this plague is a weapon, directed by evil."

"That's my fear also, just a gut feeling, but after Berhetzel, nothing would surprise me. I just hope Tristar can get us a vaccine so we can limit the causalities. And for the record, no one wants your rat chewed socks!"

"D'accord, Mon Chérie, please tell the attendant I would like to see my doctor. It's time to get the hell out of here. We have a serious investigation to start!"

CHAPTER 19

General's Metro Park

Atlanta, three days earlier
3.23 AM

Karl Rimer carried three burlap feed sacks over his shoulder as he entered on a shortcut into the far end of the two hundred acre rocky hilled city park. Surrounded by quiet neighborhoods, the park was a refuge for a large resident wildlife population. Deer, fox, coyote, skunk, opossum and raccoon were commonly out and about, having lost any fear of human contact. A ten acre pond was stocked with bass, bream, and catfish and was a popular family fishing spot. Mostly wild, the park had nearly two miles of trails and often trail riders on horseback moved along with joggers through the park. It was a popular urban oasis.

Inside each bag were two raccoons he had purchased a week before. He had injected the animals with a combination of ketamine and diazepam forty-five minutes before. The coons were immobile within ten minutes and despite his being vaccinated orally against the disease, he gloved and wore a protective respirator hood as he injected them with the engineered live rabies strain. Each animal was now a biologic time bomb and would explode, terrorizing first the park, and as the virus replicated and spread from these primary vectors to other mammals, the residents of Atlanta.

Rimer was a co-opted white supremacist who had been a New World Nazi for over thirty years. He had always been filled with hate, having been beaten nearly daily by his alcoholic father until the day he ran away and turned to the 'Party' at age seventeen. He was part of an occult group directly linked back to the Third Reich-those -- anonymous survivors that escaped Nazi Germany to start a new life in America while remaining loyal to their evil cause. He had waited in the shadows his entire adult life, through a thirty year Army career for this moment. Now he commanded forty-one party members, all ex-military that shared his politics and hatred of all nonwhite minorities and Jews. He was a soldier and when given this assignment to use a military quality drone, equipment he was expert in, to capture the wolves, then to infect the D.C. area raccoons and the crazy feral cats in Boston, he literally jumped at the chance. His youngest boy Max, an active duty solider at Fort Eustis, Virginia, had stolen the drones and was his sole confidante. No one outside the two of them was involved in this initial bioterrorism and none of his other family even had a clue they were terrorists.

Their timing and placement of the infected animals was executed with military precision and they were extremely diligent not to do any-thing to bring attention to themselves or trip security cameras. He had secretly purchased live raccoons in Northern Virginia, a violation of Game Regulations, from nuisance control trappers under the guise of stocking a hunt club. False names and disguises were used and they were careful in not leaving any trail or witnesses.

He carefully placed these raccoons inside trash bin that he tipped over slightly. There they would be safe until they recovered from the sedation and found their way out. The virus he injected now had its home, its victim, and would replicate at an astonishing rate, being shed in urine and feces even before the animals reached full clinical signs. They would feed with other raccoons on back porches and at bird feeders, raiding garbage cans leaving the virus behind for several days before the fiery rage of disease would hurl the crazed animals at anything near them. Death would end their suffering but the mammalian scavengers who consumed their remains would become the next host multiplier. Thousands would die.

Rimer removed the night vision head lamp, rolled it up and shoved it into his camovest's side pocket. He walked back up the trail bumping up two deer that went crashing away through the scrub oaks. He stopped and listened as they pushed through the brushy trees, panicked that their usual quiet private night had been invaded. Rimer pulled out his cell phone and texted Max a simple message-- 'Ready three minutes.' His son would have the pickup in position on the residential street above the park when his father exited through a back yard.

On schedule, the father and son terrorists slowly pulled away as neighborhood dogs barked their alarm. Too late. The seeds were now planted and when the crop grew, this would be a toxic area of death.

The countdown to Armageddon stood at 8.

CHAPTER 20

Paris

Home of Jules LeClerc
June 23

Jules Leclerc resided in what was arguably the wealthiest neighborhood in Paris---Neuilly-sûr-Seine. His townhouse or 'hôtel particulier' was surrounded by gardens on a quiet side street. This area was home to the elites of Paris and was a city unto itself. Crime was unheard of in this serene place as hidden private security was everywhere. Kate was now Jules and his wife Simone's house guest.

"Please excuse the clutter my dear," Simone said, "but with Jules being rushed to Saint- Lazares and with everything else going on yesterday after the attacks, I sent the staff home. They had their own families to reconcile."

Kate didn't see anything that wasn't perfect and smiled at the thought that this elegant Parisian home was in the least bit cluttered.

"Your home is lovely, perfect I would say. I live with a farm veterinarian and a nearly one year old boy so I know clutter. Your home is so beautiful and elegant! Thank you so much for inviting me to stay. I had reservations at the Midi, but I really can't thank you enough for your generous hospitality."

"It is our pleasure," Madame LeClerc answered, "I appreciate your concern for Jules and your love for Paris. These are tragic times but this city has survived so many challenges like the Black Plague, the Revolution, the Nazis, the Socialists, so we will survive these cowards who attack us like crazed dogs biting at our heels. Prisons will be built and I dare say the guillotine's blades will be sharpened again. No one has been executed since 1977, but public opinion now favors the return of capital punishment. It is time to take back our city, our country and our culture!"

Kate heard the passion, and felt the pain in her words. Their wonderful life was under attack and Jules' narrow escape put everything in vivid perspective. The citizens would rise up making the words to La Marseillaise, the anthem that played endlessly with passion on all the radios and televisions since the attacks, come true:

ARISE CHILDREN OF THE FATHERLAND, THE DAY OF GLORY HAS ARRIVED. AGAINST US TYRANNY'S BLOODY STANDARD'S RAISED.

LISTEN TO THE SOUND IN THE FIELDS,

THE HOWLING OF THESE FEARSOME SOLDIERS, THEY ARE COMING INTO OUR MIST

TO CUT THE THROATS OF YOUR SONS AND CONSORTS.

CHORUS.

TO ARMS, CITIZENS! FORM YOUR BATTALIONS,

MARCH, MARCH

LET IMPURE BLOOD

WATER OUR FURROWS!

Kate had heard the anthem on the plane, seen the tears in passenger's eyes as they watched their inflight televisions, then she heard it on the taxi radio and now into so many words, as the passionate vow of Madame LeClerc. Yes they were wounded, but no, they could never be defeated. World War Two taught the French a valuable lesson, never capitulate again!

Jules had sat mute through the conversation, his pain meds making him a silent observer. He now burned with the same anger that his friend Jean DuBois had shown after his father had been murdered and he was nearly killed by the Nazi Berhetzel. His physical pain would go away as he healed, but the emotional scars of so many dead and the loss of his beloved, historic Pasteur facility would haunt him for the rest of his days. The building could be resurrected but would never be the same. Thank God the Institute was more than just a Parisian headquarters. The remaining branches around the world would carry their mission forward.

He smiled as his wife exposed passion that had rarely surfaced. They were devout Catholics who abhorred divorce but tolerated each other despite his philandering, which had placed a quiet divide between them. Jules had had many mistresses over the years and spent untold euros on their needs, but Simone did have this wonderful home, a prestigious husband and personal wealth. None of his 'friends' could ever loosen her grip on that. She had even managed one long affair with a Parisian banker until he had died suddenly two years before. His untimely death devastated her not only from his loss, but from the realization she didn't want to invest any more of her life into a loving relationship. She would now live alone, unloved but active in her social causes. Perhaps her husband would return to her as he had many times in the past. Simone was an asset for him, a beautiful blond, trim and fit but still sixty and she understood that Jules preferred women that made him feel thirty. Their marriage lifestyle was widely accepted in Parisian society, so the only person critical of it was her. She hated that.

The women enjoyed Kir Royales that Simone made as Jules struggled with a small expresso, not wanting to mix alcohol with his pain meds. The expresso only helped make him more aware of the throbbing discomfort in his side, but his brain appreciated the wake-up call. He joined in the conversation the women were sharing.

"Simone, are all our friends and family accounted for? I am worried because so many were lost."

"As far as I can tell," she replied, "all family is safe but the Renvoir's can't locate Paul, he was possibly on the Metro and Marie and Andre's daughter was on a field trip to Notre Dame with L'école Saint-Marie and she is in serious condition and may lose a leg that was crushed when the roof and south wall fell. The poor baby is only eight years old! What kind of animals attack innocents?"

"The same bastards that behead, drown or burn alive their victims," Jules angrily voiced. "They are all murderers, abortionists of life. Nelson Blackfeather's culture deemed them 'Destroyers' and rightly so---they are perennial killers, like noxious weeds that you spray or pull up but never get all the root so they eventually reappear to spread their poison. The Lakota understand that it is the 'Creator' that controls when those weeds are located and eliminated but that persistent scion of evil that exists in the world is always waiting to present the world with a new crop of offspring!"

Kate's iPhone rang. It was Dr Fred Garrett calling from Ohio.

"Good morning, Fred. I'm at Jules' home. ...wait, I'll put you on speaker. Ok, go ahead."

"Jules, mon ami, comment ça va?" the Nobel Prize winning geneticist - microbiologist asked.

"I am emotionally wounded but physically I am very, very lucky. I should be getting around well in a few days," Jules answered. "Our Paris is the same but much stronger than any one person or ideology."

"I will pray for both you and God's mercies on your city and people that this madness stops. To that, I have completed the comparative analysis from the CDC tissue sample and the two distinctly different fur samples Joseph found on those air dart needles. We were also able to get the wolf's original puppy DNA taken in Montana almost a decade ago."

"What did you conclude ?" Kate asked anxiously.

"One sample does not match, it is a male and not related to the other. However, the female shot in The Mall of America, nearly eight hundred miles from where Joseph found the fur samples, IS the same animal with total certainty. She also matches the puppy DNA which verifies the microchip data. She was darted within eighty miles of her birth den. Someone captured her to deliver that virus in a dramatic fashion. Now the question is, who did it and where is the male?" Fred asked.

"Maybe he died before he could be used? Wait a minute, remember the bus driver at Denver International? He said he hit a large coyote and threw it in a dumpster. What if he was mistaken and it was a second wolf?" Kate said.

"Then you need to ask the man which dumpster and scour it for any tiny piece of fur or tissue," Fred replied.

"Unfortunately, that man was delirious and gave the Colorado health authorities a general idea before they placed him in a drug coma, and they checked for gross evidence but the trash had already gone to the landfill. They did search two sites for the animal but had no luck. That driver died two days ago but maybe if we search forensically we might find some blood or fur in one of the dumpsters. Before they were looking to recover a whole carcass," Kate answered.

Jules jumped back in the conversation.

"So if all this is true, we have a manmade bioweapon on the loose, but if someone is trying to terrorize your country, why have they not reveled themselves and taken credit for the attack? It seems rather out of character."

"Because," Kate answered, "they don't want to reveal it until it is well established. Otherwise we would consider it an act of war and we would go after both them and the disease with a military style approach. They would be eliminated and the virus contained in a scorched earth policy. No, I think they want this to appear to be a natural epidemic, perhaps to take it to a worldwide pandemic."

"And what better way to assure its establishment than to disrupt the scientific community by removing one of the greatest scientific research centers in the world!" Simone postulated.

"Mon Dieu! My dear, you may be correct. In all this chaos perhaps the real target was the Pasteur. If so then your CDC, WHO, and all the other worldwide health agencies are potential targets. Kate, we need to alert our colleagues right away!" Jules said, nearly shouting.

"I'll call Ted Johnson at the CDC right now and have him contact WHO. They can then alert the British, Russians and Chinese. Why don't you call Hans Vogel at Tristar and have them beef up their security!" Kate replied.

"Beef up? What is that?" the Frenchman asked.

"Sorry, it is to make their security stronger, as a bull!"

"Yes, stronger and better! I hope we are wrong, but if we are even a little bit correct, this could be disastrous. A new 'Destroyer' on the loose? Joseph was right, something big is about to happen. God help us again!" Jules prayed as he reached for his iPhone.

CHAPTER 21

Tristar Veterinary Biologics

Office of Hans Vogel

The large computer screen was switching from one pastoral vision to another. A series of snow-covered mountains, high cliffs overlooking the greenest of valleys, sandy beaches with azure waters and fields of wildflowers slowly morphed by a countdown clock as Vogel waited for Mendoza's Skype call. This was the only time they planned to communicate by encrypted Skype until the second vaccine booster doses had been delivered to the individual veterinary practices in the United States.

The monitor suddenly flashed, 'ENCRYPTION VERIFIED,' and Mendoza appeared sitting at his office desk in Argentina. He wore a Guayaberas white linen shirt and sat at a large mahogany desk with a cigar and a liquor glass.

His monitor camera must have been panoramic and across the room to provide the exacting view of the dark, wood paneled office.

"This is the first time I have used this new computer system for Skype," Mendoza stated.

"I resisted upgrading until this project was underway to install the latest technology. Now I am super secure and sit in my father's old office, which you can see is an exact duplication of his Wolfschanze war room. Same down to the smallest detail but at about a fifty percent scale. This is the room where he relived the war, day after day, where he cursed the generals that had failed him and it is also where he died, sitting at this very desk. So now, Hans, we are on the verge of our revenge for the humiliation the Americans and so-called Allies perpetuated on us almost seventy-five years ago and usher in my Fourth Reich."

"It will be a dream come true, Mein Führer! We have incorporated the viron contaminate in the booster doses and I am personally supervising the addition of that contaminant to your specifications into the vials. Death will be mixed with those second batch doses and be distributed only to the desired targets. We just submitted the test data to the CDC on the primary vaccine to protect against the new rabies strain and with their expedited approval, will begin shipping doses to veterinary practices in the desired kill zones. We will then follow with the lethal boosters one month later. So within a very short time, Hell, our Hell, will be unleashed on the United States!"

"There is one serious problem that I needed to discuss with you," Vogel added.

"What is that?" Mendoza asked.

"My contact at the CDC said the Mall wolf's tissue samples were sent to a Nobel Prize winning geneticist in Ohio. There is speculation that the animal was intentionally infected with an engineered virus. I don't know if they have a basis for that but it seems they found the drone darts by chance in the middle of that Montana wilderness and somehow have started to connect the dots. Basically, the Rimers screwed up," Vogel said, watching the Nazi's reaction to the news. It was not good.

"Have you verified any of this?" Mendoza nearly growled.

"I have asked my CDC contact to get me as much information that she can without drawing undo attention. It seems there is small group of USDA field agents that work closely with the CDC and they made the discovery and postulated that the wolf was darted, moved and infected to dramatize the new rabies virus and to terrorize the public. Jules LeClerc from the Pasteur, also called me personally to warn us that the Paris terrorist attack might have been a ruse.

"To me it is almost unbelievable that they were able to figure any of it out. The tip off on the wolf was she had been microchipped as a puppy in the general area we captured her at. The mall is nearly eleven hundred kilometers away from her birth den. They questioned how she got there and then they stumbled onto the darts at the bison carcass. It was pure luck."

Mendoza didn't comment for a very long pause as he obviously was thinking through the problem.

"How many have this information?" he asked.

"As far as I know three different entities. Ted Johnson, director of emerging diseases at the CDC, our operative, his assistant Elizabeth Adams, the USDA group which is either three or four veterinarians and the genetics researcher at the Ohio State University. How many they have discussed it with is unknown. At least the CDC connection, Adams, confirmed at the CDC, only Johnson."

"Then get the Rimers to clean up their mess. Eliminate the CDC man, Johnson and get more information on the rest. They most likely are career bureaucrats just trying to make a living so we need to find out what they know and what they are going to do about it, if anything. We can't kill them all without raising some level of suspicion and we certainly don't want to get the FBI or any other investigative agency active until our human viron is released. Get our field people involved. Have them make discreet inquiries. Then when we know who we are dealing with, I will decide how to handle it. Rimer needs to get busy, it's his screw up and I want it fixed! Jetzt!" *Now!*

The screen went blank as Mendoza abruptly severed the connection. Obviously, this unexpected turn of events put their mission at risk and Vogel's hand was visibly shaking as he dialed up his intermediary with orders for Rimer.

CHAPTER 22

Atlanta

June 27, 7 p.m.

Ted Johnson didn't really keep a regular work schedule. Most days he started well before 9 a.m. at the CDC and normally he didn't leave at 5 p.m., but stayed each day until his work was completed. He was divorced from his wife but remarried to his job. He liked it that way.

Half of his job was pushing paper at the CDC where he had worked for nineteen years. The other half of his time was spent lecturing, running meetings or in DC testifying to congressional committees. He never took time off and had banked nearly all his paid time off so if he wanted, he could easily take nearly a year off. But he was a workaholic bureaucrat, a kind of enigma.

Karl Rimer had been stalking him for three days, learning his patterns and habits. He had to find a way to eliminate Johnson and make it appear to be an accident, a robbery gone bad or a suicide. So far he hadn't decided which path to take and was getting tired of playing cat and mouse in the stifling Georgia heat. The worst thing was the constant calls from Vogel's surrogate to finish the job, so today, Rimer had decided no matter what, this was his last day of cat and mouse.

He watched as Johnson pulled out of his parking spot and turned left out on Clifton Road, accelerating quickly in his classic 1989 Red

Chevy Corvette convertible, his one non-work related passion. The car quickly accelerated, smoothly growling as the gears were shifted. The car was near mint and should have been trophied in Johnson's garage but Rimer could see that the man was an expert driver and in love with the beauty and power of the classic car.

Rimer waited to time his fake car hijacking. This appeared to be his best approach to coverup an assassination -- a failed carjacking. The last two evenings, Rimer had watched Johnson stop and park his car at Stonehaven Rest Home, he assumed to visit a resident, probably a family member. He had both times stayed exactly one half hour and then drove home. The stately Reconstruction era cut stone mansion had no doubt been a very expensive residence, a grand estate in the Ansley Park neighborhood that had been converted in the late seventies to an exclusive residence for wealthy Alzheimer's patients. There was a thick, sprawling, old brick wall surrounding the home which help hide the limited visitor parking that was under a grove of massive white pines. Rimer would attack from under that canopy, protected from security cameras and street traffic.

On schedule, Johnson pulled into Stonehaven's entrance and parked the Corvette away from the other two cars, a black Mercedes Convertible and a silver BMW X5. He hurried to the heavy wood-paneled red front door, spoke into an intercom box and was buzzed in.

Rimer parked one block away on a short side street. He was counting on Johnson being an exacting person and would be leaving the building just as he had the last two days. He waited for seventeen minutes and then walked calmly over to the home, climbing the wall easily from the rear side and carefully made his way to the small parking area. The pine grove was cool and covered in a deep layer of fragrant soft needle litter that he knew, when silently hiding behind a massive tree and approaching Johnson, would afford him the element of complete surprise. He hid in the shadow of tree trunks, waiting, his pulse quickening in anticipation of a kill.

Johnson exited exactly one half-hour after parking the Corvette and brushed some tree litter off the black leather driver's seat.

"Don't make a sound," Rimer commanded as he pushed the hard stainless steel muzzle of his S&W 9mm into Johnson's ribs. "Move away from the car. That's all I want.

"Now up against that tree," he ordered.

"Here's my keys," Johnson offered, stretching out his right hand behind him.

"Drop your gun, scumbag!" came a strong female voice from behind them.

Rimer's mind was racing. Johnson had not seen his face nor had the woman now behind him. He controlled the urge to look back to see the woman who now controlled the scenario. He needed two things. First to eliminate his target and then escape without being identified . He had to kill Johnson and then sprint away hoping the woman would hesitate.

"Armageddon is coming!" he yelled as he quickly fired the gun into Johnson and dodged to the left behind a large pine's trunk.

No shot.

I was right, she choked.

He ran dodging from tree to tree while holding his breath waiting for the sting of lead.

Nothing.

He reached the red brick wall and scrambled to climb over it.

Relieved and confident the woman was a joke, he hesitated and turned to look back, his curiosity getting the best of him.

A mistake. The woman was fifty feet away, her gun drawn, as a bright red laser sight dot danced on his chest as she fired.

He fell, propelled over the wall, landing hard on an old moss covered brick sidewalk, mortally wounded.

Rimer pulled himself up, holding his left side, adrenaline fueling his strong survival instincts. He could only manage short painful breaths but found and pushed himself into his car, started it, and moved it into the street. He needed to go home and lay down.

Get home, lay down, pack the wound. Only thirty minutes away. I will not die, I will not die !

He made it to the peeling paint, run down, slummy shack in a poor area just inside the city's beltway. He weakly pushed past the old

rusted screened door as it slammed hard on corroded coiled springs behind him. He had lost a majority of his blood, was cold, wet from blood and faint. He shivered uncontrollably as he collapsed on the large musty sofa couch where he slept. Breathing rapidly, Rimer pulled a heavy quilt over his cold body and closed his eyes.

They would never open again.

CHAPTER 23

Paris

June 28, 2100 hours

Kate was sitting on the LeClerc's terrace, overlooking the illuminated formal courtyard garden and fountains with Simone. They had each enjoyed a wonderful glass of expensive Bordeaux and now were savoring a fine cognac before retiring for the evening.

"It is so beautiful and peaceful here, I can't thank you enough for your hospitality and friendship. When Jules is up to it, I would love to have you visit Tom and I ---- nothing fancy but a nice country location and perhaps we could spent sometime in Chicago exploring and shopping, maybe take in a show," Kate offered.

"We would love to visit. I have never been to the States, but Jules as you know goes everywhere and prefers to travel alone, or so he says," Simone answered with a sarcastic finish.

Kate's cell phone rang --- a call from Tom.

"Hi, sweetheart," she greeted his unexpected call.

"Hi, honey, everything at home is fine but I have some bad news for you. Ted Johnson was killed in Atlanta in an attempted carjacking last evening, Brad just told me. The man who tried to steal his Corvette was shot by an armed woman but he got away, although they feel he was seriously wounded. They are trying to track his get away with street cams, but so far have nothing and he's not been treated at any of the emergency rooms or hospitals."

Kate was listening in stunned silence.

"Honey, are you there?" Tom asked.

"I can't believe it, it doesn't seem possible after just seeing him for the mini - conference. Are they having a service?"

"Brad is trying to find out. I should know by the time you get home tomorrow. One strange thing was the perp shouted 'Armageddon is coming' according to the woman who shot him. Sounds like a nut case. If anything else comes up I'll call. Bobbi is in bed already but he sure misses his mommy. I miss her too! Love you! Bye."

"Love you too, Tom, bye!"

"Bad news?" Simone asked, seeing Kate's distress.

"A friend and colleague was murdered in Atlanta yesterday, Ted Johnson. Jules knows him very well."

"Yes, Jules has spoken of him on occasion. So sad. What a crazy world we live in. I think I should tell Jules straight away, this is something that he needs to know right now. Pardon, I will go wake him," Simone said.

"D'accord." *Ok.*

Jules was dressed and down to the garden within several minutes. He appeared angry and sad at the same time.

"This is insanity!" he proclaimed to Kate, his anger showing. "Ted was a kind, sincere man who always used his intellect to help others."

"Tom told me it was an attempted carjacking. The man who did it was seriously wounded but they haven't found him yet. Tom also said the man shouted 'Armageddon is coming' just as he shot Ted. Maybe he was a crazy?"

"Armageddon is coming? Insanity or prophesy?" Jules questioned.

"It does seem strange, doesn't it? Why wouldn't he just take the car and run. The woman who shot him might know. I think I will change my return flight for tomorrow and stop in Atlanta to get some answers."

"I want to go also and since I am the de facto head of what is left of the Pasteur, we can use the Institute jet. Also, I will see if Jean would like to come along. He needs to keep busy and I need his friendship right now. And you know how intuitive and intelligent he is."

"Bien Sûr. I'll call Tom and let him know the change of plans. How about Simone coming along also?"

"Non, with this rabies crisis, I don't want to take a chance," Jules replied. "Besides this trip, I fear there may be some risk beyond the disease. I'm getting that same awful feeling as last time that we are not just facing a new pathogen, but with the DNA evidence that the wolf had been darted and relocated after being infected, it looks to be terrorists at work--- or someone or group of equal mental disease. This is not going to be a pleasant visit, I think it's not a time to show Simone around your beautiful country."

"D'accord, let me know the flight plan and I will call Tom, and then check in with Brad."

"And God give us wisdom, protection and strength."

"Amen," Kate replied.

CHAPTER 24

Pet Care Plus Veterinary Services

Baltimore, Maryland
June 29

Francis 'Dr. Frank' Donnelly was an early starter each day. He would be in the gym by 6 a.m., on days he wasn't jogging to work, usually on those days when the weather made the running miserable or unsafe. That didn't happen very often.

Dr. Frank owed three total care facilities in the affluent suburbs of Baltimore and employed twelve veterinarians and nearly eighty support staff. Pet Care Plus was a clinic, grooming, boarding and pet store combined for one-stop convenience. He located his businesses in failed corporate pharmacies, like a big box drug store, where several retail giants would set up at a busy intersection, build a great open area retail space and then duke it out with their competitors until one or two would fail, leaving prime locations vacant and easily converted to a pet multiplex. While conservative risk-adverse colleagues envied his success, satisfied with the status quo, he kept pushing forward.

This morning he had received a text alert from the CDC that they had approved the new rabies vaccine for conditional release, pending full licensing. Each clinic in Containment Zone A, could order up to 2,500 doses of 'Tri-Rab' for direct shipment from Tristar Veterinary Biologics with a booster dose automatically shipping thirty days after delivery verification. The CDC message warned that no vaccine could be diverted, shared or used in any way off label or a $250,000 fine and up to six years in prison would be the penalty. The modified live vaccine only had a sixty-day expiration and all vaccine not used during those sixty days had to be returned to the CDC. The cost per dose for the initial and booster was preset at $35 a dose and they were prohibited from charging more than $70 to vaccinate or booster an animal. Only dogs, cats, horses and ferrets were approved to receive the vaccination. After the Zone A practices had vaccinated 90% of the companion animals under their care, Zone B or low risk areas would receive their doses, probably in six to nine months. Vaccine orders had to be prepaid by credit card or bank transfer prior to shipment.

Donnelly did some quick math in his head. Twenty-five hundred times three practices times $35 was $262,500. One hell of a credit card bill, but since he used American Express nearly exclusively to order and pay bills, he definitely could max out the order. Other practices on a shoestring budget would be put in a difficult spot when their clients demanded vaccines they couldn't deliver. If he used and reordered once his vaccines were all given, registered and they forwarded documentation to the CDC, he could reorder again and again, expanding his client base and making a tidy profit to boot. The only real issue would be not exposing the staff to any potentially infected animals. So far reports indicated that the disease might be self-limiting its range with possibly the disease killing the infected before they could infect other animals. Either way, the disease would be around for a very long time and much like the Parvovirus outbreak of the late seventies and early eighties, would increase foot traffic in his clinics. Great, so long as no one died.

At his desk forty-five minutes later, he ordered online the maximum amount of vaccines allowed and paid by his Amex card. He then called his advertising agent to set up an E-Blast to his clients and commissioned a thirty second 'public service announcement' about the disease and their ability to provide vaccine protection. Nothing like toddlers playing in their yard being stalked by a rabid raccoon to get the phones ringing off their hooks.

CHAPTER 25

Atlanta Hartsfield-Jackson International Airport

June 29, 6 p.m.

Kate, Jean and Jules had just pushed through passport control, not having the perks that the previous diplomatic credentials had afforded their travel, because the entire international travel team had perished when the Pasteur was destroyed. Jules also lost two good friends that were longtime flight attendants who for years had made his international travel effortless. Now they matriculated through the system with the masses.

Kate led them down to the baggage claim / ground transportation area and was overjoyed to see Tom and Brad waiting.

Tom nearly ran to her, relieved she was home and safe. Embracing, they lingered clinging on to one another.

"How's Bobbi?" Kate asked.

"He's good, at camp with Grandma and Grandpa along with Jed."

Brad had already greeted the French doctors and gave Kate a big hug. Tom expressed his sympathy for all their personal loss of friends and the destruction of the Pasteur.

"We still have several hours of daylight, so we are going into the city and checking the crime scene with a local FBI agent that Special Agent

Sullivan from D.C. arranged. Sullivan also said whatever we need, the FBI is at our disposal. I think he smells a rat also," Jules said.

"We rented a big Suburban, so I'll go pull it around and we can get going," Brad said.

They loaded up into the oversized SUV and Brad bullied his way into the stream of cabs and cars exiting one of the world's busiest airports. He restrained the wisecracks out of respect for Ted Johnson but rolled over his usual humor several times in his head before wisely passing on any potential misinterpreted humor.

By six they were parked on the street just down from Stonehaven Rest Home, and walked to the brick pillared entrance. A black Chevy Malibu with government plates was parked off to the side along with one other car, a silver BMW X5. A tall black man in a gray polyester blend suit was talking to a middle aged blond ponytailed woman who was dressed in a white cotton blouse and trim fitting designer jeans. She wore yellow semi reflective aviator style shooter's glasses and smiled at the group as they approached.

Field agent Brian Jackson greeted the group as introductions were made. The woman was Shirley Potter, the person who had shot the perp as he tried to escape. She was an avid experienced shooter and competed once or twice a month.

Agent Jackson went over everything the FBI knew and then had Ms. Potter recount the events as she remembered them. It was almost the same time of day as when the murder occurred. She spoke with a refined soft Southern drawl.

"I feel real bad about Dr Johnson. I should have just nailed the bastard as soon as I saw him pressing the doctor against the tree. I hesitated because I didn't think he would shoot, not for a damned car. He never looked at me which I think would be a normal response to being yelled at, he just shot and ran. I think Johnson was dead before he hit the ground. Funny thing was that the slime bag didn't hesitate but ran and started climbing the wall almost like the escape route was predetermined. The investigators never did find his casing but the gun was a 9mm stainless steel Smith and Wesson. I have one just like it."

She continued. "He screamed that thing about Armageddon, shot and as he ran, I was hoping to get a clean shot but he dodged these big pines and there was so much shadowing I didn't shoot. You see, I am a disciplined marksman but when he was in the clear, over there, near the top of that brick wall, I let him have it. He should have died right there. I'm convinced he's lying dead somewhere because from the amount of tissue and blood he lost and that solid 'Whomp' I heard when my slug hit, he's just got to be dead. With way he moved, there is no way he wore protective body armor!"

Jean was listening intently and suggested, "Perhaps we should rec-reate the events and maybe we could find that brass that might have forensic evidence on it. Which tree was Dr Johnson up against?"

"That one," Potter said, pointing to a nearly hidden area in the pine grove.

"D'accord, Brad, you play Dr. Johnson and Tom you be the shooter," Jean instructed.

"Maintenant, Madame Potter, would you verify their positioning and place yourself where you shouted your warning.

"Dr. Upton, you get up against the tree and Dr. O'Dell you press up against him tightly from behind, like you're trying to hide him."

They both looked back incredulously at her, not wanting to get that close.

"Just do it!" Kate shouted.

"Be gentle with me, honey," Brad whispered as Tom did what he was told, pressing his friend against the tree and using his right hand like a gun, pushed up against Upton's right side.

"That's it," Potter said, "except he was a Southpaw. The gun was in his left hand!"

"What?" the FBI agent asked, "I don't see that in the report!"

"No one asked and it never came up!" she replied.

The agent just shook his head understanding he was looking at a sloppy investigation.

"Drop your gun, scumbag!" she screamed loudly, and all heads turned to look at her.

"See," she said, "you all looked, it is a basic response to a threat. This man did not."

"Then he was a trained professional or deaf," Jean concluded. "I fear this was an assassination."

"I can't argue with that," Jackson agreed.

"He shouted that Armageddon warning, fired his weapon and dodged behind the trees, under their canopy shadow. Dr. O'Dell, run from behind each tree until I tell you to stop and at that point climb the wall, stop at the top. That's where I nailed his ass."

Tom did what he was told and stopped at the top of the eight foot brick barricade.

"Bang, you're dead, grab your left side," Jean shouted.

Tom did what he was told, making a dramatic clutch to his chest.

The sun was on the left, just behind his back. Tom caught a shiny yellow reflection on the flat top of the wall to his right, partially buried in pine needles.

"Hey," he yelled back, "I think I found that casing!"

CHAPTER 26

Lounge of the St. Regis Hotel

Atlanta
Late that same evening

The five investigators sat around a low glass table in a semi-circle. They all were tired from travel, the heat, plus their brains were exhausted from being in overdrive from the somber events of the last few days. They sat in relative silence waiting for their beer, wine and tapas style small plates they had ordered to stave off their complaining bellies.

When the drinks arrived, Jules offered up a toast.

"To our friend and colleague Ted, to all those souls lost in Paris and to our friendship ----Salut!"

"Salut!'"

"And to Jules who booked us into this wonderful hotel---Merci Beaucoup!" Kate said.

They drank in a momentary awkward silence waiting for their food.

Brad couldn't stand it any longer.

"I sure wish Joseph was here, he would have some insight into all this crap being tossed at us. You all know I'm the smallest brain here and it's doing cartwheels trying to connect the dots ---Ted was assassinated? --- a hit man was sent to murder him and make it look like a car theft gone bad? Am I going nuts or what?"

"That's a yes on the brain, a yes on the nuts thing and it's not just your brain is the smallest!" Tom teased.

"That's exactly the response I would expect from a guy that has his arm up a cow's rear most of his day."

"Ok, boys, settled down," Kate laughed, "I think you're both delirious from lack of food. Well maybe not you, Brad," noting the large man's size.

Jules and Jean were laughing as their American friends poked fun at each other.

"After we relax and eat, we can review everything from the new strain of rabies to a Ted's murder. I think it's all connected and with Joseph being contacted by his Great Grandfather once more, with your dreams, Jean, my instincts are telling me here we go again," Jules said.

"Oui, je suis d'accord," Jean said. *Yes, I agree.*

The food came and they ate quickly, their bodies absorbing the welcomed energy.

"I think we should contact Joseph and put him on speaker when we go over this one more time before we retire for the evening," Kate offered.

They agreed and Kate connected to his cell and put her phone on speaker.

The phone rang six times before the young Indian answered. "Hi, Kate, I'm in the horse barn. I'll call you back in two minutes." Click.

Kate ended the call on her end and it rang quickly back. "Joseph, how are you? I am in Atlanta with Jules, Jean, Brad and Tom. You are on speaker."

"Hi, everyone! I assume this call is about this rabies business and the CDC doctor who was murdered. I finally got an XM radio for the house and I heard about his death. You all were friends, right?"

"Bonsoir, Mon Ami. This is Jules and yes we were friends, and we wanted, as you Americans say, 'to keep you in the loop' because we feel that same vortex sucking us toward unknown evil. Jean has had dreams and I understand you also are receiving messages from Nelson."

"Yeh, Deja Moo as Walking Bald would say. Right, Brad? The feeling we've experienced this same bullshit as before."

"You bet, Tonto, except this one may be worse than before. Who blows up blocks in Paris, murders a world renown leader of the CDC and intentionally sets loose a new and more virulent strain of rabies? They would have been blown off as unrelated coincidences except for the fact you found or I guess was sent to find, by your grandfather, those syringes and we fortunately made the wolf connection. We aren't as naive this time and all of us here feel that we need to thoroughly review the facts and investigate each one of these 'coincidences'."

"So what do you think we should do?" Joseph asked.

Kate had a suggestion.

"How about this. Jules and Jean, you should take the Paris investigation and find out as much as possible that relates to the Pasteur destruction that could connect to Ted and the CDC to the rabies outbreak. Don't bring too much attention to yourself, and use your cover as grieving friends and colleagues trying to find closure. That won't be something you will have to fake."

"Oui c'est vrai!" Jean replied. *Yes, that's true!*

"Then Brad and Joseph, you can team up together and dig deeper into the wolf connection to all this and Tom and I will work with the FBI and the CDC on Ted's murder. We should Skype in five to seven days to go over everything we might uncover. Is that something everyone can do?"

Everyone was on board. Jules quickly called to arrange his and Jean's return the next morning to Paris on the Pasteur's jet. Their exhausted brains now needed recharging and an uneventful night's rest to be sharp enough to combat an evil that never rested.

They all feared the Destroyer was rising again!

CHAPTER 27

Tristar Veterinary Biologics

July 1

Hans Vogel looked at the overnight sales report that always was on his desk by 0800 hours and focused on the US sales of their Trojan horse-like vaccine. Their engineered rabies was the perceived pathogen threat and the vaccine they had prepared would protect from its effect. One out of six of the required booster doses now contained a lethal human viron, a hybrid of a prion and virus, and it waited to be shed by an unaffected host in urine, stool, and salvia. The viron was their genius, the Trojan Horse, a breakthrough, that was not detectable in even the most advanced laboratories because it didn't exist outside the walls of the Tristar facility. It was difficult to detect like a prion but had the contagious properties of a virus. The pathogenic vaccine booster now sat ready to release its unique Hell unto the American public.

Vogel's blue eyes focused on two things in the report: the total number of doses shipped and gross revenue. Yesterday nearly one half million more doses had shipped bringing the total since the release to 4.5 million doses with a gross income of 151 million Euros, more than enough to cover all the development and production costs associated with their attack on America. With reorders coming in now for additional Part A vaccines they were generating a fortune. In a very short time they could start shipping the contaminated Part B, then within two weeks after an animal receiving that viron loaded dose, the first victims would have been exposed. Then it was only a matter of time.

Mendoza was scheduled to call at 0830 from Argentina even though it was five hours earlier in South America and Vogel sat nervously waiting. *That man never rested.*

The computer signaled the Skype call and Vogel accepted.

Mendoza sat at his father Adolf's large desk looking like he always did---focused, alert and very determined. Like a hungry animal about to attack.

"Herr Mendoza, it is so good to see you once more. I have exciting news for you that our plan is unfolding perfectly and soon approximately one million companion animals in the United States will become ticking time bombs. We are about one month or so before the first human cases will manifest. Other good news is with the death of Ted Johnson, the emerging disease unit at the CDC has indefinitely shut down its veterinary division. I don't think they will even look at the vaccinated animals as vectors but attack our disease not as a zoonosis but try to link it directly to a human source. Our apocalyptic disease will overwhelm them rapidly and overload all their sophisticated emergency medical and social services. I think in less than ninety days the government will collapse on itself."

Mendoza had been staring at the screen, not acknowledging Vogel's optimism. There was a long pause before he finally spoke.

"Thank you, Hans, we will be indeed fortunate if that is how this journey unfolds. We will be heroes when we present our treatment to control the plague but we must time its release with perfection so people are begging to receive it and willing to exchange their autonomy and liberty for the protection we will provide. Any word on Rimer?"

"I have followed the news reports and so far nothing has indicated he was arrested or went for treatment for his wound. He knew to never contact me directly under any circumstance. Our intermediary at the Atlanta police keeps me posted on any current developments and she says the FBI is now deeply involved and no one understands exactly why. Something possibly was found at the murder site recently by the

FBI but they are keeping the local Polizei in the dark. She is afraid to push too hard. She is as smart as Rimer was stupid. Perhaps he is dead ---rotting somewhere."

Mendoza replied, "Do we know where he lives, because depending on what was found they may get lucky and locate his residence and God knows what they might discover there that could link him to us? What about his son?"

"He had returned to active duty in Afghanistan and will be deployed there for at least eleven more months. He helped his father trap the raccoons and cats but doesn't understand any connection to us or the nature of the plague from what his father had reported. I am a little uncomfortable about him trying to reach his father and failing to do so, maybe calling the police," Vogel answered.

"Then arrange his assassination," Mendoza ordered. "That should be easy in that God forsaken Hellhole. An accident or well-placed IED would tidy up that loose end. Hire a private contractor and get rid of him in the next two days. We are too close now for a fuckup. Understand?"

"Completely. I will take care of it. I also have the result of our final field test. I think you will be pleased."

"So tell me," Mendoza ordered.

"We vaccinated twelve dogs and six horses in a Mongolian Yuri tent village with the primary and secondary vaccine in a blind study. Three doses of that booster contained the Viron and we had a total of twenty-seven Mongols that became affected. .... a very nice nine to one redistribution. They killed fourteen that either were not affected or were asymptotic at the time of their death. The Mongolian Army came in and shot everyone and every living thing and like we predicted, burned all the bodies and possessions. Their primitive government's explanation was an encephalitic infection or acute heavy metal toxicity. They even speculated on a nerve gas attack or accident from their neighbors to the south. In reality, they did no real epidemiological investigation. I would call that a complete success."

"Did WHO, the CDC or the Pasteur Asia get any information on this?" Mendoza asked.

"Nothing. On the world scale, it is like it never happened. The carnage was so violent, so out of character for a normally peaceful people, the Mongolian government released nothing about it. A perfect experiment and corroborative result."

"Just think the chaos when you multiply that by millions," Mendoza said, showing real excitement for the first time.

"The cities we targeted are the governmental seats and economic engines of the United States, so in reality the world. We are about the open the gates of Hell, our Satan, the viron, sits ready to consume their souls," Vogel replied.

"Then let the feast begin!"

The countdown dropped to four.

CHAPTER 28

Combat Outpost Sangsar

Kandahar, Afghanistan
July 4

"You'd think they would keep us in one of those super air conditioned officers' quarters on an important day like the Fourth of July, drinking beer and eating grilled steak and hot dogs instead of us being grilled alive in this God awful heat. What is it? 99 or 100?" PFC. R.J. Haus complained.

"My nifty smart watch says it is 106 with 22% humidity. Son of a bitch, all this crap I'm wearing makes me feel like I'm in Hell working for the Devil," R.J's friend, PFC. Peter K 'Pecker' Wilson, joked back.

"I think it's reading all my evaporating sweat as humidity."

"Pay attention you morons, today every one of us have a big Old Glory target on our backs and the enemy would love nothing better than to take each and every one of us out on Independence Day. You Joes have three jobs: find T-man, destroy T-man, protect the unit and stay alive. Got it?" Sgt. Bo Rimer reminded them. He was the eldest son of Rimer, brother to Max.

"Hey, Sarge, wasn't that four things?" Pecker kidded.

"I didn't figure any of you were paying attention. Since you are so alert today why don't you take point. It's Groundhog Day, we've done this a million times. Go out, make the loop and get the hell back in one piece. Then we celebrate. Eight of us start, eight of get back intact," he nearly growled.

Their close perimeter patrol was routine in this very dangerous area, considered the birthplace of the Taliban. That was what made it so dangerous; they were infidels desecrating holy land. Because patrols occurred on a semi-regular basis and their route varied only slightly due to topography, they were almost like live bait to draw out T-man, the Taliban. If a more distant perimeter was breached, their job became critically important and riskier.

"All I want to do is get back to the CHU, shower off this moon dust and drink a sixer of PBR's. You know REHYDRATE. Maybe dream a little Margot Robbie," RJ replied as the unit moved through the arid terrain.

Two kilometers ahead was a natural chokepoint that no matter which direction you patrolled from, you had to pass through. Ambush was a constant threat and over the years, seven had been KIA and twenty-two wounded by IED's and ambushes. The dogs were now their best defense against IED's.

Sasha Diminoff was a mercenary, a hunter assassin, a left over from the end of the Russia-Afghanistan War. He had been eighteen in 1989 and had been abandoned for dead in the exodus of the Red Army when his transport helicopter was hit by one of their own SAM missiles that the rebels had coopted. The big transport went down in a fiery ball and he had been the only survivor although severely burned and broken. Scavengers from a village, the first on the scene, had found him after he had evidently dragged himself for half a kilometer. the right side of his head had been melted away, right shoulder and humerus crushed and burned and his pelvis was smashed. The recovery was a three year ordeal where the bones found a way to heal on their own and the daily goat's milk washes and goat cream butter allowed his grotesque burns to scar into a facial topographical map mimicking the area's rugged landscape. He stayed with those who had salvaged him and became part of their tribe. He converted to Islam and morphed into an accomplished warrior against those who invaded on a regular basis. He also became a hired assassin who freelanced to earn money to buy black market weapons.

He owed his life to a small group of tribesmen, a debt he could never fully pay, so now he fought and would die for a people he loved. Many Russians and Americans had fallen to his hunter's skills.

He waited patiently as he always did after disguising three small remote controlled IED's placed in a strategic triangle that would funnel his prey into its belly before triggers were engaged. All he had to do was to set the trap and wait to spring it, an unusual job as only one unknown man was his desired target, but the $250,000 bounty was enough that complete evaporation of the patrol was probably necessary to assure success.

Sasha watched as the patrol predictably coursed up toward the trap. The lead man was not too far out, so unless he pushed beyond the last IED's effective kill zone he would be able to put the entire patrol down with the blasts. He scoped the alternative routes for other Americans but didn't see any. As he watched, the patrol suddenly stopped and regrouped.

"What the hell, Sarge? Everything looks ok, nothing out of the ordinary," Pecker complained.

"That's just it. Too quiet. No sound, nothing. Not one bird and if you look carefully, this moon dust looks like it was blown over. See those goat tracks, see how the outside has been dusted over? I don't believe there has been enough of a breeze to do that. Ground's too hard to pick up much but my gut says there's a rat in this hellhole," Rimer explained.

"That would be a gerbil, Sarge," Pecker joked.

"Whatever, you moron. Taylor! Call in. I want a dog team on point to verify our passage. Just in case," Rimer ordered.

Diminoff watched the patrol intently and sat down drinking water and eating a couple of dried dates. Waiting on the patrol which had stopped was a welcomed break. He wasn't positive if they were waiting on someone or just taking a rest. He really didn't care, in Afghanistan, time was infinite.

Rimer got the word on his headset the dog team was on its way, tracking their route up. ETA was thirty-five minutes. The canine was T Rex, the oldest working dog in Afghanistan at age seven. The dog had been perfection, never failing at his job but was being retired at the end of the year.

"They're sending up the dinosaur. Thank you, Jesus!. He's about the only scout you can trust near a hundred percent. If he approves our route we could squirt though in time to have beer, Bratwurst and enter the corn-hole games before the fireworks," Sgt. Rimer reported.

They waited and rested, alert for any intrusion. On schedule, T Rex announced his approach with several barks as he winded the patrol. His handler was MSgt. Tom Haas, so they were often called Big T and Little T. The dog had had a Taliban bounty on his head for four years but both handler and his canine partner were smart, cautious and best of all, lucky.

T Rex knew the patrol and greeted each man with a wag and sniff as Haas went over to talk to Rimer.

"Sarge," Haas greeted as he walked up to Rimer. "Something giving you the willies?"

Rimer smiled, enjoying Big T's 'hero to the rescue' attitude.

"Yeah, it's just my gut —being the Fourth and all. I saw some goat tracks dusted over. Maybe T man covering his girlfriend's tracks, I dunno. You just need to have the dog sweep through this bottleneck and we will be fine."

"Roger that," Haas replied as he hand signaled the dog over, checked his Kevlar vest and moved out putting the dog to work while scanning everywhere for anything different.

Now the patrol was back up, looking up, around, a visual army of eyes and honed instincts.

Diminoff had heard the dog bark and watched as the patrol moved toward his trap. The IED's would be useless as the dogs found them the majority of time. He focused on the patrol instead, placing the cross-hairs of his Dragunov sniper rifle's scope on each man searching for his nameless primary target. He was a better than average shot but road-side bombs were his forte. His facial scar tissue and poor vision in his damaged right eye caused him to drift a little when targeting his victim at a distance, but he rarely missed This might be his only opportunity to close the contract so he moved man to man searching not for a face but Sargent's stripes.

The third man down wore the three stripes. No name was visible as he was wearing Kevlar. That narrowed his strike zone to small exposed areas of the face and neck. The solider would have to stop to give him a reliable stationary target or he would have to wait for another opportunity. The price he was being paid would assure his accuracy. Besides that, his benefactor was in a hurry. Perhaps this was personal.

T Rex alerted to the three IEDs almost immediately and Big T halted the men while the dog paced back and forth in a canine blockade to prevent them moving forward. Rimer pulled up his men who took defensive positions and just as he turned to yell an order, the shot rang out followed by two rapid successive blasts.

The man's head nearly exploded, the bullet fragmenting as it hit. Men dove for cover as they waited for more firing. There was none.

Pvt RJ Haus darted out, grabbed the fallen man and dragged him to cover. The soldier had died instantly. Pecker Wilson was gone, his death the result of a missed shot standing directly behind his Sargent.

Rimer stood over his comrade, blood dripping from the shrapnel that exploded after Wilson was hit.

"Damn, Damn DA AMMMN!" Rimer shouted, "Sons of Bitches, filthy Sons of Bitches!!"

The assassination attempt on Bo Rimer, which was supposed to be a death sentence for his brother Max, had failed. They had confused the military records on the Rimer brothers, and attempted to kill the wrong man.

In four minutes, an AH64 Apache Attack helicopter came zooming up and made a quick pass over the shooter's general location. Several short bursts were fired to try to smoke out any hostiles. Diminoff was already gone, slipping into a thin crevasse that expanded into a dark cool cave that led to a series of linked caverns. These hideaways were only know to the generations of fighters that flowed in and out secretly.

He would send his contact the rifle scope's photo stream data generated in real time showing the targeting and impact. His fee would then be deposited into his Swiss bank account. No one in the military would suspect this had been a murder for hire, or that the wrong man had been targeted.

Too bad the dog showed up. They could have had eight for the price of one!

CHAPTER 29

Fort Peck Indian Reservation

July 5

"You want me to ride that pathetic animal? I might as well walk cause my feet are gonna be dragging anyway," Brad questioned the mount Joseph had borrowed for the big man to ride, "that's borderline animal cruelty with me being the poor animal!"

Joseph could barely contain himself from bursting out laughing. The old Indian pony belonged to his best friend Billy Eagles and was a small, very old sway back mare that was a prop for young children to play on and around. The mare had a sweet nature and was an easy keeper so she stayed although neighbors thought he should have shot her years before. No way that was going to happen, the kids loved her and truth be told, so did Billy.

Billy had hidden inside Joseph's horse trailer almost unable to contain himself. The whole thing was an elaborate prank to pull one over on the big jokester.

"Look, Tonto, no way I'm torturing this old nag so get me an ATV or a normal size horse."

"How about an ATV Segway?" Joseph asked.

"You have a Segway?" Brad questioned.

"No, but Billy Eagles has a gelding named Segway— a good horse," Joseph chuckled.

"I'll take anything other than this pathetic beast."

"OK, I'll get Billy to bring him over. Only there is one more thing before that happens," Joseph announced.

"Whaaaat?" Brad groaned.

"This animal has a spirit which I suspect you have crushed. In my culture you must apologize to her and ask for forgiveness!"

"Are you friggin kidding me?"

"No, it's true. You apologize or no other Lakota horse will let you mount them!"

"Really? What?. ....they have a Union?"

"No, seriously, it's better than walking!" "Jezzus, OK. What is her name?"

"Her Lakota name means Prairie Queen but you can call her Queenie."

Brad had the feeling he was being played but went along. "Queenie, I am sorry for my callous behavior. How's that?"

"You must say please forgive me."

"Please forgive me!" Brad groaned.

Billy was waiting. That was his signal to use his best Mr. Ed impersonation from inside the trailer.

"Thank you, you big white jack ass!"

Joseph broke out in side splitting laughter and fell rolling on the ground.

Billy burst from the trailer with tears of laughter streaming down his face.

"You silly bastards!" Brad laughed, rolling to the ground to pretend punch out the young Indians.

After several minutes they settled down, holding their sore sides. "Ok, seriously, do I have to really walk?" Brad asked.

"No. Billy brought a real ride for you. His personal horse. It is a great honor he trusts you to ride the descendent of generations of ponies that have been with his family."

Billy backed the beautiful white, black and chestnut gelding out of the trailer and Brad was immediately impressed.

"Wow, that's what I call a horse!! This is Segway?" Brad asked.

"No, this is Bruce," Billy answered.

"Bruce? What kind of a silly name is that for an Indian pony?"

"There you go again! Now you must apologize to him."

"Ok, I get it, your horses have a sensitive side. Bruce, please forgive my insensitivity. You are a magnificent animal!"

"I think that will do it. We best get going. Thanks, Billy, for your help," Joseph said with a smile.

"You're welcome, Wilbur," was Billy's Mr. Ed reply.

Brad and Joseph loaded up the old trailer with the horses and their supplies. They planned an hour of travel then mounting up the horses and trying to find the two bison herds. Joseph was nervous about the apparitions he had seen on the first survey trip but needed to find the white Tatanka kill site and see if they could maybe find some evidence that might finger the wolf poachers.

The truck rocked and rolled after Joseph turned right on N 17 and pushed the vehicle as far as he felt was safe. They got out, stretched and Joseph backed the horses out of the trailer. Brad wandered off a little to take a whizz.

"Too much coffee," Brad announced, "Almost like the Indian who died after drinking too much ice tea!"

"What?" Joseph questioned.

"Yup, the poor guy drowned in his Tea-Pee."

"You know, Kemosabe, if you had any follicles, I would set you up for an honorary scalping."

"Too bad, remember I'm the only person here that can signal for help using the sun and this shiny dome. You need me, Tonto!"

"Brad, you are like a brother to me. I do need you!"

"I'm kinda getting choked up here. Is this where we slice our palms and become blood brothers?" Brad asked, trying to keep it light and not getting too emotional.

"Yes, we should. Maybe not right this minute, but it is a great honor and when we do it, it will be done ceremonially, the right way."

Brad for once in his life was speechless. All he could manage was "OK!"

The horses were excited, anticipating an adventure in the sea of grass that gently moved in the west wind. The sun was bright and

Hot, so Brad covered his head with a blue USDA cap and Joseph tied a red Western bandana to cover his forehead and keep his long hair out of his face. As they mounted the pony horses, Brad felt a shiver of rising excitement.

"I think this is how a man was meant to feel, perched on top of a beautiful horse with the sense of adventure and freedom it gives you."

"You just described the American Indian before the white man!" Joseph reminded him.

"Yeah, I know. Sorry about that."

"If Grandfather taught me anything, it was that culturally we, the Indian nations, were as responsible as the white man for the state we are in today. He said you lose the battles but win the war by being one people. The problem wasn't that we were militarily defeated but culturally corrupted by the white man. That is why he said 'never forget.' That's not a cry for revenge but a plea to be who we really are. It's why I still live in that old trailer and when I marry, will raise my children as he raised me. It is so important that they are taught who they are and who we were."

"Your grandfather would be very proud of you," Brad offered.

"He and all the ancestors live in my heart, my blood and my mind. I am inescapably connected and for that I am blessed. Now let's see what they have for us today. We are going to head northwest. The horses will smell the bison long before we spot them and they know instinctively what to do. Let Bruce do his thing."

"Meaning no disrespect, Bruce, but is that really your name?" Brad half joked.

The beautiful horse seemed to understand the question and shook his head up and down in an affirmative motion.

"Well I'll be damned," Brad laughed. "Ok then almighty Bruce, let's find those Tatanka !"

The horses moved on, up the slight rise, the sun nearly directly above them.

"How far do you think we will have to go?" Brad asked.

"This time of year, till the first heavy snows, there are two distinct herds that travel close together, usually because of the prevailing wind and storms, they are normally nearly parallel to each other. You might see them a quarter mile or so up to a mile or so apart. The cows with calves control the herd until they rut then the bulls disrupt all organization for a while. We wouldn't want to invade their space then. Those big boys have the tendency to get pissed off."

"So what do we do after we spot them?" Brad asked.

"We have a look and then go searching for that kill site. I have the coordinates on my phone from those photos I took of the white Tatanka. I put them in my Garmin etrek and when I think we are close, I'll activate it to get right on top of the spot. I probably could find it without the locator but the grass has really grown so I might be off by a few yards and there wasn't that much left of the white Tatanka anyway. What we will do is move in opposite directions in increasing circles until we are out about one thousand yards. We want to look for anything not natural— plastic water bottles, cans, trash, shell casings and the like. Maybe then we can connect the dots forensically.

"I think we are about ten minutes away from where I saw the animal so this is about where the larger herd grazed. If you kinda take in the whole area, I think you can tell the grass has been grazed and beat down some in a wide area that runs to the northwest. This time of year they kind of wander based on how dry the grasses are and where their water source is located. They could spend weeks in one area with good forage and plenty of water. My great grandfather took a lot of time teaching me the life story of the Tatanka. Never figured it would have anything else to do with other than putting meat on the table."

They rode on, letting the horses find the great beasts. Brad felt the energy rise in Bruce as he flared his nostrils and moved from a slow canter to an easy trot.

"I think the horses have scented the bison," Brad said with an excited tone.

"I know. Wakinyan is tuned in. It won't be long now. I think on the horizon about two o'clock, you can pick up the brown of their bodies. See it?"

"Kinda. Oh yeah, there they are! I think I can smell them too. It's like a cross between a zoo smell and a cattle feed lot. I see their dung scattered around and the grass is patchier here," Brad answered.

"Very good! See, hanging around me has rubbed off on you, Brother!

"My Garmin is taking us more due west so after you get a good look at the herd and understand that at one time, according to Grandfather, great herds of perhaps a million animals grazed here and sustained our people. Had the Tatanka been exterminated, so would have been the Lakota soul."

They rode up to within eighty yards, quietly watching the bison graze and the calves play. The animals weren't disturbed much by their presence but several of the herd's sentries lazily kept an eye on them ready to sound the flight alert to run for their lives. Satisfied they were not in danger, they silently went back to the never ending quest to fill their rumens. Grunts, huffs and snorting, along with the swishing of their short tails competed with the pulling of grass and chewing the cud it formed.

Brad drank from his canteen and wiped his mouth with his flannel shirt shelve.

"This is unbelievable ! So many yet so few compared to the great herds of the past! Thanks for showing me this, Joseph."

"I get a chill every time I see a herd," Joseph replied. "They are part of us, the Lakota, and suffered as we did. Perhaps because the whites wanted to starve us out, this great beast was nearly exterminated only for the skin on their back or for sport. It makes me sick to think about it."

The Garmin led them west, away from the herd and placed them almost on top of the kill site.

"I think this is it. We must be within a few yards, so go ahead and dismount and drop the reins over Bruce's neck and he will pretty much stay there."

"And what if he and Wakinyan take off and leave us flat footed?"

"My horse would never go far. Bruce, I'm not so sure. I mean you're not exactly a lightweight. He probably would rather fight the wolves than taxi your sorry ass around."

"Is that any way to talk to your big brother? Remember I'm older, smarter, have better hair and am definitely a sex symbol. What you got going for you?" Brad quizzed.

"I'm young and Lakota and this," he said, sweeping his arm out before him, "is part of me. I think I got you beat."

"I think you're right. But you better be nice to your chunky, shiny head, big brother, Little Joe."

"Ok, Hoss !" Joseph laughed.

The horses lowered their heads and were content to start pulling the prairie grass, shaking off the flies that buzzed persistently around their face and neck. Joseph led Brad away toward a slight rise. He stopped and found a tuft of yellowed white hair. He showed Brad.

"This is the general area. Place that surveyor's stake I gave you right here and we will move in circles about ten feet apart till we are out one to two hundred yards, then we will grab the ponies and ride the bigger circles real slow, getting off if anything looks promising," Joseph instructed.

They found nothing on foot, so Joseph whistled and Wakinyan trotted over with Bruce following close behind. The men mounted up and continued their search pattern. The grasses continued to roll up to a wooded rise overlooking the original kill site, about eight hundred yards to the east of the kill.

"Let's head over there," Joseph said pointing to the treed oasis, "we can rest, eat some lunch and give this some more thought."

"Sounds good, my stomach is starting to complain. It's like having two wives, always bugging me," Brad joked.

The small wooded patch contained a small spring and was surrounded by some very large and old Cottonwoods and Elms. There only were about two dozen mature trees and most of the underbrush had been grazed to the ground.

"The pronghorns love this kind of cover and will burst out of spots like this at fifty miles an hour. They wait till the last second and BAM! they scare the crap out of you. They can see you long before you find them. Beautiful creatures and tasty too. They are in my good dreams and nightmares."

"Yeah, I remember that Berhetzel dream," Brad replied.

There were no surprises bursting from the small woods today and Brad noticed the large Elms.

"I bet these are original American Elms, isolated up here away from Dutch Elm Disease. My town growing up was full of huge rotting stumps where they had cut the dead trees down in the nineteen fifties and sixties. I saw photos of my grandmother's street and her house that was once lined with those majestic trees. You didn't even need air conditioning, the streets were so cool!"

They sat against the trunk of an old Elm and Joseph pulled two Cokes, cheese sandwiches and chips from a small soft sided cooler. They ate in silence, listening to the west wind gently rustle through the leaves and branches.

"You know, I doubt it gets any better that this!" Brad confessed again.

"Grandfather taught me everything he thought was important for a Lakota. This is only a small fraction that helps define us. God, I wish he were here!"

"He is. He is in you," Brad offered.

"I know that, but he would have insight into all of this. He helped me see the white calf. He knows there is another Destroyer rising, told us there always would be a new one. I just didn't think it would be so soon."

The wind started to blow a little stronger and was obviously cooler as the men finished their lunch.

"I think we are in for a storm. We don't want to be caught out here under these trees or even on those ponies with their metal shoes if there is lightning," Joseph warned.

"What was the weather forecast?" Brad asked.

"I don't know or care. Never look at the weather in the hot months, it's not reliable. Stuff comes and goes when it wants to."

"So what do we do?"

"We get off this rise and make one more pass to the northeast. Anyone stalking or waiting over a bait would want to be downwind and that would generally mean to the east if your bait is west of you. The point is those darts have a limited range and the wolves are real savvy so unless they used a plane or some sort of booby trap they never could get close enough for a shot, let alone two shots," Joseph said.

"Look to the left, north, is that what I think it is?" Brad asked.

Joseph pulled his spotting scope from his saddle bag and took a long look.

"Here, you take a look," he said.

Brad looked through the scope, fiddling a little with the focus adjustment.

"That's the same looking animal as when I was out here before. A white Tanaka, same age and size and standing alone. Get your phone out and record this as we approach, I bet this one vaporizes too. We are being sent a message from Grandfather and the ancestors," Joseph told Brad.

They moved toward the animal slowly, the horses snorting, testing the air, their noses not believing their eyes.

They moved slowly, focused on the pure white calf.

Suddenly the air was filled with the howls of wolves, directly behind them. The horses startled, their eyes wide with fear. The men turned to look but saw nothing.

"Just like last time!" Joseph shouted to Brad.

They turned back and the calf was gone. The wolves' vocalizing stopped just as fast as it had started.

"You think the wolves frightened it off?" Brad asked.

"No, neither the calf nor the wolves were real, at least in a worldly sense. They were spirits sent to guide or instruct us. Let's check out the spot where that Tanaka was placed."

They galloped up the last 75 yards and Joseph pulled up Wakinyan.

"This is it. Look around carefully. There must be a clue somewhere," Joseph instructed.

It only took a few seconds to find a green plastic BIC lighter in the grass and the filter butts of about two dozen cigarettes. Brad carefully pushed the lighter with a twig into a plastic baggie and Joseph gathered all the butts they could find and put them in a baggie.

"Someone was here for a while waiting," Joseph explained, "but it was not a meat hunter because they would never smoke and hunt.

No, whoever was here felt comfortable— perhaps observing his prey. I bet he killed that calf as bait. But there was no possible way to dart the wolves from here, that's better than a half mile!"

"Do you think you could get close enough to them with a drone?" Brad asked.

"Only if either they were at max range for the darts or the wolves were accustomed to the drones," Joseph answered. "Maybe the CIA or the military would have that capability. Commercially available drones....I doubt it."

"Let's head back and turn this evidence over to Jules. Maybe he could have Sullivan look for a print or some DNA," Brad suggested.

"Good idea. You can stay at the trailer tonight and I'll grill some bison steaks. I'm going to bring Billy Eagles over and we can see about that brotherhood thing. Then maybe Grandfather will include you in his oversight!"

"It would be an honor."

And Brad meant it!

CHAPTER 30

Pet Care Plus Veterinary Clinic

Baltimore, Maryland
One week later

Dr. Frank Donnelly was pleased. His advertising campaign had resulted in his multiple offices administering over ten thousand initial doses of the new rabies vaccine and another thirty-five hundred of the all-important boosters so far. The best news was the spin off business from the physical exams, blood testing for heartworm disease, dentals and other problems that had been discovered had increased the clinic's revenue month to month by nearly one hundred fifty percent. So much business was coming through the doors, that he had to increase staff and expand their office hours till midnight. They were now 7 a.m. to 12 a.m., seven days a week. Lots of caffeine and promises of big bonuses kept the staff fired up. They were a well-oiled machine.

He had been the first in Baltimore to receive the Tristar vaccine and was the largest single user that Tristar shipped to in the Mid-Atlantic states. He estimated that by the end of the year, he would have purchased fifty thousand first and second vaccine doses. Enough profit to build out three more stores. Size did matter.

He finished his shift at the original store and picked up the deposit to night drop at a local Wells Fargo Bank branch that he used.

Years before he would never have dreamed of physically carrying cash to be deposited in the evening but he wasn't comfortable leaving a sizable deposit at the office either. They were making two runs to the bank each day because the deposits were so large. He had thought about using an armored car service but disliked the image of an armed guard picking up a locked bag deposit. He could only guess what the snide client remarks would be upon seeing guards with shotguns entering the reception area.

He dropped the bag and headed home. He lived in the old Locust Point area, one of the wealthiest neighborhoods in Baltimore. Many of his clients also resided in the old Georgian style brick homes and walked their dogs each night as he passed, traveling home.

This evening as he turned onto Towson Street, he saw the road was blocked by Police, Fire and Rescue. Cars came in behind him, blocking any turn around.

Donnelly pulled over to a tree lawn parking spot and got out of his Yukon Denali and walked toward the commotion to check it out. There were dozens of bright police vehicle warning lights flashing blue and red and fire and rescue flashing bright red. LED headlights strobed on and off making the houses and trees look like they were part of a huge dance club. The veterinarian walked up as far as he could, stopping at the yellow plastic police line tape, peering in for a better look.

"Please stand back, sir. You need to go home. This area will be cordoned off for quite a while," a black female police officer politely requested.

"Sorry, Officer. ...," Donnelly started, and seeing her name tag, "Kane. I live right around the block and was trying to get home. Can I ask want happened here?"

"We are not sure but it seems a couple was out walking their two dogs when a man with a camping hatchet started to attack them. He hacked them up, killing both of them. The dogs finally took him down and basically ripped his throat out. The poor dogs are in tough shape."

"My name is Dr. Frank Donnelly, and I am a veterinarian. Can I see the dogs, maybe I can help them."

"Hey, Sarge," she yelled, "this man is a Vet, wants to see the dogs."

"They are behind the ladder truck, the paramedics are working on them right now. Walk him over there."

The cop lifted the Police Line tape and Donnelly ducked under. He could see three covered bodies with multiple investigators snapping photos and typing notes on tablets. He could see pools of dark blood pooling around the plastic covering the corpses and thought he could detect its metallic smell mixing with the fire trucks' diesel exhaust. He felt a cold repulsive shiver move up his spine.

Two Golden Retrievers stood and wagged their tails when the veterinarian reached the paramedics. They were covered with streaks of blood which the first responders had tried to wash off with bags of saline. Donnelly recognized the pair immediately and gasped.

"Oh my God! That's Millie and Copper. They live with my neighbors Spencer and Gabriella Swanson."

"Lived," Officer Kane replied. "We think they are the victims based on ID the male had on him. After you check the dogs, would you be up to confirming that by looking at the remains?"

"I think so. How bad was it, the attack?" he asked.

"I would describe it as brutal and crazed. I hope you have a strong stomach," she answered.

Donnelly looked the dogs over.

"Millie is the worse off. She is gonna need a lot of sutures but Copper only has the hack over his pelvis so that will be an easy repair.

"Here's my business card. I'll call over and let the staff know you are on the way so they can get these dogs on antibiotics, pain meds and fluids. Once they are stable we'll get them patched up."

"Transport them as soon as Detective Saffick gives the OK," she ordered. "Dr. Donnelly, would you come with me please."

They weaved their way around to where the bodies laid on the old brick pavers. She signaled to a man with a clipboard.

Chief Detective John Saffick was in his early forties, dark wavy hair interspersed with streaks of gray. He was tall and slender wearing a yellow nylon vest with BPD prominently marked. He looked stressed and angry.

"Detective, this is Dr. Donnelly, local veterinarian who lives in this neighborhood. He recognized the dogs and has agreed to ID the vics if you would like," Kane offered.

"Doc," Saffick greeted, extending his hand.

"You got a strong stomach? 'Cause it's not going to be pretty. They are hacked up pretty bad on their heads."

"I think I can do it," Donnelly replied, now morbidly curious about what lay under those cadaver shrouds.

"Ok, let's have a go at it. First the male."

He slowly peeled back the plastic and Donnelly barely recognized Spencer Swanson. The retired engineer's skull was cleaved in half, a mass of blood, hair and brain tissue. Both eyes had been driven from their sockets from the force of the attack and laid out on each side of what had been a face. Only one thing made the ID possible— Swanson sported a large sweeping waxed handlebar mustache which had some- how endured the attack.

"That's him, Swanson. My God, who could do such a thing?" Donnelly asked.

"Over here is the woman. Please tell me what you think."

Saffick pulled back the shroud. The hatchet was sticking up from her forehead imbedded full thickness.

"Yes, that's Gabriella. Son of a bitch! What kind of crazy does this?" Donnelly questioned.

"I want you to take a look at him, if you don't mind. That male Golden did a number on him. He's over here." Saffick led him over to the third shroud.

"He was wandering for maybe twenty minutes and staggered stiffly. Two drivers called 911 on a 'drunk on the streets.' By the time the patrol car cruised in, all this had already occurred. What a mess!"

The detective lifted up the cover and Donnelly gasped again.

"That's Father O'Connel from Our Lady, just south of here. My parish priest. He was retiring in the fall. That's the outfit he wore when coaching the community youth basketball league. God, look at his eyes, he always had peaceful, kind eyes - - now he looks possessed-- evil. I don't get this," he lamented.

"Me either," the chief detective grumbled. "I guess his crucifix was his only ID. The real question is why? Maybe a brain tumor? We won't know till the coroner finishes her work. Don't think any of us will sleep well for several nights."

Saffick was prophetic. No one would sleep peacefully till the unfolding nightmare was over.

CHAPTER 31

Mendoza compound

Argentina
July 25

Mendoza paced the cobbled courtyard from corner to corner, back and forth, hands held behind his back, head down, in virtual mental overdrive. It was a posture and habit he had inherited from his notorious Nazi father and he could pass hours of time traveling back and forth. When he saw a clear solution to a problem, he became suddenly animated, aware and activated. This was that moment and he returned to his office, typed his secure sets of computer passwords and waited.

After three minutes, Hans Vogel appeared on his screen wearing a simple cotton terry bathrobe. He looked worried and surprised.

"Sorry to have to pull you from your bed at this hour but I needed to check on a couple things," Mendoza said.

"Of course, Herr Mendoza. How can I assist you?"

"I have of course been following the reports out of America and they are a little confusing. It seems we only have pockets of the population where our creation has manifested. Is it possible we have underestimated the incubation to shed time frame or do we have a launch failure? There must be an answer so we can better understand how to correct the problem. Now, how many secondary doses have been shipped?"

"As of yesterday's overnight report, over two million. Every three days, the CDC sends their finalized administered totals which last was half of that number. There is a lag of course of about ten days for the CDC to receive the label bar codes from each dose. That means with our new three out of eight contamination ratio, we have nearly three hundred thousand exposed carriers, each a ticking time bomb, each with the potential to infect dozens of people," Vogel answered.

"And most of those bombs have not gone off. Why? According to our preliminary work, replication to conventual shed time was well under seven days. We are at twenty days minimum from those initial second dose administrations and counting. Could our initial field work been flawed?"

Vogel answered nervously.

"Our conclusions were based on four trials. The two individuals directly infected, and the two canine or horse to human via the secondary dose. I can't think of a reason we are not seeing a better result."

"Then you need to investigate it. Perhaps it is a handling problem when you mix in our viron or a shipping problem that attenuates it. Regardless, put your best man Schmitt on it. In the meantime, re-label all secondary doses as first dose vials and that way we will be sure both doses are infective. Maybe our agent is too diluted."

"Perhaps," Vogel replied, "but our work suggests otherwise. The object was only for the animals to be vectors carrying the agent. The rabies vaccine was approved for dogs, our primary carrier, but cats, ferrets and horses are also on the label because the CDC wanted it there. So far we can't connect any specie to transmission other than the dog. We know the rabies fraction is competent because there has been only a small handful of cases in raccoons in Northern Virginia where vaccinated dogs were bitten, put in isolation and so far all of them are ok. Maybe it will take longer to manifest than we anticipated. A typical prion can take years to manifest. Our hybrid is new territory, we may have to be patient."

"That is not possible. The whole idea is to acutely overwhelm the governmental services, produce chaos and bring that nation to her knees, so she begs us for our inactivation treatment. So far they are postulating it is a new mosquito borne encephalopathy but the only thing being brought down to its knees is the bug population. We have induced nothing but a panic to buy insect repellents!" Mendoza complained.

"I will put Schmitt and his team on it. I think I would consider this a real world problem, in other words, how an biologic agent acts under multiple variables like time, temperature, shipping conditions and the like. Even though we gave specific instruction on handling and administration of the vaccines, you know a percentage of those people won't follow them, like storage temperature range, time from mixing the diluent into the viral cake to administration, wearing gloves when handling and others. That's human nature and our rules may be broken because people will be in a hurry to get the animals vaccinated to make money. That might cause attenuation of the agent. Perhaps we are just overanxious," Vogel answered.

"Regardless, I want that answer. If the Americans get lucky and connect more of the dots, they could be on your doorstep and then mine. My interest is to create an overwhelming panic with disruption of all normal infrastructure support services with quarantine and isolation. As the smaller diseased pockets expand into larger areas, they will morph into massive dead zones where there is no normalcy. That's when we announce our discovery and put our people in place to administer our treatment after we secure each zone militarily. Time you can see is of the essence."

"Yes, I understand all of that. We will request a return of some doses that are already in America for "quality control" purposes. That way we can see if there is a handling problem," Vogel replied.

"You have exactly one week. I would also check the original viron we created here in South America to see if your incorporating process is returning a suitable infective agent. Leave no stone unturned, understand?" Mendoza asked.

"I will get the answers, Mein Führer!"

CHAPTER 32

Conference Call

Same Day

"Sorry it to so long to get this call started, but everyone's investigation took longer than we originally anticipated. I guess Tom and I will go first with the FBI investigation into Ted's murder. Tom, why don't you fill everyone in on what we found out," Kate said.

"Ok, hello or bonjour to all. We have been able to follow everything in real time thanks to cooperation with the Atlanta FBI arranged by Special Agent Rick Sullivan. By the way, he is taking early retirement before the end of the year because his wife's ALS is progressing rapidly and he needs to be with her more. I made a note on our calendar to send a card and I will make sure all of you have a chance to sign it. So here's what Agent Jackson of the Atlanta FBI told us just last night.

"They found the shooter. He had died at home, probably right after he escaped the murder scene and basically was found to be nearly totally decomposed. A real mess. The slug they recovered matched the woman's gun from the rest home. The murderer's name was Rimer. They then were able to match the DNA on those cigarette butts that Joseph and Brad found near the bison remains to him. Amazing that they could recover anything from them after being exposed to the elements for all those months! Turns out one of Rimer's sons, who is in the Army, stationed in Afghanistan, had called the local police on his dad not answering his cell two weeks ago, but they only did a cursory check at his house which was locked down and secure. His son figured he had gone offshore commercial fishing so he wasn't overly concerned when they reported that his residence was secure. The Sargent is on leave now and will be returning with his younger brother to bury their father and the FBI will have a lot of questions for them. There is the open question on who funded or hired Rimer, why and when. They are picking apart his bank and phone records right now. By the way, Ted's mother who was in Stonehaven passed away last Monday. They said she never stopped asking for him."

"Wow, that's sad," Brad said. "Here's what Joseph and I came up with investigating the wolf abduction site, the Denver dumpster search and two of the original pockets of rabies outbreak.

"We feel the two wolves were darted by a paramilitary or military mini drone. There are actually several versions out there that are used to sedate, treat, microchip and vaccinate wild animals, cattle or horses. I found one called Vet-Jett Air, which uses the exact syringe that Joseph found on the prairie. They have a seventy-five percent accuracy at under ten yards. Super quiet units and fast. I called their headquarters and was told they only sold seven to private entities and zoos since that model was released, but they delivered over fifteen hundred to the government and another three hundred to foreign governments, mostly African nations. They forwarded the names of the private buyers to the FBI and Jackson said they were all legitimate buyers. He feels if a drone was used, it probably was stolen from a government source. He is checking to see if it is even possible to get an accounting of the US units because the military has half of them and the CIA has the others. He said neither would confess if a unit went missing. They just don't want the hassle of dealing with investigators. So the bottom line is we will probably never know. Rimer worked for someone or entity, the job now is to find out who. Possibly his sons would have an idea."

"On the plus side," Joseph added, "we were able to find what we needed to link Rimer directly to the darting area through help from my ancestors. The white Tatanka apparition was placed where

we found the cigarette butts and the wolves howled, seeking their revenge, pushing us forward. We both were amazed at the strength of the message!"

"I would," Brad interjected, "describe it, sitting on a horse, looking over the beautiful wild prairie as surreal, exciting and a little spooky. Wait a minute, I just described my first date with Kate!"

"Ha, Ha," Kate teased back "that was definitely scary!"

"Jules, what did you and Jean find out about the Pasteur attack?" she asked.

"Mes amies, we spent a lot of time with my friends at the DGSI, as you know it is like your FBI combined with Homeland Security. They feel the eleven men and two women conspirators were not political or philosophical warriors but a well-trained, well paid mini army of mercenaries sent to do this evil for profit. They would have never been found had they dispersed immediately because they would not have matched any profile or have had a political agenda that could be traced back. It wasn't the DGSI's extraordinary detective work either that exposed their location but a timely anonymous tip. The DGSI is currently investigating why all thirteen died, not even one survivor, and the two women were killed by someone other than the government agents. The fire that consumed the majority of their building was no accident either, it appears there was a detailed plan in place to destroy most of the physical evidence. My friends said their demise was predetermined and planned, the terrorist mercenaries obviously didn't have a clue or they would have dispersed like roaches when lights come on. France is still in mourning but the good news is the Metro is up and running, Norte Dame is cleaned up and the damaged portion supported and under tarps with a screen painted rendition of the damaged facade. From a distance it appears as nothing had happened but it will be at least two years to restore it. My Pasteur is being cleared and we will build a replica of the original historic building, but with new infrastructure, actually effective air conditioning and

IT services. The new hospital will be one of the most advanced in the world. Our government is providing forty-nine percent of the funding only because we wouldn't take more. It is a matter of pride and remembering that we are a private enterprise. The good news, because I am one of the few senior staff survivors, I am the de facto head of the Institute. The bad news is the restoration project will take at least four years and keep me very occupied. Not much time to spend with my lovers. They will be so sad and lonely."

"I will be happy to keep them entertained while you do some work for a change my friend," Jean teased.

"No, I will sacrifice so I may find a way to continue pleasing my friends. To deny them would be criminal!" Jules laughed.

"You are so French!" Kate chuckled.

"Maybe you can take Joseph on as an intern," Brad joked.

"Peut-être. I am sure he would be very popular. Lots of nice hair."

"Ouch, that stings," Brad said as the rest laughed at his expense.

Kate reminded them why they were on the call.

"Ok, so let's see what else the FBI and DGSI come up with after they interview Rimer's son. Any one of us should put together a conference call if something arises. Tom and I are heading next week for a few days at Cape Ann in Massachusetts, so if you need us use our cells. Au revoir, mes amies."

The goodbyes were sincere as the countdown to Armageddon held at two.

CHAPTER 33

Boston Logan Airport

AmeriCar Rental Booth

The rental agent was unusually slow, Christian L. Schmitt thought. Perhaps she was new or just not used to walk up customers. It seemed other clients were just heading to the car livery and picking an automobile and driving off. He appeared to be an anomaly, standing alone at the service desk.

"Here you go, Doctor Helwig, sorry for the delay but I took the time and enrolled you into our Preferred Club which will allow you next time to bypass this counter and pick the car you choose from what we call the 'Livery'. Your Black Card Visa also upgrades you automatically into our Executive Club so you can either reserve a luxury vehicle in advance or do a grab and go if you like. That Mercedes you wanted will cost you considerably less on this program so I hope you will find the delay I put you through worth it. Here is a paper map of the greater Boston area, but you have voice activated navigation. I will have William escort you to your car. Any questions?"

"No, Fräulein, Danke. You have been very kind," Schmitt replied in a light German accent.

He was escorted to the car by an older black attendant whom he attempted to tip with a twenty dollar bill but was surprisingly declined with a polite 'my pleasure, sir!' response.

Christian Schmitt was Tristar Veterinary Biologic's Head of Research and Development and the brains behind their biologic attack. At age forty-three, he was the only man in Europe holding doctorate degrees in three advanced sciences —Doctorates that included: Veterinary Pathology, BioChemical Engineering and SubGenetic BioEngineering. He also was the father of three boys and three girls, each blond, blue eyed; perfectly beautiful Aryan prototypes. Each child had been exactly engineered as he planned, creations developed *in vitro* and then surgically implanted into his wife. Schmitt was fit with an athletic build, and was also blond with deep blue eyes. He was a multitalented genius, produced as a third generation result of Nazi experiments during and after World War Two. Experiments that had vigorously continued after the war, which for the Nazis never ended, to perfect the ideal Aryan—physically superior and intellectually dominant. He was that unassuming pedigreed blue blood Nazi who would never have to physically go to war to claim his birthright but would take control of inferior people's lands when they offered them up for salvation from his engineered plagues. Then he would breed them out of existence.

He was now both 'Creator and Destroyer' and his given middle name was Lucifer.

His mission to America was to find out why his plague was sputtering, only kindling tiny sparks of his genius that sputtered, refusing to ignite into the flames of Hell. He was in the Boston area to observe the way the booster or Part B of the vaccine was handled in various veterinary clinics after it was delivered from their Leipzig production facility. Using a false identity, he would collect samples to take back to Germany for quality control testing. Vogel had already contacted six random clinics announcing Schmitt's 'compliance' visit to the United States with a promise of 250 free doses of the vaccine in return for their cooperation. So far, thank God, no veterinary staff employee had been infected, but that problem was only a matter of time. If there were suddenly a disproportionate number of veterinarians or their staff showing psychotic neurological symptoms, the profession would be targeted by CDC epidemiological investigators. Once that connection was made, all his work would be for naught. Millions of companion animals would be slaughtered and the infection would be dead ended. So far the viron was mostly impotent, only infecting a minuscule number of those exposed. Nothing like the field trials. He needed to find the answer, schnell! *Fast.*

He made plans to stay north of Boston at a small B&B in Essex, on Cape Ann. There he could be semi anonymous, a tourist mixing business with pleasure. He hoped that there might be multiple reported savage, insane human on human attacks around these small town clusters so he could get himself into a the good graces of a small county coroner or health department. His goal would be to be invited to a necropsy where he could collect brain tissue samples to test back in Leipzig. For anonymity, Schmitt carried fake credentials using the name Peter Helwig, M.D, Ph.D. Public Health, that identified him as a medical pathologist / epidemiologist who was representing the Federal Republic of Germany. All he needed was a major incident to occur before he traveled back to Germany.

Essex was the very small village he chose to work from because it gave him access to several other villages and towns and easy access to Boston. There had already been one unexplained local attack on a couple riding bicycles by an old hermit like man who lived in a small fishing shack just off a popular bike path. The recluse suffered from lung cancer from years of chain smoking unfiltered cigarettes and had surprised the helmet wearing couple attacking them with a baseball bat. The woman died in the attack, taking two powerful blows to her chest rupturing her aorta, but her male companion, who came to her rescue, took two blows to his protected head before he wrestled the Louisville slugger out of the old man's grasp and swung a death blow, cracking his skull. That unprovoked attack fit the profile of what should be happening times millions if the viron was being shed properly by the vaccinated dogs and cats. The country should be overflowing with reports of his 'attacking Zombies'.

He pulled the black Mercedes sedan into the Resthaven B&B in the late afternoon. The converted old house was a two story, Cape Cod gray, Federal style, cedar shingled residence, surrounded by flowering perennial butterfly gardens and colorful hand painted swallow houses sitting on tall rusted metal poles. He could see a large deck wrapping around the side to the rear and the telephone pole like pilings that lined in the shallow estuary located directly behind the house. Two flags, one a 1776 Revolutionary Flag and the other a modern US flag, guarded either side of the front entrance.

"Welcome, Dr. Helwig to Resthaven B&B. I hope you had a safe and pleasant trip," Mary Townsend said as she removed her large straw gardening hat and cotton gloves. She was a short, portly woman in her late sixties with a cheerful cherub like face.

"Thank you for your welcome. This is very nice," he said. Now until he returned to Leipzig he would use Helwig as his identity.

"We enjoy it," she answered, "I have all of your information on file so I can show you to your room. We only have three rooms and yours is on the first floor and is our nicest. You even have your own small private screened porch. If you come in at night late, our two chocolate labs, Hersey and Cadbury, may give a couple of barks, but they won't bother you."

"Are they vaccinated?" he asked.

"My yes. Everything, including that new expensive rabies. We had a ton of raccoons that were always trying to get in the house garbage, but the county sent out nuisance animal trappers to thin them out. So you have nothing to be worried about," she replied.

"Any dining suggestions nearby. Regional food?"

"I'd drive into Ipswich. It's a straight drive in, only takes about fifteen minutes or so. There is a small Italian restaurant called Fratelli's that serves great Italian but also has fresh daily seafood caught locally like scallops, cod, tuna and lobster. You can't go wrong. Just park on Main Street and you'll see it's red, white and green lettered sign near the East Street intersection. There may be some police activity because I picked up on my police scanner that some heroin or LSD druggie attacked an old lady in Bialek Park. He strangled her with his belt maybe because she wouldn't give up her purse, then he went after the cops with a broken wine bottle. Now he's dead and the old lady is dead so that's eight within twenty miles in seven days. I listen to late night radio so I believe either it's some aliens messing with our minds or that Planet X they talk about. Either way there's never been this much trouble around here and I've lived in this county for sixty-five years," she puffed nearly out of breath.

"So here is your room. Let me know if you need anything else. Good evening, Doctor! Oh by the way, I serve a great breakfast; seven to ten."

"Danke, I am looking forward to a good American breakfast. Good evening also to you."

He carefully checked the room, examining it for security and closing the blinds. There was a small room safe in which he placed his authentic identity documents and credit cards. Then after a quick visit to the bathroom to freshen up, he left to go to dinner but more specifically to investigate the incident at the park.

Maybe I have lucked out and have a case to investigate.

The fifteen minute trip into Ipswich put him directly into the center of the village. He parked in a small municipal lot and fed the meter four quarters, ignoring the fact that it wasn't necessary after 6 p.m. He briefly orientated himself finding the small restaurant and started to cross the street to move up to where he figured the park was located. He passed the small restaurant and as soon as he reached the intersection corner, saw the cordoned park entrance with a sheriff's car and a coroner's van. He darted across to the park to talk to the deputy.

"Good evening, Officer, I heard what happened here. I hate to bother you but here are my credentials and letter of introduction from my government and your CDC. I would appreciate the opportunity to talk to your coroner. This incident may be part of a pattern of strange events that I may be qualified to assist in."

The deputy glanced at the paperwork and handed back the false documentation, lifted the yellow police line tape and let the nouveau Nazi pass through.

"You will find Doc beyond the picnic tables, just before the playground area. Follow the cinder path and you won't miss the crime scene."

Schmitt was enjoying his ruse as Helwig, the deception fueling his endorphin level. The real test would lay in his ability to fool the coroner. He hoped it would be an older man that he could intimidate with techno jargon. He crunched down the path, batting at the swarming mosquitos.

About two hundred meters in he saw three people. One policeman, a photographer who was busy documenting the scene and a red haired woman with her hair pulled back into a ponytail, that was wearing gray surgery scrubs under a long white lab coat. She was leaning over a partially shrouded corpse, wearing a pair of safety goggles and heavy blue nitrile gloves. She glanced at the handsome German in a confused manner, pulling her hands up against her chest like she was going into surgery.

"Who are you?" the policeman asked with a very official tone. "State your business please!"

"Sorry for the intrusion. I am here representing the Federal Republic of Germany to help your CDC with the Rabies containment effort. I heard about this and several other strange incidents around the greater Boston area and was asked to offer my expertise to frankly see if there may be some connecting factors." He handed over the letter and his 'Official' identification from the German government to the young coroner.

Dr Jan Robarts eyed the man who had appeared out of nowhere suspiciously. She strained to read the documents using a small white penlight to help see them.

"Sorry for the attitude," she offered, "but I am the only coroner on Cape Ann, plus it is a part-time position and I still have to run my OB-GYN practice. On top of that, it's been a full moon, so you know what that means. Lots of false labor and s'more than usual number of babies. I already have two DB's in the morgue and these two will max us out. I was thinking of shipping these out to Boston. The other two are already on ice but I need to be at the hospital for the living. I only took this 'honorary' position because old Doc Wilson died suddenly after falling off his roof. The old fart should have been smarter than that."

"Perhaps I could assist you. I am a fully qualified pathologist and could help do the gross necropsies to help you catch up and then you could determine which tissues and tests you needed. All I would want in exchange is some CSF, and some small bits of brain tissue. Would that be helpful?" he asked.

"I read your letter basically ordering my cooperation but believe me, if you could assist me in catching up, I would be very, very thankful. How would eight tomorrow morning sound. You could do as much or little as you like, but even knocking off one would be a huge help. The coroner's office is in Gloucester and I only have one technician, and he knows all the protocols and rules because when he's not processing tuna, he processing for the coroner's office. Been doing it for twenty years, humans, not tuna."

"Sure, I'll be there. Here's my card, you can text the address and your contact information. See you at eight."

He turned working his way back out of the small park. *That was way too easy!*

CHAPTER 34

Fratelli's Italian Restaurant

Ipswich, Mass.
Forty minutes later

"I will order for both of us, like a real man, if that is okay with you, honey," Tom announced.

"Just so you don't feel emasculated, you can order the meal and appetizer, but since I am the sophisticated world traveler, I will order the vino. Capisce?" Kate teased back. "But noooo chicken parm."

"I forgot that you are multi multilingual. Show off! I was thinking since we are on the shore, we try Pasta Pescatore/ frutti de mare with angel hair spaghetti but first we do the Mussels and white beans in light oil and white wine. How does that sound, il mio amore?" Tom said with a Italian accent.

"Tom, for an Irishman, you are, how can I put it, so sexy, so Italian!" Kate giggled.

"Grazie, leave the gun, keep the cannoli. That's just about the extent of my Italian." Tom grinned.

Tom ordered the meal and soon they were enjoying succulent Prince Edward Island mussels and beans. The small restaurant had only ten checker tablecloth tables and each was full. Just across from them sat the Nazi. He ate slowly and exactly, not looking up or making eye contact with other diners.

The belled front door jingled and Jan Robarts walked up to the register to pick up a to go order. She paid and started out but recognized Kate and nearly squealed with excitement.

"Kate. It's me Jan, from the CDC Zoonosis certification. Remember we had diner together? How great to see you!!"

"Of course I remember, I think we polished off a couple of bottles of wine before we all went out bar hopping. What was that? Seven or eight years ago?"

"Seven years this October. I still remember your bird joke — you know— dump the booze in the marsh so we would leave no Tern unstoned! That still makes me laugh."

"That was Brad's joke," Kate said, explaining to Tom. "Jan, this is my husband Tom O'Dell, he's also a veterinarian in private dairy practice."

"Nice to meet you, Tom. You got yourself quite a girl here!" Dr Robarts said, extending her hand.

"She sure is, now watch her blush!"

"Stop it you two! I can't help that I blush easily," Kate said, laughing as Tom dodged her playful jab.

"So, what are you doing here in my neck of the woods?"

"Well, we were supposed to visit here and stay at the Inn at Crane's Beach about three years ago when we were dating but we were unwittingly involved in the pursuit of that Nazi Berhetzel through a USDA investigation and then later we were really thrust into the thick of it. It was a total surreal experience. Now it seems like a dream. What are you up to?" Kate asked.

"Well, I 'm still a practicing OBGYN, but when our local coroner died after an accidental fall, the county commissioners asked me to assume his job, probably after asking all the other MD's in the county. They told me it would only be four to five hours a week and would pay a thousand a week. Seemed like a smart way to pay the mortgage. But now we have had six deaths in less than a week; two of them murders, one a suicide and one killed by cop. I have four on ice waiting for necropsies. See that man sitting by himself over by the wine rack.... he showed up out of nowhere when I was in the park cleaning up the last murder scene, about an hour ago. Turns out he is a German pathologist that is here on official government business. He has a letter from the CDC giving him Carte Blanche to assist, investigate and collect tissue for something they're working on. He offered me help tomorrow in completing those bodies, and I accepted. Otherwise I would never get done with all the paperwork! If I pass them off to Suffolk County, which is Greater Boston, it would be worse than doing them here. Here he comes."

The German had seen the coroner talking to the couple at the table and finished his meal quickly, paid and decided to say good evening to the young woman. He walked over to the three.

"It seems we meet again, Dr. Robarts. I just had a delicious seafood pasta but I guess the flight is catching up with me because I was suddenly overwhelmed with the need to sleep. I want to be fresh for tomorrow's work!" He smiled.

"Dr. Helwig, I would like you to meet two friends who are visiting the area on holiday. Dr. Kate Vensky and her husband Dr. Tom O'Dell. Both are veterinarians, Kate works for the USDA and Tom is in dairy practice. They work as field investigators for the CDC so they have done a lot of forensic work. Maybe they know your CDC connection. Who issued your letter of introduction?" Robarts asked.

"I think it was. ...." he hesitated, "I better check."

He pulled the paper from his sports jacket pocket and unfolded it. "It looks like it was Theodore R Johnson. Do you know of him?"

"That's Ted. He signed it Theodore? That's weird, maybe he used Theodore since it was the German Government. May I see the letter please?" Kate asked.

"Sicher." *Sure.*

Kate briefly looked at the letter and confirmed it was from Ted. "Gut. Well, I need to get some rest. It has been a long day. I left Germany very early in the morning your time. Dr Robarts, I will meet you tomorrow at your office in the City Hall?"

"County Courthouse. The Sheriff will escort you to my work area. Eight a.m.?"

"Sharp!" he said firmly with a German's precision as he walked away.

Tom turned to the two women and said, "He seemed nice."

"I agree but that letter was strange," Kate replied.

"Why?" Robarts questioned.

"Ted was murdered a few weeks ago. That letter was dated two days after he died. Let's keep that between ourselves. Tomorrow I will call Atlanta and see if there is an explanation for the dating on that letter.

"You see, Jan, Tom and I have trust issues with Germans."

CHAPTER 35

Cape Ann

"Good Morning. Department of Emerging Diseases, Sue Ann Meyers speaking."

"Sue Ann, it's Kate Vensky. How are you?"

"Kate! Great to hear your voice. I guess I'm ok. I keep expecting to see Dr. Johnson walk through that office door with a big smile carrying a bag of Kripsie Kream donuts, but the fact is, no one walks in here. We are looking for a new director. We couldn't pry you away from that farm, could we?"

"Not unless Tom decides he's had enough of freezing his butt off five months out of the year!"

"Too bad! We could use someone like you and I know that would have made Ted very happy. You did know he had a crush on you?"

"Don't be silly, Ted? All the years we worked together he never once indicated any interest."

"That's just how he was after the divorce, afraid of getting rejected again. Nice guy— really too nice."

"The reason I called," Kate explained, "is Tom and I are on Cape Ann on kind of a second honeymoon and I ran into Jan Robarts who is the local coroner. She has been fielding a lot of weird murders and was unexpectedly approached by a German pathologist who carried a letter of introduction from Ted. I read it and it looked legitimate except it was dated two days after Ted's death. I checked, it was dated on the Monday after he was murdered. What do you think?"

"That's an easy one. He left all his completed work on my desk and I would do my thing and return them to sign. On that day, he was running a little late seeing his mom so he left without signing his correspondence. We had no one to rewrite his work so we ran them through the computer on Monday which auto signed them. Not real ethical but I don't think any of us were thinking too clearly then. Sorry for the confusion."

"I guess that explains it. Sorry, I got to go, Tom's motioning to me, he wants to get on the beach. Stay in touch, Sue Ann. Please!"

"You too, bye!"

Meyers put down the phone receiver and thought for a moment. Then she removed a secure cell phone from her purse and dialed a series of three sets of numbers. Her phone buzzed and squealed as voice and data encryption initiated.

"What is it?" a voice asked as the call connection.

"Sorry to disturb but this may be important, sir."

"Then get on with it. What is the problem?"

"I just had a call from a friend and colleague of Dr. Johnson. She by chance met Dr. Helwig, using his fake credentials, on a pleasure trip to Cape Ann. Not a big problem but she questioned why the letter of introduction from this office he carried was signed by Dr. Johnson two days after his death. I made up an excuse and she seemed to accept it. I don't anticipate there being any further problem but she is real intelligent and resourceful, a potential problem. I thought you should be informed immediately so you can warn Helwig."

"Danke, you keep your eyes and ears open and I will pass this on." Click.

Hans Vogel was worried. This was the last thing he needed to hear. After he warned Schmitt, Mendoza would have to be told and that never was an easy conversation. Especially since the carefully planned zoonotic catastrophe was little more than small pockets of unexplained craziness. No crisis or panic, just focal areas of diluted potential chaos. They needed answers and hopefully Schmitt would find them. He called Schmitt.

"Dr. Helwig speaking," Schmitt answered.

"Can you talk?" Vogel asked.

"I am assisting in a necropsy but if this is important, I can step out for a few moments."

"Yes, and when we converse, even with the encryption, auf deutsch sprechen." *Speak in German.*

"Dr. Robarts, I have an important call. May I step out and take it?" Schmitt asked anticipating the answer by pulling off his other thick nitrile glove.

"Off course, Peter, just leave your gloves and gown over in the biohazard bin and Ted will get you set up with fresh gear when you return. Take your time, we are making great progress."

Schmitt peeled off his gown and exited the morgue and went under the shade of a large pin oak that bordered the parking lot. A light misty rain hung in the air and he brushed squirrel chewed acorns off a curved concrete garden bench, that sat near the large tree's trunk.

"I am ok to talk now," he said in German.

"My contact at the CDC received a call from a woman you met last evening, a Doctor Vensky. She noticed your letter of introduction was dated after Johnson's 'unfortunate passing'. She was given an explanation why and seemed to accept it. I just want you to be vigilant and careful on who you talk to. Get your mission done and return as quickly as possible. I have to call South America and relate this information and the updated field reports. That will not be an easy call. Get your samples, check out the veterinary clinics and how they handle the vaccine and get back to the lab! I will inform the CDC that we are behind in production and are slowing our shipping. We then can find out why the viron is not expressing its potential."

"What about this Vensky woman?" Schmitt asked.

"I will let Mendoza decide that. Perhaps an accident of some kind. Or we infect her family with the real thing. I will let you know. But for now you must pray my head does not end up on a platter!"

CHAPTER 36

Cape Ann

Two mornings later

Kate just started her third day's predawn run from the Inn, past the beach entrance, up to the wide and long Crane's Beach. She pushed herself hard at the water's edge on the wet compacted sand that had been exposed by the low tide. The sand resisted her forward push but she felt energized as endorphins were released, her body responding to the extra effort she was asking it to do. She ran north, the orange rising sun at her right, while the cool, light onshore breeze pushed the smell of salt and sea life across her body. Often she did her best analytical thinking while in the focused runner's 'cocoon' when her body pumped and burned energy. Like an automobile in cruise control, her brain separated from that engine and became sharper, allowing Kate to do more effective thinking. She was a problem solver and her intuition was telling her that Tom and her surprise meeting with Jan Robarts and the German pathologist was more than just chance. It was almost like when they met Joseph Blackfeather at the Fort Peck cattle kill, an event that likely saved the world from wholesale destruction of the human race by the Nazi Berthetzel. The more she thought, the more uneasy she felt about that chance meeting, two days before.

Her multifunction 'watch' signaled she had run three miles after what seemed like mere seconds from where she had started. Kate had been lost in her thoughts, her trained runner's body fixed in auto mode. Focusing on a distant small jetty, she sprinted hard about two hundred more yards and then decelerated to an easy walk, shaking her arms and hands in a typical athlete fashion. Kate stopped, stretched and turned toward the east, facing the rising sun, absorbing its energy as the air warmed. She raised her arms skyward rotating her palms toward the fiery ball and then turned clockwise, arms extended fully to the south, west and finally north mimicking what she had seen the old Indian shaman Nelson Blackfeather, Joseph's great grandfather, do. Refreshed and recharged, fully connected to the world, she walked an easy pace back to the south where she saw a few others on the beach, walking their dogs or shell hunting.

Kate moved past them, continuing south, passing bits and pieces of beached sea life and flotsam exposed by the tidal change. She checked her watch, programmed it for another four miles and started off working into an effortless, rhythmic stride. The gulls drifted lazily overhead, dipping slightly as the cloud of air they glided on shifted. They called out to others as Kate moved down the shore bumping small foraging plovers and sandpipers that scurried ahead of her, nervously poking into the wet sand, extracting small crustaceans to eat.

She ran south from where she had originally started and it seemed that today, the beach had become much more deserted as she pushed on. She had the cold Atlantic on her left, dry sand on her right that had been blown into hilled waves of sea grass dunes and the swishy wet sand underfoot. She continued forward, leaving a running trail behind her to be consumed later by the changing tide. Kate dodged a spit of sand and sea grass that pushed out to the edge of the waves. As she ran past the outcropping, she saw what looked like a man giving another CPR. An All-Terrain Vehicle was idling nearby.

Kate sprinted up to the men to help.

"What happened?" she asked.

"I think my friend had a heart attack. I tried to call 911 but I don't have any bars out here. He's non-responsive. Maybe I'm doing it wrong?" the middle aged man said anxiously.

"Let me try," Kate ordered, "I have advanced medical training!" The man moved off his friend and Kate straddled the body and started to check for a jugular pulse. She felt a strong bounding pulse. "Hey, he's got a great pulse and just took a breath. I guess you...."

Instantaneously, the man she straddled lunged, pulling her down to him holding her tight. The man behind her jammed an ultra-fast acting paralytic sedative into her back and then grabbed both wrists, pulling them roughly behind her, zip tying them tightly. She rolled stiffly over as the drugs did their job.

The first man pulled out a VHF marine radio and called out in German, "We have landed a prize specimen. Bring the transport."

Within two minutes a Bell 407 GXP helicopter pushed to the ground and the two men lifted the veterinarian into the machine, roughly pushing her on the floor to the rear seating. The man who played the victim belted himself next to her and gave the pilot a thumb's up. The other man mounted the idling ATV and sped rapidly back down the beach as the helicopter lifted away, creating a blast of sand.

The first man put on a headset as the pilot indicated a secure call coming in for him.

"Good morning, sir. Yes, I have the target. The GPS tracker in her shoe worked wonderfully and the intercept was exactly where we predicted based on yesterday's data. We will transport to the holding area and should then be there in three hours. Thank you."

Evil had resurfaced once more in Kate's life.

CHAPTER 37

Crane's Beach

One hour later

"Come on, answer! Pick up, Kate, damnit!" Tom paced back and forth on the lawn of the Inn. He left a third voicemail admonishing her call him.

He had that sickening feeling something was seriously wrong. Kate always answered her phone and when running wore a Bluetooth earpiece and could easily run and talk. He returned to the front desk and asked to please be called when his wife returned. Then Tom started across the lawn toward the beach entrance. He stopped at the Crane's Beach ranger station kiosk, where parking and entrance fees were paid. He walked up to a uniformed older man working the booth.

"Good morning, sir, can I help you?" he asked Tom.

"I hope so. My wife and I are staying at the Inn and she has been doing a predawn run on the beach the last couple mornings. This morning she hasn't returned and doesn't answer her phone. I expected her back over an hour ago as we are flying out of Logan this afternoon and had a pretty much set schedule. Plus she is the most reliable person I have ever met. Something's got to be wrong. Have you seen her — pretty, auburn hair in a ponytail, late thirties in a light green with silver running outfit and a Nike headband?"

"Well, sir, I was on duty here about 7:45, fifteen minutes before we technically open, but as you can see, unless you're driving a car,

you could pretty much find your way to the water anywhere around here. Get eaten by ticks though. I don't get much of any heavy traffic this time of year so she would be easy to spot and I haven't seen anyone except that group of turkey over there that hang around, and a commercial fish spotting helicopter. You want to check the beach?" the ranger asked.

"Yes, I just don't know which way she went. Could be miles," Tom explained.

"I'm not supposed to leave my post, but why don't you take my Jeep and since most run up the beach, first head up and then down the beach. The tide's out so you have plenty of room to drive, just watch for the shore bird habitat barriers. There is a point both north and south where you will have to get out and walk. Just take the keys with you. Use the two-way radio in the Jeep to call me here if you find an emergency. If you don't find her, I will call the sheriff for a helicopter search. Good luck!"

"Thanks, you have no idea how much I appreciate this!"

Tom jumped into the Wiley's style Jeep and shifted into gear, peeling a cloud of dusty sand as he drove rapidly to the water, fighting a rising panic.

Please, Lord God, protect Kate and help me find her ok!

Tom maneuvered the forest green Jeep past the parking area and onto what appeared to be a service path and accelerated on the bumpy trail. The beach spread out before him with a handful of dog walkers and shell seekers scattered around. He angled north in first gear, slowing to control the Jeep better. He glanced at the odometer and reset the day trip reading to zero and made his way up the beach trying to remember what she had told him the day before.

Kate said she ran just over three miles north and then about four to the south, or was it four and then three? No, that wouldn't return her to the beach exit. Has to be three then four south. For God's sake, where are you?

He drove three point four miles, stopped and got out, looking north. He saw no one. Tom turned the Jeep and sped at the edge of the tide the opposite direction stopping twice to ask the beachcombers if they had seen Kate. A middle aged blond in a gray sweat-suit and

large straw hat was exercising her black lab tossing a good size piece of driftwood into the surf. Tom stopped to talk.

"Excuse me, can I ask you a question?" he shouted.

The woman recognized the Jeep and walked up, dragging the young lab which was firmly attached to the piece of wood.

"Nice lab. I have an older male back in Wisconsin," Tom started, "I've always had a black lab. Best dogs ever!"

"He's goofy but I love him. I just can't wear him out! How can I help you?"

"I'm looking for my wife. She ran this beach this morning but now I can't reach her. Not like her and I'm really worried."

"I only saw one jogger this morning, a woman in I think a light green outfit with some gray on it? She ran north and then back past that point down there. Hard to see from here but the beach thins there for a little while and then opens up again. You will have to walk around it because there is a good drop off right around there. She hasn't come back this way and the only thing unusual and probably not that unusual was an amphibious helicopter in that area that appeared to drop down and then off. I thought it might be one of those news copters or a tuna spotter. They really frost me because they speed up and down the shore destroying the ambiance of this special place."

"Thanks for the information. I gotta go," Tom nearly shouted as he hit the gas popping the Jeep's gears. The dog barked loudly pulling the woman's arm wanting to chase the escaping vehicle.

Tom stopped where the woman had told him and walked around the water's edge. There was a single row of shoeprints in the sand and he followed their path. No doubt now that Kate had run past here but there were no prints indicating she had returned. Tom walked rapidly following the sandy impressions until he saw the area where the men had grabbed her. He saw the signs of a struggle and the two sets of much larger footprints leading to two indentations in the sand created by the helicopter and the sea grass flattened by the helicopter's air wash.

Tom called out for Kate, not believing what he was seeing and thinking. *My God, she's been taken! Why and by whom?*

He checked the area again and found a five ml syringe upright in the sand.

She was drugged! Please, God, don't let them hurt my Kate!

Tom ran, slipping in the sand in a panic to reach the Jeep. He grabbed the radio microphone and pushed transmit.

"This is the man with your Jeep. My wife has been abducted. By helicopter. Please, please get me some help!"

CHAPTER 38

Near Brunswick, Georgia

Twelve hours later

"Yes sir, we have the woman, we are secure here and I have started to recover her for questioning just as you ordered. I'm estimating tomorrow morning. We will let her get cleaned up, eat and explain her unique situation to her. I have Maria in the room with her and hopefully she will gain her trust. I'm just a little worried about the level of intelligence we are dealing with and her ability to deceive us," the large burly man from the helicopter answered.

"Good, I want no harm to come to her for the time being, she has to be willing to cooperate based on our threats to her husband, friends and little boy. I need to know what the CDC is up to and anything her associates are doing that could interfere with our plans. Hopefully they will spend their energy looking for her, thereby giving us a time window to fix our field trial problems. After that she will be of no value and I'm sure my boss will have terminations planned for the whole lot. Remember, Kurt, keep your profile low, use all our encryption tools and don't raise any suspicions. Limit your time outside the condo to only what is absolutely necessary."

Hans Vogel ended the call abruptly, sighed and stared out his large panoramic office window overlooking a manicured park like area surrounded by mixed conifers and spruce. He looked down at his Presidential Rolex dreading the next call with Schmitt and Mendoza because he had independently taken the bold step to kidnap Vensky.

At precisely 10 am his computer alerted an incoming encryption and seconds later Mendoza and Schmitt appeared on the large wall mounted screen. Mendoza sat in his office with a cigar in hand and Schmitt was seated on the back porch of the B&B. Both look somber.

"Good Morning, Hans," Mendoza greeted, "and to you Schmitt."

"Guten Morgen!" they replied in near unison.

"So, I need answers to explain our apparent launch failure. Schmitt, do you have any thoughts that could explain the viron's impotency?"

"Yes, the problem could be one of several things. One would be the shipping and handling of the product after it leaves our production facility. I inspected two different shipments as they arrived at two unrelated veterinary offices and in both, the refrigerating gel packs had reached a critical temperature. I ran a digital thermometer probe through each unopened styrofoam shipping container, did an instant read and both were too warm at seven point five Celsius, about ten degrees too warm. We ship daily including Friday and both the clinics I was at were closed on the normal delivery window of 36 hours, which was a Saturday. I think that our viron has a very low temperature tolerance to either heat or perhaps the initial cold packing. I have ten doses from each office on ice to test when I return so we will have to see which it is but, Dr Vogel, I would initiate some temperature trials and look for a biologic stabilizer. Also, because these veterinary facilities ran vaccine clinics to basically push the numbers through to get vaccinated, the vaccine syringes were preloaded. Sometimes for hours. Neither hospital wore exam gloves to handle the product and one was using alcohol to vigorously wipe down the injection sites. No one followed our explicit instructions on handling and administration. The human factor!

"I also collected brain tissue from four necropsies I assisted in a town north of Boston and hopefully they will show the viron infecting the tissue when we do the forensic testing. The good news is as far as I can tell no one suspects these crazed attacks are the result of the zoonotic disease process. Did hear a theory about aliens though."

Vogel responded, "We did do the original temperature trials in vitro but not in a real world situation. I will order new trials and look at better, more controlled shipping."

"Approximately what percentage of the domestic canine and feline population in the target areas have received the first non-infective dose?" Mendoza asked.

"We are estimating about forty-seven percent," said Vogel.

"And the infective second dose?"

"Only a third of those."

"Good," the scion of Hitler replied, "then we have a window of opportunity to correct this issue. We need revisit those areas infecting more wildlife with the live engineered Rabies and then focus on frightening the procrastinators into getting their animals protected. How ironic is that? Yes, we will protect you against that virus and at no additional charge make your beloved Fluffy your personal pipeline to Hell!" He chuckled.

"That should stir the pot and generate an influx of new animals to the clinics. I want to ask about the woman, Dr. Vensky, I heard she is missing and assume we are the perpetrators. If so, what is our end game? I'm afraid if the government of the United States gets involved we will be under the microscope and might get discovered. Why don't we just eliminate her and move on?" Schmitt asked.

"It's true I took the initiative and took her but at this point she hasn't recovered enough from the drugs to know anything. At this point, I'm not real comfortable with the kidnapping. Too many potential complications, including connecting me directly into this," Vogel confessed.

"I do agree, possibly I was premature ordering her abduction, but she scares the hell out of me with her group of colleagues plus all of them could also really be a problem. We should kill her and dump her in the Atlantic or possibly. ..?" Vogel offered.

"Or possibly infect her and the problem will take care of itself. She can be our poster child to vaccinate your pet. I think we keep her sedated and infect her with the engineered rabies virus. The virus can take care of the entire problem and generate more foot traffic into the veterinary hospitals once she is clinical and diagnosed. What a pity to be sacrificed in such a horrible way," Mendoza said.

"That is a good idea, consider it done. We will infect her with the reserved virus today and recover and release her tomorrow near where she disappeared from. She won't remember any details and it will be considered a miracle to be found alive and unharmed," replied Vogel.

Kate was now to be a victim of the disease she feared the most. A death designed by Satan himself.

CHAPTER 39

Tom paced like a madman after calling his parents who were watching Bobbi and Jed and then made the awful call to Kate's eighty-seven year old mother who had been in failing health for months. He felt like he had just pushed the elder Vensky over a cliff after she listened to his news, the old woman crying and screaming hysterically that her only child was possibly gone, kidnapped by some unknown evil.

The really frightening thing was Joseph and Jules calling within minutes of each other, checking on Kate. Joseph had a vision from his ancestors of Kate being in danger and Jules had heard from Jean DuBois who also had had a 'strange feeling' that something was seriously wrong concerning Kate. That gave Tom shivers but hope that they again were being protected by the 'Creator' that Joseph's grandfather Nelson had described to them the night before he died. He remembered Nelson's words almost like it was yesterday and the powerful storm that followed their brief encounter on the Blackfeathers' deck. Nelson had told them:

"I am convinced that, what you call 'God' is the balance between the Creator and the Destroyer. Lakota are not historically a traditional monotheistic people. When the good or Creator favors us with peace, love and good weather and abundant supplies of food, life is good. When we become the target of a rising Destroyer, then we struggle to survive —to exist. There has to be a balanced existence in all things including living and dying."

Tom was afraid that all the strange events of the last months, including the rabies epidemic, the attack on Paris, Joseph linking the wolves to the rabies outbreak, Ted Johnson's murder and now Kate's abduction were all connected. Had to be. The forces of good or as Nelson had related, the Creator, were again using them for some reason and that could only be to stop this new Destroyer. That had to be the reason behind the rabies outbreak and the events which Tom was convinced were conjured to specifically stop or impede their interference. Tom had originally felt that Nelson's commission of Kate, Brad, Joseph and himself was only a one-time deal to get Berhetzel. Now it appeared they were to do battle with the forces of evil again. Only this time it was personal.

Jules and Jean were flying into Logan on the Pasteur Institute jet and were arriving first thing in the morning, about the same time Brad and Joseph were landing. Tom planned to meet his friends after exchanging the Kia Sportage he had rented for a large Chevy Suburban. FBI Agent Sullivan had arranged a team of specialists from Boston to work Kate's disappearance and so far Tom had been interviewed three times, the agents verifying his version of her disappearance as they tried locating the woman with the black lab who saw both Kate and the helicopter. So far no luck at that. No one else had seen her on the beach with her dog that morning. They had the syringe and were testing for the type of drugs used on Kate. Because the husband always was the number one suspect, Tom was no exception. They took his phone's SIM card and replaced it with a new one and took DNA samples from him. He was under the microscope and didn't like it one bit.

The next morning there still was no word on Kate. Tom called into the special agent in charge and told him he was on his way to Logan to meet his friends. The agent told him not to leave the area.

Really? What kind of a person does he think I am?

Tom waited at the cell lot until he couldn't stand it anymore, then picked up the large SUV from Hertz and circled the arriving terminals like a lost chauffeur, the cops watching him suspiciously move in and out of traffic. Finally his phone rang. It was Brad.

"Tom? Tonto and I have just landed and are on our way to Ground Transportation Terminal C in about ten minutes. Jules and Jean have also landed and we met them five minutes ago. We're ready to help in any way we can."

"Thanks, Brad. I'll meet you there in a few. Bye!"

Brad's voice and the thought that he would have his good friends around for support put the first smile on his face in the last two days. He pushed the big vehicle just a little faster and squeezed into the curb with his four-way flashers pulsing a frantic automotive SOS. Tom sat there for eight minutes still being eyed by the airport police as cars and taxis honked and darted in and out retrieving their riders. Tom cracked his window but quickly closed it as the smelly contaminated air blew in. A cop waved, motioning Tom to move the big Suburban, yelling with a heavy South Boston accent, "Move it, you can't park here. Hey, Buddy, get going or I'll give you a ticket!"

Tom started to turn the wheel when he heard two thumps on the passenger side door and saw Brad's large frame filling the window. Tom rolled down the window and Brad shouted in, "Hey, Buddy, this limo available?"

"You have any money ?"

"Lord no! I have a wife and three kids. But I have well to do friends," as he pointed to Joseph, Jules and Jean. "The Cavalry has arrived, just don't tell that to Joseph!!"

The other three were talking to the cop and Jules showed some paperwork, probably his diplomatic passport.

Tom got out and shared sympathetic man hugs with his friends and loaded their luggage. Brad was still trying to lighten the mood. They loaded up and Brad started up again.

"Welcome to the Cash Cab! This is a game show that takes place right in this sorry ass man's cab! What do you say, wanna play?"

Tom looked at Brad questioning now, as he had in the past, the man's sanity. *Why was he so jovial in the face of Kate's abduction?*

"Ok, I guess by now you really think I've lost it. Jules, do you want to tell him?"

"No, I'll let young Joseph do the honors," Jules answered almost gleefully.

"Thanks. I'm pleased to do the honors. Tom, Jules just received news about Kate from Special Agent Sullivan. She's fine. They found her wandering in a park in Ipswich. She is still confused but apparently physically unharmed. She's now in the Thomas Smithson Hospital in Gloucester. You should probably head up that way."

"She's safe, really safe?" Tom exclaimed, choking back tears.

"Yes, she's okay!" Brad replied.

Tom dropped his head down onto the steering wheel and started to sob nearly uncontrollably. The others fought back tears and shifted uncomfortably in their seats.

"Why don't you change seats with me and I'll drive this tank. She's really ok, Tom, thank God!!" Brad offered.

They exchanged seats as the realization hit Tom that another miracle had just happened. He wiped his tears on a piece of paper towel he always carried in his pocket and pulled out his phone. He looked at the phone, tapping it with his finger trying to get it to respond.

"Well, I guess I forget to charge my phone. No wonder I didn't hear anything. I'm such a dumb ass."

That triggered a piling on as a series of 'Roger that, Oui's and Sure Are,' flowed his way.

"Maintenant, we need to find out the why. This was no isolated incident or unrelated to what happened to Paris or Ted. The question is why Kate has returned to us and unharmed. It doesn't fit our enemy's B.O," Jules stated.

"That's M.O." Brad laughed.

"Moe, Moe who?" Jules replied.

"And who's on first?" Brad laughed.

"What's on second?" Joseph added, jumping in.

Jules and Jean looked at Brad obviously confused.

"That's an old baseball routine of Abbott and Costello, an American comedy team from a long time ago, Vaudeville, slapstick humor," Brad clarified.

"Yeah, don't confuse it with Brad's jokes. His humor makes you so sick you want to slap him," Joseph said, chuckling.

Jules shook his head, then reached over and reassuringly padded Tom's shoulder.

"Your friends' attempts at humor are only to help you relax until we get you to Kate. After we drop you off, Jean and I will drive these two to the nearest insane asylum."

That had them all roaring with laughter.

CHAPTER 40

Thomas Smithson Hospital

Gloucester, Massachusetts

Kate was sleeping in her hospital bed when Tom arrived. Brad had dropped him off and driven their friends to the town's fishing docks for a fresh seafood meal at The Dockside Seafood House Restaurant, famous for their fresh seafood and chowder. Even though he hadn't eaten in over a day, Tom refused their offer to bring Kate and him some carry-out because he wasn't sure how Kate would be feeling. He sat down silently on a shiny beige faux leather reclining chair next to her bed. A vase of colorful Daisies, Kate's favorite flower, was on the night stand and Tom looked at the card. It was in French. *Pendant à toi, Aime, Jules.... Thinking of you, Love, Jules.*

Tom shook his head. How did he do that? Must have texted or ordered online from the Suburban. That man was always one step ahead of everyone, especially Tom.

Tom cradled her hand which felt slightly warmer than normal. She was flushed and breathing rapidly. She clearly wasn't ok. He closed his eyes and started to pray, something that Kate always encouraged him to do. After he finished up, he wiped tears from his eyes and saw Dr. Jan Robarts standing motionless next to Kate's bed.

"Dr. Robarts, thank you for coming to visit," he said, standing to greet her, "I've only been here for a few minutes. She doesn't look right to me. What do you know about her condition?"

Jan Robarts moved to his side of the bed and gave him a brief hug. Then she sat down on a black examination stool across from Tom. She looked a little distressed.

"I talked to the attending physician, Milton Fox, a great internist and infectious disease specialist, and it looks to him like she has an infection. Low white count and slightly febrile. Probably from stress but she is weak and mildly dehydrated and we are setting her up on fluids, antivirals and antibiotics. We are also testing to see if the Ketamine and Midazolam she was given has been metabolized completely. When they found her in Ipswich, she was disoriented so originally they felt she was still drugged, possibly from receiving multiple doses. Dr Fox doesn't think that's it. He has ordered complete sets of toxicology, brain scans and a CSF tap. He also is setting up an isolation unit just in case we need to move her. I'm afraid she will be here for a while or possibly transferred to Mass General."

"What kind of infection? She only was missing for what? Fifty-four hours? She would have had to been exposed before the kidnapping, right?"

"I'm an OBGYN so I'm not the right person to ask that question. You're still staying at the Inn right?"

"No, I had to check out this morning because they're fully booked with a Birding Club. We also have four friends that flew in to help so I need to find housing for them. It's a long story but they are here because they feel there is something strangely wrong about Kate's kidnapping and because we are technically an eclectic team of trained forensic investigators. Also because we experienced the loss of a good friend and with the attack on Paris, our instincts are being tested and I fear what or who we will find is behind all of this."

"Your friend—Ted Johnson, right?"

"Yes."

"Here's what I can do. My family owns a six-bedroom home on the water not far from here that we rent during the summer season. It was my husband's parents' place but they are gone now. You

are welcome to stay there, as long as you need. Just be out by next Memorial Day."

"Thanks, that's beyond generous. Are you going to be in the hospital much longer today, because our friends will be here after they finish eating lunch? I would like you to meet them."

"Sure. I have two patients down in Delivery in early labor, so I will be here for hours. Just have me paged when they arrive. Meantime, maybe you should wear a mask and gloves until Dr. Fox makes his determination; just to be safe."

That reality hit Tom hard. She must be very sick!

"I'm sure Fox will be here shortly and he will make the decisions on Kate's care. Trust him, Tom. He's a good man and an outstanding physician. He will figure it out and make her better. I gotta go." She stood and gave Tom another hug, this one firmer and longer.

Tom stared down at his beautiful wife. Her eyelids fluttered as she slept and her lips were dry and cracked at the corners. *She's not ok, she's really ill and I don't understand any of it. Lord, help her, save her!*

He sat back down and pulled out his phone to call Brad, forgetting the battery was dead. *Damn!!*

Tom pushed the phone deep back into his pants pocket, grumbling to himself. A nurse came in followed by a short balding man in a doctor's white lab coat.

"Dr. O'Dell, I'm your wife's attending, Milt Fox, nice to meet you." The middle aged physician with sandy brown gray close cropped hair that framed his balding head, extended his rough calloused hand and firmly shook Tom's.

"Your hands are like mine. You have a farm too?" he asked.

"Yes, in Wisconsin. Just a few beef cattle, a horse and some chickens. But I am a dairy vet and I'm always pulling something out or pushing it back in a cow. In the winter my hands split, crack and bleed. It's an occupational hazard," Tom explained.

"For me it's the hand washing and alcohol sanitizers. Plus in the late winter I tap sugar maples and produce some great Grade A maple syrup. Last year about three hundred twenty gallons."

"Wow, that a lot of raw tree sap to boil down. How in the world do you have time for that?" Tom asked.

"I have three teenagers who need money all the time. At minimum it keeps them busy and in the outdoors exercising for six to eight weeks. The money is secondary to the lessons about hard work. Now, how about we talk about your wife?

"Everything so far points to an infection, likely a virus. I can't be sure but she is leukopenic, febrile and a little obtuse. We ruled out Lyme disease, but are going to focus on neurotrophic viruses and bacteria with a CSF tap and blood and urine cultures. I am going to move her to a private isolation suite until we understand better what's going on. Could be something as simple as exhaustion and dehydration.

"So for now wear gloves and a mask. Rose will start getting her ready to move by tenting her, then the aides will help her get settled into our isolation suite. This hospital may look turn of the century from the outside but as you can see, we are up to date internally and the staff is amazing. Any questions?"

"When will you have some of the test results?" Tom asked.

"My resident will do the spinal tap within the hour so Clin/Path will have the majority of it done by dinnertime. You should go to Jan's beach house, settle in and be back here by five thirty. If she has any change good or bad, I'll call you."

"My phone is dead. I forgot to charge it. Use this number, my friend Brad's phone —555 512-3333. He's here and will be with me most times or know where I'm at. I will get my phone charged in the meantime. Perhaps I can I have your card, then I can call you directly?"

"Here you go," Fox replied handing a business card over, "call anytime but for now, go get a bite to eat while they move your wife."

"I'm really not hungry but maybe I can get a Coke or something."

"Elevator down to the basement, take a right and you'll see the cafeteria," Fox said walking away as he pulled out his phone to receive a call.

Tom watched Kate being draped under a clear plastic tent that zippered up both sides and encapsulated the entire bed; a small mechanical air pump pushed air in and a series of venting hoses ran the exhausted waste air past an Ultra Violet light and then bubbled into a vat of chemical disinfectants. The nurse and both aides wore caps, masks, goggles and pathogen barrier gowns. It didn't appear the hospital was going to take any chances. That scared the crap out of him.

Kate was wheeled out and Tom suddenly felt as if all the life had been sucked out of him. He sat down in the chair, closed his exhausted eyes and immediately drifted into a deep sleep. He was startled awake by Brad's voice.

"Tom, where's Kate? Everyone is downstairs waiting to see if it was ok to visit her."

"She's been moved to isolation because she's febrile and leukopenic and they don't want to risk she is contagious. Dr. Fox has ordered a whole battery of tests. We won't know anything until after this afternoon. The good news is Kate's friend, Dr. Jan Robards, is letting us stay at her family's beach house which is close to here and can accommodate all of us. We all need to stay together because this smells stinky rotten to me. All of us have been affected either directly or indirectly since the mutant rabies hit and I think we better go over everything again because I think that Destroyer thing is occurring again. Kate was targeted and I think I'm going to ask Dr. Fox to include the new rabies in his testing. She's been vaccinated against standard rabies for years and had her booster when we were in Atlanta for the original training and hopefully if she was infected she might get some cross immunity."

"God, I hope she wasn't exposed. I will go wait with the others downstairs. Find out about the house and talk to Fox. She's strong, Tom, I'm sure she will be ok," Brad assured Tom.

Brad walked out of the room, fighting back tears.

Rabies, please Lord God, not that!

CHAPTER 41

The Beach House was old but beautiful, a typical Federal style Cape Cod gray cedar shingled home, about twenty minutes from the hospital. The inside was finished in a beach style with lots of nets, driftwood, cute signs and lobster pot decor that gave the house a cozy New England Colonial feeling. There were four bedrooms upstairs, a master first floor bedroom with an attached tiny child's room, and a huge kitchen with a large windowed four season porch that overlooked a rustic deck leading to a narrow board walk onto the mostly rock and gravel beach. A small one-bedroom guest house stood just to the right of the deck beyond a large cedar hot tub. The property was private, the view exceptional and even Jules was impressed.

"This is an amazing place. How nice Dr. Robards extended us the use of it. I will need to invite her to stay with my family if she is ever in Paris."

"Bet this place rents for seven or eight thousand a week during peak season which probably only covers part of the taxes they must pay on it. It definitely has the wow factor!" Brad added.

"I'm going to get a fire going to take the chill and dampness out," Joseph said. "Anyone object to that?"

"Non, but I need something to do, so how about I help you by bringing in some logs from their woodshed," Jean offered.

"Great, thanks. While you are doing that, I'll clean the hearth and check the flue to make sure we don't burn the place down. I would be careful, Jean, about ticks around the bushes and the wood," Joseph warned.

"Oui, Bien Sûr!" *Yes, for sure.*

Tom walked out on the deck and down to the water. The tide was out and the water was clear and shallow, lazily lapping at the shore. He knelt down on one knee and picked up some rocks and tried side arming the rounded egg-sized rocks like a kid trying to skip stones on a farm pond. He wasn't really concentrating and the stones clunked, mostly falling to the bottom as soon as he tossed them. Brad came up from the house, his bulk causing the short boardwalk to groan and squeak. Tom turned to the noise with tears in his eyes.

"Sorry," Brad apologized, "I just wanted to see if you needed some company. I also want you to know all of us were talking in the house and we agreed that you're right, this is another mission, you know Creator versus Destroyer that we have been, I guess, assigned to. Joseph feels it, so does Jules and Jean. Because of that, we know in our minds, our hearts and soul, that Kate will be alright. Joseph heard Nelson speak to him on the plane ride out here while he slept and the message was 'Don't be afraid, you all are protected and will find the way.' Not a way, but the way. Jules is convinced that means Kate WILL recover and we will solve this just as we did the Berhetzel problem. This evening we need to go over everything until we get a better sense about it. Joseph found a large kids chalkboard to work from and we all have our iPads. But before that, I am going to get you back to the hospital at five thirty and then you should call us when you want to be picked up. We are not going to rest until we make some sense of this and Kate is better. Okay?"

"Thanks, Brad, that makes me feel a little better. You all are special friends. Kate loves you all!"

"We love you both. God will help to find the answer and fix Kate up."

"Thanks. I want to clean up now, I haven't had a shower in over two days."

"Then at least one of our prayers has been answered already!" Brad joked.

CHAPTER 42

Brad dropped Tom back at the hospital just before five- thirty and Tom got directions and a visitor's pass to the isolation ward. It was in the oldest part of the hospital and evidently rarely used. There was an inside corridor entrance to the room that had three lockers, a bench to sit on, scrub sink and stainless steel, glass front cabinets with supplies, blood tubes, minor surgery packs, and bottles of fluids.

A double doored pass-thru window could be used to deliver meals, medication or equipment without entering the main prep area. Inside the large room Tom could see Kate, still draped in the plastic tent. Dr Fox and a nurse stood at her bedside as Tom changed into a cap, mask, gown, gloves and shoe covers so he could enter the room. The door opened with a push of air behind him.

Fox was writing on a computer notepad and looked grim as Tom came bedside.

"How is she, Dr. Fox?" Tom asked.

"Not so good, Tom. With your permission, we need to place Kate in a drug-induced coma. She is starting to experience petite mal seizures and we don't want them to progress into a status condition. Her temp is now one hundred four but technically that might be good as that indicates her body is fighting the infection. We don't know what we are dealing with yet but we have ruled out bacterial agents and some of the easier to test viral encephalitis like Eastern Equine, West Nile and Legionnaire's, but I'm suspicious, sorry to lay this on you, that she may have been infected with what the CDC is calling Rabies X. The very stuff you have been trying to prevent with the new vaccine. We got a positive PCR saliva test for rabies but that is not specific for the X subtype. I sent the CSF, blood, urine and saliva to the Massachusetts Health Department by special courier and they are going work all night to complete the testing. I called the CDC to see if they had any new treatment and it appears they have been developing a hyperimmune equine serum from retired Cavalry horses at an Army base. Evidently those animals retire from work as part the equestrian drill teams and live out their remaining years on base. If she tests positive we can try it on her— might be her only chance. Only thing is, if we need it, we can only guess on treatment dosing. We could put her in acute renal or hepatic failure or cause anaphylaxis. The other bad thing is we probably only have forty-eight hours if she tests positive before. ..."

"Before she dies?" Tom asked.

"I'm afraid so. I asked the CDC to ship the serum immediately just in case the testing confirms my suspicions. They know Kate and love her too. They said to tell you this hyper immune serum was the late Dr. Ted Johnson's idea. He wanted to have it commercially available if the new vaccine being given now was not efficacious. Now it seems Kate might benefit from his foresight."

"You really suspect Rabies X? The only way she could have contracted it would be if she was intentionally infected. I guess that could be by any means because it is transmitted by bite, airborne short distances, and body secretions. But why would anyone kidnap only to infect her? It could have been done a lot easier without drawing attention to themselves. Now you have the FBI and State Police involved. It just doesn't make sense like everything else that has occurred in the last eight months. What in the hell is the end game?" Tom questioned angrily.

"You best not drive yourself nuts on that and concentrate on your wife. Just understand we are going work like hell to save her along with the full resources of the CDC. That serum will be here by six in the morning whether we use it or not. They have been collecting the blood, separating the cells from the serum and giving the cellular components back to the horses. The Army has stock piled only fifty-one hundred ml frozen units so far and that was specifically intended to be used only if the government's leadership were exposed. The President had to sign off on Kate getting it. If we confirm she has been infected and the serum cures her, because there is no human equivalent vaccine, the CDC will have to license it for commercial use through a major biologics company like Novartis or TriStar. Whoever lands that contact would make a boat load of money if the virus becomes a pandemic. The CDC also now suspects the current companion animal vaccine from TriStar is not providing the greatest protection with even the company indicating the efficacy in field may not be as good as predicted from the initial field trials. They are now calling for a third dose booster which probably will be hard to sell to the public," Fox explained.

"That's an ominous development!"

"And it's not public knowledge, so keep it within your group of colleagues," Fox warned.

"You can stay with her but you have to honor her pathogen barrier. Don't reach in, try to kiss her and the like. Don't forget you have a baby to think about," Fox reminded Tom.

"I think you should only stay ten minutes or so, then go to Jan's place and get some rest. Tomorrow will be a long and trying day and you will need your wits around you."

"Thanks, Dr. Fox. I appreciate your thoughtfulness and care you are giving Kate," Tom said nearly breaking down.

"No problem, we'll get her through this. I promise."

"You are taking a giant leap of faith saying that," Tom replied.

"My job mandates faith as a primary resource. Sometimes that is all we have."

CHAPTER 43

10 p.m. at the Robart's Cottage

Joseph had a good crackling fire going in the deck's open fire pit and the assembled group sat in a close circle of forest green Adirondack chairs. Brad, Jules and Jean were drinking a Bordeaux that they liberated from the house's wine rack and Tom and Joseph sipped on piping hot mugs of black tea. There was an awkward silence as the friends waited on Tom's report on Kate's condition.

Jules was the first to ask.

"Tom we are worried about both you and Kate. I understand this is difficult but would you share with us what's happening at the hospital. We can't bear the fact she's going through this."

"You all understand that she is insolation in grave condition. Dr. Fox feels she may have been exposed to Rabies X. If so, she only has hours to live. Damn near a zero prognosis. The Massachusetts Department of Health is rushing through some diagnostics that will answer that question of exposure. If she is infected we have one hope and that is a hyperimmune serum that Ted Johnson decided to investigate using. Only problem is they have no real idea on dosing, side effects or efficacy. We really won't have a choice." Tom dropped his head down and started to sob.

Joseph got up and stood behind him and placed his right hand reassuringly on Tom's left shoulder. Brad stood next and used his left hand on Tom's right shoulder and the two Frenchmen stood between the two blood brothers.

Joseph started to pray an ancient Lakota perennial prayer for strength and protection, the haunting chants springing from his lips, breaking the silence. The men watched as the fire pit suddenly flared, alive with red, yellow and blue plumes of color and intense heat as if the young Indian's words were a combustible fuel. Each man absorbed the heat of the fire fed by his passionate plea and closed their eyes and opened their hearts and minds. Joseph was channeling his great grandfather or perhaps generations of Lakota. As suddenly as the words started, they stopped. The only sound left was the crackling of the fire and the gentle lapping of an incoming tide against the shore rocks.

"Mon Dieu! Incroyable!" *My God! Incredible!* Jules exclaimed.

Not one hand lifted from Tom. They had become a unified, collective force.

Brad spoke next.

"Tom, all of us *know* Kate will be alright. Joseph here, my blood brother, has generations of Lakota affirming that. Jules, a man of great faith affirms that. Jean has dreamt of her being healthy and well and as far as me, my gut tells me the same thing. And we all know how accurate my gut is, never misses a meal and speaks to me often. Anyway, the bottom line is we all know it in our souls. She will recover."

"You all are the best friends anyone could want. I believe you all. She *is* under God's protection. I remembered what she told me about Psalm 91 and His promises of protection from all sorts of evil, including pestilence. Earlier this evening I found a Bible in her room and prayed that Psalm over her. Afterward I felt reassured that the Lord would care for her whether it be in this world or the next. But now, I'm convinced. Kate will be returned to us."

"D'accord," Jules said. "Now we need to discuss finding the bastards behind all of this. Here is my thinking on what's going on. First, the obvious purposely infected wolf with the Rabies X, and I would suspect the general wildlife population cases were also created to induce a wider panic. The broad attack on Paris, in my opinion, was really a decoy to cover the specific target of the attack —Le Pasteur. Then Ted, Director of CDC's Emerging Disease Unit, is murdered and now Kate, and gentlemen we have to admit, the real brains of our eclectic group, is kidnapped and probably intentionally infected with the same deadly virus. This can only mean that we must quickly find and eliminate whoever is responsible for these attacks because they are ramping up their plan."

Jean, who typically listened and only offered his input when he had something important to say, had an opinion.

"There are five primary things we need to focus on, which are the basic investigation principles I learned when I was an aspiring young journalist studying at Le Sorbonne. Qui, Quoi, Quand, Où et Pourquoi? *Who, What, When, Where and Why?* We already understand When, Where and What which leaves us with Who and Why. I suggest we postulate on the Why first. "Why would someone, some organization or government set loose a new deadly disease, kill an innocent man, Ted, and turn loose Hell on Paris, and then infect Kate with that same disease? Joseph, would you please man that chalkboard you found."

"Bien Sûr, Monsieur Du Bois," the young Lakota answered. *Of course, Mr. DuBois.*

"Très Bien, Très Bien Mon Ami!" Jean answered. *Very good, my friend.*

"Terrorism," Jules offered.

"Power or use as a weapon," Brad said.

"Profit," Joseph added to his list.

"Control, but that's just like Brad's," Tom added.

"Any others?" Jean asked.

"Peut-être se venger!" Jules almost shouted. *Perhaps revenge!*

"Like Berhetzel?" Brad asked.

"Why not? There are millions of Nazis around the world that would like nothing better than to dominate their targeted 'weaker races.' If we think Berhetzel was a freak or a fluke then we are fools. My father and his generation understood how evil breeds evil as did Joseph's grandfather, the Creator versus the Destroyer. Just when you think it's safe to take a walk in a park with your children or grandchildren, these evil-doers return with new ways to attack normalcy. Bastards!" Jean said.

"So we are looking for a group or government, possibly Neo-Nazis, that have developed a deadly bioweapon, released it to create terroristic chaos for revenge, power or profit. They have assassinated, kidnapped or murdered hundreds. That would surely cover both the Who and Why. Any other thoughts?" Jules asked.

"After my grandfather's wisdom was analyzed, we found the truth and that gave us the answers. I for one will ask my grandfather and ancestors for the truth. Then we will use that to find the answers to these questions."

"Sounds like a plan. We need to now think in terms of revenge, our revenge. I am fed up with this Destroyer business, I don't want or need this crap in my life or head. I can't believe how uncomplicated my life used to be. Now I feel like I'm on the outside looking in on an out of control plastic ant farm. The queen controls the colony and shouts *off with their heads!* Déja Moo all over again," Brad complained.

Tom's phone rang, shattering their concentration. He nervously fumbled with the phone as he pulled it up to his ear. He listened without saying a word.

"I will be there in twenty minutes." He put the phone back in his pocket.

"Kate tested positive for Rabies X at MDH. Dr. Fox wants me at the hospital ASAP. He said the Highway Patrol is now flying the serum from Logan in one of their helicopters and will be there soon. They have begun premedicating her with large amounts of Benadryl, so as soon as I get there they will administer the serum. I'll stay there until she recovers. I thought a lot about this and because this was Ted's project, his salvation, and the likely reason he gave his life. It will work, I am as sure of that as I am of my love for Kate."

Brad grabbed the Suburban keys. "Come on, Tom, I'll drive you my friend."

CHAPTER 44

Thomas Smithson Hospital

1 a.m.

Brad dropped Tom off at the emergency entrance and he was buzzed in to the emergency reception area then escorted by a waiting orderly up to the isolation ward. The room seemed darker, the lights dimmed. Kate who was out of her plastic isolation tent, was being ventilated on a closed circuit respirator. Four large fluid bags hung from poles, each with small piggyback bags. Each ran to different limbs. She was pale and gray and her extremities nearly cold to the touch.

There were four attendants in the room in full isolation gear along with Dr. Fox and one other physician that Tom didn't know stood off to the side talking, also fully protected. The orderly made sure Tom was suited up properly and then exited before Tom pushed through the air-lock into the room. He made a beeline to Dr. Fox, who looked tired and stressed.

"Tom, this is Dr. Rebecca Young from the CDC. She is an infectious disease specialist who flew up here with the serum. She will be supervising Kate's treatment. So far we have lightened her sedation so we can better assess her response and have given her two hundred milligrams of Diphenhydramine. Based on the Ebola outbreak of several years ago where serum from recovered patients was used to treat those infected, we are going to bolus one hundred milliliters and then put her on a constant rate infusion of the serum. The nurses are going to each monitor differ-ent aspects of the treatment and we brought in rapid blood analyzers to watch for renal or hepatic issues. So we are ready to go. If you don't mind we are going to say a prayer before we start," Milt Fox asked.

"Dear Lord," he started, "We humbly ask Your healing hand guide our efforts in treating your faithful servant Kate. Guide us and lead us to make her better. Give her husband strength and peace that she will recover by Your merciful healing hand. Amen."

The group which had circled Kate's bed, linked hand and hand, af-firmed that prayer in a loud 'Amen' and then took their assigned positions.

"First the bolus," Dr Young said, connecting a sixty ml. syringe to one of the IV ports while Dr. Fox did the same with a forty-two ml. dose on a different port.

"I want time called every thirty seconds; we will push six every thirty. I want BP, heart rate, and temperature every minute. Start the clock."

The room went quiet with only the respirator, IV pumps and blood pressure monitor as discordant background noise.

"Thirty seconds."

"Sixty seconds —BP one-o-five over fifty, seventy on the heart and temp forty Celsius."

"Ninety seconds."

"One hundred twenty —unchanged."

At the end of the five minute treatment, Kate's vitals were unchanged. No reaction had been observed.

"Ok, now we wait. Start the CRI pumps now," Dr. Young ordered.

"Tom," Fox suggested, "I want you to get yourself over to that lounge chair and get off your feet. It's going to be hours before we know anything.

"I'm going home for a few hours but Rebecca will be in the room supervising the treatment. Any questions?"

The Trojan Plague

"No, just my heartfelt thanks."

"Then you get yourself over to that chair and try to rest. Anything changes, one of the nurses will wake you. See you in the morning."

Tom dragged himself to the hospital chair and plopped down. A nurse took a warmed blanket and draped it over the exhausted veterinarian.

Tom fell into a deep, deep sleep.

CHAPTER 45

Robart's Cottage

"You must understand why you are here. The story has not changed only the characters. They seek to destroy us, not our people but all the peoples. They are of the same scion as the Destroyer Berhetzel and now you think of them as allies. Do not be confused, they are our enemy and are plotting Armageddon. Focus on the lessons I taught you and how the Tatanka greets his foes. He does not expose his flanks or rear. He keeps his enemies in front of him and attacks them. Do like the Tatanka and go on the offensive. If you turn away, you will be eaten. Remember all the lessons of your blood!"

Joseph was suddenly wide awake having clearly heard his great grandfather's warning. He stared up at the whirling ceiling fan mulling the message over in his head.

He restlessly flipped over on his side and looked to the east facing window at the slight glow of early sunrise. The lace curtains blew inward with the cool morning ocean breeze and Joseph could smell the incoming tide. He had briefly slept without a sheet or blanket wearing only his boxer shorts. Now he was hungry and wondered how Kate's treatment was going. He went into the ensuite bath and took a steaming hot shower. Then he dressed in denim top to bottom, ranch boots and a heavy brown leather belt with an oversized silver 'Lakota Nation' belt bucket. He tried to sneak down to the living areas silently but his boots clunked loudly on the old wide plank pine floor despite his effort to be silent.

"Damn Injun', you could never sneak up on Custer or anyone else with reasonable hearing," Brad complained, chuckling.

Joseph pushed open Brad's bedroom door and stuck his head in laughing softly.

"Sorry, it's the boots, man."

"I thought Injuns' wore moccasins. You know, chew the leather into a subtle QUIET softness. Then you can ambush any scalp with confidence," Brad teased.

"I would gladly pull some follicles from your shiny head except I would be violating the endangered species act!" Joseph shot back.

"Ha, ha," Brad replied sarcastically.

"I'm going downstairs to start the coffee and get the fireplace cranked up again. You coming?"

"I need a shower, then I'll be down."

Joseph walked the hall and down the narrow stairs. The house coffee pot was an automatic twelve cup machine with an Italian name. He loaded the coffee and water and pushed start and watched the trickle of black liquid start filling the glass pot. Joseph searched around for some cookies but only found stale potato chips, so he left to light a fire in the great room. Jean was seated on the big black leather recliner writing on a yellow legal pad. The fireplace was already lit and burning at a good clip. He smiled at Joseph and pushed himself up out of the chair.

"Bonjour, Joseph!" he greeted.

"Bonjour Monsieur DuBois."

"Please, Jean."

"Okay, Jean. Didn't you sleep last night?"

"Maybe, perhaps an hour or so. I just couldn't leave our group analysis go and ran the scenarios over and over in my head. I think I might have some possibilities that we can focus on."

"I didn't sleep too well either and had another vivid dream with my grandfather advising me about the very things we discussed last night.

There is no escaping his wisdom. Tell me what you came up with and then I'll give you what he told me," Joseph said.

Jean sat back in the chair facing the fireplace while Joseph brought two black coffees from the kitchen. He handed a mug to Jean and then laid two more split apple wood logs on the dying embers.

"My apologies my young friend, but this coffee is horrible — even much worse than our French brands. For a good cup you really need Italian coffee brewed by an Italian."

"Sorry, it was in the pantry and probably not the freshest. So what are your thoughts?"

"I kept thinking about what my father would do and how he would think it through. First he would put down his pen from the love letters he wrote daily to Bridgette Bardot," Jean mused, "then he would start a list and one by one remove the possibles that aren't probables and then organize the most possible, ranking them from one to say five. I did that last night and I think we have a direction to take this: Profit and Revenge through power. Who will gain the most economically and who becomes more powerful? And who has the resources to produce a new lethal virus, infect a country and then exert control over a population. I think I know, but it could be extremely difficult to prove. Once Kate recovers and I'm *sure* she will, we can go on the offense and stop these bastards."

"I think you're right. Grandfather told me to keep our enemies in front of ourselves, like the bison. Don't expose our flanks or rear. He also said they are of the same scion as Berhetzel — possibly he meant Nazis, so I think you are right on target, Jean. Who do you feel is responsible?"

"I would bet my father's hickory cane that Dwight Eisenhower presented to him, that they are German, also probable Neo Nazis. They have the brains, financial resources and always the desire for revenge. Everyone else I looked at like Islamic terrorists or say the North Koreans didn't have all three. Nazis are where we need to focus," Jean said passionately.

"Then that fits what Grandfather would have us do. But who is Brigette Bardot ?"

"She is an old lady now, beautiful and still sexy, but a very long time ago she was considered the sexiest woman in the world. My father received a signed photo from her wearing what today would be considered a very modest bikini, at a time when he was perhaps one of the most famous men in France, thanks to his tenacious hunting of war criminals. He never met her in person, only in his dreams," Jean explained.

"He dreamed of a beautiful woman. It seems everyone is haunted by something!"

The fire was now roaring.

CHAPTER 46

The Isolation Ward

Noon, the same day

By nine a.m., Kate's general vitals had recovered to near normal, so Dr. Fox had started to withdraw the coma inducing medications to better observe her neurologic status. She was now almost out of her coma and the treatment team surrounded her, observing her assent while Tom held a vigil, praying Psalm 91 over and over again. He was exhausted after getting only a couple hours of broken sleep but finally at least had hope.

The room was very calm, lights lowered, respirator disconnected, vitals monitors turned down. The forced silence was only interrupted by the shuffling bootie covered feet of staff as they pulled blood from Kate's IV ports and took it to the hematology machines. All signs now pointed to Dr. Ted Johnson's gamble to produce a serum as being a success. He might have given Kate back her life.

At one thirty nine, Kate woke up, stretching her right arm up before she opened her eyes. She suddenly was nearly coherent and pushed herself up to get out of the bed. The nurses gently restrained her movement and started asking questions.

"Dr. Vensky, do you understand what happened to you and where you are?" the older nursing supervisor asked.

"I'm, I'm. .." she hesitated, confused, looking around the room finding Tom's tear covered face. "Hi, honey, do you know where I'm at?"

"Sweetheart, you are in an isolation ward at Thomas Smithson Hospital in Gloucester, Massachusetts. Thanks to Almighty God and with Ted Johnson's foresight, you are the first person to recover from Rabies X. I don't know if you remember but you were kidnapped and drugged while you were out jogging on Crane's Beach, went missing for over two days and somehow infected with the Rabies X virus. You were very, very ill when they found you wandering in that park near the Italian restaurant in Ipswich and you were brought here where you were diagnosed by Dr. Milton Fox. There he is to your right."

"Welcome back, Kate. You gave all of us quite a scare!" The physician was smiling from ear to ear.

Tom continued.

"About twelve hours ago you were given an experimental treatment serum that Ted thought up and commissioned production. You are only here because of God's mercy and protection, Dr. Fox's expertise and Ted's foresight. You, my love, are a true miracle!"

"I don't remember any of that except some lines I think from Psalm 91 that ran over and over in my head," Kate confessed. "I think;

Whomever dwells in the shelter of the Most High will rest in the shadow of the Almighty.

I will say of the Lord, "He is my refuge and my fortress,

Surely he will save you from the fowler's snare and from the deadly pestilence.

He will cover you with his feathers, and under his wings you will find refuge; His faithfulness will be your shield and rampart."

Two black nurses shouted, "Hallelujah, Praise God!" over and over again and everyone was crying tears of joy understanding they had witnessed a true miracle.

Dr. Fox took her hand giving it a gentle, reassuring squeeze.

"We work our profession; the nursing staff, support staff and the rest of the physicians for moments exactly like this. You my dear have been cured by the Great Physician, we who surround you are only His mechanics, some of us are possibly guardian angels who administer His will. You were spared for a greater purpose, saved from the destruction of this horrible disease. You are under His wings of protection just like a mother hen protects her chicks from storms and predators. Take His gift and your gifts and find out who is doing this!"

The nurses now enthusiastically shouted, "Amen!" several times.

"We are going to leave you alone with Tom for now and then in an hour or so do some tests to confirm what we already know. I think you will stay on the serum another twenty-four hours and then we will 'spring' you. Thank you both for your faithfulness. This has been truly unforgettable!

"Now everyone, let's scrub out and give these two their privacy. Tom, as much as you want to, don't kiss her on the lips till we receive the ok from MDH," Fox instructed.

Tom couldn't stop smiling from ear to ear, he was beaming, almost as much as the moment Bobbie was born. Kate seemed normal in all ways with her color returning and her eyes alive again.

"Tell me again exactly what happened because I don't remember anything beyond seeing a man giving CPR on the beach. After that I can't remember a thing. Total blank. But you know, I feel great for someone who's basically been sedated for what?— nearly four days. I guess we will be getting back to work reviewing the rabies epidemic and now since it's personal, won't rest until we figure it out and stop who's responsible.

"Psalm 91? Who prayed it?" Kate asked.

"I did for hours. Over and over again. It's etched in my mind and I'm going to pray it every day. A lot of people were praying for you! Crap, I need to call Brad, your mom and my parents. I better do that now, so why don't you try to rest while I phone ? These are calls I'm going to be thrilled to make!" Tom smiled.

"Wait a minute, Buddy, you better order me a meal before you do that. I am starved."

"I'll be happy to take your order my lady. What can I get you?"

"I would like a McDonald's Big Mac, super-sized fries and a large chocolate shake, God help me!"

"Wow, a healthy start to a full recovery. Anything else, like a six pack?"

"Yes, only that you never leave me, except now. I'm starved. Please feed me and make it snappy, Buddy!"

CHAPTER 47

Next Day, early morning

TriStar Biologics. Leipzig, Germany

Schmitt has just finished his analysis on the brain and nerve tissues he had harvested in Massachusetts at the necropsies where he had assisted Dr. Robarts.

His two trusted TriStar associates just had finished their work on the vaccines he had brought back for analysis. Vogel was about to call Mendoza so Schmitt could report his finding. It was two a.m.

Vogel dialed in the encryption codes and waited for Mendoza to answer. Every time they communicated the encryption software delayed, reset, delayed, and finally patched a safe line for the men to communicate on. The software was proprietary, something Mendoza had had developed to protect his identity and location. His real plans were a complete secret, something only he knew. Vogel and Schmitt were pawns, simple tools to get from point A to point B. Tools that were going to be disposed of when the time was right. Sacrificial lambs or better yet sacrificial goats that would be vaporized when he deemed it advantageous. They believed he was now secreted somewhere deep in the jungles of South American. The reality was he was only two hundred kilometers away in one of his father's hidden Führerbunkers that was such a complete secret that it had not been discovered for over eighty-five years. A secret passed by his father and protected by successive single male heirs of now three generations of the Hermann Goering family. Only Mendoza and the oldest great grandson of Goering currently knew the location and the complex combination of steps needed to enter without triggering the bunker's self-destruct mechanism. For Goering's loyalty and dedication, a handsome stipend was paid each year in gold looted long ago from the death camps. Buried deep in the side of a mountain, naturally camouflaged and nearly inaccessible, the bunker ran lateral and parallel to a natural cavern that was visited routinely by Spelunkers, so activity around the area was very common. Mendoza's access to the bunker was from an eight meter wide, one hundred twenty meter deep perpendicular shaft that joined the bunker's natural cavern. Five hundred meters of solid rock separated the bunker from similar sister caverns. A pure spring provided all the water necessary and gravity carried waste to an exterior small septic leech bed. A single cable of electricity had been fed in long ago and was tapped in secretly from a nearby transmission line. Never used, only maintained, the bunker's secret had been well kept. An office exactly like his father's South American outpost had been arranged from furnishings placed there in 1942. It was now essentially used as a stage for deceiving Vogel and Schmitt into thinking he was thousands of kilometers away, not right in their backyard, a deception that should protect him from anyone who would destroy him or if a weakling gave up information. He reviewed the bunker, making mental notes on things he would do to make it his safe hiding place if it became necessary.

Encryption complete, the screen in Vogel's office lit up. Mendoza was seated as usual at a large desk with a drink glass but no cigar which was customary. Vogel greeted his leader and benefactor.

"Guten Tag mein Anführer!" *Good afternoon, my leader!*

"Yes," Mendoza replied in German, "it is."

"We have some answers for you, sir. I will let Schmitt explain." Schmitt moved from the sideline to a large whiteboard.

"Good afternoon, sir! I have summarized our findings here for you. It appears our viron is very temperature sensitive, so while we store the vials appropriately, once it is shipped using CDC required protocols, it only has approximately 24 -30 hours of stability en route. Some orders don't even get to the clinics for three days because there are no standardized business hours at these veterinary offices. The next problem is the handling once received. Lackadaisical or carelessness might be the best description. The temperature in the refrigerators where they stored the vials also varied wildly, from 2.55-5.55 degrees Celsius and we required exact storage at 1.66-2.15. On top of that, vaccines are often premixed and left out where they warm even more. It seems our creation is very heat intolerant or temperature sensitive."

"Or intolerant of the human factor?" Mendoza lamented.

"It appears so. All that work for nothing. Here is the good news. The individuals that were necropsied from Cape Ann showed a replicating viron population. So we can succeed if we control the process and distribute our product ourselves from controlled US offices and deliver the rationed quantities ourselves. Labor intensive but necessary I feel to establish our plague. I estimate with our concentrating on major metropolitan areas, and I would suggest every state capital east of the Mississippi and every city over three hundred thousand and we would establish the plague quickly. I ran the numbers and we would need twenty million doses ready to distribute and four warehousing centers with one hundred eighty delivery vans to deliver eighteen hours a day, some clinics receiving two deliveries a day. All orders would be filled to the exact appointment scheduling, no more or less."

"How many employees?" Mendoza asked.

"I estimate we will need to transfer three hundred TriStar employees to lead the warehouse centers and drive the majority of the routines but possibly an equal number of subcontractors driving vans," Vogel replied.

"I don't like it. The CDC might shut us out if they think our product is that unstable. They picked TriStar, the largest manufacturer of animal biologics in the world for our expertise. We had already stockpiled millions of doses, unknown to them, and our studies indicated to them near one hundred percent efficacy after our infective booster dose. Now we are going to change our conclusion and inform them our vaccine is fragile and unstable. They will do their own testing and prove the vaccine is protective and temperature stabile. There is a real chance during that process they may discover the viron contaminant. No, we can't come in and suggest the product is shit because they will pull it off the market immediately. Americans, if nothing else, knee jerk react to news like this to protect public safety. In an instant, TriStar has no credibility and therefore no market. You need to find another solution.

"Explain to me how the viron is incorporated into the vaccine," Mendoza commanded.

"We produced a modified live vaccine that contains a two-vial mix to hydrate the freeze-dried cake containing the attenuated Rabies in one vial and a second with the sterile water diluent. In our booster vaccine, the water diluent is contaminated with the viron and when mixed with the cake, becomes our weapon."

"Would the viron be more stable incorporated into the dried cake ?" the Nazi asked.

"We never tested that because we felt adding it to the diluent was more efficient. We can test that but we would need to retrofit the manu-facturing process," Vogel answered.

"Do it! Start now! I want an answer on this in forty-eight hours. We will meet again then."

The screen went black.

"How in the world?" Schmitt questioned.

"That doesn't matter. Get on it now. We have two days to mix, test viability and infect some primates. God help us if we fail!"

"God help them if we succeed!" Schmitt grumbled under his breath.

CHAPTER 48

Thomas Smithson Hospital

The next morning

Kate had been moved out of isolation into a private room on the same hospital floor, a kind of step down room, when the preliminary test results from MDH were returned negative for active infection. An antibody titer had been submitted to the CDC for Electrophoresis to confirm those results. Milt Fox arranged for Tom to invite Brad, Jules, Jean and Joseph to wait just outside her room until the final test results were transmitted. At nine thirty, Fox's phone rang with a ring tone of Curly Howard, one of the Three Stooges; 'Go ahead, Doc, take a chance, whatta you got to loose.' He pulled up the phone and answered.

"Milt Fox, yes, results for Dr. Kate Vensky. You are sure? Thanks, all of us appreciate your diligence."

"Tom, call your friends in so we can share in the news," Fox requested. The four friends poured into the room, grinning in anticipation of good news. Kate was beaming and looking very healthy. Tom was nervously waiting for the report from CDC.

"Ok, here's the results," Fox teased. "Not what we hoped for."

"What? She's not cured?" Brad gasped.

"No, she's more than cured. CDC said they have never seen such high antibody numbers. Some were equine but most were Kate's own response. They called it a bona fide miracle. So, gentlemen, you may kiss the bride."

One by one, they kissed a crying with joy Kate. Jules, then Jean, Joseph and finally Brad placed loving smacks on Kate's lips, forehead and cheek. She looked to Tom.

"Your turn, Buddy!" she ordered.

"After all those guys? I could catch something Dr. Fox might have to diagnose." He laughed as he embraced her, kissing her passionately. They both were crying joyfully.

"This was a true miracle," Fox said. "Not my first but certainly my most interesting. If you don't mind I want to read you a rather long email I received from the Army Colonel who was in charge of the horses which were used to produce the serum that neutralized the Rabies X virus. He was informed by the CDC that they were involved in a life or death efficacy trial of his serum. He also is a veterinarian.

"He wrote:

Dear Dr. Fox,

My name is Colonel Martin H. Milne and I am in charge of the 1st Cavalry Division at Fort Hood, Texas. I have twenty-eight years of service in the Veterinary Corps, twenty-five preserving the legacy and the proud history of the horse mounted solider. All military horses whether active duty or retired will eventually live out their end years at Fort Hood.

I was good friends with Ted Johnson since we met at a CDC conference fifteen years ago and shared a love of offshore fishing. Twice a year we got together with two buddies and fished around the world; Alaska, Florida Keys, Australia, Hawaii, Costa Rica to name a few. Even when the fishing was mediocre, the beer was cold and the comradeship priceless. We always had fun!

Ted had the idea to hyper immunize our retired equines to develop a potential treatment for the new rabies strain. I

saw no problem or risk to the horses so we immunized ten horses with the primary dose TriStar vaccine weekly for ten weeks. We then collected and proceeded to separate serum from blood cells and send the bulk serum to the CDC for refining, and freezing into dosing units. We never really expected to use it in a treatment so soon and those initial vials were intended to be used only for the national leadership if a crisis developed. I am so glad they allowed it to be used for Dr. Vensky.

Our horses have been part of our nation's military since the country's founding. They have served, been wounded and killed in the line of duty, just like our human veterans.

I thought you might like to know some of the names and lineage of the ten veteran horses that donated their serum.

Pershing— 27 year old stud horse, descendant of General Pershing's horse Kidron.

Winchester— 31 year old stud horse, descendent of Union General Sheridan's Civil War Mount.

Black Jack — 29 year old gelded horse, descendent of Pershing's Kidron.

Neopolitano— 27 year old stud horse, Lipizzaner, descendent of George Patton's horse from stock saved from Nazi Destruction in World War II.

Traveler— 33 year old gelded 'Gaited' horse, descended from Robert E. Lee's famous mount.

Washington—39 year old gelded horse, descendent of George Washington's horse Blueskin.

Cincinnati— 26 year old stud, direct descendent of General Grant's horse of same name (and a headstrong SOB just like Grant was).

Ginny — 30 year old mare, descendent of J.E.B Stuart's horse Virginia. (interesting note: ninety-five percent of war horses for officers were intact males, ninety percent of enlisted soldiers rode geldings. Only a few mares were used in combat because they disrupted order when they cycled. The Confederacy as a rule held superior horse-men, so as resources depleted, their Cavalry held prob-ably more mares because till that desperate end time their value was in producing the next generation of fighting horses — a nearly three-year process.)

The last two are very interesting because on our last trip together in February, Ted explained in great detail the hunt to find the Nazi Berhetzel that Dr. Vensky (who I think he had a crush on), her husband Tom, the two Frenchmen whose names escape me, 'Big Brad' as he described Dr Upton, and the young Lakota Joseph Blackfeather were involved in. He told me about Joseph being a descendent of the Sioux who crushed that idiot Custer at the Little Bighorn. Here is a strange connection to that.

We have two horses that are descendants of that battle. Comanche— 30 year old descendant, stud, from the only military survivor of the Seventh Calvary at the Little

*Bighorn—soldier or horse. That meant the horse that sur-
vived was an officer's horse and an intact male.*

*White Buffalo — 26 year old mare, Indian 'Nokata' horse,
descendent of Sitting Bull's horse Shadow Fear. Very
strange events, I would say cosmic events, have led us
to Dr. Vensky's cure. I thank God for His loving mercy and
for Ted's inspiration. I hope someday to meet all of you,
have you visit Fort Hood to see these magnificent animals
and maybe if you have the time, fish the Gulf.*

Respectfully, all the best,

Marty

Fox closed his iPad and removed his half readers and pushed them
into his white lab coat's vest pocket. He surveyed the group.

"You all look stunned. I suppose it has to be the connection to your
last adventure, Ted's chance meeting of Colonel Milne and those horses
that have a blood connection to Joseph's tribal history. Just so you
know, I gave up drinking in college so I would always have clear thought
processes. Today if I drank, I would propose a toast to Ted, Marty, those
wonderful horses and to the forces of good which you folks must be
connected to. Now I need to get some rest.

It is the weekend you know," he added with a smile. "By the way,
Kate, you can pack your bags!"

There came a gush of gratitude.

"I can never thank you enough," Tom said as he gave Fox a man hug.

"Merci Beaucoup, Docteur," said Jean as he shook his hand.

"I hope you can visit my wife and I in Paris once things get back to
normal. My gift, all expenses paid," Jules offered.

"Thanks, Doc, you were amazing," Brad said nearly shaking the man's
arm off.

Joseph simply shook the physician's hand with Lakota sincerity. That message was clear— I will never forget.

The men waited in the reception area while Tom checked Kate out of the hospital.

There was no bill. The CDC had paid all the expenses.

Kate and Tom met their four friends and walked to the Suburban under bright sunshine and a cloudless blue sky.

As they drove back to the cottage , Jules set the tone.

"Jean wants us to meet after *déjeuner,* lunch, to discuss what he and Joseph worked on to get to the bottom of all this *destruction.* First, we eat and drink then we make a plan. After lunch we set course to find these bastards."

Brad groaned, "And here we go again!"

CHAPTER 49

TriStar Biologics

Same day

Schmitt was a genius, a bioengineer that when given enough time, could come up with anything. The solution he was trying to accomplish was to marry his lethal viron into the dry cake fraction of the rabies vaccine. The key could still be temperature stability and so far in the last eighteen hours they had run four trials four times. In each test of the viron, one was mixed and held at optimum temperature, one test held at room temperature, one was heated to canine body temperature and a duplicate set of the current product subjected to the same test except the viron was in the diluent. The old product versus the new. But he could not replicate the results from Massachusetts or improve on efficacy. Whether the viron was incorporated into the diluent or in the dry cake, there was no observable advantage one versus the other. In desperation he mixed the viron diluent with a placebo desiccated cake. The viron was stable in all the tests even when he raised the temperature to almost forty-nine degrees Celsius and held it at that temperature for two hours. That temperature was just below Pasteurization temperature, so he raised it to seventy-two degrees Celsius for fifteen seconds, the Pasteurization protocol, and the viron was unchanged. The problem wasn't temperature related, it was something to do with the mixing of the agent with the Rabies X. All they would have to do was to fake the cake to give the same appearance of the rabies vaccine when rehydrated with the diluent. They could ship pure viron that would appear to be the actual rabies product. By the time the CDC figured it out, millions in major metropolitan centers would be infected from their pets. Untold numbers of zombie-like citizens would be unleashing chaos at every level. Now he was sure, this would destroy America. He asked Vogel to contact Mendoza and tell him he was in production and could ship in one week. He would flood the country with two million doses, fulfilling all their back orders He was now prepared to unleash a very special hell on the United States of America.

CHAPTER 50

The Robarts Cottage

Just after lunch

They sat outside on the deck, cool, but in the brilliant sunshine. Joseph started a warming fire and they circled the fire pit. Jean and Joseph stood to offer up their theory.

"So," Joseph started, "Jean and I have had dreams and visions on what the heck is going on and he and I went over what we discussed as a group two nights ago. Since Kate is now with us, we would like to offer our thoughts. Please bear with us."

Jean seemed nervous but resolute as he spoke.

"It is possible my thoughts on this are tainted from being the son of a nearly lifelong Nazi War Criminal hunter, murdered by the Nazi Berhetzel and then being nearly killed twice by the bastard. Stop me if you think I am off the track.

"Profit and revenge through power are strong motivating factors. Who has the financial resources, the intellect and the need for revenge? Perhaps Neo-Nazis? We just need to determine who has the most to gain from profit." Jean looked to Jules who wanted in on the conversation.

"Profit places Euros in the hands of terrorists who can use those funds to assemble armies and buy weapons. I can only think of one company who is profiting in a big way from the current crisis and that would be

TriStar Biologics. They control a majority of animal vaccine production worldwide and have strong multinational ties even though they are head-quartered in Leipzig, Germany. I think they are likely generating hundreds of millions of euros of profit. They also have the scientific brainpower to create a superbug. I met Hans Vogel at the CDC and I guess he seemed normal enough but it is possible he is out of the loop. It is a large enough company that a subgroup could be operating out of their production facilities and he might be oblivious to it," Jules postulated.

"That makes no sense. Create and unleash a plague and then pro-vide a cure? That fits the profit motive but not revenge. The vaccine will save lives, if a motive is revenge, why not let the disease run its course?" Brad asked.

"And also why release me after infecting me? If I die, that could drive vaccine sales which then shortcuts the disease," Kate asked.

She continued.

"The only recent German I've had any contact with is the German Government pathologist Helwig that Tom and I met in that Ipswich Italian restaurant. But he did have that CDC letter from Ted dated the Monday after he was murdered. That never has set well with me."

"Then we need to check him out more thoroughly. I wonder if Dr. Robarts might have anything he used with his fingerprints on it?" Jean replied.

"I'll call Jan and ask. There must be something he touched without gloves on, but it is a medical facility so they probably have disinfected and wiped down everything. Once we finish, I will call her," Kate affirmed.

Kate asked, "Tom, honey, what do you think?"

"What do I think? I think I am exhausted, feeling guilty for being away from Bobbi, Jed and the practice so long but elated that I have such a great group of friends. So what do I think?" he repeated, hesitating. "I would concentrate on the evil which describes Nazis, old style or Neo to a T. Joseph, your grandfather is warning you again about a Destroyer and Jean, your father sends you messages also. That's good enough for me. I say check out the man who was helping Dr. Robarts and based on that result direct our efforts at TriStar and wherever else it leads us. My instincts say we better do something quickly. One Berhetzel in a lifetime is enough. We have a child for God's sake, and granted we need to do something to protect his future against evil, but I also can't risk him growing up an orphan. That's what I think."

There was an awkward silence as Tom's words sunk in.

Kate looked to Jules who was having a quiet side talk with Jean. He smiled at her and spoke.

"Mes Amies, we are all tired. I think tomorrow I will visit Dr. Robarts if Kate will open that door for me. Jean will research TriStar through our resources in Paris and run some background on TriStar ownership and executives. Brad and Joseph, if you don't mind, I need more information on that shooter of Ted Johnson, and anything else to see if we can tie him to TriStar or the CDC. See if the FBI has finished interviewing the son, Sargent Rimer. If they have, get what they have discovered and maybe visit the son in Atlanta. Kate and Tom, go home. Rest up and we will conference Monday. Jean and I will stay in the country till after we talk. Hopefully by then we will have relevant information."

But time was running out. Mendoza had just approved Schmitt's new plan.

CHAPTER 51

Next Day

TriStar Veterinary Biologics

Vogel didn't often visit Research and Development Bio-Secure Lab X at the ultra-modern facility but Schmitt had requested he come down to see the results of new viron laden Trojan horse 'vaccine' on the primate community that he had infected. TriStar usually kept four species of simians, the world's largest private research colony of monkeys and primates, and that allowed rapid test challenges to be repeated and adjusted before they exhausted their test subject populations. This was a hidden, triple security area, protected and open to only four high level researchers and Vogel. To gain entry you had to receive a small mechanical finger stick to prove your identity by rapid DNA analysis. After that initial test, there were two additional corridors, air-locks, that required biohazard protective clothing and the use of numeric security codes that changed daily. The actual lab was totally mechanized so that food, water and sanitary service were automated and mechanically computerized. Each of the larger primate test subjects was implanted with a miniaturized syringe pump that could be activated remotely to drip small amounts of a tranquilizer 'cocktail' into the animal's bloodstream to facilitate safe handling. It was a twenty-five million Euro best kept secret laboratory in the world.

The initial viron testing had been run four times and then repeated when contaminated into the rabies vaccine. Those preliminary test runs had left eighty-four animals dead after suffering various levels of animal 'insanity'. The worse affected mature chimps ripped through steel partitions that divided animals to get to a nearby animals, using the steel rods as weapons to mutilate their victims before turning the chards of metal on themselves. Every second the closed circuit cameras recorded, and the carnage was documented. Now based on the previous testing, Vogel and Schmitt wanted to be eyewitnesses to the expected rage that was imminent.

Dressed in self-contained Level 2 protective biohazard, air -conditioned protective suits, supplemented with sealed oxygen delivery, they were protected totally from the viron's deadly action. One other senior technician, Ian Yeager, was present in the room in case an accident occurred which might threaten Vogel or Schmitt. He was armed with a .45 caliber Smith and Wesson revolver and a lethal solution-tipped titanium syringe push pole, one of six he had loaded and ready to go in case of an immediate crisis. Yeager had reported that morning that several small capuchin monkeys were exhibiting symptoms of agitation, aggressively charging the cage barriers and challenging cage mates. The chimps were expected next to become symptomatic as was the pattern from the initial trials. Titanium cage bars now replaced the steel that had previously guarded the housing units from the adrenaline fueled rage when the aggression caused the chimp's brain neurons to start firing in unison. In the end, there would be nothing living to escape from the chimp enclosure.

"Yeager, we need to observe the chimps the closest, because three of the five have received the anti viron medications, so turn on the cameras so we can see the interaction between the infected and protected. Give them something to eat to see what their response is," Schmitt ordered.

The large flat screen monitors lit up showing four adolescent chimpanzees huddled together in one corner and an adult male separated and perched on an raised platform. One arm partially covered the chimp's face with one amber brown eye, staring directly into the camera's flashing green LED light. The adult's arm was involuntarily twitching and the chimp's pupil suddenly dilated fully and his body went rigid. The fifty kilogram ape screamed out with guttural rage and pain.

Aghgrrrrr! Aghgrrrr!

The roar exploded into the lab. The observers felt the tingle as the hair on the nape of their necks rose up.

"Here we go!" Schmitt excitingly announced to Vogel, taking a step closer to the monitor focused on the younger chimps.

"How fast?" Vogel asked.

"Not long, now watch the juveniles' response to him."

The four younger chimps had pushed back to the enclosure's farthest corner, plastered together in an amorphous tangle of arms and legs. Not one head was visible. There was an obvious quavering of fear from the group as the large male attacked the bars of the cage. Suddenly he turned to the terrified group and in two powerful leaps he was upon them, ripping the huddled group apart. With one in each arm, screaming in fear, he dragged the sub adults to the front of the cage and swung each repeatedly into the bars reducing them to bloody hair-covered piles which he then ripped limbs from. The one juvenile remaining that had been infected, now manifested the viron's effects and raged out to attack the larger chimp. He was no match as the adult quickly subdued his aggression, pounding him into the bars so hard the juvenile broke into pieces like he had been pushed through a meat slicer. He then tore into the terrified surviving chimp.

"I've seen enough. Yeager, activate the biopump to max to euthanize the beast," Vogel ordered.

"Sorry. sir, he was not implanted yet. Just came in three days ago. He was a wild capture as the other four were and he came in through the back door so to speak.

"I'll get him with the pole syringe."

The tech grabbed the long pole, looping the wrist strap to one arm to help control his quick stab and jab technique that he had performed hundreds of times. The chimp instinctively withdrew from the cage front as the man approached. Yeager waited for the exact moment the primate would certainly charge the bars. The males always did. The secret was to dodge the extremely long powerful arms that were one and a half times the height of the animal's body. Misjudge and you could be dead in seconds, pulled onto the bars. The problem here was this animal's behavior was disease-driven, unpredictable, but seventeen years of experience made Yeager confident.

The chimp predictably started his charge and Yeager made his feint and dodge to thrust the pole. The problem was he had never used the pole fully garbed. Almost always euthanasia was performed by a dump of the syringe pump but this time when he extended his arm, the biohazard suit limited his reach. The chimp grabbed the pole pulling the technician to the bars breaking his wrist and releasing the pole. Then like a ninja, he whirled the pole and thrust it through the protective suit into Yeager's abdomen. Yeager fell backwards, the pole spinning away. He pulled the .45 sidearm and at near point blank range unloaded the revolver into the chimp just before succumbing to the drug.

Vogel and Schmitt were stunned at what they had just witnessed. "I'm convinced," Vogel announced. "Go ahead and release the reserve doses held from shipment. I'll inform Mendoza. I suspect within seven to ten days we will truly see the beginning of the end of the United States. No more deception by hiding the antigen in a tainted base vaccine."

"And think what we are about to unleash. This," Schmitt said gesturing to the carnage in front of him, "multiplied by millions. Möge Gott den amen Bastarden gnädig sein!"

May God have mercy on the poor bastards!

CHAPTER 52

Medical Examiner's Office

Gloucester, Massachusetts

Jules rested on an old heavy oak church pew like bench which likely had sat in the same place on the polished stone floor for decades. It seemed to him coroner's offices were always in cold, poorly lit basements, secreted away from the public view, hiding their often dark secrets. Robarts was already running forty minutes late for their appointment but she had called to apologize before starting an emergency cesarean section.

He got up and stretched, eyeing the coffee vending machine that occupied the opposite wall. He needed some caffeine but was leery of what he would receive from the beat up machine for his dollar. He decided to chance poisoning since he was at the ME's office and reluctantly let his dollar be sucked into the machine that immediately spit it out. And again. On the third try the dollar was digested and a styrofoam cup plopped down receiving the steaming hot liquid. Water? No coffee darkening the clear liquid.

Et Voila! He thought shaking his head.

"Bonjour, Doctor LeClerc, je suis Jan Robarts. Comment ça va?" "Ça va bien, except for this monster eating my dollar," he said reaching gently for her extended hand, "Enchanté, Docteur."

Robarts accepted his hand and felt strangely attracted to the suave Frenchman. A common female response to an uncommon man.

"I wish I could have gotten here a little earlier but that baby wouldn't wait. Then I could have saved you the dollar because that machine hasn't worked since I've been here. I do have a Keürig in my office so all is not lost." She slipped her key into the old brass deadbolt which engaged with a solid click.

"Sorry for the mess but with all those strange deaths, I've fallen seriously behind in my paperwork. This is normally a part-time position, or at least is paid that way and in the last three weeks, I've had more non-natural cause cases than the previous coroner had in the last six years. All this on the temporary table are our triplicate formalin fixed tissue samples from those cases."

Jules looked at the trays of large and small formalin jars of brain, heart, liver and other organ tissues with fluorescent orange and green labels in small clear Ziplock biohazard bags.

"Mon Dieu!" he exclaimed. "That looks overwhelming"

"If I was only doing this, not keeping a more than full-time OBGYN practice running, not raising a young family, that table would be clear. This is a somewhat honorary position," she said as she laughed sarcastically.

"Then I won't take much of your time. Did you think of anything that possibly would have Dr. Helwig's DNA or fingerprints on it?" he asked.

"We sat in here on a coffee break and he used that blue mug with the French Bulldog on it. It hasn't been washed or handled since. so it's pretty gross."

"Très Bien, DNA and fingerprints. That was much easier and faster than I thought I would get. We need to see if this German was who he said he was."

"I wouldn't know. He seemed legit to me and was very competent at the necropsies. You know he took a bunch of tissue samples with him."

Jules's ears perked. "What tissue types did he harvest ?"

"Only neuro, brain, spinal column and peripheral nerve. I thought that was a little strange," she said.

"Did he give you any reason for that?" he asked.

"Just that forensic neuropathology was his area of expertise, a personal interest, so that when a potential novel neurological disease manifested, it was something he took great interest in. The new rabies strain outbreak in the US has the German government concerned, so he said he was here to gather information to better understand the mechanics of the epidemiology and pathology surrounding it. It all seemed reasonable to me."

Jules wasn't so sure.

"I don't trust anything on the surface anymore. It seems there is always a new evil or evil person manifesting their designs on the innocents. I don't want to sound racist or prejudiced, but I have a real problem with Germans, particularly those who call themselves Nazis. Many would like history to repeat itself which means millions could die. Genocide without conscience."

"I must really be out of touch because I thought all that disappeared at the end of the Second World War. To think it still exists frightens me," Robarts offered.

"You have no idea," he replied. "If this man is not who he said he was, then perhaps Pandora's box has been opened once more and we all may be in grave danger!"

The two talked about Kate's miracle for a few minutes then Jules carefully placed the coffee mug into a small plastic biohazard bag. Helwig was a man who was likely back in Europe, so this evidence investigation would continue in Paris. All his trusted government resources were there. They would find his answer.

CHAPTER 53

Mendoza's Fürherbunker

Same day

Mendoza was restless. Too many complications now potentially existed since that woman had survived their rabies virus. Survival? Not likely, most likely a treatment had been developed. Vogel's perfect plan seemed to be falling apart as they waited, and waited and waited for an explosion of viron infected Americans. Impatience was the worst trait he had inherited from his infamous father. Not the best gene to manifest, because his father had counseled him over and over again that impatience and poor counseling by his generals led to errors, which first cost them battles, then countries and eventually the war and Reich. Now his General, Vogel, was exhibiting similar poor judgement in that each time he made an error, he left the door wide open for their premature discovery. But Mendoza was in hiding, right under their noses, protected from discovery but planning on tidying up those TriStar loose ends after the viron finally manifested its full potential on the United States. He ordered the new viron laden doses be divided specifically to hit Baltimore, New York, Boston, Washington, Atlanta, Miami, St Louis, Los Angeles and San Francisco. Each dose had an unlimited multiplier effect depending on the number of people living in the family. Each person exposed then might infect a couple dozen others through cough, colds, kissing or any other fluid exchange during the immediate forty-eight to seventy-two hours post exposure. Urinals and public toilets would become reservoirs of infection and fast food restaurants would be serving last meals. The viron, Schmitt estimated, was ten thousand times more contagious than the most virulent influenza with a prepatent period of only forty-eight hours. So if you were unfortunate enough to be exposed, you would become clinical in less than two days. Dead in another two or three days, unless you had access to the cure and preventive and he alone directly controlled supplies of his antiviron drug, VironX. In the development of the pathogen, Schmitt who was likely the premier bioengineering scientist in the world, chose the virus fraction to be specifically interfered with by an antiviral agent he had accidentally discovered when running therapy trials on chimpanzees. This drug was unknown to the scientific community and would become Mendoza's golden ticket to control the terms of surrender of the United States of America. He would make sure the arrogant country was on her knees begging for the relief only VironX, which would have the public name SaveR, would provide within hours of administration in a single loading dose and monthly maintenance. Mendoza had stockpiled nine hundred million doses deep in the cavernous mountains of Bariloche, Argentina. Simple to manufacture, the real beauty of the drug was that the tiny fifty grain sublingual dissolving tablet was smaller than an aspirin, so moving the product would be easy to accomplish. The medication was the magic bullet that people would need to restore their souls, souls that would be indebted to him in fair exchange for their lives and disposable income. The citizens would become his drones, living and laboring primarily to purchase SaveR to stave off the effects of the viron. He initially would remain hidden as their government fell and then activate his designated 'administrators' to disarm the nation prior to releasing the cure. The treatment would be required to be taken monthly and distributed based on his determination on who would be a valuable enough asset that once the major metropolitan centers collapsed or were depopulated, he would repopulate them with loyal party members. The biggest issue would involve the speed in which the collapse would occur and the millions of corpses that would need to be disposed of in a very short time. He planned on filling sports stadiums with the bodies of the dead. When they filled, he would use military style accelerants to cremate the remains, turning the sports -entertainment centers into giant ash trays. His control outside those major population centers would occur militarily and economically by nationalizing banks, food supplies and medical facilities. The United States was a house of cards waiting to fall in a massive social media panic with real time scenes of walking dead neighbors and families coating streets in blood and brains. Only when unaffected people turned in all their weapons, passed a compliance inspection and signed a loyalty oath, would they receive the medication to treat or prevent their infection. That was the catch. No cooperation, no meds. He smiled to himself at the possibilities and looked forward his public burning of the Constitution and the Nazi Swastika flying over the capital and White House, his future residence.

CHAPTER 54

Paris

Two days after returning to Paris

Jules' driver pulled up to the DuBois home, a place that held countless fond memories of time spent with Jean and his family. Time spent as children playing in the streets and alleys, as young adults in Université dating, keeping limitless hours; as professionals building careers, families and fortunes, and in the last years, the trauma of facing off against the evil that cost Jean's father, Robert, his life. The battle to remove that evil, Berhetzel, had been an exhausting adventure that had led them across three continents with their commission to stop the 'Destroyer,' which the centurion Sioux Shaman Nelson Blackfeather had given Kate, Tom, Brad and Joseph just hours before his death. Now they again were locked in on a quest to find this new source of evil.

The DuBois home had thick, oversized, double, dark oak doors with a pair of old tarnished brass lions' head door knockers. Jules gave a solid rap to the door. Jean soon appeared wearing a herringbone sports jacket over a vest with a tan turtleneck cashmere sweater shirt. He looked like the extra day's rest since returning from the United States had done him good.

"Mom Ami, you look like you are going on a date. Very dapper!" Jules exclaimed, teasing his best friend.

PIERCE ROBERTS

"Our friends at DGSI will think I am being accompanied by a movie star."

The DGSI was the French equivalent of the United States Homeland Security Department, located in a northwest suburb of Paris, Levallois-Perret. Jules was a long-time friend with Bernard Redare, the head of the massive French bureaucracy. Jules knew his friend would keep their inquiries confidential, putting loyalty to friends ahead of government regulation. He had personally processed the blue coffee mug that Jules had brought back from Massachusetts. They were about to find out if Helwig was who he said he was.

They entered the stone walled exterior through tall reinforced iron gates after presenting their government ID's to the armed security. The driver parked and Jules and Jean walked to the large unpolished granite block building to pass the second level security, which included full body scans. Jules could see Bernard waiting behind the last laminated glass blast barriers. They finally entered the secure zone.

"Bonjour, Monsieur Le Directeur. Comment ça va?" Jules asked. "Bonjour, Mom Ami. Je suis bien, et tu?" Redare replied.

"We are fine. It seems you are working at a much heightened level since the attacks. This seems totally different from the last time I visited two years ago."

They followed Redare and his bodyguard to a hidden private elevator as Le Directeur replied, "Oui, we are fully engaged but only working with a budget that the socialists have nearly cut in half. We work day and night and only accumulate hours of compensation equivalents. If everyone decided to use all those hours at once we would likely be out of business for two months. I am trying to find a way to buy back those hours. Damn socialists will ruin this country if they have their way, let me rephrase that, continue to ruin the Republic."

Both Jules and Jean understood exactly what he meant. They exited the private elevator and entered directly into Redare's office.

He dismissed his security and offered the two men a drink.

"I have coffee, wine, port or cognac. It is nearly Midi so any one of those would be acceptable."

242

Jules smiled. Redare must have some significant information to be prefixing it with an offer of alcohol.

Jean nodded and quickly answered, "Cognac, s'il vous plaît, Bernard."

"Et moi aussi," Jules affirmed. *Me too.*

Redare poured three glasses with the very expensive Courvoisier L'essence de Courvoisier Grand Cru Cognac, retailing for over two thousand Euros per decanter. They silently contemplated their snifters, expert noses inhaling the liquor's bouquet, waiting for a proper toast to bless the amber liquid.

"Gentlemen, we need first to raise our glass to good health!" Redare proposed.

"Santé," they all voiced in unison.

"Now to wisdom that we solve our current dilemma," Jean added.

"À la sagesse!"

"Last, I suggest humility in God's plan for us," Jules suggested. "Humilité!"

With that they finished their glasses, warmed by the spirits. Redare put down his glass and walked the men over to a large computer screen. He typed in a password and they watched as the screen brought up a picture of Schmitt.

"Now down to business. I have some interesting information that you requested I keep confidential so I wanted to give you my analysis personally and then I will destroy everything at this end.

"The person you see here is the man calling himself Helwig. Dr. Robarts provided it from the morgue's video documentation system. We tested the DNA off her coffee mug and we could not link it to any database whether it was Interpol or FBI. We also did not find any information, passport details, birth certificate or any other documents that support that identity."

"So he is an imposter," Jean asked.

"Bien sûr!" *Absolutely!*

Redare smiled. "We did however find a match to his fingerprints we pulled off the mug. This man studied at the Sorbonne and we found his prints linked to his student ID. He is a very big fish and after I give you the database I will be experiencing amnesia and everything I have will disappear. I must have plausible deniability, otherwise you may not be able to do what you must without interference. Government here is not the answer."

"So who is this man?" Jules asked.

"Dr. Christian L. Schmitt, German citizen. He is a scientific and medical genius with three advanced Doctorates in genetics, bioengineering and biopathology. Can't find anything negative on him, not even a traffic ticket. No debt, mortgage or traceable bank accounts. He is one of the principals at TriStar Veterinary Biologics."

"I knew it, I just knew it," Jean exclaimed. "It makes perfect sense, they are creators and profiteers from the new rabies outbreak. Bastards, I bet they are Nazis also!"

"D'accord Mon Ami," Jules addressed Redare. "I believe you have provided us with valuable information that will likely save many, many lives! Is there anything else you feel we should know about the man?"

"Only that his middle name is Lucifer."

CHAPTER 55

TriStar Veterinary Biologics

Next Afternoon

Vogel and Schmitt sat in the CEO's office checking inventory invoices ready for shipment and reviewing Mendoza's distribution plan for the viron laden vials.

"So, if we are comprehending his orders exactly, the initial doses will arrive tomorrow in the Washington-Baltimore area so they will be the first region to fall into Hell-like chaos," Vogel started.

"The secondary targets will follow in three days and those are Boston, New York, Miami, St Louis, Los Angeles, San Francisco, Dallas and Denver. In four days, Mendoza has arranged for this facility to be destroyed from a massive 'terrorist' attack. Afterward, you and I will be assumed dead but in reality, relocated to a currently undisclosed location. Mendoza told me we will be picked up twenty minutes prior to the attack by a trusted contact and the actual time of the attack will occur on the overnight shift change break, around 0800 when most of the employees will be either going to or from their automobiles. That will minimize causality numbers to perhaps twenty or thirty. Your family is to be picked up and relocated to your sister's home in Berlin before the attack for safety reasons. We unfortunately will be assumed dead and incinerated in the attack so we will need to check in through the Alpha

Security corridor on that morning so there will be video documentation and therefore no doubt we were on site at the time of the attack. Your family will rejoin us at some point."

"That's all well and good but how do we escape the plant undetected? The cameras will surely record all our movements around the plant except the excluded super secure labs and those areas require providing DNA and fingerprints."

"There is to be a three-minute total power failure before the generators fully engage which will allow us to get to Lab X which is currently unsecured for cleaning and sanitizing. We will exit the at the receiving door where there will be an ATV waiting to get us over to the pickup point. Mendoza said the ATV has an autopilot function so once we are to the North Service road where the pavement starts, all we do is press the yellow button and it will self-drive us to the rendezvous point."

"Seems like he's thought of everything. What do we do for money, clothes and the like," Schmitt asked.

"Mendoza said the non-primary corporate account has been swept daily for the last four weeks so the only money left in the general operating account will be paid receivable invoices for the last week, about ten million euros. We are to be compensated monetarily and also are promised positions of power in his new government. That is what I was told."

Schmitt was too intelligent not to question the plan.

"And you really trust him to take care of us? Seems to me it would be easier just to get rid of us to tidy up all his loose ends," Schmitt questioned.

"I didn't work, subjugated, for all these years without receiving my reward. Either he keeps our bargain or I will find a way to notify Interpol and the FBI and stop the administration of those Trojan Horse doses. It's a tiny window but we could make sure it doesn't go beyond the Washington-Baltimore area, possibly in exchange for immunity from prosecution and a nice reward. I do want what he wants, the resurgence of the glorious days of our forefathers, but I'm not willing to be cheated out what you and I were promised; fame, fortune and glory. Nothing glorious about an early grave!" Vogel replied.

"Agreed, and if he fails to completely overwhelm the government of the United States or they refuse to accept his ransom cure then we are all exposed and I am sure will be hunted down like dirty dogs. We know better than anyone the power of this disease and we've heard his theoretical scenarios, but so far nothing has gone off smoothly as planned. Now if this business is destroyed, we might be directly linked in an investigation here in Europe that will leave us scrambling to escape the continent. On the flip side of that, we are probably in too deep to outwardly double cross Mendoza. He has thousands of party members waiting to pounce on anyone or thing that stands in their messiah's way. I think we need to trust him for now but have a plan B ready just in case."

Schmitt continued.

"I would suggest then we send the four wheeler on its way after we get off the property safely and then later contact Mendoza and tell him the machine threw us off when we hit a road bump. Getting into a car and being whisked away to God knows where, by God knows who, would be silly stupid. My family will not be home either when he sends for them. A simple miscommunication will be my explanation."

"So where do you suggest we go to hide if that is our decision?" Vogel questioned.

"Where better than right into the middle of the chaos? We go to the United States. Mendoza won't be there initially and if his plans work we can justify our presence as a last minute decision after we lost contact with him, not having properly encrypted communication equipment. We can also explain we went hoping to contact his representatives directly."

Vogel suddenly saw the benefit of Schmitt's plan.

"Yah, that way we can go either way. Mendoza if he is successful, the Americans if we experience less than an optimal manifestation of the disease. Besides, that's the last place he would expect us to be."

Vogel walked over to his hidden liquor cabinet and pushed an obscure lever which caused the beautiful oak paneled bookshelves to rotate, morphing into a bar service holding only five cut crystal decanters and a dozen small sparkling crystal glasses. He searched the bottles and found the best of the best and poured two fingers of the perfected liquid. Schnapps, but not ordinary; a rare bottle from the last Kaiser's collection.

"This liquid," he announced, "is older than both our ages combined. It deserves a proper benediction before it warms our souls. Christian, would you do the honors please."

Schmitt thought for a moment and then raised his glass up and even with Vogel's glass, only inches separating their sparkle.

"We are on the precipice of our new world order and the defeat of enemies past and future. No person can control or defeat us as we are the architects of this plague and controllers of the masses. We are now independent contractors, Mendoza be damned."

They silently swallowed, feeling the fortifying burn that had warmed the soul of Kaiser Wilhelm. They put down their glasses and shook hands creating their affirming bond.

"Now let's walk and talk, refine our plans," Vogel said leading Schmitt out of his office.

The motion sensitive lighting automatically dimmed as the system sensors recorded their exit.

Less than two hundred kilometers away, the son of the most evil man of the Twentieth Century, exited his Security spyware, closed his encrypted laptop and stood up to start his methodical pacing, stewing over what he had just witnessed.

Bastards figured out their immediate future, rather lack of future. Now I see them clearly, traitors! They must be terminated before they execute their betrayal.

CHAPTER 56

TriStar Veterinary Biologics

0800 hours, the next morning

"Doctor Vogel, there are three men to see you in the receiving area. Looks like something important. One knows you from your trip to Atlanta, Doctor Jules LeClerc. There is one other Frenchman, Dr. Jean DuBois, and another is an retired inspector from the BND, Johann Hammerstein. Will you see them?" Anna Riche, his forward security receptionist asked.

What could they want ?

"Give me a few minutes. Tell them I will be down to greet them shortly. Please offer them some coffee and refreshments and if they ask about Dr. Schmitt, tell them he is not in today."

"Jawohl!" *Yes Sir!*

Vogel left his office and took out his secure personal cell phone and called Schmitt who was in the R&D Secure Laboratory. Schmitt answered on the second ring.

"Christian, we may have trouble. There are two Frenchmen here, one, named LeClerc, I met him in Atlanta at the CDC meeting, he is the man we targeted but survived the Pasteur attack. The other I believe is the son of the famous French Nazi hunter Robert DuBois and the third is named Hammerstein and is retired BND. I have no idea why they are here but I told Anna to explain you were out of the office if they ask."

"Why would they be concerned about me?" the researcher replied.

"I have no idea, but they have not traveled all the way to Leipzig on a social visit so you best get out of here. Use our primary plan and leave through Lab X since you are close. Don't go home, go instead to David's farm and stay there. Use no phone or anything else of yours they can trace. David has encrypted phones so take one, activate it, text me the number and wait on my call. It will be a text— 000 if no problem —666 if there is one or if I'm unsure. Only return my call if you get the triple zeros. Otherwise, unless I am under arrest or dead, I will call you later with instructions. Got it ?"

"Yes, I'll leave now. Viel glück!" Good luck!

Vogel returned to his office, sat at his desk reviewing rapidly anything else he needed to do and looked out his panoramic office window and verified Schmitt was off to the executive parking area. Satisfied Schmitt was out, he code locked down the security system effectively restricting entrance or exit from any of the facility's ten working zones. Everyone inside the plant was now trapped until he reversed the security lockdown. He contacted Anna to bring the three visitors to his office.

She brought up the three men and Jules went straight over to shake Vogel's hand in a cordial, friendly French manner.

"Doctor LeClerc, I am so happy to see you in such good spirits. You look well considering how close you came to dying when Paris was attacked. I was shocked at that attack and followed Le Monde reporting which described your ordeal. I heard today they moved Pasteur and his family remains from their crypts under the destruction and moved them to the National Archives until they can be reburied. You were indeed fortunate considering the complete destruction that occurred at Le Pasteur," Vogel offered.

"Yes, I was spared by merciful God so I can locate and destroy the perpetrators of such evil," Jules replied.

"What do you mean? I thought your police found and eliminated the terrorists?" Vogel questioned.

"The mechanics but not the architects. But let's not dwell on that, let me introduce these two gentlemen to you.

250

"This is my lifelong best friend, Dr Jean DuBois, Directeur Archives Nationale Française, son of Robert DuBois, world famous war criminal hunter. This other fellow is your countryman, Johann Hammerstein, retired BND inspector extraordinaire. The reason we are here is to interview your employee or partner, Dr. Christian Schmitt."

"Unfortunately, Christian is out of the office on a personal day but what business could you have with him? He just recently returned from an excursion to America for the company investigating complaints about the condition of our vaccine products, especially the Rabies X vaccine were in when they were received. We were concerned about possibly selling a compromised product," Vogel explained.

Hammerstein stepped forward directly in Vogel's face. "Then why was he using counterfeit credentials including his credit cards, passport and a fake official letter of introduction from the Administrative Department of Public Health. Also, he participated in several human autopsies, collecting tissue samples primarily on the brains. I am here as a personal favor to Dr. LeClerc so none of this for now by necessity runs through official government channels. You understand if we contact the government what that would mean?"

Vogel's mind was reeling. *Did Schmitt get away or are more investigators waiting to intercept him? How do I spin this?*

"Yah, we would be overwhelmed with paper pushing bureaucrats. All I heard were the reports he generated on his visit which indicated the vaccines were being improperly handled— premixed and then not administered, shipping delays, storage at incorrect temperature and alcohol being used at injection sites. This is an ultra-modified live vaccine, not a typical killed virus product that the American veterinarians are used to. It has to be handled and administered in an exacting manner. Too many doses were not being given correctly and the patients may not be fully protected. That is all I knew he was doing over there. Are you quite sure your information is correct? I can't imagine why he would hide his identity unless.... unless he is going to jump ship with our propriety intellectual property. Son of a bitch, that's the only thing I would consider even a possibility."

"This is the problem," Jean spoke for the first time, "you, TriStar, are profiting from a disease process and we are certain, that is the result of an engineered virus. Man-made, produced to create a panic and generate millions, perhaps billions of Euros of profit. Terrorism for profit, pure and simple. Now the question is, did Schmitt develop this disease with your corporate blessing or is he an independent contractor that released the disease to spur TriStar's development of a vaccine solely to increase his wealth? It makes sense, he is one of possibly a dozen people in the world capable of producing an engineered virus, so it would be an easy leap for him to create the antidote — TriStar's vaccine. Exactly how much of the business does he own?"

Vogel sensed an opportunity.

"He has controlled seven percent, which was vested just last year. He did however purchase another eight percent option this January when he passed his fifteen year anniversary. Fifteen percent represents one percent per year he has worked. For that last eight percent, he paid cash, ten million Euros, a real bargain. At the current stock price, he has quadrupled that investment. I see what you mean, but I still can't believe it."

Vogel was playing the part of an out of the loop Executive very well.

Jules tried to reassure the CEO.

"Regardless, we will need to interview him before we return to Paris and we would prefer to do it discreetly, so as not to create unnecessary problems for your business..."

Suddenly the sound of rolling thunder shook the building nearly putting the men off their feet.

"Whaaat the hell—" Jean shouted.

Loud alarms and siren klaxons wailed with flashing emergency exit lights throbbing as more explosions followed. Hammerstein moved to the large panoramic window and shouted, "Mortars coming from the edge of field, many of them. Here come more. Take cover!"

Jules and Jean instantly dove for protection under Vogel's massive oak desk slipping under just as the huge glass window exploded showering the room with lethal shards. Hammerstein was blown away to the far wall, shredded, nearly skinned alive. He slumped to the floor dead from shrapnel to his heart.

Vogel was lifted off the floor, bouncing off the ceiling, landing on a modern cast iron LED pole light, impaled like a martini olive, his blood flowing pimento red. Alive but unable to move or feel anything, shock began overwhelming his senses.

As quickly the attack started, it was over.

Smoke started filling the office as the automatic sprinklers rained down on the flames ignited from the explosions. They produced a surreal fog of steam and smoke as Vogel floated above it on the pike. Jules and Jean were unharmed, coughing, and covered their faces with their handkerchiefs. They rushed over to Vogel, to check his condition.

Vogel was surprisingly alert but practically incoherent. Mumbling, he garbled his words as he tried to respond to their questions.

"Don't move, Dr. Vogel, it is critical you don't move, you will bleed out rapidly if you move at all until the paramedics get here. Please try to not move," Jules pleaded.

"Move? Are you kidding me ?" He laughed weakly. "I don't think I am going anywhere."

"Hammerstein is dead, bled out from a wound to his chest. Near instantaneously, I think," Jean said after checking the detective.

"I can't believe it, two attacks and I've survived both. Who was the target here, TriStar, Vogel or perhaps all of us? God help us!" Jules exclaimed.

Vogel's blood ran down the spiral post like an old-time barber pole. He paled and started having difficulty taking a breath. In agony, he called Jules over, blank eyes pleading.

"This is more than it appears," he warned. "You need to warn the United States CDC. Armageddon is coming and Mendoza is the scion of the most evil and the author of a Trojan Plague. There is no escape, find him or Schmitt, and you find your solution."

With that, he exhaled a long rattling breath and slumped flaccid on the pike.

"Merde!" Jules shouted in frustration. *SHIT!*

"Jules, my friend, are you ok? How is it possible we both yet again survived disaster?" Jean asked.

"Obviously, we are being spared again for a greater purpose. Possibly your Papa and Nelson Blackfeather lifted that desk and not the explosion so we could get our sorry old rear ends under there like a couple of young kids," Jules answered.

"This place is going to be swarming with police in a very short time," Jean replied. "What do you want to do, stay and get directly involved or leave and remain anonymous? We only have a very tiny window. I think Redare could explain our visit when they review their security footage if any of it survives the fire. I vote to leave toute suite!"

"D'Accord, we leave."

The smoke was continuing to fill the office as the sprinklers failed to keep up with the volume demand of fires spreading throughout the massive complex. They pushed out of Vogel's heavy front doors, past a large crater in the reception area. No survivors. The emergency exits were barely lit and visible through the increasing smoke. Mouths covered, they pushed into a stairwell and gasping for air, and made it to the outside exit. They burst out into the visitor parking area where Jules' Mercedes appeared undamaged. They jumped in and Jules sped off like he was driving at Le Mans.

"I'll take the SR 45 and we can loop back around to avoid the rescuers coming in from Leipzig. God, what a mess."

Jean was quiet, wiping the ash from his face and eyes. He handed Jules a couple of wipes from the glove box.

"What are we going to do about Hammerstein when they ID him and start an investigation on what he was doing at Vogel's office," Jean asked.

"I'll ask Redare to monitor the situation and if needed create a false paper trail of some kind if there is any problem. Perhaps Hammerstein was just visiting an old friend at a real bad time."

"Yes, I would call that real bad timing. What do we do now?" Jules thought for a second.

"We bring our American friends over so we can team up to find Schmitt and find out who this master of evil Mendoza is. At least we have a direction to go. There must to be some connection to the Rabies vaccine, so I'm going to call Kate to see if she can stop those vaccines from being administered. God help them if they can't."

CHAPTER 57

The Fürherbunker

That afternoon

The security footage Mendoza reviewed showed everything up to when a mortar destroyed the primary security and communication center for TriStar. A perfect direct hit that obliterated all the current, non-archived data.

Since security data was stored offsite on a rotated time schedule, he had nothing to see in real time and nothing of value from the morning except the footage of three visitors that had made it to Vogel's office just prior to his attack on the facility. In less than seven minutes, his band of mercenaries had deposited fifty mortar rounds and six incendiary shoulder missiles into TriStar and then immediately dispersed, vaporizing into the surrounding forests. It was a surprise attack intended to permanently sever his relationship with the traitors Vogel and Schmitt. He had however recorded the destruction by using a small bird like drone that had hovered at five hundred meters and the carnage appeared to be complete, total. Only one employee appeared to escape unscathed, running away from the building and driving off before the attack. Maybe a person with ESP or someone just playing hooky for the day.

He called a friend in charge of the local BND who was the son of the son of one of his father's secretaries. The man was one of his trusted secure government contacts patiently waiting for his ascension, a soldier that would do anything to restore his father's honor and place in history.

"Heinrich, this is August. It appears that from the news reports that your department will be very busy for the foreseeable future. You know what I'm talking about, yah?"

"Jawohl, Mein Führer," he answered. "We are receiving data and news feeds now but it initially appears the perpetrators have vanished leaving very little forensic evidence if any. I would call it a masterful, well executed attack."

"I like that word—masterful," Mendoza replied.

"Yes, the first of many *MASTERFUL* events that will launch our new world order," the younger man replied enthusiastically.

"Are there estimates on the casualties yet?"

"Preliminary reports are indicating a half dozen with injuries from minor to critical with the rest in the facility dead, assuming what we were told by a fireman is accurate. Survivors are estimating approximately one hundred and seventeen deceased based on the normal census. Some may never be identified absolutely because the fire in the production warehouse and laboratory R&D area became a cremating inferno when the attack's explosions severed the sprinkler main. All that cardboard, wood pallets, paper and styrofoam along with the propane used for the forklifts went up nearly instantaneously. No one in those areas escaped. Nothing but a pile of melted metal and ash."

Mendoza asked, "What about the executive offices?"

"I asked that question to Paul Rogust, who I believe you are familiar with, he was OUR first agent on the scene. He described total office destruction but not incineration like the majority of the facility. In the CEO's office there were two bodies which are cooked or as he put it 'steamed,' but not destroyed, so identification should be pretty straightforward."

Mendoza was confused. He knew three had entered Vogel's office from his spyware immediately prior to the attack. He had witnessed the greetings but then lost the video feed. There should have been four bodies. Who died and who had survived?

"I'll need that information as soon as possible today, as my near-term plans are very critical to our common goal."

"I will have that information for you in the next four hours, sir."

"Make that two hours and do not fail me!"

"I will not!"

Mendoza stood, stretched and then started his characteristic pacing, head down, hands clutched behind his back.

Soon, the first newly infected would hit the streets of Baltimore and Washington. After two days, that number will quadruple and after that, direct human to human transmission will spread the plague from neighborhoods into counties and then to entire states. After that, the secondary targeted regions will initialize. The explosive expansion from there would terrify the nation as she collapsed into chaos.

Schmitt and Vogel must be dead, if not, would they actually notify the authorities?

He decided. Time to leave Europe and return to Argentina just in case one of the two had survived the attack and it became impossible to return to safety in South America.

His jet could be wheels up in three hours to carry him home.

The United States would have only four days before she came crashing down to her knees.

CHAPTER 58

Jean DuBois' Paris Home

Evening the same day

"Bonjour, Mon Cherie," Jules greeted Kate, "Jean and I have just returned to Jean's home after another near death episode while we were in Hans Vogel's office at TriStar. A very close call."

"My God, I had no idea you had already visited TriStar, I thought that was to be tomorrow. I heard the initial reports on the morning news but I had forgotten that it occurred at 8 a.m. your time. I just now received an alert from the CDC that the producer of the Rabies vaccine was attacked and supplies would likely be unavailable. Are you both ok?"

"Other than inhaling some smoke and our ears' persistent ringing, we are fine. Vogel, however, is dead and we are not sure if Schmitt was in the plant somewhere and is dead or is on the loose. Vogel died right in front of us and I believe fingered Schmitt and someone named Mendoza as perpetrators of the Rabies epidemic. He pleaded with us to stop the administration of any doses of vaccine they shipped because there is something wrong with them. Jean thinks that possibly they are contaminated with something far worse than the rabies and from the despair in Vogel's voice, it is likely going to happen soon. Both of us were spooked because Vogel said in his final words 'Armageddon is coming' which is exactly what Ted's murderer shouted as he fled. Something cosmic is about to happen."

"That's crazy! So what do I need to do here?" Kate asked Jules.

Jean interrupted.

"Kate, you have to get the CDC to intercept all shipments from TriStar. Also, an emergency declaration to all veterinary practitioners to not administer any products from the company or open any shipments they have received. This is critical and immediate. D'accord?"

"As soon as we get off the phone I'll call Atlanta. Anything else I can do to help?" she asked.

"We need you and Tom here in Paris to help us find these two, or if Schmitt is already dead in that attack, this Mendoza fellow. He is likely the man in charge. For Jules and I, we are two old guys that are aging faster than we should because everyone keeps trying to kill us. We need young blood here to elevate our efforts and I know how much you hate Paris!"

Kate laughed both at Jean's joke and about the joy she found in the city she called 'my Paris'.

"You both are not so old and you know why you survived these attacks. You are under God's protection with the help of Joseph's ancestors and Jean, your father Robert. I'm sure they have a hand in what most people would call just good fortune. We know better than that. We survive, I survived, to root out these Destroyers of life. So if I have to sacrifice to fly to Paris to root out these evil-doers then I guess that is what I have to do."

She could almost see the smiles on their faces at her anticipated response.

"Bon, then I will arrange everything with your supervisors and you can use the charge card I provided to arrange your travel. I would like Brad and Joseph to travel to Massachusetts to see if they can backtrack Helwig or Schmitt through the car rental agency. Most of those luxury models have a sophisticated GPS Time Data function that will allow the agencies to monitor their rental's use and abuse. Maybe we can find more out about him and exactly what he was doing in the US by retrieving that data, maybe lead us to where Mendoza is. I checked earlier with now retired Special Agent Sullivan and he said he would pull in some favors owed and arrange the warrant that would be needed to access that information and then meet them in Boston to get them started. He said retirement is the toughest job he ever had. He also is sad because the Bureau has had so much bad press from a handful of tainted career bureaucrats, he would do just about anything to improve their image. He sounded a little regretful and melancholic. I don't think he has been the same since his wife passed so suddenly," Jules offered.

Kate answered, "I can understand that. So once you know what happened to Schmitt, we go looking for Mendoza. How in the world does that happen? Vogel could have been blowing smoke and making up the whole Mendoza thing. You don't even have a first name, or remote idea on age, where he resides or even what part he has to do with all this. This is much worse than finding Berhetzel because at least then Robert was able to put a name to Nelson's journal's drawings."

"That is why I have Bernard Redare working with a confidential contact in the BND who has allowed him into their road surveillance software. If Schmitt violates any automatic traffic control cameras, we can confirm he is alive. But that may be the only way because for a very wealthy man, he has only driven a very old 1999 black Mercedes sedan which has no satellite tracking ability. I thought that the age of the car might help us but evidently there are forty-two thousand similar looking Mercedes still on the road in Germany. We will have to locate him by his license plate on a camera or some other occult means. We have his cell information but it is out of service and his home is vacant. His family is God knows where. All that leads us to belief he escaped and is on the run. Possibly he is with Mendoza, the question is where and why?" Jules answered.

Jean had his theory.

"The question nobody has asked is who and why was TriStar attacked. I think that irrespective of any terrorist motive this was a coverup attack to destroy evidence which means whatever they meant to accomplish, to put in place for a greater purpose, is complete. We have no time to waste. Terrorists attack public venues to create terror.

They don't go after private businesses when public governmental targets are plentiful and attacking them validates their ideology. This action on TriStar was paramilitary with sophisticated technique, superb accuracy and created total destruction. The perpetrators attacked and then vaporized without leaving any gross forensic evidence. No, this was the work of professionals, an army with a chain of command. There is no other reasonable answer."

There was a moment of dead silence when no one spoke.

"I believe Jean is correct," Jules offered. "Kate, let me know when you and Tom are arriving. Jean and I are going to Chez Paul for dinner and then on to our homes to get some rest. It has been a very long day and we have exhausted our brains trying to figure this out on the ride home. If this doesn't fit the definition of Evil and Destroyer that Nelson gave us, then I don't know what would. I apologize for yet again interrupting your lives but I know this is not only a professional obligation to solve this but also so very personal to you and Tom. Justice with a slice of revenge. We are all obligated to solve this mystery. Like I said before, who better than us!"

CHAPTER 59

Pet Care Plus Veterinary Clinic

Baltimore, Maryland 07:23 the next morning

Dr. Frank Donnelly was going to be an even wealthier man. His multiple offices were vaccinating on average over five hundred animals a day and since they were open seven days a week that amounted to between three and four thousand animals a week. That success was due to Donnelly's persistent 'public service' announcements on radio and television coupled with the fact he was likely the only private practice owner within two hundred miles with the financial resources to purchase by credit card the large quantities of vaccines required to fill the overwhelming demand created by the public panic. That left him the only real player profiting wildly from Rabies X. He also was the only major practice visited by TriStar's quality control officer, Dr. Helwig, that was found to be in so-called administrative compliance. For that he received a complimentary thousand doses which translated into seventy thousand dollars of pure profit which he shared one hundred percent with the staff. They were tired but happy for all the overtime and those surprise bonuses.

Now he sat in his office reviewing a CDC Emergency Communication to cease vaccinating and not to even open any shipments arriving from TriStar. No explanation was given, just not to utilize anything received. He scrutinized the email carefully.

There was no expressed penalty for non-compliance. His offices had received and placed into inventory over five thousand doses late yesterday and there was no way he was going to interrupt his business without a better explanation. He had seen the last day's news reports about the attack on the German facility, so these would have to be the last doses arriving to the US anyway. The value of these new vials were easily double the original product and therefore while he could not technically double the vaccine price which was prohibited by the CDC, he could double his examination, administration and biomedical waste fees. Also, now was the time to finally booster vaccinate all the staff pets while they still had product. They would appreciate that gesture and he would send home doses for all those that needed it for their animals. He was truly a magnanimous person.

His office manager Debbie interrupted his planning with an intercom question.

"Doc, we are receiving all kinds off calls about the availability of the TriStar vaccine, the phones are ringing off the hook. There is a real panic out there to get their pets that final booster. I have been threatened by numerous people including some very cranky old women and just heard words that even made me blush. What are we going to do?"

"Interesting, so the panic is finally on. I guess tell them all to just visit one of the offices and we will vaccinate on a first come first served basis excluding those already with scheduled appointments, until we run out of stock. Then we are going to shut down for two days with pay for all the employees. Today we work till it's all gone. Tomorrow we rest. Now please call and get the entire staff to report to work. Bring their children if necessary, but today we run the table on the Rabies X. Ok?"

"Sure, Doc, but I better get some security on site because when we get down to those last doses, there could be problems."

"Do whatever you feel is reasonable and prudent. Go to Holier than Thou Donuts and get some donuts and coffee for the office and have the other managers do the same. We will order in all the meals til we close for the day. Today will be a veterinary marathon where we all will come out winners!"

Little did he know he was about to unleash Hell on Baltimore.

CHAPTER 60

Village of Honfleur, France

14:25 Same Day

Schmitt had been transported safely to the scenic seaside village of Honfleur by David Gerber, brother in law of Vogel who was paid by TriStar to solve a multitude of different 'problems' as they arose. He could help someone disappear or make someone disappear. All of it done without question or conscience. Schmitt paid ten thousand Euros cash for the emergency confidential ride and a new set of identity papers as Ernst Straub, medical apparatus salesman. His new persona had dyed dark brown hair eliminating his natural blond, dark cosmetic contacts to hide piercing blue eyes and a well-placed fresh cautery burn on his right forehead about the size of a walnut. A clear bandage patch covered the wound which was just transparent enough to allow the wound seepage to be noted. Human nature would cause people to focus on that wound or avert their eyes so as not appear to stare, rather than scrutinizing the rest of his face. A painful sacrifice to help him easily slip through most security checkpoints.

He planned to spend the night in Honfleur and then go by private driver to London via the Chunnel. From there he would fly to Washington to a reserved luxury hotel suite at the Trump International Hotel, where he would wait on David's confirmation call on Vogel's death. After that, he would travel into Baltimore to wait on the anticipated explosion of infected citizens flooding the streets with violent acts. He had been taking the antiviron medication monthly since developing the drug and he would only observe from a safe distance assuming he could find a safe distance. The manifestations would likely cross all social and economic levels so he would travel first to the Locust Point neighborhood where the only other true episode had occurred, where the infected priest had murdered the couple walking their two golden retrievers and then was killed by one of the dogs. If he stayed in his rental car, he would be able to observe in relative safety and document on a cell phone and send an encrypted field report to Mendoza using an old emergency-only phone number. That hopefully would get him into Mendoza's good graces and since Vogel was likely dead, and upgrade his stock in the Nazi's planned Neo-Reich. If he couldn't read Mendoza's response he would simply turn himself in to the FBI, exchanging his knowledge for immunity and cash.

The private chauffeur got Schmitt to London's Heathrow Airport late the next morning where he entered Virgin Airline's Executive Lounge to wait for his flight to Washington. He would gain hours of time flying west arriving in DC around 20:00 so he could relax at the hotel, or possibly visit some the national monuments until the next early afternoon, when he would drive into Baltimore observing for any activity spurred by the viron. He calculated that the improved, more potent viron would be shed rapidly by exposed animals receiving it and then incubated to create clinical signs in the human host within the lab predicted twenty0four to thirty-six hours. Eighteen thousand doses had been shipped in the first wave of the pure product, so at minimum if all were immediately administered, which was the usual, and only one person per pet was exposed, there would be already eighteen thousand ticking human time bombs waiting to explode just like the chimps in the laboratory at TriStar. That thought sent a cold shiver down his spine.

Schmitt sat in a private corner of the lounge and set up his secure laptop and accessed the TriStar website which only showed the company logo with an overlay statement that the website was down due to technical problems.

I think that is an accurate statement, he thought sarcastically. He emailed Gerber with a simple question— *Word on CEO?*

He closed the laptop figuring his contact might be at dinner because of the time difference but the 'burner' cell the Neo-Nazi had provided rang back almost immediately.

"Yah? Ernst speaking," reinforcing his new identity.

"How was your trip to London my friend?" Gerber questioned, "uneventful I trust?"

"Yah, I am waiting now to connect to Washington. I was curious, any word on our mutual friend and his poor health?"

"I am sorry to tell you he has passed away in an awful fire at his place of employment. It was a horrible death and he had no chance to escape. He had to be identified through his dental records and thumb ID. His family is devastated and have left to be with relatives to mourn."

"When I have returned I will have to visit them to share my condolences. Keep me informed on how they are doing please."

Gerber replied, "No problem, have a pleasant trip!" He ended the call.

Schmitt then pondered the message. *What thumb ID?* Suddenly he remembered. *That damn transponder microchip!*

Before TriStar had gone to biometric security measures, upper level management used a sophisticated microchip technology implanted in the 'meaty' underside of the right thumb which was cutting edge technology that restricted entry to secure zones to only those possessing those tiny transponders. When the systems evolved, the chips were obsolete. They never bothered to remove the grain of rice sized units, not seeing a need, but Schmitt remembered they would show on radiographs and might even trigger sensitive radio scanners. He could feel the unit just below the skin as he probed his right thumb. He had to find a way to remove it before he went through airport security in the US. They missed it on his last visit but that was Boston. Security around Washington might be more exacting.

Schmitt thought about the problem and then walked over to the lounge concierge desk and requested a toiletry kit in which he knew would be a plastic razor, styptic pencil and assorted adhesive strips. He was going to do a little surgery.

At the bar he ordered a Chivas Regal, tall on the rocks, and made his way over to the men's room. The attendant reached for his drink but Schmitt faked a belligerent drunk and made his way to an empty 'handicap 'stall. He placed the drink on the wash basin and unwrapped the razor and broke it apart. He gulped down the majority of the scotch and rubbed ice from the glass over the inside of this thumb. Locating the chip, he took the blade from the razor and sliced a small incision over the location of the transponder. Immediately the incision spurted bright arterial blood obscuring his locating the chip. Blood covered his hand, and stained his shirt's French cuff and sports jacket. This was not going to happen. He pushed the remains of the razor into an insulin needle Sharps container on the stall wall and then dropped the glass to the floor, where it shattered. He yelled out with a choice German curse word. *Scheisse! Shit!*

That cry caused the attendant to rush over.

"Sir? Are you all right?"

"No, I have cut myself on broken glass and am bleeding quite a bit. I will need a doctor please," Schmitt replied.

"I will get you to the medic at the first aid office, please open the door so I can help you."

The attendant saw the blood and made a facial cringe. The small cut was a virtual geyser of blood and Schmitt was grumbling to himself about his stupidity and the amount of attention he was bringing to himself.

The medic put in a clotting powder and cleaned the wound after the bleeding had stopped. Two small sutures under the skin closed the cut and a couple drops surgical glue provided a final sealing. She then applied a foam-lined moldable aluminum thumb splint to immobilize the digit. Schmitt was relieved to see the splint and understood the splint would likely interfere with visualizing the chip radiographically and block the transponder.

"There you are, sir. It will be a little tender for a while but the cut isn't that deep and it should heal in a couple days. Use the splint at least for three days or the seal possibly could break open," she said reassuringly.

"Danke, Fräulein," he replied.

Schmitt returned to the lounge and found a new safe space. He googled Baltimore television stations and chose WBAL-TV and went to their website. He then selected the breaking news stories section and clicked on it.

Nothing. Fires, car jackings, and robberies but no crazies running the streets. He bookmarked the site and closed the laptop. He was relieved that so far they were still within the expected incubation -shed period so 'things' were likely on 'schedule'. He really wanted to be present for that initial manifestation, and eagerly anticipated the adrenaline rush watching his creation explode as it had with the chimps, and also so he could record the historic event for Mendoza's benefit. He had already memorized a long numeric sequence needed to contact an intermediary of the Nazi leader that could then have Mendoza return the filtered communication if he wished. No return call meant he would have go to the FBI and finger Vogel and Mendoza as his employers who subjugated him by threatening his family and were the true architects of the plague. Either way he stood to be rewarded handsomely but there was absolutely no room for error.

He boarded on schedule and arrived well rested having slept nearly the entire flight in a first class seat that morphed into a near horizontal bed. The deep dreamless rest recharged him so that when he finally arrived at the hotel he was ready to go out and explore the capital. He had decided to skip the rental car so he picked up a map from the concierge, got some tips on what to visit and where not to wander into for safety reasons.

He stepped onto the street, looked around and saw a black SUV idling just up the street from the old stone building. He waved and flagged the driver who pulled up. The driver was dressed in a white dress shirt, black slacks and black tie. He stepped out and opened the passenger side rear door and Schmitt climbed in.

The faintly pigmented black driver had blue eyes, was lean, of slight build and had a Haitian French accent.

"Where can I drive you, Monsieur?" he asked politely.

"I would like a mini tour of this fine city, I have about four hours available. Are you a private driver?" Schmitt answered.

"Yes, Monsieur. This is my, well mine and the bank's, very fine Cadillac Escalade, with all the bells and whistles. I am available for anything you need. Only one hundred American dollars an hour. My name is James."

"Then I want to contract you for two days. I will pay you six thousand dollars but you must be waiting for me outside this hotel or within five minutes of my call when I need the car. Also you are to keep my confidence, no discussion of my business. Is that something you are willing to do?"

"Absolutely! I will call my wife later and explain that I have a very well paying private charter. She won't be happy because we have a new baby but the money is very appreciated and needed," the young man replied excitedly.

"Good, then here is a deposit," Schmitt said while handing over ten one hundred dollar bills.

"Merci, Merci Monsieur! Now where do you want to start?"

"I think the White House, then you can drive around the city and afterward I want to travel into Baltimore to a specific neighborhood so I can orientate myself for a surprise visit to my Aunt and Uncle for their seventy-fifth wedding anniversary tomorrow."

The driver started to over explain his understanding of the history of the landmarks and monuments. It was obvious he had studied and prepared for his job. Within ninety minutes they had seen most of historic Washington.

"Now do you want to travel to Baltimore, Monsieur?" he asked.

"Yes, put 407 Towson Street in your GPS. Once we arrive we will drive around the neighborhood slowly so I can decide how I can best surprise them."

An hour and two minutes later, they pulled into the old stately neighborhood. The roads were deserted in the predawn hour and they cruised, zigzagging the streets for nearly forty minutes.

"Ok, James. Let's head back to the hotel. I think I am well orientated now."

"Yes, Monsieur. This is a very nice and quiet neighborhood. Your Aunt and Uncle are quite fortunate. So peaceful."

"Don't be fooled, young man," Schmitt explained lying, "this area has been called by the local Catholic priests, *ET PORTAE INFERNI*, the proverbial Gates of Hell."

"Mon Dieu!" the young man exclaimed, crossing himself and then pulling his silver crucifix up from under his shirt, giving it a tender, respectful kiss.

They drove back to the capital in total silence.

The countdown to Armageddon stood at zero.

CHAPTER 61

Logan International Airport

Boston 10 a.m., the next morning

Brad and Joseph had flown out of Chicago's Midway Airport on Southwest Airlines because it was the only way to get a fast direct flight into Logan and the larger Boeing 737 jet was more comfortable for the oversized Brad to fly on. It was worth the extra drive because the small regional airport flights required connections, more wait time and those smaller jets were cramped and uncomfortable.

The plan was to meet retired FBI Special Agent Rick Sullivan at the AmeriCar rental office at 11 a.m. to review their computer and surveillance systems records. He had no official warrant but had called in some favors and the company agreed to give them complete access to their monitoring systems. The Mercedes Schmitt had rented under the assumed name Helwig had been shipped back to Boston from Hartford, Connecticut and was waiting for their forensic inspection. Also the car's navigation system and on board computer records had been downloaded, printed and available for them at the business office.

Brad and Joseph were surprised when Sullivan met them just as they disembarked the 737 jet.

Sullivan was almost unrecognizable as he was dressed casually in a navy blue short-sleeve polo with a miniature FBI emblem on the left side pocket with gold small letters *Retired* scripted below the emblem, ivory dockers and a causal navy canvas style boat shoes. The biggest surprise was his salt and pepper well-trimmed goatee that framed his mouth. He was standing with a young uniformed TSA officer.

"Gentlemen!" Sullivan greeted. "How nice to see you again. This is TSA Officer Thad Donovan, eldest son of my best friend at the Bureau, Bill Donovan."

"Thad, this is Dr Brad Upton of the USDA and Joseph Blackfeather of the....."

"Of the Lakota Nation," Joseph finished, smiling proudly and extending his hand to the agents. "Nice to meet you, Officer Donovan and to see you again, Special Agent Sullivan."

He was not the shy young man of a couple years earlier.

They exchanged their condolences for Sullivan's wife's death for a few uncomfortable minutes. Then Sullivan took charge.

"So, unless you fellows have to use the john or have luggage to grab, we have a shortcut to take in this old person's golf cart, then we will take my personal car over to the rental lots."

"I think we are ready to go," Brad replied.

"Good, hop in and I will fill you in on what I have been able to find out so far. Be aware a lot of this will depend on what else we get from the rental agency.

"Christian Lucifer Schmitt masqueraded as Dr Peter Helwig, not making any real effort to disguise his normal appearance. As you both know, this guy has a genius IQ with three extremely advanced genetics slash medicine slash biology slash engineering doctorates. The letters after his name contain most of the letters of the alphabet and so to address him it would be Dr. Dr. Dr. Schmitt. A stutterer's nightmare."

"Good one, Agent Sullivan," Brad chuckled.

"And I'll have none of that — please call me Rick."

"Ok, Rick," Brad affirmed, "what was his real purpose for the visit?"

"He had the fraudulent letter from the CDC that supposedly was signed before Ted's death, but was faked by Ted's secretary, Sue Ann

Myers. It didn't take long to figure Ted's long-time assistant was involved and occultly on TriStar's payroll and likely spied for Schmitt or even possibly Vogel through an intermediary, likely Rimer. She denied any part in Ted Johnson's death and for what it's worth we believe her. She basically reported the CDC agenda and breakthroughs as she heard them. She never met any of them personally and had no idea who Vogel was when Vogel was invited to the CDC. She was evidently insulated from them purposely. An unsuspecting but well paid single mom who was an unwitting pawn. Too bad, she likely will go to jail for espionage since the CDC is a government agency.

"So, to answer your question, Brad, he was here ostensibly to find out how the vaccine TriStar shipped, was being handled and stored. TriStar had required veterinarians administering the Rabies X product pull vaccine titers which were part of their field efficacy studies. The CDC did the same, only there were vastly different results. The tests completed in Atlanta show very good protection and only failure to achieve protection in the twenty thousand tests run was well less than one half of one percent. The tests done in Leipzig showed ten times as many failures. Those results probably were faked."

"Why?" Joseph asked.

"Possibly only to increase sales by recommending an additional booster, but I agree with Jean DuBois that TriStar manufactured the rabies plague with plans to taint it with some other bioweapon that would be shed by the animal vaccinated vectors. The problem with that theory is none of the 'protected' animals have gotten ill or for that matter even had anything other than a very mild allergic reaction because as a highly refined modified live vaccine, they purposely eliminated the use of preservatives normally used to extend the product's shelf life. Their excuse was they would produce only what could be used immediately and worry later about vaccine stability. The in question newly shipped third boosters have been intercepted and administration halted by the CDC and will be forwarded to Atlanta for analysis. That along with the destruction of the TriStar production facility and Vogel's death, all we have to do is find Schmitt, have him finger Mendoza and close the book on this puppy."

"Why am I not feeling that?" Joseph remarked.

"My Indian blood brother is right. That just seems way too simple to me. When we get tangled up with evil, it's not your run of the mill type. It seems to be the worst of the worst. There are supernatural forces in play including spirits that involve us and we aren't done until they tell us we are done. We don't even have a gnat's ass of a clue of who this Mendoza fellow is, where he is and what his role in this cluster thing is. We really have far less than we did looking for Berhetzel," Brad added.

"Except this time you have the help of the FBI, albeit retired, but I do have a lot of people who owe me favors. I am your ace in the hole," Sullivan joked.

"You must find retirement extremely boring," Brad teased back.

"You have no idea!"

TSA Agent Donovan had dodged and weaved the TSA cart with orange light flashing though the amorphous migration of passengers until they found a way to a sub level secure exit. Sullivan's white Yukon Denali XL with Virginia license plates was parked among a line of TSA Black Ford Explorers. They loaded up, Brad riding shotgun. Donovan opened the security gate and waved to them as they drove off.

In six minutes they were at the car rental office. The manager was waiting.

Francis Yoe was the senior regional manager and had driven in from New York to expedite their investigation. They exchanged introductions and got down to business.

"Most people don't know that most of our fleet is equipped with electronic governors that record your location, speed, driving habits and some proprietary marketing markers. I guess technically we profile our customers which allows us to determine which automobiles they prefer and pricing tolerance. This data is generated, downloaded and is centrally processed and algorithms developed to understand our customers and business better. We also can isolate an individual who abuses the car, smokes since every auto is a smoke free vehicle, or hauls anything hazardous that could damage the rental. We had one fella that was hauling live goats in the rear seat of a Range Rover. No rule against it —yet. Your

Dr. Helwig never exceeded the posted speed limits and used his GPS for nearly everywhere he went which was Cape Ann, Boston, Baltimore and Providence, then dropped off here. Here is his printed GPS map with locations, and businesses labeled with minute by minute expired time logged. So it's easy to see on that Thursday he left the Essex Bed and Breakfast and traveled to the Gloucester Coroner's Office and was stopped there for six hours and twenty-three minutes.

"His entire trip where he used the rented Mercedes is archived on this log. The only thing we don't know is what he did outside the vehicle."

"Big Brother is watching," Brad lamented.

"You have no idea," Sullivan affirmed.

Francis handed over the paperwork and flash drive and walked them over to the Mercedes which was parked in an isolated corner of the agency.

"Here are the keys but I seriously doubt if you will find anything because it has been rented seven times since Helwig had the car, but have at it. I'll be in the office for two hours more before I drive back." She turned and walked away.

Sullivan opened the driver's door and looked in the glove compartment and inspected the truck.

"She was right, this is a dead end. I think we should go today to the B and B in Essex, where he stayed, rest there for the night or wherever and then head into Providence and Baltimore tomorrow and find out what he did at those veterinary practices he visited. The more we investigate the better we will understand his real motive for being here."

The three drove in silence, unwittingly timing their schedule to coincide with the manifestation of the viron in Baltimore.

CHAPTER 62

Mendoza Compound

Bariloche, Argentina

Mendoza was tired of waiting. His field agents, and there were hundreds in the targeted areas, were on alert to report any unusual crimes, attacks or other strange episodes. Not one of the group had any direct knowledge of any member team other than the local clan, and all the reporting was through strict encryption programs that went to another highly encrypted server and then went around the world through a series of electronic filters that eventually trickled back to the Nazi. The problem he faced was all this critical data was not received in real time. The process to hide his identity slowed his receiving these messages by two to four hours as each unit of encryption had to be tested for purity before it was forwarded. He vented this frustration, resigned to watch the travails of his targeted major metropolises of the eastern United States unfiltered through the local media delivered by satellite, but that entailed having to endure all the reports that really had nothing to do with his plague. Vogel had provided a timetable and Mendoza expected German precision in the execution of his plans. Too bad Vogel was dead and Schmitt also likely future food for worms, otherwise he would savor berating the incompetence his subordinates had exhibited.

He left his communication room and walked through the dark Bavarian style hallways, half-timbered with dark oak beams and trim and light cream stuccoed walls and ceiling. Even though the mansion exterior really had Spanish style architecture, the interior would lead one to believe they were in the forests of Germany.

He was slow and deliberate in his movement, mulling over in his head what should be exploding soon across the United States. He walked out to the courtyard where massive live oaks filtered the light from the bright, nearly full moon. He looked up at the clear cloudless star filled sky and caught the flash of a shooting star from the corner of his eye. His security moved quietly along the outside of the tall thick perimeter wall with their panting Alsatian Shepherds, the only non-ambient sound disturbing the midnight silence. The peacocks observed from their high perches in the oaks and the cool night air had muted the usual insect chorus. Mendoza stopped at the portico and found his small table with one cut crystal glass and a liter decanter of a well-respected port wine. He filled his glass half full and opened a thick encyclopedia sized Humidor with an elaborate hand carved hunting scene that had once belonged to his father. He selected a dark large style Cuban cigar and slid it under his nose savoring the dried tobacco's aromatic bouquet.

It lit with his smooth draws of delicious smoke and he slid down into an old Ratan chair that was cushioned firmly with local plant material cushions. The chair had gradually conformed itself to him just as it had his father, more than a half century before.

"Are you sure your generals are competent and your enemies targeted for destruction?" came a question from his right.

Mendoza looked to the empty chair next to him and saw his father seated, middle aged, dressed as if he was about to inspect his troops or give a great speech. The hallucination stared back at him, a Disney like hologram.

Mendoza swallowed hard then blew a plume of smoke up away from the vision as he subconsciously straightened himself stiffly upright, at near attention.

"My father, it is you! Are you here to consult me ?" he asked with a childlike incredulous tone.

"I am in you, so you are me. Your future will soon be thrust upon a nation of weaklings and I will guide you from this side. You are not going insane but using insane behavior often surprises the enemy. You are to be ruthless, unmerciful to man, woman or child to fulfill your destiny. It will come to pass but realize this, trust no one, accept no compromise. Remember who I was and who you are. It will be done and I will be right at your side."

With that, like a ghost of Christmas past, he vanished. Mendoza's phone flashed an automated message to return to the communications center, new critical reports were arriving. He nearly ran back to the room.

He opened the message. It was short and simple.

Streets of Baltimore bloodied as violent riots erupt for no apparent reason. Sixteen reported killed as more citizens pour into our street with machetes, baseball bats, axes and other weapons. Police cordon off major area but violence spreading, even among the law enforcement teams.....

A second message received was signaled: *Southwestern Airline Flight 2351 from Baltimore to Tampa crashed in rural North Carolina after several passengers 'go crazy' attacking other passengers and opening emergency exits after which the plane crashes. Passenger videos of the attack received by family members prior to crash.....*

He smiled, finally it had ignited, the viron drawing life just like the cigar he had just lit.

Things could not be better, his father was at his side to guide him and now Armageddon was birthing at The Gates of Hell!

CHAPTER 63

Paris

Jules' driver sped quietly on the A1 enjoying the non-typical lack of automobile congestion and delay that was common returning from Charles De Gaulle Airport and the northwest suburbs of Paris. The Pasteur Institute jet that brought the three Americans, still traveled the world despite the tragedy that had struck the Institute. Jules was the interim leader of the prestigious scientific organization and had access to all her available resources without question. The jet now flew as it always had, but without a full crew and the Michelin Chef who had died in the terrorist attack.

Kate and Tom had traveled on the jet with an old friend, Dr. Fred Garrett, a Nobel winning geneticist from The Ohio State University, who could decipher and analyze genetic code faster than nearly anyone in the world and would work all the way down to sub DNA particles. He was the only person in their eclectic group to ever have met Christian Schmitt in his real persona and had shared hours of ideas over dinner at a WHO Symposium held in Brussels three years earlier. The quiet university professor was medium build, middle fifties with salt and pepper crew cut hair and was dressed in his signature white short-sleeve shirt, khaki slacks and a scarlet and gray bowtie. His head was nearly always buried in his laptop computer.

Kate stared out the automobile's window thinking back on her and Tom's brief encounter with Schmitt when they met him as Dr. Helwig in that Ipswich restaurant a few weeks back. She remembered his voice, accent, but had been so focused on the fake letter from Ted Johnson, she wasn't able to fully recount the man's appearance. Maybe that was the result of her infection and treatment for Rabies X, she wasn't sure. Tom also wasn't very good at names and faces unless they wore the hide of a dairy cow. No, Fred would give them a distinct advantage plus his unique analytical scientific mind might rival Schmitt's genius level thought processes.

The driver drove straight to Jean DuBois' home and they exited the vehicle and again stood at the massive old oak front door with their ancient tarnished paired lion's head door knockers. Tom gave a solid rap on the door. Jean was at the entrance nearly before Tom's hand left the brass handle.

"Bonjour, Mes Amies!" Jean exclaimed. "Comment vas -toi?" "Trés bien Merci, et tu?" Kate and Fred replied in near unison.

"Great! We are back in Paris, again looking for another potential 'Destroyer'. What could be better?" Tom replied slightly sarcastically.

"Jules is in the garden in my father's favorite chair. We have a very nice *petite déjeuner* ready to be enjoyed on this lovely morning."

They cut through the beautiful home with its *trompe l'oeil* hallway which led past the office/library where Berhetzel had murdered Jean's father Robert and nearly killed Jean as well. You could still slightly detect the smell of smoke clinging to the books that survived the fire Berhetzel had set to cover his escape.

The garden was an urban oasis with fountains, bird houses and feeders, sculpted horticultural masterpieces and colorful perennial beds. Bees and butterflies zoomed and fluttered on their pollination tasks. It was the first time Tom, Kate and Fred had been in the garden since the young couple's wedding three summers before.

"Jean, your father would be so proud of the state of the garden. He loved it so much. I can almost see him sitting at the fountain holding beautiful BB's hand while he proposed," Kate said referencing the old man's obsession with the famous sex symbol.

He chuckled. "I see him everywhere. His soul is in this place, he is its guardian angel and along with Nelson, quite possibly our guardian too!"

Jules was up from the old wicker rocker and straight at Kate with his usual embrace and whispering kiss. And as usual, Kate's face was flush with a rosy blush. He then warmly embraced each man.

"Welcome to Paris again my friends. I don't know if you have heard but there are developments in the US which might be related to the vaccines. It seems the streets of Baltimore are alive with, as the news media are calling it, a 'Zombie Apocalypse'. There are planes leaving Baltimore crashing from passenger rioting on the planes. All very strange. Because of that, we are going to only be in Paris for a couple hours then Bernard Redare will be flying us by turbo copter to Leipzig where we will revisit the TriStar facility, or what's left of it. We also will be flying to a farm that he feels might be where Schmitt hid, possibly waiting to exit the country. My friend has several armed agents in place there, waiting our arrival. His office was able to identify the only vehicle leaving TriStar at the approximate time Jean and I were being escorted into Vogel's office, about five minutes prior to the attack, by getting Schmitt's rear license plate from the reflection of his car onto the front of a new black Mercedes at a traffic control light. An unbelievable bit of police work. Once they had that sliver of information, they did serial scans of one hundred kilometers until dark that day and that is how he located the farm where Schmitt stopped. Funny thing is Schmitt's car had a large amount of bird excrement on its roof which was the identifier that allow Redare to track it. The next morning the satellite sequencing showed the vehicle gone or possibly was garaged somewhere close by. Schmitt could still be at the farm but surveillance can't verify that. Redare has two BND retired agents who are also off the books to assist. They all have credentials but really are working with us and for us. All these agents were or are part of a bureaucracy that stifles patriotism and efficiency. If you put this investigation under pure socialist care, whatever evil that is on the way will be beyond anyone's ability to stop it before you could say presto! The men working with us are patriots and defenders of freedom. They, the professionals, feel this thing we are dealing with promises to dwarf

PIERCE ROBERTS

any evil the world has ever experienced. Funny thing is that we are once again the ones being sent to stop evil and these other men, including Sullivan, are taking tremendous personal and professional risk to help us."

"Helicopter?" Kate gulped, expressing her fear of flying and reliving her kidnapping.

"Oui, Mon Cherie, but the pilot has promised not to, as you say, do any 'hot dogging'," Jules assured.

Tom grabbed her hand and gave it a gentle squeeze.

"It will be fine, honey," he said smiling, "I won't let anything happen." She smiled back.

"Why don't you enjoy some of these wonderful breakfast delights... fresh squeezed Blood Orange juice, croissants, pain au chocolate, fresh seasonal fruits and of course Champagne," Jean offered.

"French food is one of my weaknesses, that and Ohio State Football," Fred announced.

They ate enjoying the beautiful morning, small talk about Bobbi and grandchildren and how Brad and Joseph were. Jules stood up just as his phone rang. It was Redare. Jules spook in affirmatives and ended with Merci!

"There is a private military soccer practice field about a kilometer north from here where the copter will land in about twenty-five minutes. We should finish up here and if you need the toilet, you best go now. My driver is waiting out front and I will go with Jean in his car. D'Accord?"

No questions. Kate visited the *salle de Bain,* followed by Tom and then Fred.

They arrived just as the Eurocopter X3 Hybrid 255 landed in a swirling cloud of dust. Two crew members lowered the boarding stairwell and stood on either side assisting the six passengers board. Then almost immediately Europe's fastest helicopter leaped from the field and then sped to the north, turning eighty degrees to the east just as they exited the Paris suburbs. The helicopter was extremely fast, smooth riding and was more like a hovering plane than the copters any of them had flown on before.

288

Kate started to relax as the city disappeared behind them and the fields, farms and vineyards sped past.

Jules tapped her on the shoulder and pointed downward as they crossed a river and the land started to morph into hills and forests.

"Allemande, *Germany*," he explained. "How many souls have perished over the centuries for that soil?"

"For some reason I don't find that very comforting," she replied.

Tom was sleeping, trying to adjust to his jet lag and Fred had his head in his laptop as usual.

Soon they were approaching the remains of the TriStar headquarters and the pilot made two quick passes over the property and put the helicopter gently down in the old abandoned parking lot. He gave Redare a thumbs up and after they were safely distant from the chopper, he lifted up and away.

"Where are they going?" Tom asked Jules.

"To refuel and then meet us at the farm where we think Schmitt is or was. He has to land about two kilometers away so as not to spook our prey. We are driving to that farm from here taking the same route Schmitt did, about a forty-five minute drive. I don't think we will be here for long but Jean and I wanted to see Vogel's office once more, probably more from curiosity than fact finding. I also want to check out the animal labs where the testing was completed."

The entire property was now fenced with a three meter high chain link fence with a razor wire crown. Official signs prohibiting trespass were prominently displayed at a uniform distance. They walked over to the armed security guard controlling the front gate and the BND officer and Redare flashed their identity cards and signed in. The guard lifted the latch and pushed open the gate. They walked to where the reception lobby had stood with its huge panoramic tinted reflecting glass panels. The scorched glass laid crumbled, layered over the polished dark marbled floor. Steel girders still remained but the roof and walls were blown away. It smelled of smoke, and cordite. A single water Lilly that had survived in the reflecting pond bloomed a bright pink flower, the only sign that once the business had been alive with activity. The building seemed shrunken, its rubble only a hint of what had stood there a few days before.

Jules spotted the protected stairwell he and Jean had escaped down from Vogel's office and they made their way up to the skeletal remains of the CEO's office. The furniture was melted and charred, the once hidden liquor service was open, exposing the decanters of fine alcohol that had exploded in the fire. The iron lamppost that had pierced Vogel's body lay on the floor with remnants of abdominal fat melted and mixed with his cooked blood. No computer or files were present, likely removed by government officials. They saw nothing of value but the thought that Jules and Jean had survived such complete destruction protected by a desk, sent shivers down Kate's spine.

Next was the area where the main animal lab had stood and other than evidence rats, lab or otherwise, feasting on the remnants of the Rat and Monkey Chow, there was nothing of value. They exited through Secure Lab A receiving doors and were outside in the sun on the north side of the property. An ATV stood ready next to a loading dock platform. Redare inspected it and had a BND agent take a look.

"This is where Schmitt ran out from the building and then around the east side to the executive parking area. No one mentioned this ATV in any of the reports I saw, which is strange. Even more unusual is it has an Autopilot system and the keys are still in the ignition. Who puts an autopilot on a recreational vehicle?"

Fred unlatched and lifted the hood.

"This is very similar to the one I have at home," he said, "except this unit has a lot more wiring."

He dropped to one knee and used a small penlight to look around the engine. He suddenly jumped up.

"Get back everyone. This thing is wired with explosives. C4 if my hunch is correct. Wire runs to that yellow button."

They ran, clearing the area. Redare shook his head solemnly.

"Thanks, Fred. That thing could have killed us all. Lucky no one tried to move it or steal it from here. And I bet that was intended for Schmitt, Vogel or both of them. Jules and Jean, I suspect your surprise visit to

Vogel precipitated a change of plans and Schmitt ran off, likely planning to reconnect with Vogel at the farm we are heading to."

"So why were they attacked? Certainly they didn't arrange it or they would have taken the day off. Or if they had knowledge of it

maybe they were planning to escape on this ATV. Possibly they were told to use it by a third party?" Jean asked.

"Perhaps Mendoza ?" Jules questioned.

"That's what I'm thinking," Redare answered. "They would have prior knowledge of the attack and the escape was planned on the ATV which could have be detonated either by the GPS unit or some other remote means. What that tells me is there is a much bigger fish involved, likely Mendoza. So we need information, an informant to fill in the blanks. Maybe at the farm we will get some answers. Schmitt likely is far from there and if he thinks Mendoza is trying to kill him, he will be very hard to find. We need to capture him alive and well."

"We can't leave this vehicle here to blow up someone," Jean protested.

"I have an idea," Garrett said.

He pulled a white cotton handkerchief and removed the petrol cap from the fuel tank and pushed one ended into the tank and gently reset the cap loosely on top of the wick.

"Anyone have a problem with this?" he asked.

"Then everyone get down behind that dumpster barrier wall and I'll light this sucker."

They ran and kneeled behind the cinderblock barrier and Fred dove in just as the tank blew followed by the plastic explosive. The boom sent shrapnel flying skyward and knocked the men off their feet.

"Holy crap! Damn!" Fred laughed. "Maybe we should have called the bomb squad!"

They stood and looked at where the vehicle had been parked. There was a meter deep hole in the ground and the handlebars were the only thing left of the bike. They starting laughing, patting the professor on the back.

"Where in the world did you learn about Molotov cocktails?" Jean asked.

"Is that what that was? I guess I must have read about it somewhere, seemed like a good idea."

"Just like a swift kick to the gonads!" Jules chuckled.

CHAPTER 64

Old Locust Point

Baltimore, hours prior to the chaos

Dr. Frank Donnelly was happy. They were closed for the next three days and his staff certainly deserved a rest. His marketing team was going to develop some new public service 'spots' that would explain why the vaccine was unavailable and how clients should continue to isolate their pets, not feed birds or wild animals and not to approach any wild or feral animals. They also were going to recommend twice a year examinations and boosters of all other vaccines until a replacement for Rabies X was made available. Since the outbreak of the disease, his revenues were quadruple year to date and he had enough reserves to hold them for nearly eighteen months. Best of all American Express had just issued him a Centurion Black Card. Move over, LeBron!

His home was on a short side street just off Towson; there were only eleven old but restored homes in the exclusive neighborhood. There was no violent crime, just the occasional property crimes that were hushed up to preserve property values. Most of his neighbors were clients and had a mix of Goldens, Labs, Frenchies and King Cavaliers that could be seen walking around the neighborhood. He was the only resident on the street without a cat or dog because his wife had extreme allergies that required he shower in the basement and put his work clothes directly into the washer before he could come into the main house. A bit of a pain but it saved a lot of money on EpiPens.

His office looked over the Inner Harbor and Chesapeake Bay and a shoreline walkway promenade that was used by dog walkers, joggers and old people. There usually was someone moving up or down the bricked walkway except when a NorEaster blew in with sheets of salt spray and ice. That is when he enjoyed the office the most; a drink in hand and a roaring fire in the hearth and ocean spray freezing on the old leaded glass window panes, creating rivers of ice. It made him feel like the captain of a great whaling ship, steering into the teeth of a raging sea storm. The only thing missing was a dog, likely an Irish 'calm' Setter warming with her back against the hearth but his wife's extreme allergies quashed that part of the dream.

He stared out the window drinking his morning coffee, dark, thick and black just as the sun broke the horizon, sending warm rays into the wood paneled room. He stood, stretched and moved over to the window and cranked open one of the tall leaded casement window panels. A pair of ponytailed joggers in matching blue and gray running gear, one male, one female, moved in unison, hair swinging in rhythm, northward at a steady pace. More came out and soon the regular fitness fanatics were pushing themselves in different ways. Mrs. Roberts was out walking Madeline, her overweight Frenchie, who was panting heavily. She looked very put together with her overcoat and fancy hat, despite the middle sixty near shore temperature. She looked up and waved, gave a thumbs up, demonstrating she was following his exercise and weight control plan for the chunky canine.

He waved back. "Hi, Wilma, Hi, Maddie!" He returned the thumbs up.

He sat down in a worn leather recliner that he had positioned strategically by the window and opened the Wall Street Journal. Several minutes later, bloodcurdling screams erupted from outside the window. He jumped up and tried to see what was happening.

Wilma Roberts was attacking a female jogger with something in her hand. The jogger who was younger, stronger, was on the ground in a near fetal position, hands covering her face as the older lady straddled her stabbing with short thrusts with what appeared to be a large needle. Alerted by the screams, bike patrol park rangers ran up and pushed her off the bleeding jogger and jumped back as the woman thrust the weapon at their face. She clearly was out of control. One of the rangers fired a Taser that put the old woman down but only for two or three seconds. Up again, demon-like, she became more aggressive as her neurons fired in near unison, and thrust the weapon into the female ranger's left eye. She screamed in pain falling to the ground as the attacker plucked it from the eye and lifted and stabbed again, penetrating deeper. That was enough. The second officer fired his service revolver, killing Mrs. Roberts. Maddie was huddled, pushing herself against the stone wall shivering and whining. Donnelly got out of the house just as the shot was fired.

The female ranger had a large hat pin sticking out of an eye. She was crying in excruciating pain as she pressed both hands over her left eye to stop the blood flow. Donnelly ran up, confused at what happened and picked up Maddie, who was salivating in fear, shivering and crying. The vet pulled his handkerchief out of his rear pocket and wiped her down before replacing the white cotton cloth back in his jeans.

A crowd had gathered, circling the scene, jockeying for a better view. Some were crying and others trying to snap pictures with their phones. Police and EMS arrived and removed the injured ranger and started taking statements. While the crowd dispersed, a middle aged man suddenly lunged at one of the police and grabbed at his service revolver which was loose in the holster. The man was manic, screaming, biting at the officer's nose and ears while pulling loose the 9mm and started firing at the crowd. More screams and panic ensued. Three were hit and of those two looked critical.

The police partner fired one round and the man's head splattered on impact. Donnelly ran to the safety his house cradling the panicked dog in his arms. His face was covered with blood and bits of brain and hair and he gagged in response to what he had just witnessed.

He pulled his handkerchief again from his jeans, wiped down his face and then phoned his wife's cell, told her what happened and not to enter the office because of Maddie. He told her to lock the doors, let no one in and set the alarm. He was frantic, in near tears, sweat streaking down his face. He wiped his face once more with the white cotton cloth.

That was his fatal mistake.

CHAPTER 65

Rural village outside Münster, Germany

Staging to raid the Gerber Farm

There was a small army of French and German investigators waiting on orders covering every direction from which anyone on the farm might try to escape. The plan was for Redare, Jules and Jean to pull up in their automobile, feigning being lost trying to locate the farm of a friend. Probably a poor excuse in the age of GPS systems. Thermals indicated only one person in the farmhouse and only assorted animals in the outbuildings.

Jean knocked hard on the front door, rattling the old peeling gray paint.

No answer but they could hear someone moving in the background.

"Wer ist es?" *Who is it?*

"Drei verlorene Reisende aus Frankreich." Three lost travelers from France, was Redare's reply.

The door opened and Gerber stood wearing a long sleeve beige shirt and faded denim jeans and dirty red suspenders. The man was heavy with a large beer belly, barrel chest, unkempt reddish blond beard and blond thinning hair. His eyes were pale blue and he wore thin wire rim glasses.

"What can I do for you?" he asked in a non-threatening but non friendly way.

"Our GPS keeps taking us in circles trying to locate Franck Mueller's residence. He is very old and doesn't answer his phone because he can't hear and we are trying to have him sign some paperwork for a release of his war memoirs. We talked to him last week and he gave us pretty straightforward directions and an address but no one so far anyone has any idea who we are looking for," Jules offered.

"Never heard of him, so if you don't mind I have work to do." Redare now took it up a notch.

"I also have the name of his nephew who might be able to give us some help. Frederick Helwig? He is an medical doctor."

Gerber paled and staggered back a step. Redare reached back and subconsciously placed his hand on his hidden service weapon.

"No idea," he muttered pushing the door closed.

The three Frenchmen turned and walked away, got into the car and pulled away from the house.

"Now we wait," Redare instructed.

"We have the parabolic microphones focused on the house and we are prepared to intercept any cell transmission he makes. It did not look to me there was a landline so I'm not sure about an internet connection, likely he uses satellite to make connections. If that's the case, anything he says or does will be intercepted immediately and if it is incriminating we move in. If not, we play a waiting game. He knows Schmitt, looks to me to be undisciplined and I'll bet a hundred Euros he will either make a run for it or send a message within twenty minutes."

"Oui, I saw that tiny instant look of panic when you said the name Helwig. So now we wait," Jean agreed.

Fifteen minutes later two encrypted messages were sent through a satellite connection and captured by Redare's men. The encryption was so complex the field software was unable to decipher it, stalling the program. It was immediately forwarded to Paris, captured so the intended receiver would not see the transmission.

Jules subconsciously checked his Rolex every few seconds, uncomfortable with the delay.

"Why don't we just take him for interrogation? He might have a tunnel or something to escape us," he said.

Redare chuckled. "You watch too many American movies my friend. No, he is waiting on orders, he is conditioned not to make any decisions on his own without consent. He is German you know.

"When my people have the encryption deciphered, we will send him a message to call directly for clarification. Then we can connect the two ends. We are pretty good at what we do, Mon Ami."

"Bien Sûr!" *Certainly !* he replied.

In forty minutes the answer was received from Paris. "The messages went to two different parties," Redare explained. "One went to a secure cell that is currently somewhere in the Washington Baltimore area, the other is super encrypted and likely belongs to the brains of the group. I was told that my staff couldn't break the second level of protection so it will take some time and possibly some unique software to process it."

"How long will that take?" Jean asked.

"Likely days, but weeks, months or never is a possibility. The process is cookbook but the recipe is in a language we never saw before. A genius at work!"

"Merde!" *Shit!* Jules complained.

"Don't worry. He will soon make a run for it because we sent a simple message. Vacate immediately! Followed by the initials, CLS. Christian Lucifer Schmitt.

"Expect to see him leaving the house within a few minutes."

Almost on cue, Gerber came out the rear of the house and placed a duffle bag in the back of an older Nissan pickup truck. He then opened the large barn, turning the cows out to pasture and hastily dumping two full bags of feed on the ground for the ducks and chickens and tossing a half dozen bales of hay into the cows' fenced pasture. He then ran to the idling truck and rapidly drove to the main road.

"Are you going to get him ?" Jean asked anxiously.

"No, we will follow at a safe distance using the tracking device we placed under the truck while he was preoccupied talking with us because he may vacate to another rat's hole so we can find out more players. But now we can examine his home once my men are positive there are no booby traps waiting to ruin our day."

Five minutes later, they entered the simple farmhouse. One of Redare's men pointed to a stairwell leading to a basement where the smell of sulfuric acid was strong. They creaked down the old stairs onto a compressed clay dirt floor basement, with fieldstone walls. A type of computer room was set up with laser printers, scanners, servers and other equipment. Most had been smashed to bits and some more critical parts dumped in a large yellow plastic vat of sulfuric acid that was hissing and popping with sulfur gas that was choking the men and burning their eyes. It was obvious that Gerber had made sure he left no evidence behind and they quickly left the house to breathe in fresh country air.

"That man was well trained and likely we will gather nothing of value from there, but you never know," Redare explained.

"You have a phone number for the US contact, so while you work on this end, we will again travel back to the US along with our American colleagues who we just left back in Paris to rest up and enjoy the city. Too bad they basically just got here and now must return. C'est la vie!"

Fifteen kilometers from the farm Gerber stopped alongside a quiet pull off by a rocky stream. He pulled his phone to retrieve the texted instruction code he had just received from Mendoza. 20041889. He swallowed hard and rubbed his face in frustration.

He pulled his cell and typed in a code, verified the command and pushed "execute." The farmhouse was no more, booby trapped, and he had just triggered its destruction.

Hands shaking, he reached under the car's dash just below the steering wheel and pulled a matchbox size tin loose, and laid it next to his lap. Small beads of sweat formed on his forehead as he contemplated his orders.

Resigned, he opened the miniature tin and pulled a small glass capsule the size of a Lima bean and rolled it around in his hand. He opened his mouth, pushed the toxic vial between his left rear molars and bit down hard, exploding the death warrant.

Forty seconds later he was dead, the code, Hitler's numeric birthday, sending him convulsing into Hell.

CHAPTER 66

Trump International 'The Old Post Office' Hotel

7 a.m. Same Day

Schmitt stepped out and walked to James' idling black Escalade. The young driver jumped from the SUV to open the second row passenger door but Schmitt waved him off, seated himself in the front row passenger seat and shook the young Haitian's hand. He then pulled an envelope from a small backpack and handed it to the man.

"Today is the last day I will need your employment as I must move on. This is the balance of what I contracted you for and a little extra for the baby's future. Thank you for your assistance," he said without emotion.

"Merci, Monsieur, you have no idea what your charter has meant to my family. I prepared my contact information for you in this envelope, you know, for the next time you are in town. Where are we going to this morning?"

"Back to Locust Point, there is something occurring there according to the news and I am worried about my Aunt and Uncle. People are going crazy."

"The Gates of Hell?"

"Perhaps, or maybe some bad sushi?" the Nazi chuckled.

"Maybe something in the water?" James postulated.

They traveled in silence from that point, no real traffic heading into Baltimore but bumper to bumper heading away from the city with multiple fights occurring as people attacked each other jamming up the busy divided highway. Schmitt noticed the young man seemed very nervous, small beads of sweat forming as he turned the temperature down on the A/C.

"How will we get back to the capital, sir? The westbound traffic is insane."

Schmitt smiled. "If this is what I think it is, I would have your wife get in a taxi and vacate to a small rural town. Then you go pick up your family and get somewhere away from here. I think this may be a plague of some sort. Get away from the coast. Maybe travel to the Blue Ridge Mountains. There is enough in that envelope to help you escape. I fear Armageddon is here."

Now the driver was speeding, disregarding the posted limits. He called his wife with his orders and it seemed she was explaining what she saw on the news and was afraid. He told her to use their GM business credit card and take an Uber out to Winchester, Virginia and find a hotel room and wait for him. He explained to Schmitt that she was crying, sobbing and very afraid, but agreed to flee the city.

"It is done, Monsieur."

"Good, you can thank me later," the Nazi said in a rare moment of compassion.

They drove into the general area of Old Locust Point and pulled over when police blocked their entry. Multiple house fires were burning and some people were wandering in what appeared to be a blind stupor, staggering and mindless.

Apparently a dumb manifestation of the viron, Schmitt thought.

"I will be leaving you now, James. Good luck to you and your family. By the way, do you have any pets – dog or cat?"

"No cat or dog but we have a parakeet. I'm sure she will bring the bird."

"Good, remember this, no contact with any dog, cat or any strange acting human.

"I am leaving you now. Bon Chance, James!"

Schmitt was wearing a Washington Redskins sweatshirt, jeans, a good Reebok running shoe, Orioles ball cap and dark reflective sunglasses. He used a small backpack to carry everything he needed to survive until either Mendoza summoned him or he flipped to the FBI. The only weapon he carried was a folding camping multi tool that had a knife along with seven other useful parts. But most important were his life protecting pills, three units, enough to last ninety days.

He walked over to the Baltimore policewoman walking the restricted taped off street and she stopped him.

"Sorry, sir, you can't enter this neighborhood or should even want to. It is chaos in there, so unless it is life or death...you want to die?" she asked rhetorically.

"Of course not!" he shot back. "But my mother is trapped in there and is on oxygen and I need to change her tank, get her hooked up to the portable and get her out before the whole neighborhood goes up in flames. She's over on Towson. My driver is going to wait on my call and then I'll wheelchair her over to wherever he is."

She reached under her Kevlar and pulled out a business card and wrote a number on the back.

"Call this number and I'll send a black and white to get you when you're ready. You need to avoid any contact and whatever you do, don't engage anyone. Just get there and get out fast. This whole neighborhood has gone insane!" She lifted the tape, letting him pass.

"Thank you, Er, Officer Ulle you are very kind!"

"Just be careful, sir."

He nearly sprinted in, observing everything that was going on. Fires, fights, panicked screams, and coagulated blood in large pools collected by the cobbled street curbs. He started taking cell phone video and photos. The deeper he went into the district, the worse it got. In twenty minutes he had had enough. He quickly reversed course to escape. He dodged affected children, men and women of all ages. It made no difference who you were, where you lived or what level you lived at. The plague reduced everyone to vicious subhuman assassins. Their brains were burning with pain and they only saw demon-like enemies.

This is only the germination, once the roots are established, this nation will collapse.

Out of the corner of his eye he caught movement, an attacker that soon had him from behind. It was an impossibly strong man who had Schmitt in a chokehold while aggressively biting down on his shoulder and scalp. He could feel warm blood running from his torn flesh and could hear the man's teeth grating down on the bone of his skull. He struggled, unable to breathe but managed to reach the knife in his right jeans pocket. Schmitt couldn't see the knife and dropped the hand he was using to try to pull off the attacker off his neck. Gasping for air, he finally sprung open the blade and thrust it into the attacker's hip near the groin, over and over again. Stick and twist, trying to hit a major vessel. No luck. He was losing consciousness and reversed the knife and folded up his arm jamming the blade into the right side of his attacker's neck twisting the blade deeply. Immediately the attacker's hands went reflectively to his painful wound and Schmitt whirled and slashed back and forth at both carotids. Blood sprayed in a crimson fountain. The man dropped to his knees, moaned, eyes dilated widely and jerked over backward hitting the ground with a thud.

Schmitt, gasping, also fell to the ground pulling deep breaths into oxygen starved lungs. He reached to his torn scalp and poked his index finger around estimating the size of the wound. It was about the size of a plum and hurt like hell.

He got up and stood over the blood covered dead man, scrutinizing the result of his creation. This man looked strangely familiar. Then it hit him.

I know him. The veterinarian. The owner of all those offices who had purchased so many thousands of doses. What was his name? Donaldson? Dennison? No, it was Donnelly, Frank Donnelly. Poor Bastard!

He pulled the card out the cop had given him and dialed the number.

"Hello, this is the man you gave the card to. My mother is unfortunately already dead and I have just been attacked by a crazy man. I am injured and need medical attention. Is that ride offer still good?"

In three minutes the patrol car pulled up and Schmitt was rushed to a nearby paramedic station. He had his evidence of his success for Mendoza. Now it was time to secure his future.

CHAPTER 67

Essex, Massachusetts

That same evening

Retired Agent Rick Sullivan was looking solemn as he got off the phone. Brad and Joseph were out on the waterside screened porch of the B&B eating some homemade chocolate cake. Joseph had a massive scoop of Edie's Vanilla ice cream on top the rich double dark chocolate layers.

"You know, you really shouldn't eat that!" Brad admonished the young Sioux.

"What in the devil are you talking about?" Joseph asked, suspecting he was being set up.

"Everyone knows, you can't have your cake and Edie's too!" Brad laughed out, nearly choking on some milk he had just swallowed.

"Good thing we're brothers, otherwise I would have to report you to Comedians Anonymous, you know, that you fell off the wagon!"

"Yeah, a covered wagon with one pain in the ass Injun' stalking my sense of humor!"

"That's senseless humor!" Joseph corrected.

Sullivan came in from his bedroom side onto the porch and likely prevented a chocolate cake food fight. He asked the obvious question.

"Is there booze in that cake or are guys just that wacky?"

"Guilty as charged," Brad replied." We are definitely wacky and it's no laughing matter."

That had them all roaring.

"Ok, Ok, I have some information and change of plans for us."

"Alright, but remember, the facts, nothing but the facts," Brad said, doing a pretty good *Dragnet,* Joe Friday impression.

That got another burst of laughter.

"Ok, here are the facts. We are to meet Fred, Jules, Jean, Kate and Tom at ten a.m. tomorrow at Logan. They're coming in on the Pasteur Jet. We are then going as a group to Baltimore where in the last six hours, all hell has broken out in some kind of End of the World scenario. Two neighborhoods are under martial law and a large portion of the population that could leave, has. The problem is the chaos is being transmitted like a disease with the affected spreading it, so it is becoming more widespread. Half of us, likely myself, Jean and Joseph will ride with the police to review the street situation. Believe it or not, in an Army HumVee, converted into a riot control vehicle. The other half will also go in an armored transport to three of the clinics that Schmitt visited, so that group is primarily in charge of back tracing Schmitt's trip and will be interviewing those people or veterinarians. That might be both dangerous and difficult. One owner is already dead, possibly infected, and he had multiple clinics so you will meet with his office manager. Jean, Fred and Jules, have postulated that this is biological warfare linked to the TriStar vaccine, so if we can prove that theory or perhaps some other agency determines it, then we will be out of the picture. Then full force of the military will descend with a scorched earth approach. They will effectively take out the affected residents and eliminate them and the diseased area with a little extra destruction for safe measure. This has the making of a gigantic cluster thing that could carve out a large portion of the original thirteen colonies. My friends at the Department of Homeland Security are estimating a maximum three-day window before it totally hits the fan. As of ten minutes ago, no one without DHS credentials can get in or out of Washington and they are creating a two mile wide secure perimeter and have shut down all roads including the outer belt beyond that two mile zone. The city is now isolated, just as it was during the Civil War."

Brad interjected, "Is it going to be safe enough for us with families to go in there?"

"Getting in and out won't be a problem and DHS wants all of us in Hazmat Level B equipment and assuming we can get into the clinics to inspect them, we should be in and out of the hazard zone in less than two hours. Then we go through decontamination and we run Schmitt down and hopefully he leads us to this Mendoza fellow. So, to answer your question, you won't be contagious and probably, relatively safe."

"Gee, that makes me feel so much better!"

"Remember, Grandfather, our ancestors, Robert and the Almighty will be looking out for us. That's better than DHS or any other governmental agency," Joseph offered.

They sat back down in the wicker rockers, contemplating the task ahead. The tree frogs were trilling, crickets chirping and the harsh squawk of the night herons was resounding in the distance. This was a place of peace and they understood that what they were experiencing at that moment could soon become an anomaly.

Joseph started softly praying ancient words just under his breath but they seemed to engulf the air. Brad felt them enter his being and it sent a shiver up his spine. Sullivan also felt power in those incantations. They listened in resolute silence.

Joseph's prayer seemed to intensify, filling the space around them but his words never rose above a whisper. That ancient power had a multiplier effect and consumed their being. Suddenly as Joseph's had words flowed, they stopped.

Sullivan crossed himself and Brad patted Joseph on the back.

The Destroyer, the evil Joseph's great grandfather predicted would always lurk, waiting for a chance to end life, had been again empowered, this time aggressively expanding that power. Joseph would have to continue to pray more timeless prayers to protect his family of friends.

CHAPTER 68

Baltimore

Dawn the next day

Smoke filled the air as police and National Guard helicopters, surveying the carnage below, zoomed to and fro across the chaotic neighborhoods. Fires had taken out over fifty stately mansions and several blocks of row houses. The injured stood at over three hundred and the total death estimate was impossible to guess because likely many died in their homes locked away from the awful street violence. Eighty-two were confirmed dead, some the infected and some simply victims of the violence, in the wrong place at the wrong time. The problem was the level of violence was exponentially increasing despite the National Guard presence and martial law being declared. Now the only ones on the streets were the diseased, mentally disconnected, attacking each other and law enforcement. The sane, unaffected, sequestered in their homes, leaving only if the threat of incineration from the fires flushed them like rats onto the streets.

Schmitt was on the tenth floor of an Inner Harbor hotel with a French name and had a bird eye's view of the fires and helicopters. He watched as large Convair 580 tanker planes swooped into the Chesapeake, filling their bellies with brine and then showering it down on areas where the edge of the fires were threatening unaffected zones. He smiled at the scene before him believing at this very time it was being repeated up and down the East Coast.

He had submitted the photos to Mendoza with the following attachment:

Mein Führer,

I hope you are well and enjoying the results of our efforts in regard to the project we started. You have the evidence that the creation will expand into new areas once the timing is correct. I was seriously injured while in pursuit of this evidence for you, but will be fine.

After Leipzig, my hope is you will take this as my expression of loyalty and allow me to continue to support our noble cause. I am ready to be a warrior for you and as your architect of the agent and its control, I can redirect my efforts into new areas that would benefit the cause. I am on the front line now and will continue to be your eyes and ears here.

I trust you will contact me.

C.L.S

Schmitt relaxed now, understanding that in the next twelve hours either he would be redeemed and elevated or likely he would be hunted. One or the other. So be it.

The maximum time he had to move out of Baltimore to a secondary location was eight hours, figuring in the time for his message to go through the encryption and filtering process. He would then wait several hours for that signal of Mendoza's intent, whether it be welcome back or goodbye — forever.

He decided to call David Gerber to see how his family was. Gerber has supposed to accept the call with a choice of three two words phrases. *Not now* —meaning he had no information to report. *Better now*— they are safe and in no danger. The last was the phrase that would signal they were not safe, captured or dead— *Not here.* Simple codes to shorten communication time to prevent detection.

The cell number rang and rang. He ended the call, waited five long minutes and resent the cell call. This time it was answered on the ninth ring cycle. Schmitt waited for one of the codes but received a different greeting.

"Hallo?"

Immediately, Schmitt ended the call. The phone protocols were precise and never were violated. Gerber was compromised, so Schmitt needed to leave immediately. He packed his new small duffle style backpack and headed out of the room to the elevator. He saw a housekeeping trash chute, took the SIM card out of the phone, and dumped the phone body down the chute. The card would be flushed down a lobby men's room toilet and he would head out to leave the city.

Where was it James told his wife to flee to? Winchester? He needed to pick up a burner phone so he found a Walgreens Pharmacy and bought two. Activation was simple for the basic service on one and on the other phone he purchased a data plan with an Application package that included Google Earth and Navigation. That one was only to be used for data. His map to Winchester, Virginia.

He walked to an outdoor bus stop bench and pulled a business card out of his wallet. He dialed the listed number.

The young Haitian answered on the third ring.

"James?" Schmitt asked.

"Oui?"

"This is Ernst Straub and if you are willing, I need your services again."

"Monsieur Straub, how nice to hear from you. Because of you my family is safe and secure. We will be eternally grateful to you. Merci!"

"You are welcome. Are you in Winchester now?" "We are, I just arrived last evening. Where are you?"

"I am in Baltimore. I was attacked after you dropped me off and almost was killed but I am better now but need to get out of these populated areas. I have need of your service again."

"Absolutely!" came the excited reply.

"Excellent. Then I will take a Greyhound Bus to Arlington. I leave in two hours and will arrive supposedly in three hours but with all the road closures I could be late. Baltimore is in chaos."

"No problem, I am available for anything you need. There is a very nice B&B about two blocks from where we are renting an apartment. If you wish, I can book you in there."

"Thank you, that would be very nice. I only don't know how long I may need it."

"I will book you in for several days and have them give you the option to extend on a daily basis. I will warn you that prices may be steep because of what is going on in Washington and Baltimore."

Schmitt laughed.

"Money is no obstacle. You soon will be able to start your own livery business. Serve me well and you will not be disappointed."

With that the German ended the call. He would have to check with Mendoza using the burner phone in eight hours. Gerber was likely dead as he had, as all the new Führer's followers, committed himself to never be taken alive. No, Gerber was dead, and unless they were able to trace his phone in microseconds, Schmitt was still safe.

Safe to watch a great nation fall to her knees and beg for his deliverance!

CHAPTER 69

Mendoza's Compound

Bariloche, Argentina

The weather in the far Southern Hemisphere was the mirror image of the Northern climate on a monthly basis. Bariloche was in the Southern tail of Argentina separated from Chile by the Andes Mountains and its climate was a reflection of the latitude and proximity to fronts of Pacific weather crossing the mountains with clouds and misty wet days. It never was too warm or too cold. Something Mendoza's father Adolph treasured as Alpine like, but for Mendoza, he preferred to be somewhere where the days and nights were near equal in length and the climate warm and toasty. Perhaps he would move the White House to Miami and rule the world from there.

He had just reviewed Schmitt's message and viewed his graphic videos of the violence on the streets of Baltimore. Mendoza had been monitoring CNN and knew generally what was manifesting in the United States and so far the Baltimore explosions of violence was the only gestated plague birthing on its due date. He questioned why? Without a nationwide disease explosion overwhelming all the infrastructure and public services, he would not have the political leverage to negotiate the terms of surrender. He decided he needed Schmitt's intellect and resourcefulness to stay ahead of the massive effort that would be brought forth against them. Stockpiles of the viron were stored on every continent except Antarctica in enough doses to infect ten percent of the population by several means: aerosols by drones, food contamination, direct infection by injection or surface contamination were some of the possible infective methods. He had developed a container designed to look like common disinfectant cleaner wipes or hand sanitizers so he could have agents wipe down public doors, stairwell handholds, subway grabs, grocery carts, restroom doors and school bus seats and after a couple of days, the exposed would be infected and out on the streets, spreading the viron plague from violent street interactions. If the rabies connection was eventually discovered, then these other sources of infection could be summoned up quickly with a quick series of execution codes. You always needed a backup plan and since the pathogen was demonstrating at some level its efficacy, Mendoza was ready and able to continue spreading the viron by alternative means if the primary attack failed to manifest the degree of chaos he desired. Schmitt developed the primary occult form of infection with the viron hidden in a rabies vaccine to prevent a disease that was meant to create the panic that would assure a controlled distribution of the viron into population and power centers. These were plans to cripple the United States so completely that its leaders would beg Mendoza for the treatment and exchange control for survival. Without the cure, the major population centers would eat their own, consuming all life until only an underground population existed, surviving by avoiding contact with anyone else. Truly survival of the fittest.

Those that fit into Mendoza's plans.

According to protocol, Mendoza needed to send Schmitt a message through his intermediary, and then through a series of contacts explaining his desire to continue working with the scientific genius. The message was to be encrypted to only be deciphered and delivered by the final contact and then only in the presence of Schmitt.

Mendoza executed the series of commands to make contact. Now he would wait and plan the next step.

He walked out to the courtyard and started his methodical pacing, thirty-three perfect paces back and forth stepped off precisely, exactly.

His military style, spit shined black leather riding boots counted off the paces as the hard leather heels struck the cobbled ground. Thirty-three up and thirty-three back, he walked with mindless precision with head lowered and hands folded together behind his back. Thirty-three — a magical number representing the year, 1933, when his father finally ascended to power.

When would his magical number be revealed?

CHAPTER 70

Logan International Airport, Boston

Dawn the next morning

Tired, they rode silently to the airport in a pounding rainstorm. Sullivan had updated them on the overnight reports from DHS and his friends at the FBI and it appeared the initial wave of street violence was slowing as anyone who wasn't ill, was in virtual lockdown inside their home. The police and National Guardsmen were under strict orders to shoot to kill after six of their brothers and sisters were KIA. The television, radio and internet reverse 911 calls repeated warnings that anyone venturing onto the street would be shot. The warnings were given in English, Spanish and a half dozen other languages, nonstop. The death toll stood at six law enforcement and military, three hundred seventeen confirmed attackers and their prey, with over one thousand cluttering city hospitals, each one, whether it be child, adult or senior were shackled to their hospital beds. One by one they were becoming clinical and succumbing at an accelerating rate. All hospital personnel were in advanced protective gear which helped, but here or there, a staff member would suddenly exhibit bizarre behavior and attack patients or other staff. One woman had given birth after becoming clinical and that tiny premature infant was in a NICU isolation room. So far that baby was struggling but was expected to live. Sullivan didn't sugarcoat anything and Brad and Joseph rode silently, eyes closed while awake, their brains trying to understand what they were heading into.

The traffic was heavy when they approached Boston as the morning rush hour push of commuters washed in like the morning tide into the city. Sullivan reached into the Yukon's large utility between seat box and pulled out a blue police strobe flasher, rolled down his window and placed the magnetic light on the roof of the large SUV. Traffic began to part as they saw the flasher and suddenly they were slipping through at a good rate.

"I bet they would really move if you had a siren," Brad said a little sarcastically.

"You mean like this?" Sullivan shot back as he flipped a switch.

The piercing siren seemed to catapult them forward but in reality it was only the other road warriors, slowing to clear a path. "I'm surprised they let you have all that nifty stuff—you know, being retired."

Sullivan smiled.

"The badge says retired, not dead. At least not dead yet. You may yet appreciate my decades of experience as we see what this soggy day brings. At least the fires may be less of an issue."

"After we get to Logan, how long to Baltimore? I mean we pick them up and then it's what, at least six or seven hours even with the siren blaring. I think you keep Brad in here with the siren running for all that time he is going to be confessing to all kind of closed case crimes. Could be the high water mark for your career," Joseph teased.

"No, the high point of my career was when I took your group seriously when we met prior to that last Inauguration ceremony. I went up one full grade in pay and with my retirement that translates to more money in my checking account each and every month. And just so you know, the Coast Guard is flying us right to the Inner Harbor. We split up from there and meet up later for dinner and group analysis."

"Gee, Brad, more group therapy!" Joseph teased.

"Well, since Lakota blood runs in my veins, why don't we call this a powwow ?"

"Man, you two are a regular Abbott and Costello!" Sullivan joked.

"Or Martin and Lewis, my great grandfather's favorite comedy team," Joseph added.

"The guys that explored the Louisiana Purchase with Sacajawea were comedians?" Brad hit back.

Joseph capped it off.

"No, my shiny domed brother. That was Lewis and Clark. I prefer to think of us as classics like Desi and Lucy and guess who USED to be a redhead!"

"Whipper snapper!" Brad laughed.

Sullivan pulled into the same secure area they had left from two days before. TSA Agent Donovan was waiting with the cart and started to weave in and out of an overflow of passengers in the terminal. Sullivan pointed to the density of people and asked, "Why are there so many people in the airport this morning?"

Donovan had the answer. "We are getting a lot of the diverted traffic from both Washington airports and Baltimore because that entire area has been shut off since eight this morning. Nobody in, nobody out. The flights are diverting to other airports but they will not allow them to go to New York. The word is the Federal Government is taking over the UN and moving to the city. A temporary center of government until this blows over and probably to reassure Wall Street."

"So is that why we are coming in the backdoor of Baltimore?" Brad inquired.

"Yes, you will land on the Chesapeake and be motored to shore, with your military escort to protect you, but your time will be severely restricted because also since eight this morning, that whole area is under strict quarantine. That's why your colleagues are flying in here instead of us flying down to Baltimore to meet them, they can't land there. My mission is to limit your exposure on the ground, expedite any airport security issues and hopefully help you learn something of value to narrow the search for Schmitt. They made me a type of concierge for you," Donovan answered.

"You seem to know a lot about what we are doing," Sullivan told his friend's son.

"My title is a little fuzzy but I am to travel with you, to help if needed but I am also assisting because we are evacuating several government VIPs trapped at the airport. My uniform should help me get them out a little easier, plus I am carrying a letter, really a pass from the President, so I am your Carte Blanche to get you anything you need. That pass will be priceless because nobody trusts anyone right now!

"Because of the quarantine, you guys, and Doctors LeClerc and DuBois, Group A, will be doing the general evaluation of ground conditions and a quick drive through and then you will visit Johns Hopkins Hospital to evaluate the patients under care, both the injured and affected. Then a trip to the hospital morgue where you will pick up all the blood, tissue and culture samples the CDC requested. Group B will only be able to visit one veterinary hospital, Pet Care Plus, because so far all the rest of the clinics we feel Schmitt visited based on his car's GPS data, have had no staff affected although several have been burned out of their homes. The clinic you will visit was owned with a number of sites by Dr. Frank Donnelly, who did become infected along with ninety percent of his staff. Donnelly is now dead along with the majority of the staff and their families. You are to meet with his office manager who lives directly next door to where she was employed. She will slip out the back of her place and into the clinic from the rear, protected from the street. We will call her just before the meeting and afterward meet with the rest of the group at Johns Hopkins. Any questions?" Sullivan explained.

"Where will we go afterward, back to Boston?" Brad asked Sullivan.

"No, we are going to Columbus to The Ohio State University and wait on Dr. Fred's analysis of the tissues and then hopefully he can define the pathogen and tie it back to Jean's theory on the contamination of the vaccines from TriStar. Then we have to come up with a reason why that facility was destroyed and if they were producing the bioweapon with or without their actual knowledge. That could explain why they were attacked as a way to cover the production records and other evidence of involvement," Sullivan answered.

"How long in Columbus does Fred think it will take? I may want to head home for a few days and I think Tom and Kate will also want to see Bobbie and Jed," Brad asked.

"You will have to ask Fred but my guess we might be in quarantine for two or three days unless they feel the protective gear you will use in Baltimore was adequate protection," Sullivan answered.

"You better stay put and hope Fred finds a fast answer. I wouldn't want to have to shoot you like Old Yella when you start foaming at the mouth," Joseph joked.

They continued to move though a group of travelers that were obviously distressed, standing in long lines trying to reconnect cancelled flights to Washington and Baltimore. One woman was screaming hysterically about her cat that probably had no food or water. No one knew for sure if they could get home or even had a home.

Donovan got them to the tarmac where a large red and white MH-60 Jayhawk Coast Guard Rescue Helicopter sat ready for takeoff, rotor spinning lazily. The entourage from Paris was already onboard and in minutes the friends were reunited.

The large copter lifted off and headed south at an incredible rate, racing toward those flames of Hell that were waiting to greet them and maybe keep them for a while.

CHAPTER 71

Walmart Super Center

Richmond Highway, Arlington/ Alexandria Virginia/ Noon

Schmitt stood just inside the exit side of the massive retail store protected from the pouring rain. Thunder shook the building and flashes of lightning brightly lit up the parking lot like someone was snapping a gigantic photo of the people running for their lives to keep from getting soaked or electrocuted. The stream of customers was steady and regular as citizens purchased food and supplies in anticipation of possible evacuation orders. The shopping carts were all being used in the store or scattered around the parking area as people filled their cars and left the carts right where they emptied them. A young man in a yellow poncho struggled to keep up with returning the wire carts to the storage areas. It was a losing proposition.

Schmitt stood close to the door and watched for James' black Escalade. The glass was steamed up from the high humidity and the Nazi strained for a better view, anxiously waiting to be picked up. So far, the Haitian was seventy-five minutes late and Schmitt had loitered in the store vestibule for nearly two hours and was beginning to worry that he was not going to be picked up. Then he saw the Cadillac pull up and stop by the automatic doors. He grabbed the umbrella he had purchased from the store and stepped out and got into the second row passenger side seat.

"Bonjour, my young friend. I trust you had an uneventful journey?"

"Bonjour, Monsieur Straub. I apologize, I am always early, never late, but the traffic was horrible and there were a number of weather-related accidents and two detours due to some flooding. I think the world has gone mad."

"That, James, is perhaps a perfect description of what we are experiencing. Insanity."

"I think I will take a different route to Winchester with your permission. I want to travel south for a short distance toward Richmond, then west to the Blue Ridge Parkway which will get us to Winchester a little later but safely. My wife prepared a picnic lunch for us which I guess will now be a dinner which we can eat at one of the scenic overlooks on the Parkway. I even found you two bottles of Bitburger, if you enjoy beer."

"Of course I like beer, it is the mother's milk of Germany!"

The traffic improved as they left the congested Northern Virginia suburbs of Washington and soon were on a two-lane winding road heading north and west.

"I am grateful you had us leave DC because our friends are telling us that people are acting in bizarre ways, fighting and even the so-called normal people are near rioting, demanding answers and a way to escape the city. All those cell phone videos from Baltimore that are being posted are scaring people to death. It is very, very bad in my old neighborhood. Even the police are refusing to get involved now."

"Sorry for your troubles, James, but I am a scientist by trade and my analysis and instincts is this will get much worse before things settle down. I am famished, how long before we can stop?"

James pushed his navigation screen a couple of times.

"My very nice deluxe navigation system indicates about ten miles to a picnic rest area. Less than fifteen minutes."

They pulled into the secluded rest area with large oak trees and giant black pines. The ground was littered with a layer of pine needles and acorns and the air was scented with a clean piney smell.

James cleared a table and laid down two towels to cover the damp benches. He then pulled a medium sized cooler from the cargo area of the large SUV.

"I hope you don't mind the food selection. My wife prepared a variety of cold sausages, cheeses, pickles, heavy dark bread, fruit and an apple strudel she baked for you. I hope you are alright with that."

"Wunderbal!" *Wonderful!*

They enjoyed the food, Schmitt drinking the beer, James, iced tea.

"I am expecting an important call in ten minutes, is it alright that we rest here till I get it? Won't take long," James requested.

As they waited in the isolated part of the rest area, whitetail deer appeared out of the shadows, unafraid and looking for a handout. Schmitt watched, hungry for the venison he enjoyed regularly in Germany. James' phone then buzzed loudly and he answered, listening without reply to a message. Still listening, he stood up and doing as he was directed pulled a Smith and Wesson M&P Shield 9mm compact pistol from under his jacket and pointed it directly at Schmitt's forehead. Schmitt froze, staring down the abbreviated barrel of the weapon.

"Oui, Oui, I understand," he acknowledged the caller and ended the call, pushing the phone into his jacket.

"I apologize for the charade, Monsieur *Schmitt,* but our benefactor has unique methods of doing business. Every order must be followed without question, every task completed effectively and those who are traitors or incompetent eliminated. Simple but effective.

"I am part of the party, even with my atypical Aryan bloodlines, I assure you I am seven eighths pure blood and one part contamination. I am the great grandson of a top leader of the Third Reich, Artur Axmann who was, as you know, in charge of Hitler Youth. A most important position as all those boys became men that bled and died for the Motherland. My ancestors fled to Argentina but then left when the Mossad closed in. They settled in Costa Rica where my great grandfather met my Haitian great grandmother. They had two children and then diluted the Haitian blood by importing other true Aryans. The same with the next generation, my parents. All those years, they only produced male heirs. My father was the last male parent heir and he died when I was a baby, but my Mama still lives in Costa Rica. I am linked to the party genetically but assure you despite my complexion, I am as committed to our cause as anyone ever has been. Also you should know, I am a pretty good actor, am I not, Monsieur Schmitt?"

He put the gun down and placed it back in the concealed holster.

"I am confused," Schmitt said, thinking the worst, "who is your boss and what is going to happen now?"

"Your boss and my boss are the same. It is destiny of our forefathers to control the world through the blood of one man. But to answer your question directly, David Gerber was my only named contact. I was recruited to be eyes and ears on politicians and their often alcohol loosened tongues or sexual dalliances that might provide a blackmail opportunity. So, I wait outside hotels and watering holes for the politicians and have developed a very nice list of wayward judges and legislators. For citizens that supposedly uphold the values of a nation, they hold very few personal values. Gerber arranged your credentials and itinerary to escape Europe, so I was assigned to watch you and assist you in anything you needed."

"So, why the gun pointed at my head?"

James smiled wildly showing his brilliantly perfect white teeth. "You passed the loyalty make-up exam my friend. Had you failed, we would not be having this conversation as I would have pulled that trigger without question. You however have been reborn and now you are my boss."

"Now what?"

"We travel on to Winchester which David had told me was my prearranged liaison point. Evidently, there are over eight hundred of our political persuasion embedded within ten miles of there. I suspect there must be at least one good German restaurant in the area."

James' phone signaled a text.

It read: *17X1.*

"The message is from a friend in the BND. 17 X 1. Seventeen, Gerber is dead, the X. One, a suicide while he was being pursued. I suspect that now we will receive new orders."

"So, are we still going on to Winchester?" Schmitt asked.

"Our orders haven't changed yet. So, yes, we continue on to Winchester."

"I am looking forward to meeting your wife and baby," Schmitt said trying to be cordial.

"I have no wife or child. I am married to our cause."

Damn. He is a good actor!

CHAPTER 72

Baltimore

Late afternoon

The Coast Guard pilot came in low over the sea quarantine blockade of Baltimore Harbor and made a pass over the Locust Point neighborhood and by the burned out buildings and vacated streets. There was no life on the streets in the original burned out zones and the cordoned areas were delineated by police and military vehicles with flashing emergency lights. The copter then made passes back and forth over the city proper and again there were no signs of normal life. The city was in shutdown.

No one said a word as they looked down at essentially an assassination of a city. Sullivan offered his opinion.

"I don't see a good reason now to visit at street level. The risk benefit is too high and there is probably nothing more of value to see. So how about we have the pilot drop a minimum number crew to visit the veterinary clinic, I think there is a soccer field just about three blocks away so we can have you picked up there by the armored transport and then you can get to that office safely. The rest of us will go on to Johns Hopkins, walk through a couple of wards and go to the morgue. I think Jules, Jean, Kate and Tom are most suited to visit the clinic and interview that office manager. When you are finished you can meet us at the hospital and then we will move on to Columbus."

Everyone was in agreement. The big helicopter swung around and in one minute was hovering above the high school soccer field creating a dust storm while they waited for the armored transportation. It arrived shortly and the pilot put down the big mechanical bird.

They waited while Kate called, confirming the meeting. The woman was already in the office, had been all morning. They each put on a respirator shield mask and nitrile gloves and then left the copter and ran over to the transport. The pilot lifted up just as they got in the National Guard vehicle.

"My name is Dr. Kate Vensky-O'Dell, this is my husband Dr. Tom O'Dell and these are our colleagues from Paris, Dr. Jules LeClerc and Dr. Jean DuBois. How are you today?" she said shaking hands of the soldiers.

"Not bad except we are patrolling Hades and I mean that with all sincerity. I'm Sargent Beth West and my copilot is Sargent Bill Rector. Our gunner is Corporal Red Rouge. Yeah, don't ask, just call him Double R like the rest of us.

"Some background on us; we are the National Guard, your neighbors in uniform. I am a florist from Annapolis, Bill teaches high school sciences, and Double R sells insurance for a living and has an agency just inside the cordoned zone so he will be one busy guy when we end this thing. Just so you know, you will be passing some bagged bodies covered with ice waiting to be processed. Thank God there is a fishing industry here with the capability to produce tons of ice.

"Here are the rules. You don't leave this vehicle till we tell you to. You keep your mask on when outside this vehicle. Wear gloves and if you feel the need to vomit, then give us a signal and we will get you a bag. Do not and I repeat do not barf in this vehicle or in your mask because we do not have but one extra. Questions?"

"Are you really a florist?" Tom joked.

"She's the one who pulls the thorns off the roses. Only she does it with her teeth, right, Sarge?" Double R replied.

"Right, and then I store them in my cheek like a wad of chew so I can spit them into your sorry ass!"

They laughed, a good stress reliever under the extreme circumstances. The trip to the clinic was two minutes and they passed six piles of melting ice. It was a somber reminder of what had been going on the last thirty-six hours.

Kate prayed silently for each person they passed but lost it when they passed a pair of plastic 'Hot Wheels' tricycles with bloodied superhero helmets laying scattered on the ground.

The clinic, a large converted drug store, was a mostly bricked building with glass blocked accent windows. It was modern and clean with converted automatic doors in a double vestibule set up. The office manager stood between the double doors, key in hand. As they approached she unlocked the outside doors.

"Hi, I'm Debbie Vrable, the general manager for Pet Care Plus. I also am the office manager of this location."

Kate went through the introductions and they entered the reception area and then Vrable's office. She had laid out copies of all the invoices for the last year from TriStar.

"Here is everything I have related to TriStar. As you can see we used a bunch of their products but over here are the invoices specifically you wanted on the TriRab product. Doc was a stickler on keeping good records and as you can see I did also. I have copies of the CDC reporting sheets with the vial peel off labels along with the client animal information. The last sheets from the final doses we received are separate and over here because I hadn't scanned them into my computer yet to email them to Atlanta. I don't have one unaccounted for dose including the doses he gave the staff on the last day we had product, maybe forty-eight hours ago."

Jules asked the obvious question, "Those last doses, when were they received?"

"We got the last shipment about a day before we ran our marathon vaccine push of those last five thousand doses. In one extremely long day, our offices inoculated about four thousand eight hundred customer's cat and dogs and Doc gave two hundred doses to staff for their pets."

"What about the Emergency Cease and Desist order the CDC emailed to clinic owners not to use any vaccine received from TriStar?

That was sent right after the company was attacked by terrorists and you were prohibited from administering any more of their product or even to open the shipping boxes. That was a crucial order. Didn't you see that order?" Kate asked.

"I didn't. Anything like that would be emailed directly to Dr. Donnelly or sent to him through the USPS. A physical letter I would file, an email, only if he printed it or forwarded it to me. Are you telling me that those last doses were not supposed to be used?"

"Oui, Madame," Jules answered, "we feel that those last vials were contaminated with some sort of bioweapon and all this death and destruction around the city is the result of the administration of that vaccine."

"Christ!" she exclaimed.

Jean explained more.

"This neighborhood seems to be the primary focal point of the problem. It would also appear every other veterinary facility heeded the order and didn't give even one dose of those last shipments. Is it possible to get into Dr. Donnelly's email?"

"Sure, you can have a look." She typed a series a series of commands into her desktop computer.

"He used the dumbest passwords," she said, "this last one was makemerichnow96. Ninety-six is the year he graduated from University of Pennsylvania. Here it is, marked urgent from the CDC. It is in his read file, so yes, he got it but never mentioned it to me or anyone else. Why would he do that?"

"He got greedy," Tom replied before the others could. "Greed, pure and simple and now he is responsible for thousands of deaths, including his own, and for the unleashing of a pathogen that potentially could destroy this city forever."

"Madame Vrable, would you be so kind as to provide me with a copy of those administrated vaccine sheets so we can check it against a list of the dead. Also a list of your employees so we can see if any have been exposed or infected."

"Sure. As far as staff is concerned I am sorry to say over one hundred dead so far including one family of six. She had four dogs and three cats."

"How about you, Madame Vrable. Do have a vaccinated pet?"

"No, my Sally is a twenty-two year old cat and would never leave the house so I saw no reason to give it, thank God!" She printed the list for them with tears in her eyes.

"All this because Doc wanted to make a few more bucks? He didn't need the money, he just liked feeling important, needed."

"Don't we all, Madame?" Jules replied as they started to leave.

Kate had a thought.

"Do you still have the SHARPS containers you used during the vaccine clinic? I think maybe we can check the used syringes for pathogens."

"Yes, and Doc kept a container for the empty vials also. You can have one of each."

"Superrr...." Jules exclaimed, really rolling his r's.

Just then Double R was at the door pounding hard. Vrable let him in. "Come on, we got to go!" he shouted. "They are going to nuke this area with a lethal foam in eighteen hours. We have to go door to door and evacuate the healthy and quarantine the docile affected at Camden Yards baseball park. Any violent affected are already under a shoot to kill order. God help us!"

"Madame Vrable," Jules offered, "why don't you go get your cat into a carrier and leave with us. Corporal, get her that last mask and gloves please."

They got into the transport and weaved through the decimation that once was a vibrant Baltimore neighborhoods, finding their way to Johns Hopkins Hospital.

The soldiers pulled to a rear loading dock area of the hospital and entered an Emergency receiving area after large rolling metal doors pulled up, exposing a cavernous storage area with pallets of supplies stacked on large metal shelving.

After the door closed, Sargent West let them remove their masks and get out of the transporter. Debbie Vrable went off with Sargent Rector to be evacuated out of Baltimore and an employee working the area showed them to a set of elevators.

Soon they were in a private staff only cafeteria area and lounge. Brad, Sullivan, Donovan, Fred and Joseph were eating dinner along

With a military officer. Joseph stood as they arrived and offered his seat to Kate.

The officer was a DHS assigned Army Lt. Colonel. He smiled and introduced himself.

"Believe it or not," he started, "my name is George Allen Custer, no relation to the Little Bighorn Custer, but if I had a dollar for every time I was asked that, I would have a nice little nest egg!

"I am a Medical Doctor with a specialty in Forensic Epidemiology and I was extremely pleased to find out Dr. Vensky-O'Dell holds a similar veterinary specialty degree. So, let me fill you in on the situation.

"So far we have not identified a causative agent but the CDC and Dr. Garrett will have unlimited resources available for them, except time. We just pushed back the time for decontamination of Zone A, the outbreak area, and the ten city blocks beyond that perimeter, to forty-eight hours so we can be sure it really can't be avoided. That reprieve came directly from the White House, otherwise DHS would be have the Air Force loading the bombers right now."

"Lethal Foam, exactly what is that?" Jean asked.

"So the cat is out of the bag?" Custer replied, a little surprised. "This is not to be repeated outside our group. Lethal Foam Containment was developed to restrict spread of highly dangerous pathogens without having to nuke an area to cinders."

"Exactly how does the foam work?" Brad asked.

"Think of the expanding foam products used to caulk or insulate walls. Then imagine that product on steroids. Basically, we developed a dense foam product, compressed a hundred thousand times more than the stuff in the can, containing several viral, bacterial, fungal and aerobic organism lethal agents that will basically sterilize its contact area as soon as it is activated. It is dropped as a styrofoam packing size peanut that is very dense and heavy, spread almost like crop dusting, except they are like dropping driveway gravel. Once adequate coverage is obtained, a treated water wash with a pH of seven or below is sprayed over the material causing each pellet to expand to the size of a concrete truck. It's an exothermic reaction and not only are the chemicals lethal but the heat released is equivalent to a pizza oven set on high for sixty seconds."

"So, it's just like a grade school science project making a baking soda - vinegar volcano?" Tom questioned.

"Basically yes, but like I said, on steroids. The foam will persist for two days, then we spray on an enzyme catalyst and it breaks down over a week or so. Afterward, you would never even know it was used."

Joseph was angry. "Except no birds, bugs or babies. You are a sick bunch of bastards. Talk about a Destroyer, I thought we were the good guys."

"We are. If this is not contained then evil *has* won. In certain cases, extreme measures are required to protect the majority. Often the cure is as bad as the disease. You unfortunately only have forty-eight hours to prevent the release of that agent."

"Then I suggest," Sullivan interjected, "we get off our butts and find those answers."

Jules, Jean, Kate and Tom each wolfed down a sandwich and cookies. Custer led them down to the isolation wards in the second sub ground level, just above the morgue. It was a converted laundry and sixties civil defense shelter that had been developed for the next pandemic, which till this point had never occurred. There were fifty ten by ten foot self-contained mini isolation rooms in ten parallel rows of five. The area between each row was a decontamination zone, in effect a prep and prepare zone, to service those individual isolates. Two double sized rooms were used for families with small children. They stood outside the wards in a kind of a television director's room with fifty room monitoring video screens, and layers of vital sign monitors. Seven technicians sat in a semicircle, recording data and barking orders to the treatment staff. Four screens indicated flatlined monitors but the chief technician explained they had nowhere to move the dead to. The morgue was overflowing and the CDC had not yet prescribed a way to store, move or dispose of the dead.

They then walked down one floor to the morgue and donned protective gear. The brief visit was so they could visualize how the affected appeared after death.

Thomas Brown was a giant of a man, the morgue technician who assisted Custer in selecting the bodies to view. Each had a painfully contorted visage but each had a fraction of a smile that seemed to suggest death was welcomed. Custer then had a specific body he wanted them to see.

"Here lays your villain," he indicated as Brown effortlessly slid the gurney from the refrigerated crypt, "Dr. Frank Donnelly."

They peered at him somewhat out of disgust but also with pity. A colleague that was a modern version of Typhoid Mary.

"He cut his own throat?" Joseph asked.

"No, he attacked a man with a blade of some sort and that man, a German, was able to wrestle that instrument around and did a number on the Doc," the large black man explained. "I was in ER when the guy who killed him was brought in for a bad scalp laceration. He was a mess, blood everywhere and I know I wasn't supposed to but I got a picture of him before and after he was cleaned up and sutured. Weird, I know, but I felt compelled to do it."

Jean asked, "Perhaps you were compelled by the Almighty God. Can we see those images on your phone please."

Brown said, "Better yet, I'll send them into our clinical database on Donnelly and you can see them as attachments in high definition."

In half a minute Brown had the image of a bloodied man on the screen, only his eyes clear of crimson. The second image was the cleaned up and sutured patient. Jules and Jean studied the images carefully.

"I might be wrong but I think that man is Christian Schmitt. What name is his chart under?" Jules asked.

"The name I have is Ernst Straub, German National. Not Schmitt," Brown noted.

"We are going to need a copy of those photos so I can forward them to Redare for analysis. I think this is our man. The question is why would he be here in the middle of all this chaos, risking his life?" Jules asked.

"Maybe he wanted to meet with Donnelly or like a pyromaniac, witness his creation. That still doesn't help us with the question, *Where is Mendoza, and who exactly is he?*" Kate answered.

Joseph was silent, clearly thinking and trying to find something that would make sense.

"I think after we make it to Port Columbus Airport," he explained, "I need to return to Fort Peck for a couple of days. Unlike with our search for Berhetzel, right now I feel totally disconnected. I need to reconnect to the ancestors and Great Grandfather. We are missing something and he will guide us."

"Ok, then I will arrange for you, Brad, Kate and Tom to head home for a few days. No reason for you to hang around Columbus anyway," Sullivan agreed.

Kate and Tom were both visually relieved and Brad was smiling at the thought of seeing his family.

They were now scattering, leaving the infant Armageddon still nursing on the teat of Baltimore. They had forty-six hours to find the answer.

CHAPTER 73

Fort Peck Indian Reservation

The next evening

There were only a couple of hours before the sun would be setting and Joseph needed to get out and ride Wakinyan and this was a perfect evening for a trail ride. There were only a few high thin clouds and the wind was a gentle cool breeze; the prairie grasses would be moving in soothing waves and the animals that existed in and on them would be active with the late day cooling.

The horse was excited, vocalizing impatiently when Joseph entered the small barn. Billy Eagles had been caring for the horse and his new stablemate 'Bob', a Paint miniature horse. The small horse kept the larger Wakinyan instincts to be part of a herd satisfied without requiring a lot of extra feed or care.

Their pre- ride routine was more of ritual than a chore. The horse was curried and brushed to remove the dust and loose hair not only so the gelding would look his best but so that when the horse heated up and lathered sweat, there would not be stream dirt down his whithers or crud on the saddle blanket and tack.

Joseph cinched up his old butt worn saddle and did a quick mental checklist. He grabbed his hoof pick and cleaned each foot, checking each steel shoe. Billy had cleaned the stall earlier in the day and picked

Wakinyan's feet clean so Joseph's inspection was done more to satisfy that checklist. Just like an airplane pilot's preflight routine, the safety of the ride to both rider and horse was critical.

Wakinyan hadn't been saddled in nearly three weeks, so Joseph knew they would have to take it slow. The horse was an athlete but slightly out of shape from lack of work. Too much, too hard, too fast might injure the horse causing muscle damage.

As usual when Joseph mounted the horse, he could feel the energy stored in the animal, almost like riding a giant battery. Also as part of his routine, the young Lakota prayed, his words a mixture of old prayers and new pleas to the ancients to open his mind and his friends' to find this 'Destroyer'. It was a prayer he could have uttered anywhere, but here, on this land, the spirits moved with the wind, the grass, the clouds and the animals. Here the words were magnified and empowered.

Wakinyan was ready to go. He shook his head up and down and shuffled his feet in anticipation. Joseph smiled, understanding the horse's soul was to run, with a rider or not. He leaned over, his body over the horse's strong neck and as he had done countless rides before, gave the horse permission to move on.

"Let's go find Custer," he whispered in the horse's right ear. That was the signal the horse was waiting for.

Joseph held the horse at a fast walk for the first mile or so then on at a medium canter. Wakinyan weaved himself carefully up the trail they had taken so many times before. A loop to the west was followed, then north, west again before heading south and slightly east. It was a trail they had followed on moonless nights or in blinding snowstorms. He reached the end of this modified fish hook trek and went north to a bluff overlooking a vast span of grass. A replacement herd of mixed Angus and Hereford cattle grazed peacefully while calves with white faces and black bodies of various sizes pranced in play in a kind of bovine game of tag. It was a far cry from the carnage of nearly three years before that he witnessed when Berhetzel's device had slaughtered all the females of that herd. He looked on through his spotting scope and was satisfied that for now, this peaceful place was safe from evil.

They turned to leave, the sun now on their right, disappearing slowly into the west. A fading ball of yellow and orange lowered, promising that it would rise again at dawn tomorrow and then repeat its vanishing act, just as it had for countless eons. Something most took for granted.

The trail was near invisible as they moved forward reversing their trip in. Wakinyan didn't need to have light, his instinct and eyes moved them securely forward and as they neared the barn, Joseph gave the horse his head and that last three hundred meters was a joyful burst of energy that fed both their souls.

Joseph rubbed down his riding partner, checked his feet and fed him a much appreciated small meal of grain. 'Bob' complained wanting to be part of the fun, his small stature belying his full equine spirit.

Joseph put the barn lights on the timer so they would go off in forty-five minutes, not that the animals would care one way or the other. Their friend was home and that was all that mattered.

The young Indian crunched the cinder path back to the double wide trailer that had belonged to his great grandfather. It was where he was raised by his great grandfather after his father died, drunk driving on an icy road. This was where he learned to appreciate their culture by his grandfather's invoking the legends and truths about the Lakota's history and culture. This was his inheritance, both physical and spiritual.

He went to the tiny kitchen and poured a tall lemonade over ice and made three cheese sandwiches with the sharp French Dijon mustard that Jules had sent as part of a Christmas Gourmet gift basket last winter. The cheese was Wisconsin cheddar, the bread a whole grain, but they were only the palate for the fine mustard. Joseph grabbed a bag of wavy potato chips and pushed out the old creaking screen door onto the weathered wooden deck which faced west into the faintest remaining rays of sun on the horizon. The young Lakota placed three apple wood logs and two honey locust wood pieces in the open metal fire pit on top of a compressed sawdust and wax fire starter and lit it with a Zippo lighter. Soon he had a good fire dancing skyward. Joseph sat back in his grandfather's old handmade Adirondack chair and put his feet up on a chunk of tree stump, which had served as a foot stool for nearly forty years. He looked down at his worn ranch boots, between bites, and made a mental note to go down to the general store and buy a new pair; these were nearly worn out after three years of hard use. He dreaded the thought of breaking in a new pair of boots.

The fire danced with warm hypnotic waves and Joseph drifted into a deep sleep.

"You really don't have a lot of time left to be daydreaming or night dreaming, boy," came the resolute voice of his great grandfather Nelson.

"Your friends in Columbus are at great risk. You need to warn them. The Destroyer and his angels are on the move and will do anything to stop those whose faith is with the Creator. One who is with them is the Destroyer's agent. You must call Kate and put up a shield of protection against these evildoers. Remember the lesson of the Tanaka and prepare to do battle. *Wake up, Akicita!"*

Wake up, Warrior!

Just as fast as he had drifted off, he was wide awake, his grandfather's warning sounding an alert.

Joseph checked his phone. Nine twenty-three. One hour later in Wisconsin. He called Kate prepared to apologize.

"Hi, Joseph," came Kate's cheerful greeting.

"I'm sorry for calling so late, but I just received a warning from Great Grandfather and it seemed urgent. He said 'our friends in Columbus are in great danger.' Clear as a bell. I had just returned from a trail ride and had just fallen asleep on the deck. I'm scared, it sounded urgent. He said to put up a 'shield of protection.' What do you think we should do?"

"I will call Jules immediately... so one of the group is from the enemy? There are only two outsiders from the group that are possible; Sullivan or young Donovan and I seriously doubt it is Sullivan. I have to reach Tom, he's out on a call to deliver a calf. If Donovan is the problem, we have a real issue; the man has a service revolver. I gotta go and call Jules! I'll get back to you as soon as I know something."

CHAPTER 74

The Ohio State University

Dr. Fred Garrett's research lab. Ten minutes later

The group was gathered for their final time of the day. The only person absent was young Donovan who was 'checking out High Street,' where most of the student bars were located. Everyone was exhausted except an energized Fred Garrett who was in his element, closing in on an answer, seeming optimistic that he was near to identifying the mystery pathogen.

Jules' phone rang and he answered cheerfully.

"Bonsoir, Mon Cherie. ...Oui, nous somme ici...Tout le Monde, mais Donovan."

"Good evening, my dear...yes, we are here. ..everyone but Donovan."

Kate explained that Nelson Blackfeather had yet again issued a warning to Joseph that there was a rat in the group in Columbus and that they were in grave danger.

"Wait, I need to put you on speaker so everyone can hear this. Just a second, I need to pull them closer."

"D'accord, we are listening."

"Hi, everyone, I am not surprised you are working at what, nearly midnight. Anyway, we have had a serious development. Nelson has warned Joseph that you are in eminent danger from someone in your group.

That only really leaves Donovan, I think, and since you know him, Rick, it doesn't really make sense."

Sullivan interrupted her.

"Wait a minute, I know his father and that his son worked for TSA in Boston. I had called his dad and got his apartment and cell phone number but it was his father that set up that first meeting at Logan Airport."

"Call the number, see if he answers," Jean suggested. "Hold on, Kate."

Sullivan punched in the number and reached Donovan's voicemail.

"This is Thad. If you are a telemarketer, psychic, ex-girlfriend or Yankees fan, my voicemail is full. Everyone else go for it."

"That man has a strong South Boston accent," Sullivan explained. "Our Donovan has no accent at all. Something is seriously wrong here. I need to call his father."

"Jim, Rick Sullivan, sorry for calling so late, but it's important. Have you talked to Thad in the last week? Because we have been working with a TSA Agent Donovan from Logan, but I am unsure it's your son Thad.

"About six three, dark curly hair, small tattoo on his right forearm with a skull and crossbones with the word Destiny below it. Blue eyes.

"I see, ok. Sorry to bother you. If you talk to Thad, ask him to keep this confidential. Thanks."

Sullivan pocketed his phone to explain the call.

"Jim said that Thad has been on temporary assignment in Houston for the last two weeks. He had told Thad that I might call and this could be his opening into the Agency, but then he had to go on assignment. He said I described Thad's roommate who flunked out of their TSA training at Logan and now is a bartender and a little weird according to his son. He said the man must be impersonating Thad because they are about the same size and Thad always kept one extra clean uniform in his apartment. He didn't know the roommate's name but will call his son and text it to me."

Sullivan's phone rang back.

"Yes, Jim, I see. Christ, that's weird. Ok, I will. Thanks."

He turned to his friends. "Thad said the roommate's name is, get this, Richard Donoven... E N. They got harassed in training about being a couple. Thad also told his father that he had mentioned to Donoven that if someone called on the apartment landline with the name Sullivan, it was a friend of his father and it might be his ticket into the FBI."

"So the man we have been working with is a fraud and a threat?" Kate asked.

"I don't know, but anything is possible at this point," Sullivan said.

"Rick, call him and ask him to meet us tomorrow at the Bob Evans Restaurant on, what's this road called, Fred?" Jules asked.

"Olentangy."

"Olentangy, at eight for breakfast because we have our answer and cure and we are headed back to Baltimore right after that, D'accord?

"Kate, you call Brad and tell him please about this and I want all of you to buy flamer phones and only use them, not your personal cells; in fact, I would pull out the SIM cards and dump the phones in a river or lake. We will confront this man tomorrow."

"What's a flamer phone?" she asked.

"I think Jules means a burner phone, you know disposable, from Walmart," replied Sullivan.

Fred Garrett spoke up.

"I nearly have this nailed down, Kate. Most of those vaccine vials in the SHARPS container contained the pure pathogen which looks like an engineered prion, structurally like BSE, Mad Cow, married to a highly neurotrophic virus which is or similar to West Nile. Cutting edge stuff with Schmitt's fingerprints all over it. The funny thing is the vaccine vials containing the RabiesX product only contains fractions of the pathogen. Something in those vials didn't allow the pathogen to exist. This organism could easily cause the rapid onset of a disease, so I am going to work through the night to see if I can determine exactly how it works and how we stop it."

"That's great, Fred, I knew you could do it!"

Kate ended her call and immediately phoned Brad.

Sullivan had Garrett lockdown the lab as he left to go to arrange a new different hotel, just in case Donoven was the enemy.

He stepped out of the lab and as was his habit, Sullivan remote started the Yukon and walked toward it.

The vehicle suddenly exploded, glass and metal shrapnel flying. Sullivan blew backward, slammed against the building. Wind knocked out of him, he was doubled over, small cuts bleeding, ears pulsating.

Jean, Jules and Fred burst out the building door, the men seeing Sullivan stunned, unable to stand. The campus police, whose station was one street over came running and summoned campus paramedics.

Sullivan looked to Jules and with an overly loud voice, groaned, "You know, I never got hurt in all those years of service. This retirement thing is a bitch!"

He sat on the ground shaking his head trying to dissipate the ringing as the paramedics tried to lift him onto a gurney. He refused.

"Remember, I am a stubborn Irishman, so I am going nowhere." He turned to Fred and said, "I have that mobile App to make my insurance claim, wait till they get a load of this. Bet they will try to say it's not totaled —"

He pointed at the mass of burning rubble and began laughing hysterically.

"Good thing I have accident forgiveness..."

That got everyone else but Jean also laughing hysterically.

He walked a little closer to the debris, sniffing the air.

"Plastique!" Jean announced.

"Gee, you think?" Sullivan roared. "I was thinking more along the lines of a meteorite!"

The paramedic again tried to get Sullivan on the gurney to transport to him to University Hospital but he flatly refused.

"I know you think my brains are scrambled but I have no pain or headache, just these little cuts. I'm fine, just overwhelmed by the depth of this investigation's hole we are trying to climb out off. This incident will have all my brothers from the Bureau, the ATF, and DHS swarming here after they grab their Starbucks."

The Trojan Plague

That had him laughing again.

Students and onlookers were gathering now and the paramedics gave up on transporting Sullivan. Columbus City Police arrived with their forensic team and started to work. Fred had already returned to work and Jules decided they stay put, safely locked in the building till the morning when the normal staff would return.

Sullivan went to Garrett's private office and rested on a worn leather couch that had served as a bed many times for the research professor. He quickly drifted off.

Jules called Kate and explained what had happened. He followed with a warning.

"You must call Brad and Joseph and all of you get on the next flight to Atlanta because Fred is going to bring what he has to the CDC. But you get out, Donoven knows who you are and in general where you live. And I think he is just the teat of the iceberg."

"God love you, Jules, but it's the *tip* of the iceberg." "Non, Mon Cherie, this is a *teat that is sucking US in.*"

CHAPTER 75

Mendoza Compound

Bariloche, Argentina
Next morning

Mendoza closed the last of his father's war journals, understanding a little better the depth of despair his father suffered from after his generals' attempted assassination at Rastenburg, Prussia. His father always required absolute dedication and loyalty. The 'rats' that attempted the overthrow were hunted down and five thousand so-called conspirators died; shot, hanged or by their own hand. That was his father's last real wartime victory over his enemies but also was a true wake-up call that not only was his Reich crumbling internally but the so-called Allies were unequivocally going to crush Germany militarily. At the start of the war, his father's writing waxed eloquently, positively, even romanticizing the sacrifices made in the war. After D-Day, his entries were mostly rants against the incompetence of his generals. He never blamed the foot soldiers, possibly because in World War One, he had been a lance corporal in the Bavarian Army and had been once wounded in the leg and another time gassed. He also had been famously spared by a British soldier that could have easily shot him, but refused because young Hitler was wounded at the time. Mendoza's father had been a man who had been mercifully spared but would never be merciful to any enemy, real or imagined.

Mendoza had only had that one 'visit' from his father under the portico and although he had returned at different times of day, smoked the cigars and drank the fine Schnapps, there had not been a reappearance. He longed for another few minutes with his father to advise him.

He had just received word that the disease had been restricted to primarily parts of Baltimore and that within twenty-four hours the United States would be decontaminating the city, effectively ending his plans. The other small eruptions of the viron were being contained in airports, train stations and isolation wards of hospitals all throughout the country. There had been no quavering of the government, no collapse of infrastructure because there had been really only one successful area contamination. He now knew the why. The rest of the doses had been intercepted due to a warning issued by that woman, Vensky-O'Dell, and her team of investigators. Four separate times he had the opportunity to disrupt all or part of their group; Paris, Leipzig where they were not a target, the woman's incredible survival of Rabies X and now the failed bomb in Columbus. They would have to be eliminated and he hoped he would pull the trigger personally as his thanks for their interference.

Mendoza had rethought the original plans and was now ready to release the disease around the globe using the reserves that had the pathogen disguised as common cleaning products, hand soaps and gel hand sanitizers. This the Nazi hoped would act to take attention away from Baltimore and the connection to the Rabies outbreak and the TriStar vaccine. He targeted four major world cities with dense populations that had never used any TriStar vaccine products. All had large airports with thousands of international travelers in and out daily. Once he ordered it, his followers would make sure the viron laden products were in London Heathrow, Shivaij International Airport in Mumbai, Beijing Capital International Airport, and Haneda Tokyo Airport restrooms, restaurants and lounges. Also, the security checkpoints had wipes and sanitizers and the janitorial staffs were also fully supplied. Work done months before allowed his followers to create counterfeit labels in each country's language to mimic cleaning agents already in use. It was a simple matter to replace existing supplies with the tainted ones. This was his genius, because as the new outbreak manifested, more disinfecting and hand sanitizing would occur, spreading the disease and panic. He would divert the attention from the United States for a moment of time and as the international panic rose, he would use the same distribution method to attack the United States just when she felt her crisis was contained.

Mendoza had put in an encrypted request for Schmitt to call and gave him a specific time to do it. Soon his RTEncrypt Sat phone signaled an incoming call with Schmitt's verification code displayed correctly.

"Christian, you are as punctual as always," Mendoza answered as a cordial greeting.

"Danke, Mein Führer. It is good to hear your voice once more."

"And to hear yours, Doctor."

That was the first time Mendoza had ever acknowledged Schmitt's title.

"Where are you now?" Mendoza asked.

"We, James and I, are still in Winchester, waiting your orders. I am disappointed that the pathogen was unable to be disseminated to maximize its effect but I have been informed, by calling two veterinary clinics outside of Baltimore, that the vaccine was unavailable because the CDC issued an emergency order that none of those last shipments, our fortified pure product, be given. Interestingly, the man who attacked me on the streets of Baltimore was an owner veterinarian and our largest purchaser of the RabiesX vaccine on the East Coast. Because he was infected, I assume it was he who disregarded the CDC order and spread the disease...or he never received that notification.

"So are we to do, Mein Führer?"

"We are abandoning that path and are going with a general contamination plan. Plan B as Vogel put it. Maybe this is the approach we should have started with but Hans was correct in that by controlling the distribution of the diseases and selling the RabiesX product we would generate large profits and in that respect he was right— we have banked ten billion euros of profit and invested another two billion in our new products to spread our pathogen. I also have ordered several billion more doses of VironX be produced to treat and prevent the disease process. When we see what happens, we may need still more massive manufacturing capability. Once the Viron is well established, you will need to create another unique disease to keep ahead of these countries' ability to fight us. We cannot rely on our initial treatment formula to be unraveled for very long. Someone will figure it out."

"I created it so it would difficult to decipher, with the actual active ingredient hidden in a plethora of common medications combined in ways that will make it a Chinese puzzle with traps and false leads. We need to be sure the tablets are only administered by our agents, paid for by the affected and since they are sub lingual and dissolving no person should ever possess any actual intact tablets beyond the dose he or she is taking that day."

"In theory that is great, but look at our plans with Rabies X, it's that Murphy's Law thing, whatever could go wrong, did go wrong."

"If it wasn't for the interference of those Americans and Frenchmen, we would have already been in Washington," Schmitt grumbled.

"They are our Murphy's, but we will be the law and they will be condemned to death. We did everything correctly, how they got involved and connected the dots is beyond reason. Almost supernatural, but I will end their run of luck. You my friend will be returning with honor to join me in my home in South America. We won't be here long, just long enough to prepare new plans for the future and watch the viron or your new creations express themselves internationally. Our colleagues will then secure local power in exchange for the treatment, but again since we likely will not be able to overwhelm these nations, we won't be able to holdout forever. Eventually, we will need that one two punch to grab the reins of these governments. Unknown to you or Vogel, when I built TriStar, I duplicated the laboratory and production areas exactly as they were in Leipzig near to where I reside. Literally everything is the same including the eight managers that called in sick that day of the attack on TriStar; they are to be your staff. Only thing is, this time we are invisible, underground, buried into the side of a mountain. It is secure and protected in ways that you wouldn't believe possible. Billions of Euros spent to prevent Mr. Murphy. So now your genius will have a home to safely spread its wings. Am I not brilliant?"

"Brilliance cannot begin to describe your genius, Mein Führer! I also have good news."

"And what is that ?"

"In the process of developing the viron, I discovered that there are endless numbers of viruses that can be hybridized with the BSE prion. Also, there are other prions that could be used. I chose the BSE prion because most of the reliable research had been on the Mad Cow Prion. Some current work is being conducted on Chronic Wasting disease in Odocoileus, native deer, in the United States. I already have sixteen possibles and models in virtual form that are ready for laboratory and field trials. We could have and release a half-dozen unique diseases within three months, the only issue being finding a preventive or treatment to protect the desirables while eliminating quickly the rest. This time I would suggest a quickly lethal combination and overwhelm the nations just enough to cripple them and then seize control. Our current viron was selected to scare the crap out of a nation and disrupt her infrastructure to the point of collapse. I think we need a pathogen that has both high, ninety-five percent or higher morbidity and nearly one hundred percent mortality in first twenty-four hours post exposure. There cannot be a treatment, just a durable way to protect our followers and the desirables."

"The ultimate Ultimate Solution?" Mendoza pondered. "Yes, and we are closer than you could ever imagine."

"Here are my orders. You are to fly to Havana and call the locator number and put in your code. A man named Pedro Garcia will contact you and arrange your safe transport to Santiago, Chile and you will repeat the process and I will arrange your final leg of the trip. You need to be here in no longer than two days. Timing now is of the essence."

"We are on our way, Mein Führer!"

Little did they know, so was the supernatural.

CHAPTER 76

Baltimore

Zero hour

The Maryland Air National Guard had twenty-four in service helicopters of various ages from trainers to the latest largest versions staged, armed with the lethal pellets, waiting the order to fly to their assigned GPS co-ordinates to start their zigzag overlapping distribution patterns of death. The only problem was the weather.

Two hours prior to the mission's initiation, an unpredicted storm of tremendous power blew out of the Atlantic and into the Chesapeake Bay. High winds, thunderstorms, lightning and torrential rain made flying impossible and because of the hydrophilic nature of the anhydrous pellets and acidic adjunct, it was a hazard to safely distribute. If any moisture reached those pellets before they left the helicopters, the sudden exo-thermic reaction would cause the copters to burst into flames. On top of that, crews had to wear heat protective suits to load the fifty pound bags of pellets into the sealed plastic spreader hoppers that were used to evenly distribute the material. They looked like giant seed spreaders with a phalanx-like arm than would hang well below each aircraft. Each aircraft was loaded with between ten to forty bags or five hundred to two thousand pounds of purification, death and hopeful salvation.

The helicopters sat clustered, waiting, rotors idling, in four separate staging areas, waiting their orders. The rain was endless, but once it stopped and flying conditions improved, they would start their distribution runs to destroy all remaining life and sanitize the designated areas. The mission had to be timed exactly because with standing water on the ground, the product would be expanded to maximum in seconds, killing all life nearly instantly. A thick smoke like cloud of steam would be released by the chemical reaction and would blanket the area like a shroud until it cooled and rained down with nearly distilled water. That steam cloud made safety coordination of the copters critical, getting caught in it would be extremely dangerous.

The storm continued for ten hours, drowning all of Baltimore but little else. With the changing tide rising, water rose, storm sewers filled and backed up. In some areas two to three feet of flooding was occurring and the helicopters were ordered to move to dryer alternative staging areas. One small helicopter was ordered to do a test run and treat the Locust Point neighborhood epicenter to make sure they could spread the chemical successfully. That single helicopter took advantage of a break in the downpour and sped up and out to the Chesapeake to start a run over the targeted streets, the presumed origin of the outbreak. As the four person helicopter approached the edge of the neighborhood, a violent gust of wind pushed the aircraft back, away from the shoreline in the exact opposite of the storm's prevailing gusts. The pilot struggled to maintain control into the teeth of the wind but was unable to safely move forward. He wisely turned the craft away and made a wide circle to the original staging area and expertly set the copter down.

The rain restarted with increased violent lightning and thunder. Safety orders were given to shelter in the aircraft until the storms abated.

Two hours passed and an urgent new operating order was received; Stand Down Immediately, Mission Canceled.

As suddenly as the storm appeared, the rain ceased, the skies opened to brilliant blue and rainbows arose as clouds split and the sun broke through.

The President had canceled the mission.

Dr. Fred Garrett had found his answer and the cure.

CHAPTER 77

That afternoon

Logan International Airport

Jules, Jean and Sullivan landed near the restricted area where the Pasteur jet was waiting.

A small Ohio State University Embracer Executive jet had been loaned to the men by the University upon request of Fred Garrett. Sullivan slept the entire flight as he had a mild headache and persistent ringing in his ears but swore to his friends he was 'good to go'. A light misting rain greeted the men as they exited the small jet and were picked up by a covered oversized golf cart and driven over to the 737 belonging to the Institute. The stairs were extended and the cabin door open but no crew member stood as usual at the top of the stairs, a little unusual.

Sullivan went up the stairs first, followed by Jean and Jules. They saw no crew in the galley or cockpit and the plane appeared almost deserted. The men worked their way to the tail of the plane and when they looked in the first of the two bathroom suites, suddenly behind them, Donoven appeared. He had been hidden behind a privacy curtain, a small machine pistol in his hands.

"Well, we meet again my friends," he announced startling them, slightly waving the weapon across the group.

"What the hell?" Sullivan exclaimed.

"Retired Agent Sullivan, I will need your weapons... all of them. The Glock, the Smith & Wesson and that Kimber mini you keep on your right calf. No monkey business now or you will be the first to go. Messieurs, please empty your pockets and lift your trousers to your knees just so I can be sure Sullivan hasn't deputized you. Also I need your cell phones please, gentlemen."

"Mon Dieu, Jules, just like when Berhetzel surprised Papa and me!" Jean exclaimed.

"Donoven," Sullivan asked, "where is our crew and what is your end game here?"

"So you figured out my real identity. Good work, Sullivan. To answer your question, the crew, except the co-pilot, who is in a safe place, are currently on an Air France flight back to Paris, their orders given very early this morning by you Dr. LeClerc. Your impersonator gave a fictitious new mission for them in Senegal and they are going to supposedly provide transportation for a full medical team to handle *LA CRISE* —the crisis. By the time they figure out what is going on, you will have disappeared, perhaps forever!"

Sullivan glared at the young man, who was wearing a TSA uniform with the silver name tag T. DONOVAN above his right shirt pocket.

"You're a punk, Donoven, surely you aren't the brains behind this. I suggest you just give this up and cut your losses. Otherwise you will end up in prison for the rest of your life or even better, dead!"

"No wonder they retired your sorry ass, Sullivan, you have no clue the forces that are behind all of this. I don't even know for sure, but I can guarantee for what I am being paid, it has to be enormous. I'm just a mechanic, really a soldier, following orders, but I think you may be bait for the rest of your group so you all can be gathered together for an 'interrogation' of sorts. My job is to let our flight crew take you to an undisclosed location, then I will receive my commission and possibly a permanent position."

"Probably six feet under," Sullivan mumbled.

"Perhaps, but that more likely describes your future or lack of future," Donoven snapped back.

The men were taken to the on board morgue and shackled to three separate wall anchors that were titanium welded handholds. They were sequestered deep in the belly of the plane and no one would be able to hear their cries for help or even suspect they were in there along with the unconscious pistol whipped co-pilot.

Two retired freelance ShipX pilots arrived to contract fly the large jet to the so-called undisclosed former Russian military airbase on the island of Cuba where the jet would be handed off to a different crew. That's when Donoven would trade off his responsibility and get paid in cash by the second leg pilots. The captives in the plane's morgue would have no idea where they were or what was happening and by the time the jet made its and second and final stop in Chile, the men would have been gagged, hooded and made ready for the two-hour small plane ride to Mendoza's hidden landing strip outside Bariloche. They then would be sedated and sequestered on the compound grounds where Mendoza could control them. Next he would extract the veterinarians and Indian after they arrived in Atlanta. Fred Garrett would not be targeted until the Nazi understood exactly what the others knew or were willing to give up. Mendoza needed to understand first how these people were able to interfere so successfully in their plans and after Schmitt arrived, he would use whatever means necessary to stop these interfering SOBs and eventually Garrett.

As soon as the jet was airborne Jean looked at his watch. He wanted to time the flight and because they knew the cruising speed of the jet, he might be able estimate where they were. He wore a Rolex on his left wrist that had belonged to his father but on his right wrist, he sported a biometric device that constantly monitored his blood pressure, heart rate, temperature and had a biomedical alert function that could be activated in case of emergency. In that watch there was GPS transponder built in that had advertised 'can locate your emergency anywhere in the world and call immediately for help.' The miniaturized computer had been a gift from his daughter Susan and also featured a compass function. The small screen was now flashing yellow indicating his blood pressure and heart rate were out of normal range.

"My *ALLEZ* is telling me I'm upset. Isn't technology wonderful?" he asked his best friend.

"Oui, I wish I had one, I'm usually fairly stable but so much has happened since the attack on Paris, my tolerance level to stress is near zero."

"Jules," Sullivan asked, "is there an intercom in this part of the plane? I see a phone over by the door with a speaker. Could Donoven listen to us remotely without our knowledge by activating the speaker?"

"Non, c'est pas possible." *No, that is not possible.* "Good. Jean, is your watch a medical alert device?" "Oui, my daughter gave it to me for Christmas."

"Then we have a chance of being found after we land. That 'watch' acts like a cell phone and pings off cell towers or satellites. You will need to send an emergency signal at least several times anytime we land. Is the device based in Europe?"

"Oui."

"Then the signal may take a while to run through the cell connectors and satellites but they at least will have a record of where we have been. Your daughter will likely be notified and after she can't reach you she would call..."

"Jules."

"He doesn't answer, then who?"

"Simone, Jule's wife."

"And she would call?"

"Kate, and she would try to reach the three of us, failing that I bet she would call Bernard Redare. He has the all resources of the French government to find and rescue us. Suddenly, I think I am feeling much better."

"Moi aussi," Jules agreed.

"Good, so we need to concentrate on staying alive and keeping our mouths shut."

"My watch had us flying east toward Europe but now we are headed southwest. That's very strange."

Sullivan thought for a second.

"Likely as soon as Logan handed this bird off, Donoven cut their communications and changed course. Probably disabled the transponders and are blocking the radar image. Logan might think this jet crashed in the Atlantic. Perfect way to explain our disappearance, never to be found. Ingenious!"

The co-pilot was starting to moan and move his arms a little as he began to regain consciousness. His face was swollen and black from bruising.

Jules spoke his name to test the man's mental state.

"Henri, Henri Sabo, levez la main si vous pouvez m'entendre." *Raise your hand if you can hear me.*

Slowly the man raised his right hand and gave a small flip wave of his fingers. He also smiled slightly at the corners of his mouth.

"Bon, je vais parler anglais maintenant, D'accord?" *Good, I am going to speak English now, ok?*

Sabo nodded affirmatively.

"There are three of us here with you in the morgue of the jet, Jean DuBois, Agent Rick Sullivan and myself and although we all are in the morgue, all of us are very much alive. Are you able to answer any questions?"

Henri gave a weak, "Oui" and a thumbs up.

"D'accord, how many attacked you?" Jules asked.

The co-pilot held up his left index finger and made a hatchet chop toward the back of his neck.

"That is all I remember," he replied painfully.

"They have no real interest in you, so I would think you are the most disposable of all of us, so here is my suggestion. When they return for us, you must play dead. Staring eyes, mouth open, breath held firmly. I will explain to them you had a seizure and stopped breathing. Hopefully they will release you from your restraints to bag you or whatever and when that happens you must try to overwhelm them. It will be our only chance. Push them toward one of us so we can help you. If we can get hold of that set of keys, we will have our chance," Jules instructed.

Sullivan added, "Push your thumbs into the bastard's eyes. Then just shove him away toward one of us. If I get my hands on him, he's done for."

"Moi Aussi," Jean said. "We must be in control of this jet before we get to wherever we are supposed to end up at or we will ultimately be dead."

They continued to refine a plan to retake the plane and find out who was behind all of this.

It was now or never!

CHAPTER 78

Atlanta Hartsfield-Jackson Airport

Private Charters Lounge That Evening

"None of them are answering," Kate complained, "they should have been here three hours ago. All their phones are going to voicemail. That's the sixth time I've called."

"I really expected them to call or text us and leave a message that they had arrived and were waiting for us. Something is wrong. Jules is real anal about communication," Brad said.

"I just called Fred and he hadn't heard anything from them either. He is under protection by the FBI as requested by Sullivan so he will be fine. He is not leaving OSU as he has solved both the cause of the of the plague and is in the middle of formulating the final treatment and prevention plans. The order to use the lethal disinfectant on Baltimore was cancelled by the President based exclusively on Fred's work. The President has extended his thanks to our entire team. The only thing left to do is to find the perpetrators and that is still our mission but I have a sickening feeling they might have found us first," Tom reported.

"It won't do us any good just standing here. I don't know about you but I am starved. Let's find a place to eat," Joseph almost pleaded.

"There is a Buddies Seafood in the main terminal. They serve decent seafood and steaks and I've eaten there a couple of times," Brad offered.

They walked for nearly twenty minutes with Kate calling and texting Jules and Sullivan every couple minutes. No luck.

They were seated and soon had drinks and appetizers. No alcohol, just ice tea and soft drinks. As usual Kate prayed but this time they all joined hands and bowed their heads.

"Dear Lord, please bless this meal we are about to receive and we ask Your protection and guidance for our dear friends, Jules, Jean and Rick. Help us locate them and please keep them safe."

"Thank you, Kate," Joseph offered.

She smiled and wiped tears from the corner of her eyes with her napkin. She was tired like all of them and feeling real guilty not being home with Bobbi. Also there was no question that all of them were at risk of injury or worse but then they all understood the stakes they were playing for and most importantly they felt reassured that they were under the protection of the Creator. That was probably the only thing that kept them moving forward; Divine Protection.

The appetizers had just arrived when Kate's cell phone chirped like a cricket, her default ring for incoming calls from an unknown source. Kate recognized that the area code was European, from Paris.

"Bonjour, Kate Vensky – O'Dell parlant. Ah, Susan, comment sa va? Anglais? Oui."

She put her hand over the phone and whispered to the group, "Jean's daughter."

"I am going to put you on speakerphone, Susan. Can you hear me alright?"

"Yes, I can. Hello, everyone!"

"Bonjour, hello," came the mixed reply.

"I called because Papa's medical alert device sent a distress signal three times from somewhere around Cuba of all places. It was picked up by the communications system at your Guantanamo Bay Prison and relayed back here to the watch servicing company. Your Army said he had to be within fifty-five miles of their facility for a civilian based unit to be detected. The third distress signal faded away indicating he was on the move away possibly to the Southwest. Papa was last seen going through diplomatic security in Boston and that was about four and a half hours prior to the call. Also the Pasteur jet disappeared from radar and communications including the transponders about one hour after the departure from Logan. No distress signal had been received and the FAA was investigating when his call was reported. Because it is a private jet, they are somewhat limited on what they will do but there are satellites scanning that area where the signal was lost for evidence of the jet, but if the jet was below a certain altitude, they likely could miss it.

"I am sure they are alive but I have no idea what is going on. Do you know anything that can reassure me ?"

"No, Susan, we haven't heard anything. I will call Jules' friend at the DGSI, Monsieur Bernard Redare and see if he can help or knows anything. I will call you back after I talk to him. Au Revoir, Susan."

Kate went into her wallet and found Redare's business card on which he had written his personal emergency contact number. She called. "Bonjour, Monsieur Redare, Kate Vensky-O'Dell parlant. Je suis désolé, mais il y a une problème, Jules, Jean et Rick Sullivan manquent. *I am sorry, but there is a problem, Jules, Jean and Rick Sullivan are missing.*"

"What exactly do you mean 'missing,' Doctor?" he asked.

"We don't know exactly where they are since they were to arrive in Atlanta before we got here and that was over three hours ago. No contact of any kind with them or the Pasteur jet since before they left Boston. Jean's medical alert device watch was activated somewhere around Guantanamo Bay prison on Cuba and his daughter received a notification from the company that sold the device called *ALLEZ.* It appears the jet is off course or unable to communicate..."

"Or has been hijacked. That seems a more reasonable explanation than that jet with her expert crew getting lost."

"That is why I called you. Something is very wrong."

"I will call this *ALLEZ* company and see if there is a way to send a signal back to Jean, like a reverse 911 call. Possibly we can then verify that the device is still in range and working. All these devices are based on a GPS locator system so there are a lot of possibilities. Give me a couple hours and I'll get back to you. Are you still working on the plague scenario in the United States?"

"Yes, but Dr. Garret has evidently nailed down the cause and treatment. He was able to stop the Army's destruction of most of Baltimore," Kate explained.

"Bon chance, my friends, I'll see what I can do."

Redare ended the call.

"Now what ?" Brad asked.

Joseph waved the server over and they ordered their entrees. Then they ate in silence, all of them silently trying to reconcile what was happening.

In the natural world they would seem defeated, but they were protected by supernatural forces. Little did they know the supernatural was guiding each decision they made.

CHAPTER 79

Pasteur Jet

One hour later

Donoven had not been relieved or paid because the second crew that was to meet them on an old Russian airstrip, unused since the end of the Cold War, never arrived in their allotted thirty minute window. The crumbling concrete airfield was surrounded by overgrown sugar cane fields but the highly toxic herbicides that the Russians had used constantly for the thirty years when the base was active, had permanently sterilized the ground so that weeds on the perimeters grew better in the cracks in the concrete landing strip than on the adjacent soil. It was common knowledge that the abandoned air base was used regularly by drug smugglers and in the recent past had been a location set for several Spanish movie productions.

Donoven settled in soon after the jet had retaken to the air after the brief stay. He had no idea where they had landed at the first destination but figured now that he had earned at least double the fee he had been promised. Also since he was a non-pilot on the plane, he would need to continue to stay in control of his captives and therefore continue to be of value to his 'benefactor'.

The mercenary pilots indicated a flight time of approximately five to six hours after which the jet would have to land to refuel again. Since the jet was flying essentially empty, the aircraft was only burning approximately seven hundred gallons per hour of airtime. After the refuel, they would have to fly at least one more segment to reach their final destination.

Donoven decided to check on the men held in the morgue and give them some bottled water and cookies he had found in the gallery. This was to be his second time he had checked on them since he shackled them to the wall of the jet.

"Hello my friends," he announced gleefully as he came down the stairwell to the morgue. "I have brought you some water and these St Michelle Butter Galettes so you can maintain your strength."

"You are too kind," Sullivan said sarcastically.

"We need to pee," Jean complained, "this is cruel to make old guys hold it so long."

"Then when I go back upstairs, I will see if I can find a very nice bottle of Pee No More wine. Get it, not Pinot Noir but Pee No More," he chirped, laughing loudly.

"The boy wonder is a comedian as well as a reprobate!" Sullivan replied.

"And you are no Elliot Ness, old man, so I would shut up," he snapped back.

Jules pointed over to the co-pilot and said to Donoven, "That man is nearly dead. Why don't you just unshackle him and cover him with a blanket. They are in that closet over there."

He pointed to a cabinet on the far wall near the autopsy table. "Besides, we are tired of watching the poor man struggle for breath. Do something decent for once in your life."

"I guess it wouldn't hurt any to do that," Donoven replied.

He went to the aluminum glass front cabinet and pulled out two large navy blue cotton autopsy drapes that could serve as a blanket. Then he went to the wall and unlocked the shackle that held up the copilot's left arm and then released the shackle on his right foot. He nudged the man's chest with his foot. There was no response.

"If you have flashlight function on your phone, use it to check for a pupillary reflex. If he has one then you want to roll him on his side. At least then his breathing might improve," Jules suggested.

"This is nuts, I'm not looking but I will put him on his side," Donoven complained as he set down the machine pistol and struggled to place the copilot on his right side.

Suddenly the man was alive, grabbing Donoven by the face pushing his thumbs hard into his eye sockets. They rolled, the co-pilot fueled by rage and the survival response, and immediately was on top of the surprised younger man, pushing down harder, blood oozing around his thumbs.

He pulled out his thumbs and started to choke Donoven down, while enduring fierce blows to his back. He grabbed a shackle and wrapped it around Donoven's neck and twisted. Soon the young man was subdued, unconscious but the enraged co-pilot continued to twist, suffocating the man.

"Stop, enough!" Sullivan shouted.

"Henri, Arrêtezvous le tuer!" *Stop, you are killing him! Jean echoed Sullivan.*

Donoven was cyanotic, blue skin, bloodied eyes that bulged just beyond their lids. The man was alive, but barely. The rage subsided and Sabo released his stranglehold while flipping Donoven onto his stomach. He took the shackles and crisscrossed them onto the wall anchors, putting the young man in a very uncomfortable position. He took the key to the restraints and tossed them to Sullivan. Soon all three men were free. Sabo crouched on the floor, crying in an emotional release.

Jules checked him. Bruises, possible fractured orbit bone around his right eye; he would take weeks to heal but likely had sustained no permanent injury. Donoven however was struggling to breathe but seemed to have regained normal oxygen levels though was breathing like a bad snorer.

"The bastard will survive. I suspect we just saw an example of the power of adrenaline. Good job, Henri, I doubt any of us could have pulled that off any better," Jules said.

The co-pilot took a deep breath, composing himself, and explained, "Before I came to be employed by Le Pasteur, I was a career flight officer in an Elite division of the FFL. So I know how to fight dirty."

"What's the Ffeeel?" Sullivan asked, confused by the accent.

"Our French Foreign Legion— a bunch of very tough mothers, as you Americans would say," Jules replied.

"I guess so."

Jean grabbed the machine pistol and expertly checked the clip and the action. He took the gun's sling and expertly hung the gun from his shoulder.

"You know how to handle that thing?" Sullivan asked.

"Absolutement! Everyone in leadership positions in the Archives Nationale are required to take basic self-defense firearms training and you can request advanced classes. I did and now I am glad I did."

"Jules, can you use that MP?"

"Non, pas moi."

"I can," Sabo affirmed.

"Good, three out of four," Sullivan said, as he went through Donoven's pockets, removing a cell phone, two Swiss Army knives, and three more loaded clips from the man's dark blue and black TSA armored vest. He pulled off the vest and slipped it on.

"I guess we have two choices," he said.

"One would be to hijack this bird and force the crew to return us or land somewhere and get other transportation home. The second would be to allow it to fly to its final destination and then I could perhaps impersonate Dovoven and we see where they are taking us. They must want us for some reason, otherwise we would be dead already, same for you, Sabo."

"No offense, Rick, but you are seriously older than Donoven and beside the pilots have already interacted with Donoven so they would immediately resist anything we do."

"Except we have the gun and this jet has to land at a commercial airfield or at least a very big one. The last landing we made was extremely rough, someplace unkept or Third World. This jet was not made for that kind of abuse so I think to refuel, which will be needed very shortly, if we left with full tanks from Logan, we are going to have to land at a decent commercial airport with clean aviation fuel."

"How will we know if that stop is the last?" Jean asked.

"We will know because the pilots will do one of several things. They will not want to invite anyone of authority on board so they will

not open the cabin doors unless they absolutely have to. If they open them, we should be able to hear it from here. Then I will *persuade* them with my government credentials that they have been tagged by the United States and if they want to stay alive and out of jail, they would need to leave and remain silent about their activities, whether it be hijacking or stealing this jet or they would forever be looking over their shoulders. If they know who they are working for, which I doubt, they would need to hand it over. Otherwise, I will have to kill them."

"You could do that?"

"I think so if it becomes necessary. There is a lot at stake for us and the United States, hell, the entire world. We are in way too deep to run away. Also we are closer than anyone to discovering the author of this, so if your commission, and I guess mine also, is to unravel this who done it, then the end probably does justify the means. If this next stop is our final one, the doors will open, and someone will come looking for the intermediary which would be Donoven and his four 'guests'. Likely they will just be mules to transport us to where we will be handed off to next and them the next. I don't think anyone, at least locally, knows what we look like and no one knows or cares why they were hired. I think we can fake our way into the lion's den. You just keep pushing that button, Jean, when we land."

"What do we do with Donoven?" Jules asked.

"You see those black hoods and zip ties over there by the metal autopsy table. I saw them when he brought us down here. They were for us to wear before we leave this plane. You will still each sport one except no duct tape on your mouths, only the boy wonder. Also, I'll fix the zip ties by my cutting a small defect in the plastic so if you snap them sharply they will break. It will be a little claustrophobic for you but the hoods will be loose. I will be our eyes and ears so we need a verbal to trigger your escape.

"If I shoot or you hear gunfire, drop flat to the ground. If I sense pending trouble, what word do you want to use as a signal for action?"

"What was that Lakota warrior cry Joseph shouted in the French Embassy in Washington?" Jules asked.

"I will never forget," Jean replied, "it made the hair on my neck stand up, and cut straight to my soul."

"Good. Let's hear it."

"*HOKA HEY!*"

"He shouted it with generational passion," Jules noted. "We need to channel that energy and each shout it with all of our heart, mind and soul. Let's try it!

"On three, one, two, three!"

"*HOKA HEY!*"

Something happened at that instant, thousands of eternal miles away. A nation of ancients were stirred from their afterworld to prepare for battle!

CHAPTER 80

Noon the same day

I 95 south of Daytona Beach, Florida

James drove relatively slowly as cars and trucks zoomed past well in excess of the posted speed limit. Most were driven by senior "snowbirds" hurrying to their warm nests as the colder weather creeped closer and closer up North. He felt relieved that those old timers would occupy the efforts of the highway police and likely make their travel to Homestead, Florida uneventful. The last thing they wanted was a traffic stop because they felt that by now, Schmitt had to be on some kind of universal governmental watch list. They were going to take no chance to disturb that bear.

Schmitt was on his laptop computer working endlessly on virtual experimental data utilizing the Cadillac's WiFi system. The scientist was so focused that James had to ask him several times before he heard his questions.

"We need to stop for petrol and get something to eat very soon before we get into the Fort Lauderdale -Miami traffic. After that, I don't want to stop. We need to arrive at the private landing strip no earlier than quarter of eight and no later than eight thirty. Traffic could be a bitch so I want to take no chances that we could miss that plane ride to Havana."

"That's your department, my friend, this," he said tapping the computer with his index finger, "is mine. Without you we fail, but without me creating more infectious chaos, we both are doomed. So like it or not we are in the same boat. My job is to be sure that boat is not the Titanic. Comprendre?"

"Oui, Docteur."

James drove to just above Fort Lauderdale and exited. He refueled at a large Speed-In gas station and then drove to a fast food restaurant known for its roast beef sandwiches. They ate in silence in the car and then got back on the interstate just as the traffic was backing up.

Barely a mile down the road, James' navigation system warned of a multiple car accident several miles ahead and suggested an alternate route around the traffic that would be slow but better than waiting on the stalled highway.

"What do you want to do?" the young driver asked.

"We can't just sit here, you better follow the navigation directions."

About half a mile down the road James had moved the big vehicle over to the right and off the congested road. They followed the navigation as the neighborhoods got less desirable with rundown storefronts with boarded windows and groups of angry looking young men watching the shiny Escalade move down the ramshackle street.

"Whatever you do, don't stop. These guys want your car and possibly us. Just keep moving forward."

Not half a block from there, a large gray beat up pickup pulled directly across the street in front of them and another car came in bumper to bumper behind them.

"Merde!" James mumbled. *Crap!*

The four gang-tattooed young men jumped out of the truck and moved to the front of the Cadillac wearing dark sleeveless T shirts, wrap-around sunglasses and dark baggy cargo pants, slung well below their waists. Each held a baseball bat and swung it menacingly, tapping the hood of the car.

Thump, thump, thump.

James pulled his S&W 9mm from under its armrest hiding place and palmed it. He slowly pushed the Escalade until it was inches from the truck.

"What do you think ?" he asked the German.

"I think they are not going to leave until they get what they want —this vehicle and us, either in the hospital or dead."

"I think you are exactly right. So here is what I think. I will push that truck out of the way and shoot anyone who tries to get in the car."

James pushed the oversized Cadillac into the old truck while the men yelled and postured hitting the SUV harder, smashing the hood and windshield, cursing the two men.

"Ya dead, suckers ! HEAR ME? DEADDDDD!"

Two men moved with the Cadillac, smashing at the passenger door and window glass, pounding harder and harder with drug fueled rage.

"Push it harder, get us out of here!" Schmitt shouted in near panic. Suddenly, Schmitt's door sprung open and one man jumped on him like a hungry tiger, his hands choked up on the bat like a ball player ready to bunt but in this case the ball was Schmitt's head.

James had had enough; he pushed the 9 mm in the man's side and in two deafening blasts killed the attacker. Schmitt pushed the man out and onto his partner as James floored the SUV pushing the truck, spinning it out of the way, with plumes of smoke from the squealing tires. Schmitt grabbed the door and slammed it shut.

Blood was everywhere. Schmitt squeezed his lips tightly and closed his eyes while he searched for his handkerchief. He then briskly wiped his face and hands to remove the spattered blood.

"Who knows what myriad diseases that bastard carried," Schmitt complained.

"In the glovebox," James said, "are some disinfecting wipes. Take care of yourself, then start wiping down the car. If we get stopped for a headlamp violation or the mirrors, the blood must not be obvious. I'll ramp up the AC and roll down the windows if they work and when we are out of this area we can stop and use some black duct tape to make the side mirrors look better. I have a prepaid Amex with a hundred thousand dollars loaded on it so if we get to a shopping mall close to a Kia or similar car dealership we will leave this vehicle and buy something to get us the last few hours. If those men report us, at least they won't spot our car. Can't waste time at a car rental because we don't have any time to spare and those vehicles can be monitored."

He pushed the Onstar button.

"Nearest Kia dealership on current navigation route?"

"In four point five miles on your right is Big Sea Kia. Shall I call that number for you?"

The connection was made and rapidly James explained he needed to purchase quickly, a small SUV and the transaction had to take place within forty minutes or he would miss his flight time. The dealership had several courtesy cars prepared for quick sale and the salesman gave a price, James accepted and gave a fictitious business name and address to start the title and registration work. The car was promised in half an hour.

Schmitt continued wiping down the Escalade and reached for the door panel where he had secured his laptop before the attack. The computer was not there. He searched the floor, no laptop.

Schmitt was in a panic.

"Those bastards must have taken my computer or knocked it out of the car. Crap. We need to go back."

James looked at him like he was crazy.

"Non, Monsieur, c'est pas possible." *That is not possible.*

"That area will be crawling with police, plus a lot of angry locals. You will just have to accept the fact it is gone."

"All my data is encrypted, but none of it has been saved off the device yet because I didn't have access to a primary secure server. That represents new and old data that will be critical to developing secondary pathogens. Mendoza will likely kill me for this," Schmitt lamented.

"He will not kill you because we will not tell him. All we need is a new computer to look like the old one and you will just have to start over. Results are hard to predict. Science is not necessarily a linear path to discovery."

"Why would you want to cover for me?" Schmitt questioned.

"Because what happened back there was as much my responsibility as it was yours. I'm sure he would see our mission as a shared responsibility. You die, I die."

They stopped at a Best Buy electronics big box store and Schmitt found exactly what he needed. Two storefronts away from there was a huge sign that read Big Sea Kia. They quickly searched the Escalade for any personal items and James went to the rear and took two softball sized objects out of a locked steel case. He fiddled with one and tossed it back into the passenger row of seats. The second he put in a plastic shopping bag. He then locked the SUV.

"What was that ?" Schmitt asked.

"An incendiary bomb. In ninety minutes that vehicle will be destroyed to an unrecognizable mass of metal. Neither of us will be linked back to it since it was registered fictitiously as will be the Kia. Anyway, we should only be in this country a few more hours, after that it won't matter anyway."

The Kia dealership had everything ready to go and they were out of the showroom in twenty minutes. A record according to the salesman. The only ID needed was James' international driver's license and insurance card. Both were fake.

As they rejoined the freeway, James put their destination on his phone. They were almost three hours away and that meant they should have a one to one and a half hours extra window to get there. Plenty of time.

Miami traffic was crazier than normal but spit them out with twenty-five minutes to spare. The destination put them next to an open field and they waited for a small plane's approach. Finally, on schedule, it came in low and made two shallow passes over the field as James flashed his headlights on and off twice. The plane came down and landed within fifty meters of the Kia.

James tossed the incendiary ball into the car and locked it up. They then walked up to the small, old Cessna.

"Hola, mis amigos," said a gray haired mustached middle aged man as he opened the plane's door. "I am Pedro, your guide on this sightseeing tour. Please come in as we will need to leave before the Coast Guard realizes we are trespassing in her territory."

Almost immediately as they strapped in, the pilot took to the air, banked the plane sharply and headed due east and then over the Atlantic headed south.

"We should only be in the air about ninety minutes to two hours because we are going to fly slow and make a couple evasive turns to make us look less significant on radar," Pedro explained.

They hung on as they were buffeted by turbulence and the inside temperature hovered just shy of sweltering as there was no air conditioning. Schmitt kept his eye on the gas gauge which had read a fraction above empty from the time they had left, so it was obviously not working. Scary.

They eventually drifted onto the same airfield that the PasteurJet had landed on a day before. A larger turbo prop airplane sat at the opposite end of the runway with its engines idling. As soon as Pedro had the two men out of the Cessna, he signaled the other plane and it worked its way slowly to them.

They boarded into the state of the art turboprop and the two European pilots that were in the cockpit greeted the men heartily.

"Welcome to Getaway Airlines, where we help you get away from anyone. This is your private charter with our next stop Lima and then Santiago, Chile. From that point you will no longer be our responsibility," the pilot said and chuckled a little.

"How in the world did you get here in that piece of garbage," the copilot said as he pointed to the old Cessna.

"By the grace of God," James replied.

"Do you have WiFi on your plane," Schmitt asked.

"Yah, and more importantly we have a head, food and drinks," the younger pilot replied.

"German beer?"

"Yah, Bitburger. Our mother's milk."

"Gut, then all is not lost." Schmitt laughed as he opened the new computer and logged on to the setup menu. He would have at least several hours to configure the device and then reconstruct his research format from memory. That would require he download some advanced software from Research Education Resource, Ltd., an international leader in customizable programs to aid work flow for university professors and commercial research. It could give him a quick way to recreate his work platform so if Mendoza asked, he would have something to show him.

If you can't convince him, confuse him.

They ate and afterward while James slept, Schmitt called on his incredible intellect to recreate a reasonable looking work document that used his memorized format relinking the salient points so that only someone with an extremely advanced education could untangle his temporary charade. The only person in the world he thought of that could quickly prove the work fraudulent would be Fred Garrett.

One stop and hours later they finally landed at Santiago, Chile. The pilots signed off on them and a third contact, who again had a small plane, loaded the men for their last leg of the journey to Bariloche. They flew east a short while through a mountainous pass in the Andes and then went due south parallel to the mountain range. Two hours and twenty minutes later the small plane landed on a tiny rural airstrip in a predominately agricultural area outside San Carlos de Bariloche.

They were loaded into a Jeep and taken up and down hills, through streams and over muddy trails. Two hours later, jostled and bruised from the long ride, the wilderness opened into a Bavarian looking oasis. One armed guard stood outside massive iron and thick wood gates, the man dressed in khaki military style shorts and shirt, topped with a matching baseball style cap. The guard was restraining Alsatian Shepherds on short leashes, carrying compact machine pistols and other assorted lethal devices. One other man - dog team could be seen patrolling the outside perimeter of the high ten foot stone walls that were stuccoed over in a light cream color. Strange trees with smooth cinnamon colored twisted trunks were predominant and framed the villa-like compound. Some of the trees were budding in preparation for the far South American spring but the air was cool reflecting their distant latitude. The compound's geolocation was nearly identical in the Southern Hemisphere to the South Pole as Bavaria was to the North Pole. In 1943 when Mendoza's father had reoccurring premonitions at the height of the war that he was going to be hung publicly as a war criminal, he commissioned three trusted aides to find and develop a sanctuary where he could survive in secluded safety. They found Bariloche and during that age of poor communications and no spy satellites, they felt they had found the perfect climate, seclusion and remote location to relocate their Führer. Ships with construction teams and equipment were immediately sent and by the end of 1944, with the war spiraling disastrously downward, the sanctuary was prepared, staffed and secured, ready to receive Hitler.

Schmitt was impressed, this was the capital of the new world order where bio- blackmail would force nations to beg for relief. It was beautifully simple and unassuming, surrounded by the thick forest of those unusual looking trees. Those magical trees of the Los Arrayanes Forest now framed the heart of a new Aryan nation.

CHAPTER 81

Atlanta, Georgia

Kate, Tom, Brad and Joseph had just sat down for dinner when Kate's phone rang. It was Redare calling from Paris.

"Bonjour, Monsieur Redare, pardon, Bonsoir."

"Hello, Kate, sorry to disturb you at this late hour, but I have some information for you. Jules, Jean and I assume Sullivan have been traveling by air for many hours. First Cuba, then Lima, Peru, and the last signal received was from Santiago, Chile but after that there has been no contact for more than eighteen hours. We are unsure if the device is still working or if they are somewhere remote enough to prevent a signal to be received or transmitted. They could be anywhere in the lower third of South America. A virtual needle in the haystack. That little device sent vital signs each a long time with the distress signal and they were each time normal excepting a rise in Jean's blood pressure. My gut tells me they are still alive and need help. So I am sending three men familiar to you from the FFL to Santiago, Chile to search for our friends."

"Are they part of the rescue team that plucked us off our raft in the Amazon?" she asked.

"Oui, exactement, Paul, Eric and Dennis. They said to say hello and thank the group for providing them with some job security. It was their way of saying they would get the job done and find them."

"I hope so but this is again beyond the natural and will require the help of the supernatural. We will have to go to Chile and meet up with these brave men and bring the supernatural with us."

Redare paused for a moment.

"D'accord. I will provide everything you will need logistically, but you need to find immediate transportation to Santiago so you arrive about the time they do. Coming home won't be a problem as Le Pasteur's 737 is on the ground at the airport there. A young man named Donovan was found on board and he had been shackled in the plane morgue and is claiming ignorance on what happened to our friends. As he said, he was attacked and tied up because obviously he was of no value to the abductors. He also claimed he was a TSA Agent, who was inspecting the jet's manifest when he was subdued at Logan. Donovan was held temporarily because he had no credentials or official uniform and has been relegated to the American embassy. I suspect he is not as innocent as he professes and when they process his fingerprints and DNA, he will be arrested."

"We have our passports and the French Diplomatic badges that Jules gave us but I think they are expired. We also have our USDA credentials. Will that get it us where we need to be?" Kate asked.

"Oui, I believe any of it will get the job done but ultimately more is better. I will update your French Diplomatic credentials, it will only take a few minutes and I will forward them to your email. Just get to a computer printer, use barcode label paper and print one for each side of your badges and on each bag you are carrying. Think of it as an insurance policy. I will send everything I have on that region; hazards, language do's and don'ts and the like along with the soldiers. They can brief you but you must follow their rules. Also, if you are officially detained by a government agency for any reason, feel free to give out my contact information."

"Thank you so much for your kindness. I wondered if you are fully aware of the extent of what is happening in London, Beijing, Mumbai, and Tokyo? We have just been briefed here at the CDC."

"I have only received some preliminary reports but I suspect within a very short time we will restrict all travel to and from these areas. The Chunnel has already been closed and many, many people in Britain are not happy being trapped on an island with plague. Our Maritime Gendarmerie has brought in all their officers and will be patrolling the coastline to force back boats trying to smuggle human cargo. The Armée de L'Air, our Air Force, will also be patrolling from above with orders to sink any vessel within two kilometers of a potential landing point. This has the earmarks of a great human disaster."

"I agree but here is something not yet released that we just were told," Kate explained.

"In the outbreak in Baltimore the disease was delivered by specifically linking it to a veterinary rabies vaccine produced by TriStar Veterinary Biologics. You already knew that, but these new cases are not being delivered in that way because the vaccine was only used in the United States. These new city sources came from either the exposed leaving Baltimore to spread the disease after incubation or a new more successful means to deliver the pathogen has been developed. The CDC believes it is the latter. Mumbai and Beijing are in total chaos and the Chinese government is blaming the United States for Biologic Warfare and threatening retaliation. The world is sitting on a keg of dynamite. The good news is Dr. Fred Garrett thinks he has found a cure based on his research on BSE, Mad Cow Disease. That information has been forwarded to China in hopes they will back down. If they can quickly produce the cure in the quantities necessary, perhaps we can limit the worldwide casualties."

"Bon, I will continue then to monitor for Jean's signals and inform the FFL men you will meet them in Santiago and provide them with your contact data. I would tell you this, Kate, there is some major form of evil behind this. Use your faith as a shield and be prepared for anything. The best way to end this threat is subtlety. We can't expect armies to burst in and capture the devil. He is too smart for that. However a well-executed coup in his lair can best eliminate his presence. This is not an mission with mercy but a mission to terminate. Do I make myself clear, Kate? It is kill or be killed."

"We fully understand our responsibility and the risks," Kate answered solemnly.

There was a pause. Redare replied, "Then go with the blessings of our merciful Savior."

CHAPTER 82

Mendoza Compound

Arrayanes Forest, Argentina. Same day

Mendoza sat under his portico, satisfied, thrilled with the worldwide reports on the newly viron infected cities indicating his direct simple method of spreading the plague was far superior to their original plans. The disease was now going to be disseminated more widely and be likely harder to control. In a few days he might offer the four infected nations an opportunity to save their most important cities by cooperating with his demands for power in their government and of course pay a ransom. He would never directly reveal that he was the author of the plague but imply there might be many other pathogens ready for release. For now he was satisfied to let Schmitt get settled in and then he would interrogate the two French captives that had been delivered the night before. He needed to know how much was known in the real world about him and his plans and it never hurt to hold a hostage as a bargaining chip.

Schmitt and James enthusiastically walked over to him after entering through the gate and past the barking Alsatian. They looked exhausted and dirty but were smiling widely to finally be at their destination.

Mendoza was sitting in his customary worn rattan chair under the shaded cool portico. He was wearing his signature white linen Guayaberas shirt, crisp linen white slacks and matching white alligator skin loafers.

A large Cuban cigar drifted smoke slightly upward until it met the waves of air produced by a long belt-driven fan. The rubber belt creaked a little as the fan wobbled.

Schmitt stood before his Führer and snapped to attention, his rubber soled boots muting his heel's collision.

"Herr Mendoza, you look well. Congratulations on the success of your new delivery method of the viron, it was pure genius. The more the disease spreads, the more they will try to disinfect with the false products. They may never figure that out, at least in time enough to stop an explosion of disease. How many are they estimating are infected or dead in those cities?"

Mendoza took a drag on the cigar and causally released the plume of smoke upward, savoring both the flavor of the tobacco and the taste of success.

"James, you are dismissed, José will show you to the kitchen."

"Oui Monsieur!"

He turned and walked into the house and Mendoza watched him until he disappeared from view.

"Let's see, where were we? Ah yes, my agents in those unfortunate cities who work in public health have sent very encouraging numbers. It appears that as expected, the more densely populated, less 'clean' cities have been hit the hardest. Beijing is reporting two hundred thousand dead, a half million infected and the city in a complete panicked shutdown. Mumbai is by far the worst with four hundred thousand dead and one million clinical, that, of course, they have no way of treating. London and Tokyo have nearly identical numbers at twenty thousand dead and a similar number in hospital. Unfortunately, it appears they have started steam disinfecting pubic areas and it appears to be working. I considered releasing it into their public water system but the dilution of the viron in such massive public works would probably just waste our precious supply. We need now to work on those new disease entities and prepare a second front. I have serious questions on how we proceed and will need your counsel.

"We have two prisoners, perhaps a better word is guests, that I need to interrogate to determine how much is known about our disease. I waited to start that process to specifically include you. We all, including the prisoners will dine tonight, and tomorrow you and I will get down to business."

"Who are these people?" Schmitt asked.

"They are two very prestigious Frenchmen, if that is not contradictory. Doctor Jules LeClerc of the Pasteur Institute and Doctor Jean DuBois, son of the bastard Nazi hunter Robert DuBois. A third man was with them but he apparently is one of us; a defector, an airport cop who captured the men. I still am not sure about him. He seems a little old but he indicated that in two months he would be eligible to take retirement. He is willing to remain on in his current job and give us access to some of the governmental databases, but more importantly could help our people get in or out of the country if we travel through Boston. He also indicated that he could be transferred to a more valuable airport if necessary to service our needs, like Miami International. He also informed me that he is scheduled to work tomorrow and will need to call in this evening to leave his supervisors a message explaining he is ill. Otherwise he may lose his position. I will allow him access to one of our disposable SAT -D phones. Once he leaves his message, we will immediately destroy the phone. He betrays us, we will destroy him also."

"When will I have the pleasure to meet these Frogs?" Schmitt asked.

"Like I said, we will be eating this evening in the grand dining room in about three hours. There will be just four of us at dinner, the Frenchmen, you and me. Somewhat intimate, we will treat them in a friendly manner and perhaps they will give us what we need to know without a struggle. I think they want to find out more about us and I'm sure they think they can outwit us. Their arrogance will be their undoing.

"I suggest you get a snack from Manuel in the kitchen, get cleaned up and then rest until dinner. I want you to have your wits about you."

Schmitt was escorted to the kitchen and Mendoza sat back in his favorite chair and closed his eyes. He could hear the compound's chickens scratching and pecking at the ground insects and softly clucking as they filled their bellies and he smiled as the peacocks screamed like great raptors from their treetop vantagepoints, like feathered watchdogs. Theirs was a primal scream that creeped some people out who never had heard the strange noise before.

Mendoza was always on alert, egotistically watching for imagined assassins, a paranoid trait he had inherited from his father. It had kept his father alive against the odds through thirty-two assassination attempts and those same instincts were going to help keep him alive. He trusted no one, not even his mother who died in his prearranged plane crash when he was a young man.

Mendoza now longed for one more visit from his father. That brief vision had been an great encouragement that he was on the right path and that his father believed in him, perhaps even loved him. If his father only would reappear, then he would believe that he wasn't on the verge of insanity.

He drifted into a very short deep sleep and dreamt of wolves, bison and wild Indians. He felt panicked, and in his dream was trying to run harder and faster in snow that kept getting deeper and deeper. His legs seemed leaden, he gasped for breath. Mendoza stumbled and fell into the cold snow and a warrior Indian wearing a full headdress of long eagle feathers was instantly upon him. The Indian was screaming a bloodcurdling *HOKA HEY!* He sensed the warrior's hand push down his forehead as the opposite raised high to strike a blow to his skull with a rawhide wrapped tomahawk.

He gasped, helpless to stop the blow...

"Herr Mendoza, sorry but it is time for you to get to ready for dinner."

Startled, he gasped, sweaty from cold fear and the reality of the vision he had just experienced. He quickly stood, only slightly disoriented and thanked the servant.

"Gracias, Manuel. I must have drifted off."

The servant backed away and Mendoza took a white handkerchief from his back pocket and wiped his forehead and looked, half expecting to see blood from the realistic dream.

He jumped as the peacock screamed loudly again, looked up at the bird's roost and saw that the large male was in full tail display,

with the setting sun behind him giving a corona effect much like that Indian's headdress in his dream.

That sent a shiver up his spine but he shook his head and laughed off the silly bird and his dream.

Dummer Vogel. Dumb bird.

By seven that evening, Manuel had prepared the massive Black Forest Oak dining table that had been carefully shipped from Germany in 1944. The dark wood was ornately carved and could easily seat twenty but over all the years the most that had ever dined together was three; his father and mother and the child Mendoza. Tonight there was to be four guests, including the Frenchmen.

Mendoza and the two prisoners met in the library for pre-dinner drinks and Mendoza greeted the Frenchmen cordially as they entered the half-timbered room with its oversized stone fireplace. Old European oak was burning vigorously in the hearth.

"Bonsoir, messieurs, I hope your accommodations are satisfactory in my guest cottage," Mendoza greeted.

"Oh, I thought we were prisoners not guests. My mistake. The guard and dog at the front of the cottage must be there for our protection only," Jules replied sarcastically.

"Yes, they are for all our protection, including yours. If we can convince you to assist in our efforts, I give you my personal guarantee that you will be released no worse for wear and better yet than that, you will not have to not worry about anything unfortunate occurring to your families in Paris. Dr. LeClerc, your gorgeous wife, children and I believe four grandchildren and Dr. DuBois, your beautiful daughter Susan and two grandchildren. For now they are safe, protected from harm by my agents. If you fail to cooperate, it is a simple matter for me to bring a special kind of Hell to their doorsteps."

"Why would you need our help?" Jean asked.

"I need your expertise in research and governmental process. Also, I want to control your ongoing efforts to stop me before I accomplish my goals. It is really quite simple, you assist me and call off your colleagues and everyone will be healthy and happy."

"This place stinks to me of a Nazi palace," Jean said angrily.

"You are quite correct, Dr. DuBois, this beautiful refuge was built to house a great man, my father, the greatest world leader of the twentieth century."

"Your father was Winston Churchill ?" Jules said, kidding sarcastically.

"No more than your father was Benito Mussolini," Mendoza said, returning the laugh.

"Then who was your father? Darth Vader?" Jean pressed. "That will have to wait for now. I see Doctor Schmitt is here."

Schmitt entered the room as the two Frenchmen glared at him.

Here was the object of their quest. Schmitt walked over to the men and cordially extended his hand. They each kept their hands at their sides, refusing.

"Gentlemen, let's not be petty about this. I think it would be very wise that you greet the good doctor for both you and your families."

They slowly extended their hands and shook Schmitt's hand passively. "Very nice to meet two famous men like yourselves. I look forward to collaborating with you. I think you will find my work *très intéressant.*"

"Perhaps we will," Jules replied, rolling his eyes.

"We are good then," Mendoza implied, "we need to have a toast with some very fine cognac. What shall we toast to? Collaboration? Friendship? New World Order?"

"How about Justice?" Jean suggested.

"Yes, I think that is good," Schmitt replied.

"Alright then, lift your glasses high. ... I said high," Mendoza ordered. "We drink to a future where justice is blind, and the unjust peoples of the world, as defined by me, will need to justify their existence. Prost!"

Schmitt and Mendoza shouted the toast, Jean and Jules just mumbled the word.

The cognac was warm encouragement for the two Frenchmen, both afraid that if Sullivan was discovered to be a fraud, they all would be dead, but encouraged that the former FBI agent possessed the skills needed to get them out of their confinement. Time was their only limitation. They needed answers on exactly what were Mendoza's plans and needed them fast before they unleashed Sullivan and hopefully ended the Nazi's scheme.

Manuel came in and whispered something in Mendoza's ear.

"Gentlemen, my very excellent Chef has informed me that our dinner is ready. He will lead us into the dining salon."

The table was set with an array of breads, heavy, dark and dense, lighter croissants and biscuits. Each place setting consisted of ten pieces of ornate silverware, three bone China glazed plates sporting an elaborate hound and stag hunting motif and there were six Baccarat crystal stemware glasses. A large native flower arrangement was centered on the table and a massive candelabra held twelve tall white candles.

Each course was done to perfection. The appetizer was fresh water shrimp and sausages of different meats, the salad, a mixture of micro greens from the compound's garden, a main course of roasted duck with root vegetables, a cheese course and dessert of a light coconut sorbet with macaroons.

"I must say," Jules said complimenting the chef, "this was a very good meal by anyone's standard. Well done, Manuel!"

"Bravo!" Schmitt added.

"Well then I suggest we retire for the evening. Gentlemen, you will necessarily be locked into your guest quarters but my men will be protecting your safety just outside your doors. Please do not tempt or test them. We will move on tomorrow to the lab so we can get down to business. Any questions?" Mendoza asked.

"Yes, I have one. Whose portrait is covered with the black cloth on the Great Wall?" Jean asked.

Mendoza smiled and replied, "That is your answer to whose son I am. That my friend is a portrait of the greatest leader of the twentieth century, my father. Would you care to see it?"

"Bien Sûr," came his reply.

Mendoza walked over to the portrait and explained, "This portrait was done two years before he died of Parkinson's disease." He pulled the cloth away.

Jean and Jules gasped and walked closer inspecting the painting. They saw the artist's signature and tried to reconcile the date in their heads.

"Like I said before, the greatest man of the twentieth century, as you see he had aged significantly but then again he was very old. Do you recognize my father?"

Jean offered his opinion after carefully studying the portrait. It was the eyes, the pure evil in those eyes.

"Adolph Hitler?" he asked incredulously.

"Very good, Doctor DuBois. It is him. He lived decades after magically escaping from his bunker. Now I will finish what he started."

CHAPTER 83

Evergreen Resort Hotel

Santiago, Chile. Next day, early afternoon

Tom held the door open for Kate as they entered the old granite stone hotel as a stale mild mildew odor hit him. The inside looked like it would barely qualify as a three-star hotel in the States, but was listed on the booking website as a five-star with full amenities. Bernard Redare had booked them in and sent the link to Kate, but obviously this was far less than they had expected.

Brad was the first to complain after looking around the rundown lobby. "Of all the years we have been doing this as a group, this is probably the worst hotel we have ever had to stay in. I would prefer the old Fort Peck Hotel over this place. That place was haunted, this place is plain creepy. I would change the name to the 'Last Resort' Hotel. Five-star? Maybe five out of ten?"

"Just like you to be the complainer," Joseph teased, "maybe the rooms are better and just this part is rundown."

"And maybe the Tooth Fairy and Easter Bunny stay here when they are in town," Brad kidded.

It turned out Joseph was right, the rooms were nicer than the less than perfect lobby. This was likely five-star in a South American kind of way, not by a Parisienne standard.

They settled in for an hour cleaning up and preparation for meeting with the three French Foreign Legion officers who had the skills to help them find Jean, Jules and Sullivan. Then hopefully at the same time they would end the Mendoza/ Schmitt threat. Santiago had been the last recorded transmission from Jean's medical alert device so that was their logical starting point.

They met outside the hotel precisely at three as was prearranged by Redare.

The French soldiers were dressed casually in light colored slacks and different colored polo shirts. Other than their extremely fit physiques and short military style haircuts, they looked the part of European tourists.

"Bonjour, mes amies, comment ça va?" Kate asked as she greeted each man with a cheek on cheek air kiss.

"Nous sommes très bien, merci," Eric, the flight surgeon replied. Paul and Dennis each took a turn shaking the men's hands.

"There is a very good cafe about four blocks from here in the old town section and it is quite charming. The food is a fusion style Chilean Japanese so believe it or not you can get very good regional seafood prepared in a local manner and some impressive sushi plates," Dennis added. "And it is very private so we can talk freely."

"I'm famished, so as long as they don't try to feed me a guinea pig, I'm good," Brad joked.

"That's a Peruvian meal, dumb ass," Joseph teased.

Tom was laughing and said, "Lead the way, gentlemen, we are all a little delirious from hunger but not nearly as bad as when you plucked us out of the Amazon."

It was a pleasant late spring day and the walk was mostly downhill and soon they were seated in the nearly empty restaurant. Wine was ordered and after Eric proposed a friendship toast they ordered their meals.

While they ate a first course appetizer, Paul, their intelligence officer filled the four Americans in on what they had found out.

"Redare," he began, "gave us some very accurate data from Dr. DuBois' medical alert device so we started where the last transmission occurred, Benítez International Airport. We located the Pasteur jet which is in a private hangar the Institute is now leasing. We went over it with a fine tooth comb but unfortunately it had been thoroughly cleaned after it went into the hangar. Asking around got us two leads. One was that two men were removed from the jet with black hoods over their heads plus what looked like someone guarding them and they ended up in a smaller two-engine plane that is known by the locals to be piloted by a man with very few scruples. He evidently is a man who will take any job, legal or illegal, moral or not, just for a payday. He returned without his three passengers and the next day, yesterday, and he immediately refueled and flew two more men out. Interestingly, the man is a stickler about keeping his fuel tanks topped off and we contacted the airport petro manager and he told us the man used nearly exactly the same amount of fuel each day. The fuel manager suggested, after we paid him sixty-five thousand pesos, that the pilot most likely traveled to Bariloche, Argentina. The fuel and flight time logged each day was a close match."

"You paid him how much money?" Brad questioned incredulously.

"About one hundred dollars. A fortune down here."

Tom asked, "Did you find the man? Did you talk to him?"

"Oui," Eric answered, "and we persuaded him to discuss his charters and it appears the first flight was the one LeClerc and DuBois were on as prisoners and a third man, older, he estimated in his late fifties was in charge of them. On the second charter, he was flying a German man and a light mocha complexion male with a French accent. He thought that man was likely from a French Caribbean nation. He put down at the same landing strip both days, and was paid in cash. The fuel manager was correct, they were in the Bariloche area.

"The pilot was the ratty type with a dash of weasel tossed in and we couldn't let him go so..."

"So we locked him in the morgue on the Pasteur jet," Paul confessed. "We figured he will fly us to Bariloche tomorrow on a larger four-engine we rented into the actual city airport. The authorities will then be detaining him for a few days until we tell them to release him. We don't return he will be in confinement for a very long time. So tomorrow early in the morning he will fly us to Bariloche, but remember Eric and Dennis are fully qualified to fly, but he doesn't know that. We want him to fly us first over where he landed the two flights. Then we will land at the big airport and then find alternate overland transportation to that spot, likely onward in jeeps. Should be fairly easy to follow the trail from there since it's only been forty-eight hours. We get close and assess the situation and then take action if necessary. The main thing is we get Jules, Jean and Sullivan, if he is there, out."

"What if we run into a small army or someplace heavily defended? It might be an impossible situation," Kate questioned.

"Redare is harvesting the satellite data for the general area but we located some images taken by Google Earth and the primary entity in that region is the Los Arrayanes National Forest. It is very dense and has some small remote areas that were carved out before the forest was nationalized. We did some research and those areas are privately held, secluded, and possibly defended. It appears of the half dozen that are publicly documented, only three are active. Argentinian Army Rangers hold maneuvers in the area every two years and we contacted their regional commander and he said he would concentrate on the southwest mountainous part of the park, as that holds two of the three occupied compounds as they are the largest and most active. One is allegedly a religious cult with monks, the other has been off limits to everyone since the late forties. That off limits order is directly from the Argentine Central Government and to the commandant's knowledge, the only one he has ever heard of. We think that is where we will find them."

The food arrived and they started to eat the fresh seafood feast.

"So," Tom asked, "we start using jeeps but how is that going to get us close enough without being detected and what are we using as an excuse for even being in the area, assuming these people are hostile."

Eric had their cover.

"We are sure they will be hostile because they have two prisoners possibly three and with Schmitt likely on that second flight, we feel we have may have located Mendoza. Schmitt is, we think, the architect of the plague, likely with Mendoza's financial backing. We have really tried to keep this a low profile investigation but the area is crawling with low life that will do anything for a few extra pesos. So we are going to Jeep in halfway to the compound and then we might use some burros to pack in our equipment. That decision is pending."

Joseph lit up.

"You mean we will have rocket launchers, drones and other weapons?" he asked excitedly.

"No, food, water and cameras," Eric said.

"Our cover is that you four are National Geographic photojournalists and we are here to record the native reclusive Southern Pudú deer. It is rare and endangered and the smallest of the world's deer species. We three are your French camera crew and Kate, you are to only speak French to us. This was Redare's idea and I think a quite good one. We already have some footage loaded on the cameras, some trail cameras which really are combination camera and SAT radios. Our weapons are simple. Since firearms are prohibited in the National Forest, we are carrying machetes, assorted knives, garrote wire disguised as utility wire, some medical supplies, and of course a good supply of Plastique packed in the wall of a water cooler. We will pack everything in and then play the game by ear."

"You forgot the hummingbird drones. They're the coolest of all. We can fly one in when we are within three hundred meters, gather data and if necessary, use it to kill by exploding it near a target. It is a beautiful piece of lethal technology," Paul added.

"Oui, I can hardly wait to try it out," said Dennis.

"And Redare will send to your phones all you need to know about the National Geographic Society, for example who you work for and your work information such as when you were hired and the like. Not too hard, also Redare created two articles about your freelance wildlife work and your study of deer with CWD, whatever that is, and everything they could gather on the Pudú. You have this evening to get up to speed and tomorrow, we will quiz you on the way in. We also brought you some army style fatigues that have built-in tick and insect repelling properties which I understand we will need.

The Trojan Plague

"Any questions?" Eric asked.

No one said a word.

"Bien, then we should finish up and head back to the hotel. I have a feeling we won't rest much for the next few days."

Brad couldn't resist a final comment. "My God, it's Deja Moo all over again."

CHAPTER 84

Evergreen Resort Hotel

Later that night

Joseph was restless. His well-tuned instincts were firing off a jumbled mix of generational experiences, personal apprehensions and fears. The Legion's soldiers plans sounded good but he wasn't entirely comfortable playing another role to try to fool someone who wouldn't blink an eye at killing them, alibi or no alibi. Berhetzel, the last Destroyer, was able to figure out who they were because Kate screwed up for just a second and afterward he tried to make them a main course on an Army Ant picnic. They were only saved by his great grandfather's spirit who appeared as a grizzled rat which chewed through the ropes that had secured him to a tree. He counted on his grandfather's protection every day of his life but this was shaping up as requiring a double dose of protection. He restlessly paced the large room which seemed to be closing in on him with each pass, so he went out on his large balcony that faced east toward the Andes. He sat back in an old wicker rocker and put his feet up on the original gray granite wall that had kept guests from toppling over to the street below since 1919. He closed his eyes and started praying those perennial verses that he had memorized as a child and been a part of his being since he was formed in his mother's womb. Joseph kept his voice low but convicted, each utterance a magical message to his ancestors.

He started to feel warm, full of energy and confident, comfortable that his words were being received. He watched as the setting sun shone from behind the hotel and cast a warm orange glow on the still snow-capped mountains. It was as if his prayers had lit the face of the mountains.

"Well, I'll be damned," he said grinning. "It's going be alright." The air had cooled as the sun finally set and Joseph pulled the rocker closer to the wall and put his boots up again. He closed his eyes and relaxed in the fresh evening air and soon was engulfed in much needed sleep.

"My son," came the calm voice had he had heard nearly all his life and now was the voice of wisdom and assurance that emanated from beyond the grave.

"My son," his grandfather repeated, "you need to know some things about your mission."

Joseph was mentally connected in the dream with his grandfather but physically he was captured in a very deep sleep.

He visualized his grandfather clearly as a young warrior, dressed in beaded buckskin as if going to a ceremony or into battle, not his customary faded denim jeans and white T shirt. He was not old but Joseph's age; smooth skin, long jet black hair, clear sharp eyes, appearing lean, muscular and very fit. Here was his hero, the only man he ever wanted to be just like.

"You," his grandfather continued, "have a gift that no one else in your group of friends possess and that is our ancestors' direct guidance and protection. The forest you are entering is a spiritual, magical place. However, not all those spirits are friendly and those that are evil will use their power to create more evil. They will surround to protect this new 'Destroyer' of life so not only do you have to defeat the persons you seek, but also must get through this forest of evil first to find them. Defeat the bad magic first or you will never make it out of these woods alive. Remember to keep your enemies in front of you to protect your flanks like the Tanaka, but be aware that these evil spirits in this forest will try to push you down and if they do, you must pivot to protect any area that they can attack. Stay back from the others and guard their flanks, don't rush in."

Joseph wanted to respond, to acknowledge his grandfather but he was unable, resigned to being only a listener of his warning.

"Tomorrow everything I have taught you will be tested and you will begin to better understand the depth of evil in this world. Use all your gifts, remember the Tanka..." his voice faded away.

Joseph was suddenly flung upright like the chair had been pushed up to toss him over the balcony. He landed hands on the granite barrier that separated him from falling to his death. He sucked in a breath, gasping and grabbed hold firmly, not trusting the old mortared stone.

"Christ!" he yelled, a bad habit he had picked up from Brad and then he slowly pushed away from the edge.

He thought about what had just happened. The message was clear as a bell to him; he possessed the greatest responsibility to his friends. Also, Grandfather had confirmed they were on the right track to find the men.

He pulled out his cell and called Brad.

"Brother, are you asleep?" he asked.

"Do bears crap in the woods?" Brad quipped.

Two minutes later Brad was knocking on Joseph's door.

"This better be good," the bull of a man grumbled.

"I have good news and bad news," Joseph teased, "which do you want first?"

"Oh goody, I get to play a game. Give me the bad news first."

"Grandfather just came to me in a dream and he said the forest we are traveling into is full of very evil spirits and they are going to try to protect the persons of evil we seek. They will make our job near impossible if we aren't at our best."

"Okkkk, what's the good news?"

"If I understood him correctly I am to follow behind you all to guard your flanks. I will hang back and, I guess, be your ace in the hole. If everyone agrees, I will stay at a safe distance and call in reserves or other help if necessary. If we are wrong, which I doubt we are because Grandfather wouldn't set this up if we were, then we haven't lost anything but time."

"That's just great. How in the hell will I be able to sleep now? A haunted forest with likely a new Destroyer waiting to capture us in his spider web of evil. I think I need to find a new job. I think a dairy soft serve, a cone master, just think of the delicious benefits and no evil spirits trying to melt me.

"We need to talk to some locals about this place we are invading tomorrow. I need a beer anyway so why don't we see if we can find someone who speaks English in a local tavern who might give us some insight."

They took the stairs out of the hotel, avoiding the lobby. Five minutes later they came upon an Irish pub, Flanigan's, its sign complete with a large emerald shamrock.

The bar was busy serving liquor and food to a late night collective of locals and tourists. Brad made a beeline to the shiny brass decorative bar.

"A Guinness for me and a sarsaparilla for my Injun' friend."

The bartender smiled and poured a heavy headed dark ale and a tall ginger ale for Joseph.

"Is that pale ginger ale?" Brad asked, joking with the bartender.

"No," said the bartender with a good Irish accent, recognizing the set up, "it came from this bottle not a pail."

Brad extended his hand and laughed. "Nice to meet a man with a sense of humor."

"Nice to meet you, Yank," came the reply.

"Maybe you can help us," Brad asked. "We are working for the National Geographic Society and leaving to go to Bariloche tomorrow to document the plight of the Southern Pudú deer. Is there anyone that you know that could give us some local folklore background on Los Arrayanes Forest? We heard it is a place of evil spirits as well as one of great beauty. Someone who speaks English."

"Sure can, see that acute little strawberry blonde in the corner with her two friends. She is a graduate student entomologist from somewhere in the States. She is in that forest all by herself five or six days a week, then flies back here for a couple of days to clean up and visit her friends. She's been down in Chile and Argentina for a couple months and I think she will be heading home fairly soon. Her name is Alice, and she is super nice!"

Brad led Joseph through the amorphous mass of people that stood talking in groups, each turning up their volume to talk above the next group. When they reached the table Brad did the introduction.

"Hi, Alice, ladies, sorry the bartender didn't give us your last name but we were told you had been working in Los Arrayanes, and we have some questions for you if you have some time. My name is Brad Upton and I work for the USDA and right now I'm helping two friends who are studying the Southern Pudú deer for the National Geographic Society. My sidekick here is Joseph Blackfeather, a Lakota Sioux from Fort Peck, Montana, and he is our tracker and hopefully our survival guide."

"Pleased to meet you, fellas, my last name is Murphy, Alice Murphy. I am a Ph.D. graduate student from Kansas State. My expertise, believe it or not, is termites. Damp wood, dry wood or subterranean and now a new species I identified in Los Arrayanes, which can digest cellulose four times faster than any other know specie of Isoptera of which over three thousand have been identified. My goal is to prove a commercially compatible specie can be used to digest paper for recycling in controlled situations or say a colony of all sterile workers controlled by pheromone attractants that can be injected into a landfill to speed up cellulose decomposition and in the process release a harvestable methane gas which then can be used to power electric plants. How's that for a mouthful? Anyway, the key is the selection for the sterile male workers of the termite so it is incapable of establishing itself outside its controlled purpose."

"Good idea, will that work on all types of termites?" Joseph questioned.

"No, most won't hold as a colony without an active queen. The ones I'm investigating are unique in that the queen is only active part of the year when she is reproducing, unlike bees and ants where queens survive much longer than the so-called workers and directly control the colony, although some termite queens have been known to live thirty to fifty years. Something else that is curious is when people see termites they think ants but in reality, they are more closely related to cockroaches."

She was smart, pretty and enthusiastic. Brad could tell Joseph liked her.

"Any words of advice for us on what we heard was the evil controlling this forest?" he asked.

"No question it can be a creepy place if you let your imagination run wild. Those Arrayanes trees are both beautiful with their gnarled trunks, all twisted, their cinnamon colored bark and have their unusual growing habit from either upright or bushy and twisted. You can see all sorts of things in their shapes, hear the wind moan as it passes through a grove and mistake tree shapes for human forms. At first I was scared, even with my assistant present, until I realized it was him who was more afraid from all the years of the locals telling stories about hunters disappearing without a trace or children getting lost, never to be found. But the thing the native population fear the most, at least for the old people, are the witches they say inhabit Los Arrayanes. The young fear the stories of aliens. Scares the crap out of them. My field guide deserted me after my second trip in.

"Just so you know, you probably will have a real hard time finding the Pudú, because I only saw one all spring, and that was just a fleeting glance. They have been hunted and poached mercilessly to near eradication. You'll also see that with the density of those woods, you will likely have a very hard time sneaking up on them."

"We will be using blinds once I find evidence of their trails or droppings so I think, if we are patient, we will get what we want," Joseph said trying to sound the part he was playing.

"Now I have a question for you, Joseph," Alice said. "We know a couple of clubs nearby, how would you like to join us three girls for a little dancing. I promise to have you home early if you want."

"Go ahead, have some fun. Who knows how long we will be in those woods anyway," Brad said.

"Come on, Joseph," the other girls pleaded, tugging at this arms. He gave in after a short series of inviting smiles.

Brad paid their tab and headed back to the hotel.

Have fun, my brother, Lord knows what kind of evil is waiting for us!

CHAPTER 85

Mendoza Compound

Dawn Next Day

Two guards led the Frenchmen to the portico where a continental breakfast was set up. Mendoza and Schmitt were already drinking rich hot chocolate and each had a bowl of fruit and some strudel. They seemed extremely happy and greeted the men with a cordial 'Bonjour.'

"Gentlemen, I hope you are well rested. We have a lot of amazing things to show you and a project we will need your cooperation on. Please eat and refresh yourselves because this is likely to be a long day."

Jules and Jean ate in silence as Mendoza and Schmitt joked and laughed in German.

"Now," Mendoza announced, "we are going to travel to our subterranean laboratory where you will help us gather our data. I promise you everything you see today will change your concept of history and what we are trying to accomplish. Unfortunately, we are going to have to hood you again until we are underground but that will be a minor sacrifice for the amazing things you will find waiting there."

The men were hooded and guards drove two jeeps, one with the Nazis and one with the Frenchmen. They drove for fifteen minutes over very rough terrain and finally stopped by a small waterfall. The men were helped out of the Jeep and escorted through a very cool damp area and into a musty smelling area. They could hear some mechanism closing what sounded like heavy doors behind them. The guards then removed the hoods from the men.

"There have only been a few men who have visited my father's personal treasury and safe place. You are privileged to be able to see this."

He flipped a switch and a polished quarried stone corridor, cut with German precision, illuminated, giving the impression they were standing in a great cathedral.

"Mon Dieu!" Jean exclaimed.

"It is quite impressive, is it not? The work of a small army of German soldiers, engineers and architects that created this beautiful entrance and cut the tunnels into the hillside. This was a natural creation that was discovered while searching for a safe place for my father's retirement. He was not the first however to utilize this cavern system as you will see in a few moments. Let is take a walk farther in and I will explain.

"This part of South America was part of the Spanish Empire from the late sixteenth century to the mid nineteenth. Like most of this continent, the civilizations were subjugated, domesticated and eventually eradicated primarily from exposure to diseases carried by the Conquistadors, diseases to which they had no immunity. Unintentional but similar to our current campaign, exposing populations to disease to which they have no protection. They looted these countries and established Catholicism to control the people for centuries more. The people were poor, undereducated and kept under control of the Church and their Patriarchal governments. Just look at some of what was found in this cavern when it was excavated in 1944."

There was a small carved out side cavern that was gated with heavy iron bars. Mendoza took a large iron jailer's key from his pocket and opened the gate. It groaned on old hinges as he struggled to push it open. He flipped on the lights.

"Nothing you see here has been disturbed since it was discovered. Everything you see here is Spanish plunder from several centuries," Mendoza explained.

Jules and Jean walked around dozens of barrels containing silver coins, chests full of rare gemstones and piles of silver creations of all sorts. Three armored skeletons in full dress were seated at ninety degree angles around the treasure. Pikes, muskets, axes, chains and all sorts of period armaments were stored in piles, a testament to the power Spain once held. Each skeleton was exactly placed on a heavy wooden chair and appeared to be there to guard and ward off looters. The treasure had never been touched.

Mendoza explained, "This area was part of the Spanish empire called 'The General Captaincy of Chile' and encompassed the entire lower third of South America. Santiago was the capital and the area was ruled with ruthlessness. Pedro de Valdivia explored the region and sent ships filled with tons of silver and other wealth back to Madrid. He did however at the same time plan for his future, so what you see here is likely a small portion of what is hidden throughout the region. Those skeletons likely were men killed to keep this place secret. When he died, the locations of these places passed with him. The interesting thing is men search the oceans for treasure from those ships that never made it back to Spain but I think they would be better off searching these hills and mountains because that is where the real treasure is.

"Now let me show you this."

They walked fifty meters to another much larger cutout that was behind a more modern stainless steel door and Mendoza swiped a card key and the vault door slid open nearly without a sound. The lights came on automatically after detecting their motion and body temperature.

"This my friends is what is left of the treasury of the Third Reich. There are twenty metric tons of gold, diamonds and jewels, artwork originals and billions in cash from the United States, Great Britain and Europe. The currency is circulated in various ways but none of it is traceable and moves in and out of the stock, commodity, and oil markets. What you see here is to be dumped this fall and then played into the currency markets. You should try it, the end game is quite interesting."

"You bastards looted this wealth from millions of my people. This display makes me want to puke," Jean voiced angrily.

"Do as you must but you need to know that billions more wealth is being grown with each day our plague expands, so when we offer the treatment or cure if you prefer, those dollar figures will quickly quadruple. It was a near perfect plan, and would have brought the United States to her knees if it hadn't been for you and your friends' interference. But now you are *HERE* and *WILL* be part of the solution. Remember about your families. Now let's go to the laboratory."

The group traveled to what appeared to be a dead end and there was another door that Mendoza's card key swiped. It opened to and exposed an oversized service elevator that took them down one hundred meters. The doors opened revealing a replica laboratory that duplicated the research and production labs of TriStar in Leipzig.

"Doctor Schmitt, this is your new laboratory, only difference is we have no large primates, just the normal small lab mammals and New World monkeys. There are six private bedrooms if you need to work through the night. Doctor Schmitt, you have the presidential suite, and two are for the guards. There are staff dormitories for the assistants and there are plenty of assistants. Not one of them will return to the surface until I have a new biologic agent for my arsenal unless I order it. Everyone clear on that?

"Well then, have at it!".

CHAPTER 86

Los Arrayanes Forest

Same day, noon

The pilot had done exactly as they had told him to do and landed precisely where he had dropped his two previous charters. This time when they landed, Eric had three local police, which really was the army, take the pilot for safekeeping after a nice bribe was paid, their decision not to lock him back on the Pasteur Jet. The pilot would be in isolation until they gave the ok for his release. If they didn't return he would likely be swallowed up by the system.

Joseph and Paul took one of the extra Jeeps Redare had had brought in by the police, again with a very hefty 'rental' fee for the time they were needed. The good news was the Jeeps were in very good condition and each carried an extra two hundred liters of petro to supplement the full tanks. They carried enough water and RTE meals for at least a week and there were also three-wheel trailers each Jeep would pull. All seven would go in together and where they saw a diversion trail off the main trek, Joseph would exit and hang back to follow on a parallel foot path. He carried everything he needed in a backpack including one of the small drones. He would hang back and if a problem arose, call on generations of Lakota spirits to help.

They slowly traveled in for about ten kilometers, and pulled the Jeeps off into a raised cutout area just off the main trail. The ground was dry and moving forward more silently on foot seemed logical. It was the obvious way to get close undetected and the primary reason they had decided to pack everything in on their backs and not use the sometimes noisy burros.

"It's getting a little late so we will pack in and set up a base camp about two additional kilometers in, then we will move out tomorrow morning setting out the blinds and trail cameras to legitimize our reason for being here. Joseph, we will only use the personal communicators, what you call walkie talkies since cell service is likely spotty at best— keep your unit on vibrate only. I would like you to stay directly behind us but if you want to scout around, just do it carefully with the understanding there may be surveillance and even booby traps already set out there. D'accord?" Eric instructed.

"Got it. I'll be fine," Joseph said excitedly.

"Here is a key to the green Jeep. Hide it somewhere safe, maybe your boot. The black Jeep key I'll hide in the engine under the battery with just the tip exposed. Everyone good with that?" he asked.

They all nodded affirmatively.

"D'accord. Allons y!" *Ok, let's go!*

They sorted out the packs with the FFL soldiers hauling double loads. Kate and Brad used a walking stick and Tom traveled in the middle of the group with Dennis and Paul leading the way in and Eric in step behind the group. The French soldiers knew the target area they were heading to but also understood they needed to establish a credible alibi first before they 'stumbled' into the compound, feinting being lost or one member being ill.

Joseph watched them move deeper into the forest as the woods grew quieter. This was unlike any forest he had ever been in before. There was a good canopy in some areas where the Arrayanes trees had grown straight and tall and then just a short distance away would be a thick scrub oak looking version of the trees with its peeling cinnamon colored bark. There were gigantic ferns clustered under the taller shading wood, with vines entangling the scrubbier version, making those areas nearly impassable, like a forest version of Hell.

Feisty squirrels with dark bodies and white faces sprung from branch to branch of the larger trees which appeared like they had just finished flowering. In a weird sort of way it was both a magical and foreboding place.

The team had headed in an almost due west direction so Joseph shouldered his heavy pack and walked southwest at a slight angle from their path. This appeared the easiest way as the thicker patches of undergrowth looked to be more north and west. He planned on a zig zagging path to cover more ground slowly, checking for evidence of human activity.

The sun continued lowering in the sky and Joseph figured he better settle in for the evening and found a short mossy fern covered area that would make a nice place to roll out his heavy wool blanket and sleep under the stars. He cleared a small area of litter, found some dry moss and started a small fire with the Arrayanes tree bark and branches. The wood burned hotly with almost no smoke. He heated a small tin drinking cup with water, added cocoa and sat and listened while eating some protein bars.

The sun disappeared quickly as it fell behind the Andes onto the Pacific horizon and the air quickly chilled as he settled down on a cushion of moss. Joseph then started to scan the southern sky. Confusingly, the stars and planets were all in different positions and he made a mental note to find out what the difference was between the Big Sky of Montana and the Southern Argentina sky he was scanning now.

Joseph listened as the animals of the night started stirring, hunting and being hunted, imagining four-legged predators, the South American versions of bobcats and foxes moving stealthily, seeking their next meal. He listened for the death cries of victims of the night but it was a quiet, silent night and he drifted off to sleep, senses alert with his generational instincts protecting him.

Suddenly aware of an intruder, the young Lakota grabbed at his large Buck knife that was kept razor sharp and palmed the bison hide wrapped handle at his side. Feinting sleep he waited.

"Joseph, Joseph it's me Alice."

He sat up and sure enough a female form appeared like an apparition from just beyond the light from the fire. She was smiling widely, beautifully.

"Alice? What in the Sam Hill are you doing here? You stalking me?"

"Well, I hadn't thought of it that way, but yes, I guess I am."

"Why?"

"There are several reasons, one is personal— I had a great time last night and I'm extremely attracted to you."

No girl had ever said that to him before with the exception of Cindy Grayfox, and she was attracted to nearly every one of his friends.

"And," she continued, "I had a real strange dream last night where I saw you surrounded by wolves while you were desperately whirling around, holding that big knife trying to keep them away from a desperate looking white buffalo calf."

"Tanaka, they are called Tanaka by my people," he explained.

"Then I heard a voice, very calm, very strong and reassuring; wise and almost heavenly."

"That had to be my great grandfather. He watches over me and my friends. What was his message?" Joseph asked.

"He said, 'Joseph needs you, my daughter, go find and help him.' That was it.

"I was wide awake trying to figure what had just happened. I mean I had only known you for what, four hours? I was up the rest of the night but I felt rested and energized in a way I never experienced before."

"Grandfather has a way of doing that. Did he actually call you daughter?"

"Yes, why?" she answered.

"Because that would be a very high honor. He obviously knows something we are not aware of. How in the world did you find me?"

"Well, because I was up all night, I waited outside the hotel and followed all of you to the airport. Let me back up a little. After your grandfather spoke I googled you and Dr. Brad Upton and learned all about what happened in Argentina two years ago and the Washington attack during the Presidential Inauguration ceremony. You are quite the heroes as are the O'Dells. By the way those three cameramen don't look the part. Trim, fit and good looking."

"Like me?" Joseph teased.

"Yes, just like you but you have better eyes. Cameramen usually are scruffy, disheveled and grubby, only in love with their lens. I've worked with quite a few in the last year and your men scream fake.

"So, I followed you to the airport and my pilot told me your flight plan and about the creepy pilot who flew you in. I flew in two hours after you and then tracked you here."

"What? Did you clip a transponder on me last night?"

"No, but my dad always wanted a boy and when Mom died, he took me camping, hunting, fishing and rock climbing. I can track with the best of them.

"What are you guys, CIA?" she asked.

"Hardly, USDA."

With that Alice started laughing.

"Meat inspectors?"

"Much more than that! So seeing I'm stuck with you, I guess I'll need to explain from the being."

He threw some larger logs on the fire until it was dancing wildly and pulled Alice over to him in a relaxed embrace. They sat watching the fire, his arm wrapped around her protectively. He started to tell his story, his people's story and she was captivated by his spirit. Their souls were melting into one as they watched the warming fire. It seemed like the most natural thing.

CHAPTER 87

Mendoza Compound

That same afternoon

Mendoza had timed his visit so that he would return before dark to the compound and enjoy a good dinner. The others he left in the laboratory would be fed cafeteria style along with the rest of the staff three times a day, albeit the meals would be of excellent quality from the facility's gourmet chef and his staff of two assistants. No one working in any support capacity would complain because they would earn more in the three months they were contracted for than they could make in five years under an Argentinian economy. He knew the Frenchmen would cooperate because of his threats to their families but in reality they needed to be in the lab to be hidden from anyone attempting to find them.

With Mendoza absent, the compound was extremely quiet with most of the guards resting as they had no one to protect. Two guards had been assigned to protect the laboratory by Mendoza and would stay there to support Schmitt. Another guard had taken Manuel on a provisions run down a river that ran to Bariloche but the trek required they go one kilometer east, deeper into the forest on ATV's to reach the motorized skiff they used. They would be gone six hours. That left the one guard and his dog that slept under the shaded entrance of the compound to keep an eye on James and Sullivan, aka Donovan. The compound was virtually empty.

It was quiet and the house empty so Sullivan entered the kitchen by the back door, feinting searching for food by going into the refrigerator. He grabbed a duck leg and started to wander into the main house, munching on the meat. He was orientating himself to the floor plan, looking for cameras while acting innocent. He tried several doors which were locked but one was to a room with a warning sign marked *KOMMUNIKATION KEIN EINTRAG.*

Communications, no entry.

Sullivan tried the door handle but the lock was secure. He reached to his belt and found a paper clip from the plane he had hidden. Inserting the clip in, he tried to remember the class he had had over thirty-five years before in survival techniques. He had never used any of it but how hard could this be ?

After what seemed like a lifetime, the lock clicked over and Sullivan pushed his way into the cold room with numerous computers, television screens, and radios including security cameras scanning the compound and what looked to be an industrial warehouse. The cameras kept scrolling through screen shots and briefly he caught a glimpse of Schmitt, Mendoza, Jean and Jules. It appeared they were on a tour.

"What are you doing in here old man?" came a voice from behind him, "the house and this room is strictly off limits. No one is permitted in the house without Senor Mendoza's permission."

Sullivan slowly raised the duck leg to his mouth and took a bite. He turned to face the challenger.

It was James.

"Who died and made you King?" Sullivan asked with sarcasm.

"Maybe you," came the sharp reply.

Sullivan then saw a small nine millimeter pistol barely bigger than the man's palm. It was pointed directly at his chest.

"I came in for a bite to eat and was curious. Glad I did because I saw something on this security camera that you might find very interesting.

Looks like our benefactor is sitting on a huge fortune, something perhaps you might be interested in sharing with this poor American."

"What? Let me see!" James commanded.

Sullivan stepped back and let the younger man in front of the security screen. Briefly the rotating computer screen showed the silver and gold rooms. Sullivan's suggestion had been a ruse but now fortunately the cameras verified his fictitious claim. Sullivan's eyes widened at the reality.

"Mon Dieu," James exclaimed. "D'accord. I'm interested but how do I know I can trust you?"

"Let's call it honor among thieves, and because we are facing over-whelming odds, we need each other. Perhaps we could enlist the help of those Frenchmen and a couple of the guards. It will take some serious planning but it seems to me there is enough for all of us for several life-times, or more. Now we best get out of here before someone catches us.

"Tonight after dinner we will need to talk, you tell me what you know about how this place works and where they went today. Do you think some of the guards would help us if we asked?" Sullivan inquired.

"Probably, if we can find one who understands English or French. Let me think about it. I have talked to Manuel, the chef, he complains all the time and might get on board, and he speaks English, Spanish and German. He also knows the back door way to Bariloche, I tracked him and a guard down to a river today where they took a flat bottom skiff to pick up supplies. They keep that launch point well-hidden and secret. It would be an easy means to smuggle out all that gold and silver. Anyone stands in our way, we just kill them."

"You make that sound so easy, Mendoza must have an army of sup-porters waiting to defend him if he cries out for help," Sullivan postulated.

"I'm sure that's right but if we make our move swiftly, first taking him out and then Schmitt, we can be gone before anyone knows he's in the grave."

Sullivan knew he had to press the issue to prevent James from double crossing him. He needed to intimidate the younger man and as they were going through the kitchen, he grabbed James from behind and using his FBI training, put the man down to his knees while stripping the nine millimeter pistol quickly from his hand. James was straddled on his knees, head pulled back by his long hair and Sullivan held a butcher knife level with his larynx, pressing firmly against tender skin. A single drop of blood rolled down his neck.

"Donovan! What the hell?" he gasped.

"Just a reminder. I am the teacher, you are the pupil. Understand this my friend. I know more ways to kill than the number of your age. I am a highly trained assassin who just happens to have a day job with the TSA. From my perspective, everyone here is already dead and will have to earn the right to walk away with their lives. Remember that you are already dead and serve me to be resurrected. You can't spend all that money if you are dead. By the way, I'm keeping your pathetic gun."

Sullivan pulled James up to his feet by his shoulders and brushed the black hair back from the man's dilated eyes.

"Isn't it nice to have a friend?" he said with a cruel laugh.

CHAPTER 88

Base camp

The soldiers had found a great secluded location to establish their base camp, quickly put the tents up and had a fire going in less than an hour's time. Eric made sure the electronic perimeter sensors were up and working and Paul prepared a very good dinner of grilled Argentinian beef steaks, rice and black beans. They drank a decent local Pinot Noir that Paul had purchased to serve with the perfectly cooked steaks. Tomorrow they would have to eat the RTE rations. After the meal, evening was closing in with a sky illuminated by the brightest of stars. Everyone was exhausted, so Dennis volunteered to take the first two hour watch. Then Paul would stand watch, followed by Dennis, and Tom had volunteered for the last predawn shift.

Everyone but Brad was up as first light rolled upward and he was left undisturbed until Tom figured he had no choice but to get the big man up for their breakfast of oatmeal, raisins and brown sugar and hard biscotti. The coffee was terrible confirming Kate's theory that the French brewed some of the worst coffee in the world.

"Ok, Dennis and I have discussed how we are going to work this today," Kate announced, "and we came up with this plan. This spot is going to stay as our base camp. It's a good locations and it's only about five kilometers from here to that first compound. Really an easy walk. Tom, Dennis and I will scout out the general area of that compound and see how close we can get without risking being detected. Brad you will work with Eric and Paul and set some trail cameras to establish our alibi for being here."

"What about Joseph?" Brad asked.

"Hopefully he will show up today and we can fill him in. Look for him while you are setting out the cameras. If we don't see him, we can walkie talkie him this evening, otherwise he understands exactly what we are trying to accomplish and still can protect our rear ends," she answered.

"Just so everyone knows," Paul announced, "I received an encrypted text message overnight on the SAT phone from Redare. He said to inform everyone that Dr Garrett has figured out that an old strain of Influenza vaccine, one created to fight the Swine Flu from the late nineties, will protect against this disease of Schmitt's. It seems to generate enough of an... let's see if I can get this correct, strong immunoglobulin response that tricks the immune system to attack one fraction of the hybrid disease essentially disabling its pathogenic potential. Also works to treat those already ill. Redare said it was genius."

"Yes, that pretty much describes Fred," Kate said with pride.

"And me. Just ask my kids. I'm a genius just for being able to keep them in clothes, food and shoes, they're growing so fast," Brad joked.

"Redare also texted," he continued reading, "there are no reliable satellite images from this area that are currently available due to the overhead passes having occurred in the evenings, so he has no updated information on what we are up against. He also noted the latest death total worldwide has stabilized at just over one million so he can only keep what we are doing out of the normal channels for about three more days. I think he is only doing that because of Dr. Garrett's recent discovery and because he promised Jules his revenge for the attack on Paris. So, I guess we have to push on this a little harder because if we don't and fail to find Mendoza or Schmitt or if God forbid Jules and Jean are killed, this will be taken out of our control."

"We should be ready to go in a few minutes. Since we are in an endemic tick area, I suggest you spray down any skin not covered by the tick repellent fabric with the Deet we brought along. After the last time we were in Argentina on the Amazon, Kate and I can't stand the thought of being eaten by bugs in any manner," Tom added.

The Americans sprayed themselves down to the point of near saturation but the FFL soldiers didn't seem to care about the threat of ticks or any other blood sucking parasite. They lived the tough life. Ten minutes later the two groups split and went their separate ways.

Tom, Kate, and Dennis headed slightly southeast zig zagging around the natural barriers presented by the dense patches of Arrayanes trees. The skilled soldier used a compass and his navigator skills and after forty minutes had them stop and rest. Tom was perspiring heavily, but Kate and Dennis hadn't even broken a sweat.

"You guys can move pretty fast. I didn't think I was this much out of shape," he commented.

"You're in pretty good shape," Dennis laughed, "but we generally do this with packs full of gear, so for me this is a stroll in the woods, so don't feel bad."

Kate handle Tom a bottled water and he sucked it down and took another.

"Where are we?" Kate asked.

"I think we are real close, less than three hundred fifty meters, if my calculation is correct. The compound should be to our right so we need to rest quietly and listen for any activity or sounds. After a little while we will cut that distance again by half."

They heard nothing but squirrels moving about and birds doing bird things.

"D'accord, we will move single file forward, stay behind me. From this point we only use hand signals and go slowly looking for booby traps or perimeter alarms. Stay two body lengths apart, Dr. Kate, I want you in the middle."

They stopped again and listened. The compound peacock called out in the distance.

"That was a peacock," Tom whispered, "I hear them all the time on farm calls. They can't survive on their own so that bird must be in the compound or near it."

"We can risk getting a little closer so let's go another fifty meters, then you stay there and I'll go in for a closer look. If I'm not returned in half an hour, get out of here and return to the campsite and evacuate."

Dennis slid silently through the brush as Kate and Tom could now barely hear voices and an occasional bark of a dog. No question that they were close.

In fifteen minutes Dennis returned with some startling information. "I went up a tree and got a good look at the compound. There are armed guards with canines at the gate and on the perimeter. One way in from the front and possibly a simple iron gate at the rear, unprotected. I saw three guards, two dogs and two other men on the grounds, one of which I believe is Sullivan. It definitely is a hostile environment so we need to plan this out carefully and return this evening."

"Why this evening?" Kate asked.

"It's been proven that if they are hostile, they usually won't make any significant decisions till the next day, like whether we are a non-threat and can be trusted or if we are a problem and need to be eliminated."

"That's just great! What are the odds they kill us?" Tom sarcastically asked.

"Statistically we have a seventy-five percent chance of walking out alive. It really depends on what they are trying to protect or hide. We may not even get inside the compound. Our advantage is we have Sullivan there so our odds are possibly slightly better. The thing is, we better have every detail down to perfection."

Reversing course they headed back to the camp. The others were already eating ham and cheese sandwiches, bananas and ice tea. It was the last of their fresh food.

"Dennis, what did you discover?" Eric asked anxiously.

"We found the compound, it is not too heavily protected but they do have Alsatians and machine pistols. There is no way we can surprise them without someone getting killed. So several of us will have to 'stumble' onto their front gate and act out our parts of stupid scientists. Good news, we will have a back-up crew on the outside waiting to come to our rescue or summon help from the Argentinian rangers we made friends with. We need to get this done this afternoon at dusk; Brad, Tom and I will show up on their doorstep and plea stupidity. We just need a common understanding on how much we offer to tell them."

Just then Brad yelled out jumping back, "CHRIST!"

Joseph had snuck up behind the tree he was leaning against and had poked the big man in his side fairly hard. Brad turned to see what happened and laughed upon seeing his blood brother standing behind him.

"Jezzus, I could have been scalped by this 'Injun," he joked. "And how in the hell did you get past the perimeter alarms?"

"That's a stealthy gift from my ancestors. I was just following the reflection off your shiny dome that likely could have blinded me," Joseph said with a quick laugh.

He turned to the group.

"Hi, everyone, how's it going? I have someone I want you to meet." Joseph waved to their left and Alice appeared out of the shadows. No one had guessed that she was there.

"This is Alice Murphy and she is a post graduate entomologist from Kansas and just so you know, I wouldn't jeopardize our mission by bringing someone unknown on board, but Grandfather sent her to me," Joseph explained.

"What is your grandfather, a supernatural dating service?" Brad questioned, half joking.

Kate went over and shook the younger woman's hand.

"I'm Kate, that tall, dark and handsome guy's wife, over there, and I am the person in charge of this picnic we are on. Those three incredibly handsome men standing over by the food table are what I call the French Connection, they are our protection and muscle. That's Eric, Paul and Dennis on the right. French Foreign Legion. Did Joseph fill you in on everything?"

"We talked all last night. I know everything from Berhetzel to this mission you all are on now. I think I understand the forces behind this, the good versus evil aspect, the Creator versus the Destroyer. Joseph's great grandfather sent me a vision the evening after I met Joseph. The dream was of Joseph surrounded by a pack of attacking wolves as he was protecting a white Tanaka calf. It was vivid and his grandfather's message very clear; Joseph needed my help, and I was to go and find him.

"I wasn't sure how or why, but felt compelled to do it. I watched you leave your hotel, followed you to the airport and used my contacts there to start tracking you all down. It wasn't hard, I really was only hours behind you and since I am very familiar with this forest, I located Joseph easily. I know this area very well and I can tell you that about five to six kilometers that way, there is type of compound, defended and secure that belongs to an older man named Mendoza. He was born there and has lived there his entire life. About seven kilometers due south, there is a secure mine or cavern that has recently become a very busy place. I was on top of the rise of land directly above that cavern, looking for termite colonies and I found the largest active colony of my research sitting directly over this mine or cave. I also found two old galvanized venting style pipes about four inches in diameter extending up out of the ground. I actually tripped over one of them. That's when I searched and found the camouflaged entrance with the heavy metal doors near a small waterfall. There was plenty of indication the location was active by the ground litter but I figured it was some kind of Argentina governmental facility. I was afraid I was trespassing on some ultra-secret facility so I never mentioned finding it when I had dinner with Señor Mendoza."

"Wait a minute," Kate interrupted, "you had dinner with Mendoza?"

"Yes, about six weeks ago and even spent the night there. He had heard about my research and treated me very well. I showered, spent the night and his houseman Manuel did the laundry from my pack. Mendoza seemed sincere, kind and fatherly. I felt very safe there."

Joseph jumped into the conversation.

"I told Alice about the psychiatrist, Dr. Maria Schenk, that we met in Paris, you know the old woman that survived the Death Camps and her specific warning about being duped by the Nazi's cordiality. I will never forget her, she scared the crap out of me."

Alice continued.

"I can take you down to where that cavern or mine is this afternoon and probably get you safely into Mendoza's compound with some sort of scientific relationship lie. I was sent to help Joseph so whatever I can do to help, I'm ready. Also FYI, I am an excellent shot, can handle a knife and just about whoop anyone's ass, man or woman..."

"She's a trained MMA fighter. Top amateur in the Midwest," Joseph said proudly.

"Number two amateur female in the United States. Soon to be numero Uno."

"Wow, I would never have guessed," Brad said.

"What, that's she's so tough?" Tom asked.

"No, that Joseph would find a girlfriend in the middle of nowhere."

CHAPTER 89

Mendoza's Laboratory

That same morning

It had been a long night but Schmitt had been awake and had worked feverishly, his energy fueled by Amphetamines and thick dark coffee. His mind raced as he reconstructed his original work and by six o'clock he had thirteen trials of new viral- prion combinations undergoing virtual experimental trials. No question he was a genius that could marry two diverse pathogens into one lethal agent but as long as there were the Fred Garretts of the world working against him, he understood he might never be able to rest.

At ten, Mendoza showed up at the lab, located the two Frenchmen and asked Schmitt to join him for a picnic brunch. He refused. Too much to accomplish.

Forty minutes later Mendoza returned and gave his orders for the day.

"I am heading back to the compound soon so Dr. LeClerc and Dr. DuBois, you are still under Dr. Schmidt's direct supervision. What that means is, if you mess with his work, he has my permission to kill you. After that I will wipe out both your families and track down and kill your colleagues. I don't think you might fully understand the power and extent of our movement. Another thing is you won't leave this facility until Christian has several new bioweapons ready for our cause. Then we will develop another, then another, each more powerful and deadly than the previous. You may have limited our success this last time with the Rabies add on, but the future still belongs to us. My father's dream for a thousand year Reich will be resurrected, except it will be the Infinity Reich, and it will be created in the laboratory and not through blood on the battlefield. Really a much more civilized way to control the masses. Do I make myself clear, gentlemen?"

Both shook their heads solemnly, understanding fully Mendoza's threats. With that the son of the personification of a previous century's evil, waved to his bodyguard and turned to leave.

"Wait!" Jules shouted. "What assurance do we have you will keep your word?"

Mendoza smiled cat-like as he turned to face the men.

"I have no personal interest to kill you or your families unless you persist in blocking my efforts. I have goals which must be met, so a good effort will result in mercy from me. You see, I am not a vindictive man, just one on a mission."

With that he turned back and walked away exiting through the laboratory's massive solid stainless steel doors.

"I would take him very seriously, mes amies," Schmitt said.

"Here is what we are to accomplish today. I have thirteen active viable trials running virtually in vitro. Dr. LeClerc, you and I will have the exciting job to help find the top three prospects and start clinical trials likely this afternoon. Now here is my surprise for you. I will be creating these diseases on my biologic, if you will, 3D printer. They will be totally synthetic, replicated mechanically by the billions in a fraction of the time they would take to grow conventionally in culture media. I'm sure you know about 3D printing of replacement ears, heart valves, bone matrix and handguns. It is the future of medicine and now real with my refinements and my taking the process down to the nano level. The funny thing is nobody ever dreamed this could be accomplished at such a high level. I can produce, test and then manufacture hybrid bioweapons in a fraction of the time it took in the old-fashioned way. When the rest of the world catches up, eighty percent of it will be under our control. The remaining areas will be the shit parts anyway."

"You are an insane son of a bitch, Schmitt!" Jean voiced with anger.

"On the contrary, my dear Dr. DuBois, I am likely the most disciplined intellect you will ever have the honor to work with. It is true that my political views are not mainstream but look at the deterioration of the human race over the last century. There is no survival of the fittest or the natural selection of the best of the specie, so the human race has become generally weak and senseless. My selection process may be a little radical for some tastes but we will decide who warrants protection from my bioplagues and thus create Mendoza's new world order."

"Our Creator God will find a way to stop your efforts. Destroyers like Hitler, Stalin, Pol Pot, or Berhetzel come and go just as you will eventually. Your reign will be brief on this earth but endless in Hell," Jules shot back, his fists curled to help contain his passion.

"We will see about that. For now, Dr. DuBois, I want you take notes for Dr. LeClerc on this secure notebook. Just so you know, there is no way to use this unit to access the outside world. It feeds directly into my program so it functions purely as an extension of my computer. What you will be doing is virtual trials on the pathogenicity of each newly created disease in the human, canine, avian, porcine and simian species. The computer will also simulate real world scenarios and generate morbidity and mortality figures in six major cities. There will be real family names and units, hospital systems, governmental epidemiology services as part of the trials. Think of it as a form of video game where you will subject these cities to different exposure techniques such as water or food borne, aerosols, contact and vector borne. In the end, I will narrow these thirteen potentials down to two or three and then we will start the animal trials. This all has to occur within the next three days. If you are diligent I might even name one of these pathogens after you."

"Which cities are on your list?" Jean asked.

"The cities that are preprogrammed are Moscow, Chicago, Rome, Sydney, Mexico City and of course your beloved Paris. In the end I will only target five of those, so if you behave and are diligent perhaps I would spare Paris just as Hitler did in the last century.

"Now we need to work. This evening we are to dine with Mendoza in the main house and I want to show him evidence of our progress."

"I'm curious," Jules asked, "exactly what does this miracle 3D printer look like?"

"It's over there linked into my amazing Hitachi Electron Microscope. It's ironic that the best electron microscope in the world is not German but Japanese, also a war defeated, humiliated nation. The printer is however pure German, my engineering miracle, currently one of a kind since the prototype sister unit was destroyed in Leipzig. Once we are established as THE world power, I will produce several more to be used to fight diseases like cancer. It might be confusing, but this miracle of my intellect doesn't create new diseases from scratch but rather produces a compatible matrix of each of the targeted parent fractions and then links them together to form a unique pathogen.

"People need to think grand ideas to develop magnificent break-throughs. In my case, I thought small."

Schmitt laughed at the irony.

Jean looked over at his best friend with a reassuring smile. *I think I know now how to stop these maniacs!*

CHAPTER 90

6.8 kilometers south of the base camp

Late morning

Alice moved like a jungle cat, fast and deadly silent. Joseph trailed directly behind her keeping up with similar skill, then the older group; Kate, Dennis, Tom and Paul followed, straggling slightly, twenty meters behind the youthful couple. Brad and Eric had stayed back in camp to guard it.

Alice slowed a little and made a near right turn to the west for two hundred meters, then south back three hundred meters, then east two hundred more meters and stopped.

"Sorry for the convoluted way here," she explained softly, "but this is the rear approach that will put us over top of the cave or mine without them being able to hear or spot us. Over to our left you'll see that small piece of my green surveyor's tape which marks the main portal to that huge termite colony that works here. If you would walk directly over it, you would see that the character of the soil changes into a less compact, softer consistency. See how much greener the vegetation is along this area, that's a direct result of the termites' activity. I call it the ring of life. There have been reports of large colonies like this producing enough methane gas to easily fuel several homes or a farm. Since these colonies can exist for multiple decades, the methane has the tendency to permeate into surrounding ground structure and when located near to say where a backhoe was trying to move a boulder, and a spark was created, a flame flash or weak explosions have been reported. The premise of my work is to find the most effective termite subspecies to become methane producers and domesticate them into gas producing recycling machines."

"So just like the cows I work on except the cows require expensive feed and forage to support their rumen microbes while your termites scavenge simple forest litter into methane," Tom noted.

"And my termites could likely consume dried fecal matter from those bovines and sheep. The feces would be first rinsed until all the residual nutrients are removed from the dry matter and then the liquid evaporated in the sun to be used as fertilizer or alternatively, the liquid slurry could be sprayed on the crops or over the soil. Their methane production from the fecal dry matter would be able to run most farms and the excess sold to energy companies. I have a patent pending on the process. My big beef is the University will want their cut of my intellectual property, and I don't think they deserve it," she replied.

"What happens if these termites go rogue and eat up middle America. Puts a whole new meaning to The Terminator," Tom joked.

"They will only eat what we feed them including waste paper and fast food trash. Ten thousand can produce as much methane in a day as a medium size cow. When you consider than an average colony of this specie can support as many as fifty million workers, that would be like a herd of five thousand cows belching gas," she added as she pointed off away from the ground.

"Twenty paces south of that tape is the ventilation pipes from the cavern. I listened at them the last time I was here and it sounds to me like equipment working, possibly ventilation or air exchangers." The men went over and took turns putting their ears to the pipe.

"One is a sewer vent but the other is ventilation. I think I can hear voices faintly also," Paul said.

"I agree with that. We need to get down front and check the entrance. I'll go if everyone is in agreement," Dennis offered.

436

"Wait," Kate said, "what about that mini drone thing? Did you bring it?"

"Oui, it's in my fanny pack. That's a great idea. It can take some video and we can review back at the camp later on," Paul replied.

"That's *IF* you don't crash it," Dennis ribbed his friend.

In five minutes Paul had the tiny drone zooming around in near silence. The noise it made was slight but similar to that of a large flying insect. He controlled it from a smart phone app and made three quick passes at the massive protective doors.

Suddenly those doors opened and two men exited. Paul pulled the drone back to try to focus on their faces. He captured the images he wanted.

He signaled complete silence and waved the team over to watch the monitor as the two walked away.

Alice strained for a good look.

"The larger gray haired man is him, Mendoza. They must be headed back to the compound. It's in the general direction they are headed."

As they disappeared, Paul made one more pass at the doors and then recalled the tiny flying computer.

"Wow, that was crazy. Imagine what could have happened if one of us were down there just now," Kate said.

"We better head back. I want to review this footage some more and then I'll get closer to the compound this evening after dark. It's a new moon so that should be helpful, and I'll fly a little tour of Mendoza's home. I love this technology, makes me feel like a teenager again," Paul said as he chuckled softly.

Alice went over to her green survey tape, pulled it up and watched for several moments as the termite workers dragged organic matter down into the football sized opening. The stream was continuous and endless.

"They work twenty-four hours a day gathering and processing, never stopping unless it is torrential rains. The more I study them, the greater respect I have for such simple insects. They make us humans look like complex monstrous creatures," Alice observed.

As the Destroyer headed back to his lair, the soldier-scientists re-treated to their camp.

It was game on.

CHAPTER 91

Mendoza's Compound

That evening

Sullivan had kept a close eye on James during the day and made sure the Haitian didn't communicate with anyone that could alert Mendoza. He saw Manuel return with his guard assistant with a load of fresh fruits and vegetables, several cases of wine and four styrofoam ice chests likely loaded with fresh fish, poultry and meats. Everything was unpacked from an oversized hand cart that was pushed up the path to the compound's back entrance near the kitchen.

Sullivan knew he had to find that offsite location that Mendoza evidently had taken Jules, Jean and Schmitt. He needed greed to motivate young James and use that sense of immortality that motivated youthful men to take on great risks. It was why young men were the pawns of the great wars. He would use James in that same way.

Mendoza had arrived and retired to the house until lengthening shadows put the portico in the shade and then he went out to relax in the shade. As usual Manuel brought him a decanter of rare cognac and his humidor of grand Cuban cigars. Manuel poured the liquor while Mendoza prepped the expensive smoke for lighting. He slid back in the cushioned rattan chair and lit the tobacco, focused on blowing smoke skyward where the overhead fan dissipated the blue gray cloud. He had a lot to consider and was unusually exhausted. He had too much to consider before Schmitt and the Frenchmen returned for dinner.

He had checked his agents' communication reports from around the world and learned that the second wave of plague was stalled because a vaccine was being used, a common one kept in storage in huge quantities by WHO to stem pandemic Swine Influenza. It was being used to stimulate the immune systems to fight or prevent the Viron effects. That disease was now a dead end as far as he knew and since he never declared ownership of the plague, he was still an anonymous author. He had learned a great lesson about over estimating results and the value of being patient about declaring victory. Had he presented his terms prematurely, there was no doubt he would have been discovered and destroyed by now. Had he not destroyed TriStar and Vogel, then the focus on Vogel or Schmitt would have eventually led investigators back to him.

This time we shall release larger quantities of multiple agents into very specific targeted populations to completely overwhelm health officials and governmental workers. We will layer disease upon disease like a great pathogenic cake. Let them eat cake!

He drifted off, engulfed in sleep.

"Señor Mendoza, pardon me for disturbing you but Dr. Schmitt, LeClerc and DuBois have arrived and are preparing for dinner," Manuel said apologetically.

Startled a little, he stood and noticed the cigar was nothing more than a stick of ash.

"What time is it?" he said glancing up to the sun.

"Almost eighteen hundred," came the timid reply.

"I lost two hours just like that. Not like me to loose tract of time."

"No Señor."

One half hour later they met in the dining room, this time the uncovered portrait of an aged, plastic surgeon altered Adolph Hitler stared down solemnly over the table.

"Well, Schmitt, I understand you have been working continuously since you arrived at the laboratory bunker. You are to be commended on your diligence. How are your assistants working out?" he asked.

"Why don't you ask them," was the reply.

"Messieurs, comment ça va? Are you adjusted to working underground and doing your job as requested?" Mendoza asked, feigning interest.

"We are the good soldiers doing exactly what we are asked. Actually both of us are amazed by the level of sophistication and degree of quality work being accomplished. Also the speed of intellectual production is unlike anything we have experienced before. You both are to be, I guess, congratulated," Jules replied.

"That is an amazing conversion to a relative level of support," Schmitt observed.

"That is because I think we underestimated the potential degree of success you are achieving. Jean and I are smart enough to know when we are defeated."

"That likely is the result of your French blood," Mendoza said sarcastically.

"No, it's just that we are realists and recognize who we need to align with. Plus we need our families to be safe. I assure you on our honor as gentlemen that you will have our full cooperation as long as we are benefactors also from your efforts. We will work behind the scenes to accelerate your success," Jean added.

"You might lead the New Vichy Republic of France and my Berlin will be the epicenter of the world. You will be my loyal associates. Now a toast!

"To the New World Order, made to order by me, Caesar H. Mendoza. Salut!"

"Salut!" came the vigorous reply.

"Very nice. Thank you all."

Outside, Sullivan nervously paced the courtyard, pretending to be busy. He had seen Schmitt and the two Frenchmen walk through the gates late that afternoon. At that time he had temporarily lost track of James but he spotted him at the back gate just as James was returning from checking the trail to the river.

"What were you up to?" Sullivan asked angrily.

"I took the initiative and followed their cart tracks back to the river and found their boat. It is about seven meters long with a ten horse Evinrude motor that is at least fifty years old. There are also three cans of fuel, about twenty-five liters. We likely could make four or five runs. The problem is going to be moving something valuable and heavy without triggering scrutiny. There is a lot of treasure down there if what we saw was accurate," James said.

Sullivan thought about the right play.

"We take the gold and jewels and let the silver stay to satisfy the Argentinians. Maybe work out a deal. The silver is really theirs anyway."

"That's bullshit, it's finders keepers. The larger the haul, the more we have to split, especially if we bring on the Frenchies or any of the staff here. I could be king of Haiti with that kind of money," James replied.

"Why would you want to be king of Haiti. Why not Venezuela, they need the money and leadership. You would fit right in."

"When the Frenchmen return to their room after dinner, I will need to talk to them and see if I can recruit them to be our eyes and ears in the bunker. I think they won't care as long as we can get them out of here alive and wealthier."

"Why not me? Let me ask them, I speak French."

"Because, my young friend, this is my rodeo and I am in charge. You will be the lookout, I won't take long."

About an hour and a half later Jules and Jean were returned and locked in their cottage. Sullivan picked the rear door lock while James stood guard. In two minutes he was inside and greeted his friends.

"Keep it low, my associate likely has his ear to the door," Sullivan whispered as they greeted each other.

"I was caught by him, Schmitt's driver slash companion, who is affiliated with the NaziX movement in some fashion, in the communications room while I was doing some snooping around. Luckily, the security camera program in the cave picked up images of the gold and silver that is stored there and now the greedy little bastard wants to steal it after eliminating Schmitt and Mendoza. I played along and I think he is convinced I am going to figure out a way to solve the Schmitt Mendoza problem and get out us of here with the loot. I told him I would get you two to join us. You on the inside of the cavern and the two of us working the compound makes it a piece of cake I think."

Jules shook his head solemnly.

"It's not that easy. I think there are a dozen or so workers in the bunker. And who knows how many actual people are on his payroll around here. Jean and I pretended tonight to be on board with Mendoza in exchange for a share of world domination profits. I'm not sure he believed us or actually would keep his word. We aren't going to keep ours of course."

"My question is where in the world are Kate, Tom, Joseph and Brad. Are they being held somewhere else or God forbid dead? Redare must have his people working on our behalf or with them off the radar. It's all very confusing," Jean lamented.

Jules continued, "Schmitt is a real scientific genius, although a madman. He is on the verge of creating more lethal bioweapons which he intends on giving to Mendoza for his political blackmail. The sophistication of the equipment they have is unbelievable!"

There was a light frantic knocking on the back door. Sullivan hustled to see what was going on.

"Come on, we got to go. Are they on board?" James asked.

"Of course, what option do they have ?"

Sullivan and James went off to start their plan. They needed a plan, something to have quickly before Schmitt was ready with his next creation.

They needed Divine intervention.

CHAPTER 92

Mendoza's Compound

Paul sat camouflaged against an Arrayanes tree, his face blackened with charcoal from their campfire while he flew their tiny drone for thirty-five minutes. It deftly zoomed and zipped back and forth taking video and recording measurements. The guards never noted the light buzz of the mechanical bird as he easily surveyed the interior of the compound. The only response the drone received was the Alsatians, who watched it alertly, even though they couldn't figure it out what it was.

He stayed in the shadows and watched the guards and observed their routine. The two guards working were obviously trained paramilitary and everything they did seemed to be scripted and exacting. That meant that they would be unlikely to resist any effort to overwhelm the facility without causing significant casualties. Besides that, it would be the three French soldiers versus at least two well trained, well-armed and defensively positioned guards and those dogs. True, they would have the element of surprise, but they possessed minimal offensive weapons, other than the Plastique explosives. They would have to slip in, garrote the guards, but first they would have to find a way to sedate the dogs.

Maybe if someone yelled Squirrel.

Paul started back to the campsite, fighting a persistent swarm of hungry mosquitos.

In twenty-five minutes he came silently out of the darkness like an apparition into the camp while everyone was scattered paired off into three groups. Brad and Tom were losing at poker with Eric and Dennis, Joseph and Alice were off by themselves sitting by the small campfire and Kate, who had done some exercises, was writing in her journal. Surprised by his quiet invasion of the camp, he called to them to gather so he could give them some details of his surveillance.

"I think I need a blood transfusion from all those damn mosquitos," he complained.

"I saw Dr. LeClerc and Dr. DuBois escorted into the house just before dark. They looked well and were back in the guest cottage when I left. I also saw Sullivan moving about with the smaller man that is not a guard and my suspicions are that they are up to something, so hopefully Sullivan has allied with the man.

"I think we can surprise the guards if we are able to separate the dogs from the men. Each guard carries a machine pistol and what looks like a nine millimeter handgun. If we eliminate the dogs before their shift change which I'm not exactly positive when that occurs, then I'm convinced we can find a way to overwhelm the guards."

"What do you mean 'eliminate' the dogs?" Kate asked, concerned.

"Hopefully we can sedate them. Is anyone here on meds that might work?" he asked.

No one answered.

"Maybe we could get the dogs and the guards drunk," Brad said jokingly.

"Not a bad idea, why don't you buy," Tom shot back.

"I would but I don't think the USDA knows where to forward my pay," he laughed.

"I know about some plants that Grandfather taught me about that have powerful sedation properties like Valerian root and Kanna root that could work if we can find and grind the roots and then hide the material in something the dogs might eat. I just don't know exactly how much, what it would taste like compounded to a dog or even if it is native around here. Our people used the roots in teas to calm nerves before battles or for women during childbirth, but now very few practice herbal medicine. I was taught by the best and I think I remember what the plants look like.

"Alice and I can go out tomorrow and forage west of here and maybe we will get lucky. He taught me general properties of different plants by blind taste testing and once you taste some that vile crap, you will never forget what it is. He had about twenty primary barks, seeds, roots and leaves he had me taste over and over again and I remember the bitterness, the numbing effects on my tongue, the instant sense of nausea, and overwhelming tired sensation from the tiniest tastes of different ones. I never thought I would use it but, as time goes on I'm beginning to understand everything he taught me had a specific useful purpose. It just wasn't apparent till now."

"We need to get in there and talk to Sullivan and specifically find out what he knows. Our objective is not to kill Mendoza and Schmitt but to capture them so we can interrogate and find out how in the heck they created this disease and what we can do to prevent similar future biologic attacks. That is the only good reason I can think of why we don't just nuke that compound, plus the fact Jules, Jean and Sullivan are there," Kate explained.

"This is brain surgery and our objective has to be that our friends escape with their brains intact and that we capture the enemy so Redare can pick apart their brains."

"How about I sneak in just before dawn and talk to Sullivan, you know do the Indian thing. Paul, do you have an idea where he is sleeping at?"

"All the guards stay in the staff housing which looks to be... wait a minute, we can review the drone video."

In two minutes he had the video up and running on a small tablet. The drone images were incredibly clear and detailed and when Paul had switched to infrared mode you could 'see' heat images in the house, four in one area and another off in the far end of the house which Paul called the kitchen because other strong images were likely a stove and hot water tank. There were two more located outside which he said were Sullivan and his sidekick and then the two guards and their canine partners. In normal mode they could see what looked to be staff sleeping quarters.

"That doesn't look too difficult, especially if Joseph can talk to Sullivan and fill in the gaps," Dennis observed.

"How much time do I need to get there?" Joseph asked.

"The way you move, about twenty minutes, a little longer coming back. Go to the rear gated door which is about a forty-five degree angle north from the gate. If you can talk to Sullivan and his friend is around, remember he is Donovan, not Sullivan. Be careful what you say, don't expose us. Get in and let him know that we need to move quickly on the compound tomorrow evening or early the next morning. The only contingency would be that Schmitt, Jules and Jean need to be there and not in the cave. We men will have to take shifts watching the coming and goings in and out of there until we know everyone is accounted for and their daily schedule."

"I'll go soon and be back by dawn. Then Alice and I will go forage for herbs that might sedate the dogs. Who is going to take the first watch because I think we should start that now?"

"I think me first since I just came from there and my adrenaline is pumping, then we switch off every two hours. After me, Tom, then Brad and as daylight hits Dennis and then Eric. That would put us at early evening tomorrow to execute a plan if everyone we are after returns for dinner and the doggy downers work."

"Is there any more of that good wine left?" Alice asked.

"Yes, half a case," Paul replied.

"I think I know a way to get the dogs knocked out and the guards too.

"They know me and I think if I come bearing gifts, homemade treats for the dogs and a bottle of wine for each of the guards and one for Mendoza then perhaps I could pretend to bringing a thank you farewell gift to them explaining I was leaving to go back to the States. Joseph, how many ways did Grandfather teach you on ways to use the herbs?" she asked.

"Let's see. Dry grind, raw grind, steeped as a tea, and distilled for potency —ingest, apply, drink and inhale—and believe it or not in a sup-pository of Tanaka tallow. You have to remember they suffered injuries, headaches, allergies, broken worn teeth, difficult birthing, organ failure and some cancers. They needed medication that if it didn't cure them, at least provided symptomatic relief. They rarely confessed illness because that was a sign of weakness, they didn't believe in complaining. White man's illnesses and frailties introduced devastating diseases like smallpox and the social diseases. Grandfather rejected the new and felt the old ways must be preserved so the Lakota would keep their Souls. He was right, he always was."

Kate was thinking carefully about what her friend had just said.

"You said distill for potency. How long does that take?" she asked.

"It's not distill in the classical sense like alcohol but really evaporating a steeped liquid into a thick concentrate by simmering slowly. I guess it would depend how much you needed. At least a couple hours I think."

"Then you and Alice better hustle finding those herbs after you return tomorrow. We don't have much time if they bring in more support or if they vacate the area there may be no way we can help Jean, Jules or Sullivan.

"Except pray."

CHAPTER 93

Two hours before sunrise

The Compound

Joseph waited, listening intently for the sound of the dogs or guards moving around the compound. He was at the rear wall, between the dense thorn bushes that defended the rear wall and thick vines that were tangled in the stucco. The young Lakota waited quietly until he felt he was safe and then climbed the vines and slid down silently onto the cobbled courtyard. He stealthily hugged the wall perimeter until he was at the men's sleeping quarters and peered in through a window to the bunk bed area. Sullivan was facing him while the other man on the upper berth was facing the wall. Joseph removed his boots and pushed open the heavy door just enough to slide in, creeping over to Sullivan.

He tapped Sullivan three times before the man awoke. He gasped a little then smiled seeing Joseph.

Joseph pointed to the door and slipped back out into the shadows while Sullivan quickly pulled on his pants and followed.

Joseph met him at the back gate.

"Good to see you, sir," Joseph said.

"Remember, it's Rick."

"Yes, sir!"

"Who all are here?"

"All of us plus three soldiers sent by Bernard Redare. We are thinking of taking this compound tomorrow but only if Jules and Jean are on the grounds and since you are here, capture Mendoza and Schmitt. What do you think?"

"If you have the firepower, I think that would work, but it's the bunker that is the prize. Mendoza has twenty metric tons of gold and a huge store of sixteenth century Spanish looted silver and jewels down there, plus Schmitt has a fully equipped lab where he is running bioweapon experiments. Jules said he is using new technology and will unleash some engineered pathogens very soon. Oh and get this, Mendoza is the biologic son of Adolph Hitler."

"That's crazy nuts. Then we have a problem, because we really don't have any weapons, just some plastic explosives. Can you get your hands on some firepower for us?" Joseph asked.

"I doubt it. This place is locked down pretty tightly. There is one secure room over there away from the house with a warning sign against smoking or flames and that could be a weapon storage area or armory. It's possible more is stored in the bunker cave. You know I've been around a lot of evil in my career but this place just oozes wickedness from every pore. I'm scared shitless they are going to find out who I really am but so far they are buying my impersonation. I have to keep pretending to be calling in sick at my TSA job and so far they haven't checked out my calls, which by the way go to my old office voice mail. They're giving me burner phones to call out on and so far that has saved me. My Irish luck can't last much longer."

Just then they could hear the sound of a heavy truck down shifting gears and brakes squealing. Dim headlights shone faintly into the compound. Joseph scrambled up the wall and laid flat against the top and Sullivan pushed himself against it, under a shadow. Six men emptied from an old truck cab and rusted canvassed bed and started unloading heavy, drab, olive colored metal crates.

A stunned Sullivan looked up to Joseph.

"You better get going," he whispered, "I recognize those containers. The Bureau seized similar ones ten years ago in Delaware. They are US Army and have Stinger Missiles in them. One box looks

like it might contain grenade launchers. You can't attack Mendoza now, they will wipe you out immediately. Go back and tell them what you saw and tell Kate I will try to get my hands on some weaponry for you. Meanwhile, don't do anything aggressive. Keep a low profile."

Joseph slid down over the wall to the outside, squishing berries from the thick vines. One squirted a tiny drop into his mouth, bitter tasting and nearly instantly caused him to have difficulty drawing a deep breath. He became dizzy and rolled to the ground, gasping short labored breaths.

The young Lakota was dying.

CHAPTER 94

One hour after sunrise

Kate was worried. Tom had relieved Paul from his watch and Joseph had gone with him to try to enter the compound and talk to Sullivan. Joseph was due back over an hour ago and since Tom had no way to communicate with the group, she was concerned something bad had happened to one or both of them. Brad was the next scheduled observer but Dennis switched position with him so he could better find out what was going on. Brad moved like an elephant in the brush and Dennis could get there with stealth, not with the grace of a bull moose.

"Dennis, please be careful," she pleaded, "something is wrong, I can feel it."

"Je vais, mon cherie." *I will, my dear.*

Twenty minutes later, Dennis came up in a whisper behind Tom. Surprised, Tom jumped slightly with a gasp which immediately caused the dog at the gate to alert.

"I can't believe that dog heard that," Tom whispered as low as he could.

"They are trained to hear a pin drop. I'm here because Joseph has not returned to camp. Have seen you any sign of him?"

"Nothing is going on. I did catch a glimpse of Sullivan doing some sweeping around the back gate, but if something happened to Joseph while he was with Sullivan, then I suspect both of them would be locked up or dead."

"Or Sullivan is one of them and he turned on Joseph. If that's the case then we are at extreme risk," the FFL soldier postulated.

"I don't believe that for a minute because I know Sullivan and if they captured Joseph they would surmise he was not alone and that place would now be crawling with activity and at minimum, the gates would be secured."

"C'est vraie." *That's true.*

"I still have thirty minutes on my shift. Do you think you could check the perimeter for any sign of Joseph without being detected."

"That's my specialty my friend. I can drop back and loop in from the north and get to that rear entrance area and then check the south side. If he is anywhere around there, I will find him."

Dennis headed to the north and faded into the forest. Tom strained to keep him in sight but had to focus on new activity in the compound. Jules, Jean, Schmitt and a guard were leaving and walked into the forest toward the bunker. There were several more men moving in and out of the sleeping quarters and they were hauling around large metal boxes. Tom strained to see but the mosquitoes were relentless and with the morning warming up, the perspiration that beaded up on his forehead pushed the Deet bug repellent down into his eyes, burning them. He was tired, uncomfortable from remaining so still and extremely afraid for Joseph.

Dennis worked his way back to the walled compound, moving slowly and deliberately. As he approached the rear wall near the gate, he saw Joseph's ranch boots pointing skyward sticking out of a thicket of tangled vines.

IL EST MORT.... He is dead.

Dennis was correct, almost. Joseph was unconscious, in a near death state. His flesh was cold, his skin a pale bronze blue gray. Between his lips were two crushed bean like seeds. All around, Dennis sensed he was being watched, and he was. Scores of squirrels hung from branches, several small deer watched from the shadows, and furry tail wood rats and tiny mice darted in an out of the thick vegetation. Dennis looked around at the flowering vines believing he had seen them in some medical training he had had and pulled a handful of the leaves, berries and the vine's beans and shoved them into his fanny pack. He then checked Joseph's airway again and lifted him over his shoulder. The soldier moved, carefully picking his way back to the camp. It was a grueling fifty minute uphill ordeal where he stopped every few minutes to check Joseph's vitals and airway while catching his breath. Finally, he reached the camp and gently laid the young Indian on a blanket.

Eric, the flight surgeon, grabbed a penlight and stethoscope. "His pupils are constricted and he has a slow and irregular heart rate. It appears he was poisoned. Dennis, was there any vomit, syringes or other suspicious material around where you found him?"

"Rien. *Nothing.* He was surrounded by heavy vines, one with berries and one with a podded seed or bean. I have some in my fanny pack."

He pulled the plant material and laid it next to Joseph. A worried Kate stared at the material and spoke up. "Veterinarians receive training in poisonous plants and phytotoxins. We are tested on it and almost never use it, but those beans look awful familiar to me. I think they are Calabar beans from a plant with the scientific name Physostigma venenosum, one of the most toxic plants on the planet. It has action like atropine and physostigmine, highly toxic when ingested."

"I don't think he would eat something that he didn't know what it was," Alice said.

"She's right, no way he would do that!" Brad affirmed.

"What is that other berry? Does anyone have an idea?" Kate asked.

Eric grabbed a couple and rolled them back and forth on the palm of his hand.

"Looks familiar, I just can't place where I've seen these before, but I just don't know where. Paul, Dennis, can you place these?"

"The only time I recall being trained on plants was that field survival exercise in the Congo, about eight years ago. Remember the lessons on using botanicals to capture food or kill the enemy? That berry looks like the one that can be used to paralyze respiratory function when arrows, needles or knives are dipped in its juices. I just can't remember the name."

"Curare," Alice said, "it's called Curare."

"Oui, that's it. It's also used in surgery to paralyze muscles for delicate surgeries where the patient's respirations are mechanically supported. Highly toxic with a rapid, near instantaneous onset. Alice, how did you know?"

"I've had several botany classes as part of my undergraduate curriculum and if I remember correctly physostigmine is the antagonist."

"If we are right then, Joseph is not unconscious but immobilized from the toxin. Does anyone know what the half-life of the poison is? We can support him, sit him up, warm him and wait," Paul recommended.

No one had an answer.

"He's young and strong," Brad agreed, "besides that he's got generational support from his ancestors. How do you think those antagonist beans reached his lips. They didn't just fall from the vines and land between his lips, they were put there. I put my money on Nelson."

"It was pretty weird, we've been out here almost two and a half days, and beyond a couple of squirrels and small song birds, we've seen almost no wildlife. Joseph was surrounded by animals and this sounds a little strange, they seemed concerned," Dennis said.

Just then a huge shadow glided above them, silently, drifting on updrafts and thermal currents. They looked up through a gap in the treetops and saw an astonishing slight.

A huge vulture was gliding and circling directly above.

"That's the first one I've seen in all the time I've been working here," Alice said while fixated on the bird.

"What the hell is it?" Paul asked in amazement.

"That," she said, "is the rare, magnificent Andean Condor. He is a far distance from his usual habitat," she answered.

"No," Kate replied, "he is exactly where he is supposed to be. That's no bird. That's the soul of the Lakota Nation watching over their son."

CHAPTER 95

Inside the Bunker Laboratory

That morning

Schmitt was a madman on a mission. In less than two days he had virtually produced six new unique hybrid diseases that Jules watched on computer programs wipe out millions of humans from city to city. Schmitt wasn't interested in just crippling major metropolitan areas by killing a segment or percentage of the population, but rather depopulating it with a rapid onset, quick to kill disease with one hundred percent mortality. The fact that Schmitt had the expertise to create, test and manufacture pathogens in mere days, stunned the Frenchmen.

Jules' task was to review the generated data and select the 'best' candidates to manufacture. He had to prove to Schmitt that his training in epidemiology and statistics was as good as Jules knew it to be. Jean on the other hand was to project responses of governments to the overwhelming biologic attack based on each country's political system and hierarchy in the world order.

This morning Schmitt was 'printing' the matrixes that would link the two pathogenic components. In other words, he created a link, almost like a magnet, that when an infectious agent divided during replication, it could attach itself, creating a bond on the side it was most similar to. The other half of the matrix would be most compatible to the second pathogen and a fusion of the two diseases would occur. Each half would support the other so when it was introduced into a host, the hybrid or new disease would overwhelm the immune system causing rapid destruction of the host. Schmitt also had found a way to create two versions of these novel disease agents. One would have the capacity to replicate in and be shed by the host, if the host lived long enough. The second version would destroy the host but not have the capacity to exit that host and infect another. This gave Schmitt the ability to target individuals for death or wipe out entire regions. The only real hurdle standing in his way was the intellect of Dr. Fred Garrett.

Garrett, Schmitt learned, had found a weakness in the original plague that he had buried in the vaccine for Rabies X. That disease had been carefully developed by using old labor intensive trial and error methodology which meant identifying a new and unknown agent after 'marrying' two unique parts together in vast tissue cultures, basically a luck of the draw scenario. He had been lucky, but originally missed the fact that these two disease organisms wanted to divorce the other half and find its own kind or a different half. That is what caused the plague to be unstable and fail in the real world. There were too many more desirable choices, more biologically compatible that each half of the hybrid preferred. Thus, when Garrett correctly identified an unstable organism by seeing fractured pieces of the hybridized agent, he was able to introduce common viruses which linked with ease to the pathogenic viral half of the Schmitt's viron, attenuating it. It was genius with a lot of luck thrown in.

But now, with Schmitt's miniaturized 3D printed biologic link, that would not happen. The matrix link would prevent premature separation of the agents and negate the solution Garrett had discovered. The diffuse agents would be permanently bonded almost like the grafting of a scion to a root stock when creating a better apple variety. This time his engineered matrix would make sure the graft held and produced fruit.

Jean watched screens as Jules sent the new hybrids over to his analytical program which played out the geopolitical impact of

essentially removing one of the world major cities from existence. Each time the country would collapse when government banking systems, stock markets, universities, governmental departments, medical infrastructure and religious communities failed. The computer estimates were overwhelming and staggering.

The six viral halves Schmitt had chosen included Ebola, Hantavirus, Marburg, Dengue, Rabies and Spanish Influenza, each lethal in their own right but when paired with the BSE or Mad Cow Disease prion, the lethality increased to above ninety-nine percent, virtually unsurvivable. Jean had tears in his eyes as the computer projections became more detailed, each metropolitan area falling in days after the release of the pathogens into the general population. The one thing that Schmitt was not making the two friends privy to was how the plague was to be delivered, which disturbed Jules. The second thing Jules wondered about was how would Schmitt protect his anointed citizens from his created diseases. No man creates something so destructive that he cannot control it. That was the key because knowing the delivery system may be the only way to stop him once he released the plagues.

"This is insanity," Jules said to his best friend. "Each of these hybrids would wipe out millions of souls before anyone had a clue of what was going on. Horrible, painful but mercifully rapid death. We need to figure this out quickly because at the rate he is generating those canisters full of death, by the end of the week he would have enough agent so at least a couple targeted cities could be infected."

Jean was overwhelmed with emotion.

"How is it possible God lets monsters like this exist? Now I understand what Nelson Blackfeather warned us about when he said 'there always will be a new *Destroyer* to challenge the Creator.' However, these monsters make Berhetzel look like small potatoes. You know that Kate, Tom, Brad and Joseph are out there trying to find us and Sullivan is close by, but God help us, I don't see a way they can end this."

"I have faith that they will find a solution and particularly if Bernard Redare has been kept in the loop, then we will have a fighting chance. The astonishing thing for me is the speed at which this man is able to create and produce these diseases. I'm also sure he has developed a unique and special way to deliver these infectious agents. I believe you and I may have to kill him to stop this madness. Mendoza is a megalomaniac just like his father and he is utilizing Schmitt's ego-driven intellect by providing the unlimited financial means to help create that amazing equipment he now uses to prescribe millions of death warrants. This is the Holocaust on steroids, a nouveau genocide that in reality is a complete sterilization of human life from targeted cities or regions. That leaves all the wealth in place, all buildings and infrastructure intact, ready for repopulation by I guess, the followers of Hitler junior," Jules replied.

"The stakes here are tremendous for mankind. If this Destroyer is able to establish control of two or three major metropolitan areas we are going to be in World War III, except it will be a biologic world war where everyone loses."

Frustrated, they settled back into their duties and two hours later Schmitt called the men into his private lab space.

"I just downloaded your work and need your best opinions on the tasks I assigned you. You need to consider your answers carefully.

"Dr. LeClerc, which two primary pathogens do you feel will be the most lethal and have the highest degree of morbidity, mortality and will create the greatest amount of panic?"

"That is easy. My analysis is Ebola would be my first choice and then Marburg. Both have the lethality and name recognition to create maximum impact. If you can deliver it effectively, in three days max you would have near one hundred percent lethality."

"Good. We are in agreement," Schmitt said excitedly.

"Dr. DuBois, which two cities would you recommend to be the recipient of my gifts."

"I think Moscow and Sydney."

"Why?" Schmitt inquired.

"Because the Russians would never ask for help until it was too late and Sydney because it would lull the world into a 'too bad, thank God they are at the opposite side of world,' attitude. Complacency would give us a timed advantage," Jean answered.

"I agree with both of your assessments. Very good, gentlemen. I think by the end of this week, or early in the next, I will have the agents we need on site ready for Mendoza's order to proceed."

"How do you expect to be sure everyone is exposed quickly and in a high enough dose to make sure they expire quickly?" Jules asked.

"What are the three things every human needs to survive?" Schmitt asked.

Jules replied quickly, "Food, wine and sex."

Schmitt laughed.

"Spoken like a true Frenchman.

"How about air, water and food?" Schmitt continued.

"Oui, nous savons que," came Jean's reply. *Yes, we know that.*

"Well then you should know Mendoza owns the largest bottled water company in the world. Not Coca-Cola, but Bavarian Springs. He has bottling plants in every major city in the world. We might blow up the targeted city delivery infrastructure in a terrorist attack or poison their reservoirs and then provide at no charge, free bottled water to each and every citizen. A humanitarian response. We also can aerosolize the agents into subways, government agencies and the like."

"Seems to me that that still leaves a lot to chance. What if the government steps in with their own water sources or you can't permeate the air supplies to building or subways. It would seem to me you would have an incomplete effect, basically a repeat of Baltimore; dramatic but not earth shattering. No, you need to slow down and find a way to FORCE the citizens to be exposed without them understanding they are walking into the showers, may God forgive me for saying that," Jules offered.

"Interesting, how do you suggest that be accomplished?" Schmitt asked.

Jean jumped into the conversation.

"I remember as a child whole towns lining up in large groups to be given a tiny sugar cube carrying the oral polio vaccine, I believe it was the Sabine vaccine. Everyone was mandated to do it and everyone did. So, I think you introduce a virulent flu or similar disease into a city and then provide the cure which would be disguised as another oral vaccine but in reality be our pathogen. That assures the population receives the death dose."

"That's a novel concept. We do own a biologics producer company in South Korea which we could use as a cover for data I produce. I will bring that idea to Mendoza's attention at dinner this evening."

"I was curious," Jules asked, "how do you transport enough of the agent into a country without detection? It seems to me it would take a huge volume of agent to infect population centers of five to fifteen million."

Schmitt smiled at the curiosity.

"When I desiccate the disease slurry down to a cake, I can line one hundred twenty liter ice chests with the material, making it appear as thermal insulation. I will then have more than enough agent to wipe out three times those numbers. It will be light, a solid, and will not trigger any narcotic dogs or excessive screening. Fill the inside of the cooler with frozen fish or something unusual and no one is the wiser and the bioweapon stays in a refrigerated state and stable. Once the agent is activated before deployment, it should be infective for up to seven days. So as you can see, we will have multiple ways to expose people.

"You both have done well and I'm sure Mendoza will be pleased." Schmitt went to an auxiliary computer and typed in a series of commands.

"Here, gentlemen, are the financial stakes for you. This screen is the link to the private banking center called Exceptional Bank Services of Central Europe. EBS is owned by Mendoza, although it is not run by him. As you can see on the screen, there is an account opened for both of you in the amount of two hundred fifty million euros. Once we successfully deploy an attack, that amount will double. One half billion euros is a lot of money and will only be there if you continue to cooperate and we are successful.

"Dr. LeClerc, here is your private identity screen to access your account. There are sixteen parts to your encrypted password, you need to type in the first thirteen, at least one capital letter, one number, one special symbol. I then will put in the final three and when we are successful starting with our first endeavor, I will release to you the fourteenth number or symbol, after our second, the fifteenth, and the last number will be given to you after a very special task I will assign you both. After that I will know you are loyal and you will have full access to all your money. Be aware that amount of money represents the minimum, those numbers could increase significantly after we loot the cities we choose to decimate."

Jules knew he had to play out the game. He could see Jean was visibly upset but when he got up from the computer work station, his best friend was quickly at the task. Jean completed his password, stood and looked like a man under a death sentence.

"Come now, Dr. DuBois, does the role of collaborator upset you that much?"

"Honestly, I will do anything to protect my family. The money means nothing to me. I kept seeing my father's face with each keystroke I just performed. Each one was a slap across his face, his legacy."

"Don't live in the past, Doctor, work for a better future where a pure-bred race of men will make unemotional, intelligent political, social, medical and religious covenants," Schmitt said pridefully.

"My word of advice for you," Jean shot back, "is to watch for the Creator God's answer to your arrogance. My Soul belongs to Him, I work for you, but my God is who I ultimately serve."

The conversation was over, points taken on both sides. Jean and Jules returned to their computer screens.

Jules turned to Jean and smiled at what had just happened.

"You executed that better than I could have hoped," he told his friend.

"Not bad if I say so myself. Good cop, bad cop. But that man makes me want to puke."

CHAPTER 96

Base camp

Noon that day

Kate had sat praying Psalm 91 over and over throughout the morning after Joseph had been returned to the camp. She was convinced it was the Psalm's assurance of God's protection that had brought her back from the precipice of death in Massachusetts after she had been intentionally infected with Rabies X by Schmitt. Everyone else in camp was resting while Paul arranged lunch. The men continued to rotate surveillance on the front gate of Mendoza's compound and Brad was ready to take the next shift once he had eaten lunch. Alice couldn't stand seeing Joseph's struggle to breathe and went out to forage for medicinal plants that might help the young Indian.

They had Joseph propped up against a large soft needled pine tree wrapped in layers of sleeping blankets and Mylar heat reflecting ground tarps. His color was getting better but he could not open his eyes, speak or use his extremities and his breaths were shallow and a little irregular.

When Alice returned she was excited. She carried her baseball cap which was full of molding berries.

"I think I have the treatment for Joseph. You probably are not to believe this but I was led to the spot where these berries were collected, fermenting on the ground, by a small white buffalo just like the one in my dream. I saw the animal and knew I was supposed to follow. After a short distance it stopped, pawed with its front leg at the ground, exposing these Arrayanes' berries. It just stared and stared at me and I heard a voice come to me; it said 'daughter, take this fruit, crush it and give it to my seed.' I'm sure it was the same voice as the one I heard in the first dream about Joseph needing help. Someone get me a cup and I am going to smash these suckers up and get some into Joseph."

Alice crushed the berries to a heavy juice consistency and put a half teaspoon between Joseph's lips and his pure white teeth. Several minutes passed and his eyes twitched and legs and arms jerked a little. She gave another dose and minutes later his eyes were open but unfocused. One more dose and he spoke two words to her.

"Thank you."

It was almost a repeat performance of Kate's recovery from the Rabies X. There were high fives all around as Alice continued to spoon the syrupy liquid into Joseph's mouth. In one hour his color had returned and he was able to stand and stretch. He was hungry and demanded food and hot tea.

He explained what had happened.

"While I was talking to Sullivan, a group of men came in by truck and Sullivan thought they were bringing in STINGER handheld missiles and grenade launchers from the metal boxes they unloaded. That is some serious firepower and with the extra paramilitary types that basically turns the compound into a fortress. I went back over the wall and squished a berry on my way to the ground which shot into my mouth. It was bitter tasting and literally within seconds I was paralyzed on the ground. I could not move or speak but I was so acutely aware of everything going on around me, it was surreal. I saw clearly every animal and bird which came to visit me and there were many. Two squirrels placed something in my mouth and I started to sleep, breathing a little better and I had unbelievable visions. My Great Grandfather Nelson introduced me to Sitting Bull, my father and his father, who I never knew. They told me I would survive if we follow the same plan the Lakota, Cheyenne and Arapaho used to draw out Custer. We will have to make the guards and now the mercenaries chase us away from the compound. Then we will surround and attack them. Meanwhile, Sullivan will capture Mendoza and Schmitt with the help of a man in the compound and also Jules and Jean. Sounds great but a little short of details. But I know this, we may not have weapons but we do have those berries and can make short blowpipes out of bamboo and use the thorns from a type of Mesquite tree that Grandfather said are in this forest."

"Yes, I know where there are some of those trees. Not far from my termite colony. Long sharp thorns that will work well with some fletching. We just need some feathers," Alice said.

With that, two long primary flight feathers drifted down from the tree canopy. They were pristine, from the Condor drifting overhead.

"Now THAT is just creepy," Brad exclaimed.

"I think it is amazing and beautiful. The Creator is lining all of this up against the Destroyer," Kate said with tears forming in her eyes.

"Ok, so we draw these men out, dart them with poison darts, then what? We sit and watch them die? Is that what we are supposed to do, Joseph?" Tom asked.

"We are to subdue them and I guess disarm them. I think we make enough berry juice to recover them after they pass out. We can use the duct tape Paul brought along to hogtie them until we are finished. There is something else you should know."

"What is that, Mon Ami?" Eric asked.

"That cave bunker is not just Schmitt's amazing lab where he is cooking up new bioweapons but it is Mendoza's personal safe. Sullivan said he saw it on the security camera system, and it was confirmed by Jules and Jean — that place is full of gold, silver and jewels. A fortune, twenty metric tons of gold, he said. That is what payrolls Schmitt's work but is just the tip of Mendoza's wealth. Oh yeah, one more surprise."

"What's that?" Eric asked.

"Mendoza is the biologic son of Adolph Hitler. Hitler escaped from Germany, had plastic surgery and retired here. He fathered Mendoza and died years after he had his son fully apprenticed. Mendoza is truly Satan's son. We fail at this and the Destroyer wins."

"That is unbelievable. I thought that was just a urban myth that a double died in his place in that Berlin bunker. This is critical, failure is not an option," Kate affirmed.

"Dieu nous aide tous!" Dennis said solemnly.

God help us all!

CHAPTER 97

Mendoza Compound

That evening

Sullivan was nervous. The new paramilitary types had unloaded their weapons and had cleared several defensive positions making the STINGER missiles readily available. The old weather radar system was replaced with a new state of the art surface to air 3D radar and Sat Weather Comp2Air Detect Warning Unit. This represented a huge defensive upgrade for Mendoza, so it would take a full military attack with anti-missile technology to take out the compound. Not something that was likely to happen in this part of the world. Nazis had settled post war in South America in both remote jungles and populated cities. Many of those that needed a metropolitan lifestyle were tracked down and captured or killed by Nazi Hunters like Robert DuBois, Jean's father. Some of those war criminals hid safely from justice in remote seclusion, existing in quiet solitary confinement. Others, like Adolph Hitler, were insulated from discovery but not exiled from the world. He made a point of traveling outside the compound twice a year regularly until his Parkinson's became so bad, he could not take the rigors of long air travel. But up to that time, each New Year started with a trip to Berlin and then another visit in the Fall to cities that he had coveted all his life: London, Paris, Moscow, New York and Washington.

The new men on the grounds were obvious mercenaries, military specialists for hire who did whatever was asked of them for a fee. They all were darker skin, lean, trim and in their forties, dressed in a camo-fatigues that appeared to be patterned after the surrounding wooded environment. They spoke in rapid Spanish commands and they smoked good aromatic cigars when they took a break.

Badass Cubans!

Sullivan kept his distance doing minor housekeeping duties trying to appear to be occupied, but he profiled each man and if there were any weak links in their ability to function as a unit, he could not find it. They were a serious complication, six hardened men that made the current compound guards appear like minimum wage night watchmen. He needed to update Jules and Jean this evening and warn Kate and the others about this frightening complication.

James recognized the complication the mercenaries presented and at lunch he had voiced his concerns with Sullivan.

"These new bastards will interfere with our plans to remove the gold and silver from that bunker. Since you are the brains of our outfit, how do YOU suggest we overwhelm these six new men and also the guards. I for one, don't like the odds."

"How many people do you think know about the treasure in that bunker? A handful? I think likely anyone who worked to place it in there before the war ended was eliminated or has died of old age and anyone currently in there will suffer that same fate when Schmitt is done using them. So, with the two Frenchmen on our side it's ten versus four. The problem is we have no real weapons and those six new men are skilled assassins. I think we will have to divide to conquer them with a diversion. I need to go get some help. Can you cover for me for a couple of hours after they finish dinner this evening? I want to speak to the Frenchmen and to a couple of friends who by now should be in the area."

"What do you mean 'friends in the area'? You lied to me! I thought we were only going to bring in the two French doctors and Manuel from the kitchen."

"Don't be an idiot! The Frenchmen told me Mendoza said there was at least twenty metric tons of gold, in one kilo bricks, in that reservoir. How do you propose we move that with just a few men? Once we subdue these soldiers with the help of my friends, eliminate Mendoza and Schmitt, then we will become their new *Jefe,* the boss. We exchange their promise, on their honor, to be good boys and then cut them in. We then have their truck, the boat and packs. We just have to be able to get the treasure over the Andes to sell it on the Chilean Black Market."

"I don't want to share. What's twenty metric tons worth in US dollars?" James asked.

"I did the figures after my last talk to the Frenchmen. Twenty metric tons is about seven hundred five thousand ounces; gold is sold by the ounce. At fifty percent of the current market price, likely what we would receive for it on the black market, that's six hundred dollars an ounce or approximately one half billion dollars, tax free. Figure maybe another two hundred million or more for the silver, jewels and artifacts and there will be plenty of pie to go around. Think about it, how much do you actually need to live on in a remote paradise?"

James pondered the question for a few seconds.

"I'm not sure. You may live another twenty-five to thirty years but I am a young man and would live the long life of a playboy. Lots of wine, women and play time."

"That's your problem. I suggest we don't count our chickens before they hatch, so will you cover for me while I slip out this evening, yes of no?" Sullivan asked, irritated with the young Haitian.

"Bien Sûr. I found some cases of very nice rum in the storage shed behind the kitchen. One of two of those might be appreciated by the new men."

"Cubans, they are Cuban mercenaries, likely down from Venezuela. They drink rum like water and piss Mojitos. I'd look to see if there is any scotch in there. They may be less familiar with a good scotch and overdo it. D'accord?"

"Oui. So, after the dinner you head out and I will entertain the Cubans. Be back in no later than two hours. Then I want to be in on the conversation with DuBois and LeClerc."

That was the plan. Sullivan slipped out the rear of the compound and headed north. He could see James in an animated conversation with the gate guard, waving a lit Galloise cigarette in one hand while pointing to the south, explaining something while laughing. He seemed to be telling a funny story or joke.

As soon as Sullivan turned west he was picked up by Paul who was sitting watch on the gate. Paul gave an American Turkey gobble which caught Sullivan's attention. The FFL soldier gave a brief hand signal pointing behind and to the west behind him. He then got up and quietly worked his way over to the retired FBI agent.

"Bonjour, Monsieur Sullivan, I'm Paul, French Foreign Legion," he whispered.

"Allows y." *Let's go.*

Twenty minutes later, at a quick pace, they were at the camp.

"Hello, everyone, good to see you again," Sullivan greeted the group.

"Rick, nice to see you again," Tom said as he shook Sullivan's hand. "There are a few people you haven't met yet; this is Alice, a friend of Joseph who is down here doing a post graduate entomology study and you already met Paul and this is Eric and Dennis who are his colleagues. Bernard Redare arranged their help and we have worked with them before because they are the same heroes that plucked us out of the Amazon. Good friends."

"Nice to meet you all. I better make this quick because I have a kind of shady character covering for my butt down there and the quicker I return the better. Let me fill you in on what the situation is.

"Jean and Jules are in good shape but have been forced to assist Schmitt in his work and they indicated we are on a very tight schedule because Schmitt will be ready to deploy his bioweapons in a couple days depending on where he chooses to attack and which agent he decides to deploy. Additionally, I'm sure Joseph filled you in on the SAM missiles and other firepower that was brought in last evening. Six mercenaries are residing in the camp and I think they are Cuban and quite well trained. There is no way to storm that place and an outright attack will likely cost Jean and Jules their lives.

"How much firepower do you have?" Sullivan asked.

"We have one handgun, some knives and are working on a bow and arrow weapon and blowpipes with Curare tipped arrowheads and darts. If we can get them out of those walls and hit them with the poison, we should be able to neutralize their threat. We want to capture not kill," Kate explained.

"Nice sentiment, but you understand they will kill and ask questions later," Sullivan replied.

"We will do whatever is necessary as I'm sure they will."

"Our hope is we can use the element of surprise and use similar tactics that my ancestors used to defeat Custer. It's a work in process," Joseph noted.

Alice, who had been quietly listening, spoke up.

"I've been thinking that if I approached the gate, looking beat up and disheveled, crying and distraught, I could surely get in. They know me and about my work. I could say a band of armed lowlifes tried to have their way with me but I was able to escape. Could give them a false distant location that would take them a couple hours to reach."

"That might work, especially if they think they are facing an armed enemy. I could then meet the rest of you at the rear gate and let you in. We dart the guards, James, the house servants, if needed, Schmitt and Mendoza and take over the compound and call for reinforcements. When the Cubans return empty-handed, we greet them with some grenades and hopefully they'll figure it's a lost cause. The key is going to be whether or not they give a crap about a poor college girl," Sullivan said.

"Mendoza will care. He took a real interest in me, was very fatherly and concerned for my safety. I found him quite charming. He'll send them out. I can say they took all my computers and data and I need it back. Let's see if my two electives in theater pay off."

"What do you think?" an unusually quiet Brad asked the soldiers.

"I think it could be successful," Eric said, "but she going to have to really look the part and we need to find a spot in the vicinity where she says she was attacked and create a camp and a false trail. Leave a little trash. It needs to be at first light before anyone else leaves for the cave bunker. That gives us less than ten hours from now to pull off this deception."

"I'm going to head back now," Sullivan said. "If for some reason you pull out of this plan before dawn, fire one gunshot and they'll think it is a poacher or something. If you are ready, send Alice down after you see me at the gate doing some sweeping or raking. I will get Alice into the house, that way I can signal to the two J's that it's a go. Alice, you have to convince Mendoza to send out the men out so give that Academy Award performance. I suggest you drop a hint that they are treasure hunters looking for Conquistador silver and a 'city of gold.' That should light a fire under him. God help anyone else in the forest when they head out."

"The treasure angle is a good one. That will motivate them more than poor Alice," Joseph agreed.

"Hey! I'm a treasure, aren't I?" Alice teased.

"Careful, Joseph, it's a trap." Brad laughed.

"You are a priceless treasure!" Joseph replied.

"Awhhhh," Kate said.

With that they started working on the plan.

It was going to be a long night.

CHAPTER 98

Dawn the next morning

The rising sun split the morning fog from behind the compound and as the river mist burned off, the peacock cried out, competing with the compound roosters who seemed to sense the impending excitement, trying to roust the human population out of their bunks.

The gobbler call came, which in the intermittent silence from the birds, sounded very loud. The two Alsatians alerted and barked in confusion at the strange sound and the front gate dog, Maximus, kept watching the north access road. Soon, Alice appeared staggering hunched over holding her side. Her normally shiny ponytailed hair was dirty, caked with mud with leaf matter. Her neck was exposed, covered with what looked like scratches. Splattered blood was on her shirt which was torn at the sleeves and in the back, blood courtesy of a cut Joseph made on the palm of his own hand.

She looked injured and immediately the guard hooked the dog to the gate and ran to help her.

"Señorita Alice, what happened?"

"Ernesto, I was attacked and need some help, Por favor."

The guard slowly walked Alice to the gate and ordered Sullivan to take her to Manuel in the house. Sullivan grabbed her arm gently and slowly walked her, limping to the house.

He leaned over and whispered, "You just might get an Academy Award for this performance. Relax and don't overdo it."

Sullivan knocked on the door and Manuel answered it in a few seconds. He was visibly shocked by Alice's appearance and had her sit in a hallway chair and went to get Mendoza. The Nazi was out of his room in less than a minute.

"Señor Mendoza," she said standing to greet him, "sorry for the intrusion but I had no place safe to go."

"My dear girl, what bastard did this to you?" he asked with anger.

"Late yesterday I was leaving with my gear, wrapping up my work to head back home to finish my thesis. I ran into a group of armed, I guess I would call them bandits who quizzed me about a lost Conquistador treasure and a buried City of Gold. They spoke Spanish and I understand enough to realize they were going to steal my computer, use me, and then kill me."

"How many men?" he asked.

"I counted eight but they could have had more in the area. They had rifles and machetes and lots of empty oversized heavy duty backpacks. They had to be looking for something. They questioned me for at least forty minutes, then the guy in charge dragged me off into the brush. He pinned me down but luckily I had my breath spray size container of formic acid in my cargo pants and I was able to get to it and give him a couple of pumps to the eyes, which had him off me and screaming. I got up and ran like hell, fell a couple of times but it was getting dark and luckily I found a small windfall and hid till a couple of hours ago when they stopped looking. It was pure luck to find my way here."

"That was not luck my dear. You were guided here for a greater purpose, I think perhaps to protect us. Why did you carry formic acid with you?"

"I use it when I survey a termite colony to judge worker numbers. I just spray some on a piece of dried wood and they think the colony or really the queen is under attack from army ants. Usually in a few minutes the majority of the workers are massed around the entrance blocking it.

I can then estimate colony size from a formula developed around 1935. Works pretty good and kinda fun to watch."

"Interesting, but I must find these men, so I will send four or five of my security team out to search for these bastards. God only knows what their real motives are."

"What I really need is my laptop back. My data is on there."

Mendoza smiled almost fatherly.

"If they are still in the area, we will find them and your laptop. Manuel, have Silva report to me.

"Why don't we get you something to eat and then you can get cleaned up. I will find you something to wear while Manuel washes and repairs your clothes. I will make these men pay for violating my paradise and trying to hurt you!"

Twenty minutes later the Cubans left the compound double quick with full packs and semi-automatic weapons. Sullivan watched as the men trotted out and once they were clear, he cornered James.

"Ok, now we need to subdue that last Cuban. You have to lead him into the generator building so I can whack him in the head and tie him up. Then call in the rear guard and we can repeat the process. Can you handle the dog?"

"Hell no. I'll tell him the Cuban is having a seizure and he needs to put the dog in his run. Then we take him out. The front gate will be the most difficult. Ernesto is pretty tough and so is Maximus."

"Don't worry, I have that covered."

Their plan worked well for the Cuban and the rear guard was even easier. Schmitt and the Frenchmen had left for the bunker right before they subdued the Cubans and the rear guard and that left with them only with removing the front gate guard. Sullivan walked up and pointed into the woods where Paul stood up and waved. Then Sullivan slapped the guard on the shoulder with a Curare dipped thorn. The man dropped nearly instantly and struggled to breathe. They taped his hands and feet as the Americans and FFL soldiers rushed down from the woods. Kate immediately administered the Arrayanes berry elixir and when the man started to breathe better, she duct taped his mouth. James and Sullivan carried him to the small power building, Sullivan then told the FFL soldiers to man the gates and the rest to stand down and start a weapon search.

Now the easy part, Sullivan thought, he went to the kitchen and took the small handgun to get Manuel. The cook was washing the breakfast dishes and confused, slowly raised his soap covered hands up over his head. James came in at that moment.

"I know you understand English, so if you try anything I will shoot you," Sullivan warned.

Manuel nodded solemnly.

"Where is Mendoza, which room?" "In his bedroom I would think."

"Let's go," Sullivan said waving the gun toward the main house. The servant turned and as he did he grabbed a large kitchen knife and rotated like a ninja kicking the gun from Sullivan's hand. He slashed, cutting the retired FBI agent across his forearm which had been raised defensively. James tried to come around from the man's backside but the knife was expertly welded and he dodged the stick. The cook screamed a warning to Mendoza.

"Ayuda estamos bajo statue ve a la habitación segura!" *Help! We are under attack, get to the safe room!*

Sullivan lunged forward swinging a long handle fry pan as the cook expertly dodged his lunges. James grabbed a cleaver and swung it from the other side until he got lucky and cut half the man's left hand off. He screamed and dropped the knife and grabbed his wrist falling to the floor crying out in pain, blood squirting.

Sullivan hit him with the pan, knocking him unconscious with a 'bong'.

"Pack that wound with a kitchen towel and duct tape it up tightly, then his feet, mouth and wrists. That man is dangerous, so make it tight. I have to find Mendoza."

He found the gun and worked his way into the main house, moving slowly.

Alice was peeking out her door.

"Did you see him?" he whispered.

She shook her head *no*.

He checked each room. *No Mendoza.*

At the far end of the house, he found the safe room. Reinforced steel double doors were securely locked and solid. An above door red light was illuminated in a wire protective basket. There would be no way to get in there without an Acetylene cutting torch, and even that would still take hours.

James came to the door, his face covered with blood.

"He's dead. Couldn't stop the blood, the towels just soaked through."

"Mendoza is in here," Sullivan explained. "We will have to cut him out."

"You stay here, I'm going out to have everyone look for a torch."

Sullivan called the group together, while Eric and Dennis stood the guard positions and the rest gathered by the porch.

"Ok, the bad news is the cook is dead and Mendoza is locked in a kind of safe room. Right now we can't get to him, so here is what we need to do. Schmitt, Jules and Jean are in the lab bunker and we won't have any way to get to them till this evening. So here are our tasks for now.

"We need to firm up our defenses, so Paul, you and your colleagues set up a good defense perimeter with the grenade launchers and the machine pistols. I want everyone armed in case we experience a breech. Kate and Alice, I want you to keep the two prisoners reasonably comfortable but don't go in there without one of the men.

"Joseph, I would like you to scout the area around the lab and find out where those Cubans have gone. Tom and Brad, you need to find a cutting torch, there has to be one around here somewhere."

"We both have used one," Tom added, "on the farm."

"Next, I don't trust James. We need to tie him up, right now, he is watching the bunker door. He is our weak link."

"Or missing link," Brad joked.

"Paul, bring that machine pistol and we will go get him."

Sullivan and Paul went back into the house. Alice was dressed and out of her room.

"Go to the courtyard and get with Kate, she will fill you in," the agent ordered.

They got to the safe room and the door was open, the light off. James was missing as was Mendoza.

"Merde!" Paul swore. *Crap!*

They moved carefully into the good size room and saw a small trap door leading down to a subterranean tunnel. The men were missing.

"Damn. I shouldn't have left James here alone. We can't go down there, it's likely booby trapped in some way. Which one of you is the explosive expert?"

"That is Dennis. He can check and clear this in a few minutes. I'll go get him!"

"Be sure everyone has a weapon. If Mendoza links back up with those Cubans, we are screwed!"

Two minutes later Dennis was in the tunnel working his way out. There was only one grenade trip wire in the tunnel and about two hundred meters behind the compound there was an exit through a vine-covered oversized culvert pipe. Mendoza and James had disappeared.

"I bet the boat is gone also," Sullivan said and they worked down to where the boat had been cached.

No boat. They had escaped.

Mendoza was on the loose. They needed to get into that lab ASAP.

CHAPTER 99

Lab entrance

Fifty minutes later

Kate, Alice, Tom and Dennis stood at the steel entrance of the cavern bunker.

"I don't think I can blow this door without possibly bringing down the whole damn structure. That's a double reinforced magnesium steel alloy and it's very strong, plus the hinges I think are a titanium alloy and they are sequestered.

"We need a plan B. Let's go up to those ventilation pipes, I have an idea."

They climbed up the hillside until they were directly over the ventilation and plumbing vent. Dennis lit a match and held it over each pipe.

"There is almost no draft on the sewer pipe but the ventilation pipe has a fair positive downdraft. Alice, about how much methane does that colony produce, say in one hour?" Dennis asked.

"A super colony like this one generates about five liters an hour. Most of that is trapped in pockets underground in these heavy clay or rock pocked environs. There could be ten to fifteen thousand liters accumulated down there, depending on the age of the colony. All you need is a way to suck it out."

"What are you thinking, Dennis?" Kate asked.

"I think I know," Tom replied. "We smoke them out of the cavern just like groundhogs on the farm. Make them leave and get them on the way out."

"Oui, I think we introduce the gas down the sewer pipe, drop a walnut size piece of C4 on a wire and fire it off. The explosion would shake them up pretty good and produce enough smoke to force their evacuation. Especially when we block the ventilation system."

"I think that might work also," Tom affirmed.

Alice looked concerned.

"You won't damage the colony will you?"

"Non, they will just play the part of the Gas Company."

Alice and Kate stayed while Tom and Dennis headed back for the supplies they would need. Alice was grateful to be alone with Kate.

"I never would have guessed that all this was possible. I mean Nazis, bioweapons, mercenaries and Joseph."

Kate smiled at the comment about Joseph.

"You really like him, don't you?" she asked.

"I have had a one track mind since I left home, that was academics. I mean I have had boyfriends but in today's world, it is hard to find a decent man. Joseph is kind, sincere, gentle, smart, honest and very interesting plus very, very good looking. What is that word on how he affects me?"

"Smitten," Kate said with a little laugh. "Smitten, just like when I met Tom. When I think about all the good and bad I've seen and experienced in the last couple of years, I know it's been all worth it because I have Tom, Bobbie and that goofy dog. I don't know if you fully understand this, but when you had that first dream or vision, it was no accident. You were predestined to be here. If I've learned anything it's that we are together because we have been commissioned by what Nelson Blackfeather, Joseph's great grandfather, said is the Creator. We are here to stop the perennial Destroyer. He said the Destroyers will come and go, so I see ourselves as Crusaders in the good sense. I would say you were always in Joseph's future, it's just neither you nor he knew it."

"You know, I never ever even dreamed of getting married. What little girl doesn't dream of her prince and a royal wedding? Now I am thinking, at a church or a wedding on the prairie? He is so quiet and shy I'm afraid I just might have to ask him."

"Once we finish this up you will have plenty of time for a courtship. I would say don't push too hard, just enjoy the ride and make sure he thinks it's his idea."

Tom and Dennis returned with a long black garden hose, some fiberglass insulation, the C4, wire, duct tape, black plastic bags and an old bicycle pump.

"Alice, is that a straight shot down to the colony or do we need to pack the entrance off?" Tom asked.

"I would run the hose in about a meter and then pack it off. There has to be dozens of connecting chambers underground. Methane is lighter than air, so once the termites feel like they are being threatened, their movements should force some of the gas out. You are going to need to drop the hose well down into the pipe," Alice answered.

They ran the hose into the nest, packed insulation around the hose and sealed it with the plastic. Next, Tom measured the length of hose to the pipe, added ten feet and slid it down the pipe. Dennis taped a walnut size chunk of C4 on a detonation wire to the hose and slid the hose down the pipe and then sealed off both pipes with the plastic and duct tape.

"Now what?" Kate asked.

"Remember when I told you the ground around the colony is soft and full of decaying organic debris, so we need to stand on top of it and lightly jump up and down. That should compress the space and they will get real agitated and move the methane around," Alice replied.

In twenty minutes Tom asked, "Is that enough? I'm getting a little tired here."

"I think so. So now we get to test the Big Bang theory," Alice replied.

"Everyone stand clear, no, way over there. Get down, cover your ears and face," Dennis instructed.

"Un, deux, trios....." he made the contact with a small lithium battery.

The earth rumbled from a series of muted explosions, each a little stronger, knocking the four off onto their rumps. The hose blew out skyward.

PIERCE ROBERTS

"Sacre Bleu! There must have been a lot of gas in that nest. I didn't expect that!" Dennis exclaimed.

"I hope we didn't just kill Jules and Jean," Kate worried.

"I think they may have crapped their pants a little but that wasn't enough punch to kill them but if we are lucky, we started a fire and they will need to get out of there in a hurry. We will get them on the way out."

They scrambled down the hill to hide, waiting near the front door. All of them held weapons including the two women who had double barrel shotguns with Lugar handguns for insurance. Tom and Dennis had automatic machine pistols and Lugars.

They didn't have to wait long.

The steel doors slowly opened and smoke poured out. Ten men in white coveralls were the first ones escaping, they were unarmed and scattered like rats on a sinking ship. They let them leave unmolested, and the next one out was the guard and dog Maximus, both coughing. He dropped his weapon when he saw Dennis, wanting no part of a battle he could not win. Alice held a shotgun on him.

The last three men appearing out of the smoke were Schmitt, Jules and Jean. The Frenchmen had Schmitt gagged, hands secured with electric cords, tied tightly, and a blood soaked wrap over his head, covering his eyes. They looked soot covered but had wide smiles when they saw their friends waiting.

"Mon Cherie!" Jules said before enthusiastically embracing her. "Tom, Dennis, comment ça va ?"

Alice held the gun on the guard and Jean noticed her.

"Who is this lovely young lady?" he asked.

"This is Alice, a graduate student in Entomology who was recruited by Nelson to assist us in stopping these Destroyers."

"Alice, these fine men are Dr. Jules LeClerc and Dr. Jean DuBois. Both extremely smart, kind and generally wonderful men who would suffer from the same assigned duties as us. We are all in the same boat," Kate explained.

Jules walked over and lifted her hand and gently applied a wisp of a kiss.

"Enchanté, mademoiselle," he greeted while looking into her eyes.

"Enchanté, miss," Jean echoed, gently shaking her hand.

Tom looked around nervously.

"We need to get back to the compound so we have a defensible position. If those Cubans give up and return back before we do, there will be hell to pay."

"I agree but I think we need to disable this cavern so no one can get in easily. It's full of gold and silver, plus all that pathogenic agent Schmitt produced. If we can collapse the front entrance, then there will be no way anyone can easily get to the treasure or Schmitt's work. You won't believe what is in there," Jean replied.

"I have the remaining plastique at the compound, let's close the doors but don't let them have direct contact or they will electromagnetically lock. After we get back, Paul and I will set the charges on the inside to collapse the entrance behind the doors. That should do the trick I think. Is there anyone else in there," Dennis asked.

"Non personne," Jules answered. *No one.*

"Ok, then let's hurry and get back to the compound, lock these two up and feed the dog, since we are, as Doctor Kate said, 'all in the same boat.' So the ladies can take point."

Jules looked to his childhood friend and said solemnly, "Let's just hope that our boat is not the Titanic."

CHAPTER 100

Bariloche

Three hours later

Mendoza was infuriated at his sudden turn of luck and the fact he had to escape from the home that had been his father's. Blinded by now what he saw as arrogance, he realized that he had become complacent, allowing too many people into his world, into his plans.

Mendoza had grabbed three of his 'burner' phones plus his father's personal stainless steel Lugar when he escaped to the safe room that his father had had built before the war ended. It had never been used, but per his father's instructions, he had always kept it in good repair, functional and stocked with fresh food and water. It was Mendoza himself who had installed the tiny surveillance camera outside the door which had allowed him to negotiate with James to help him escape. James had proven himself to really be a money whore but Mendoza didn't care, he would promise the moon but in the end would deliver a nine millimeter slug to the man's brain.

He had called the Cuban Silva's Sat phone which was encrypted. It took two hours for him to respond simply with the number 11. That meant he was meeting with Mendoza at the predetermined emergency location— the Saint Stephen Chapel in one hour.

They met as the sun was setting in a tiny secluded chapel of the larger nineteenth century Cathedral.

James stood guard at the entrance.

"Silva, we have a problem," Mendoza started, "the compound has been taken over by treasure hunters. You were sent out on a wild goose chase to find men that didn't exist. I need to get back into my home and you need to eliminate the intruders. How do we do that?"

"We determined that we were being duped when a false trail totally ran out. Then we heard a very small explosion and then about thirty minutes later a much louder one. We circled back carefully and saw the compound was locked down and secured with the heavy weapons deployed so we backed off to find the source of the second larger explosion. We found a collapsed cave tunnel system which was the obvious point of the larger explosion. The entrance was totally caved in with smoke coming from inside. Was that your property?" the Cuban asked.

"Yes it was. It held my family's treasured memories, library, art work and important papers," Mendoza replied.

"Then, Señor Mendoza, I am very sorry for you. It will take heavy equipment and lots of explosives to make that entrance passable. I'm sure months of work."

"As long as I can remove these bastards from my compound and I get back in there, time is not an issue. When can you restore me to my home?"

"We need to gather some tools but realistically the best time would be around 0200. They have had a long day and we will be on them before they have any idea what is going on. Do you want them alive or dead?"

"Dead except for the girl Alice and Schmitt. Line them all up, and I will tell you who they are. The rest give blindfolds and then execute them. I am going to relish that moment, so when you are ready to leave here, text me the number two.

"I will meet you at the east entrance to the airfield. Understand?

"Si, Señor Mendoza. It will be done, I have a truck backup so we can return quickly."

Mendoza exited the chapel and as he and James left, he asked the young man a question.

"I need to ask this," he said, "exactly what are your life's ambitions?"

It didn't take James long to answer.

"I want to be one of the wealthiest men in the world and most powerful. I have no political goals but am of the Aryan bloodline so I believe we are aligned in our views. I know I need to hitch my wagon to a star, and with your royal background, I think I am in the right place to accomplish my goals."

"Good, an honest answer, I like that. Here is what is going to happen now. We are going to take back the compound tonight and eliminate our enemies. I expect you to be part of the assault, to participate as a sign of loyalty. I'm still not sure I can trust you but this will be your chance to earn that trust. Screw up and you also will be dead. Understand?"

"Oui, I will earn that trust, I promise," James assured the Nazi.

Mendoza and James took a beat up taxi to the airfield after getting a quick meal at a small German restaurant. Bratwurst and a beer only took a few minutes but it promised to be a long night to go without food.

They only waited fifteen minutes and Silva showed up with the four other Cubans in a truck that was similar to what they had brought the weapons to the compound on. They left with only the running lights illuminated.

After two and half hours they were a couple of kilometers in and parked the truck and unloaded the new weapons which were their standard issue Russian Kalashinikov AK-12 Assault Rifles.

"Here is our plan," Silva explained, "I want Pedro on the rear gate. Lay down fire to if necessary keep everyone inside the compound so they can't escape to the river. Santiago, you take Luis and James and assault from the northwest. I will go with Matías and we will attack from the southwest. The object is to get over the wall silently and then capture the sentries and the household. If they only have two or three guarding, we should have the place in a few minutes. Questions?"

"Vámones entonces, amigos!" *Let's go, friends!*

CHAPTER 101

The Compound

Midnight

Joseph couldn't sleep for a couple of reasons.

One was Alice who was in his thoughts nearly every minute. The second was an unsettling feeling that something was about to hit the fan. It didn't seem reasonable for the Cubans to abandon their associate or their employer and not return to fight it out. His instincts were telling him to go out and see if he could find if they were camped somewhere close in the area, with the hope that darkness might reveal a lit cigar or cigarette or the glowing embers of a campfire.

He pulled on his jeans, socks, denim shirt and the pair of moccasins he had brought along and walked to the back gate where Dennis was on watch.

"Where are you going?"

"I can't sleep and a lot of this doesn't make sense to me, so I thought I would go out and do some more scouting," Joseph confessed.

"My colleagues and I feel the same. It is not like Cubans to forfeit a paycheck. I'm glad your instincts are the same. They are out there somewhere and we know they will try to retake this place. Take one of the Lugars and for God's sake be careful. If you need to alert us and can't get back here, fire one round, wait thirty seconds and do a second.

If they catch you don't try to take on the group. You could pretend to be a native foraging, poaching or something."

"Except I don't speak Spanish," Joseph reminded him.

"Minor detail to an otherwise stellar plan," Dennis said with a laugh.

"Don't worry, they won't catch me unless I want to be caught," Joseph said as he rubbed some muddy dirt from the flower bed on his face. "See you in a couple hours."

Joseph slid through the gate and creeped out into the forest. He could hear the nocturnal animals sensing his invasion scurrying off or verbalizing a protest. Alice had told him of her encounters with Andean Pumas on two occasions but everything moving this evening was small and shy.

Alice had told him the Los Arrayanes Forest was considered haunted but also magical by the locals who believed strange demons or creatures roamed at night, some being good, while others allegedly consumed your beating heart to get to your soul. Interesting stories but he didn't fear folklore creatures, he feared men on a mission.

Joseph now walked quietly and stopped often to listen for voices, animals in unusual behavior or anything that his innate instinct would trigger the hair on the back of his neck. He called on the ancestors to guide him and he eventually found the Cubans right where they had made the false camp. They were not asleep and he could smell the odor of burning tobacco and very strong coffee. This time of night, not sleeping could only mean one thing ; they were planning to assault the compound soon.

Joseph squatted and listened. He could hear low voices murmuring and muted laughing. There was the distinct sound of men checking the actions of their weapons and honing knife blades on sharpening stones. There was a palpable sense of anticipation radiating from the camp. He decided to work his way around to the upside of the camp on higher ground to get a better look.

He went far to the south and then swung west following a well-worn game trail. Working slowly at first, Joseph started a brisk walk expertly dodging branches and vines and hurdling over down trees.

The terrain was forcing him further away from the camp and as he was turning to head down to the camp, he jumped over a rotted log.

The jump placed him directly over a poacher's pit trap and he fell hard into the eight foot hole, solidly hitting his head on a rock as he crashed to the bottom.

"Grandfather!" he pleaded as the world went dark.

CHAPTER 102

The Compound

0230 hours

Silva's men were in perfect position. He scanned the compound with his FLIR night vision scope and imaged three sentries with four men resting under the Portico. Two heat images came from inside the house and four from inside a room opposite the house, across the courtyard. Thirteen total.

He gave the signal to start the assault. The first wave was to quietly take out the guards and then the portico, house and that other room. One man worked to the wall and slid along the perimeter, the others on the team kept their weapons trained on the sentry.

Eric was at the front gate and his inherent radar sensed trouble. He looked down and saw two red laser dots steady on this chest. He rotated quickly to the right, his finger pressing the machine pistol's safety and was face to face with the Cuban Silva, his AK-12 level with his chest.

"Buenas tardes, my friend. Drop your weapons, por favor."

"You are very good, my compliments, soldier to soldier, man to man."

"Gracias, now you will wait quietly till my colleagues finish taking back Señor Mendoza's home."

The Cuban moved so he was right in the Frenchman's face.

"Dennis, Paul! Envahisseurs! *Invaders!*" Eric shouted.

Silva swung the butt of his rifle across Eric's jaw, breaking it and knocking him to the ground. There was a sudden explosion of gunfire.

Dennis was down, shot through his left shoulder. Paul was wounded in his left hip. Both men were prone on the ground and Jules, Kate and Alice burst from the house and ran over, attending to them, applying hand pressure to the wounds. Their three best assets were wounded and the compound captured in under three minutes. Eric was dragged over next to his two colleagues.

Mendoza was escorted back into his family compound just as Schmitt, the last Cuban and the two guards were released from the utility room.

"Good to see you are safe, Christian. Sorry for all of this. Your lab unfortunately will be inaccessible for a period of time so you will be unable to get back to work for a while. We can talk after I clean up this mess."

"I will get some morphine and bandaging material for your friends, Doctor LeClerc, in a few minutes."

"How about some antibiotics for them," Jules asked.

"I don't think that will really be necessary," Mendoza replied. "Donovan, why are you standing with these others?"

Sullivan thought about his response for two seconds.

"I'm sure James told you that he and I were planning to steal from you. What he didn't know is that my name is really Sullivan and I am an FBI Agent. These others here are my friends and colleagues. We were on your trail and also Schmitt's. The DGSI in Paris also knows where we are and as soon as we fail to report in, this place will be swarming with military and police. If I were you I would leave with your lives."

"Not before I finish my production of the new pathogens," Schmitt said firmly.

"Good luck on that, bastard, we were there yesterday and apparently there has been a landslide. I would say your lab is buried under tons of rock and debris," Jean said gleefully.

"Then we have no real use for all of you so in a couple hours you all will stand along THAT wall and meet your Maker," Mendoza said as he stormed back into the house.

Tom turned to Brad and said, "I don't think he's very happy. We only have one chance now and that is Joseph can find some help. I hope he is alright."

"He's alive, I can feel it in my blood. The question is where in the hell is he."

CHAPTER 103

In the poacher's trap

Joseph, your friends are in grave danger. Wake up, they need you. Your Alice needs you. The Creator needs you to lead an attack. You alone must lead this attack, wake up, my son, your friends are in grave danger...

Joseph's head was pounding and hurt like hell. He had no idea what happened other than he had fallen or tripped and hit his head. As his eyes adjusted, he understood he had fallen in a pit, a simple trail trap that had sent him crashing to the bottom of a poacher's hole. He sat up, orientated himself and then stood, just a little dizzy. He reached around and found the edge of the pit and grabbed a root or vine and pulled himself up and out of the trap.

Standing, he looked to where he had been going and saw no evidence of the Cubans. No smoke or voices, no flicker of light from a cigarette. Then he heard the gunfire that came from the direction of the compound. It seemed too brief for a battle which could only mean the Cubans' attack was swift and successful.

He had failed, unable to warn his friends and felt horrible. *Alice!*

"Grandfather, my ancestors, what am I to do ?" he pleaded, "I have failed my friends, I have failed you."

You have not even tried, how could you have failed? You have the pure blood of a warrior and now you feel defeated? You cannot be defeated until you are dead. You need to get back to your friends and be prepared to do battle. When you are ready, signal with a gobbler call, you will receive all the help you need. Scream it out, Hoka Hey!

Nelson's unearthly voice had reassured the young Lakota and he found his way back to just beyond the hill where he could see down into the open gate. A Cuban now stood guard and he could see his friends huddled in the center of the courtyard, the two wounded Frenchmen propped up, covered with blankets.

Joseph sat and watched. He needed to plan an attack and he had no idea what was going to happen or if he could do it. The morning sun was starting to break the twilight and the roosters commenced their crowing. The peacock joined in the avian competition from above on his roost.

Joseph watched carefully, not finding a plan on how he was going to save his friends, his Alice. Suddenly, Mendoza exited the house in a full Nazi white dress uniform. He wore highly polished storm troopers boots and carried a black riding crop. It looked as if he was channeling his famous father. He screamed some commands and the Cubans pulled his friends roughly up unto their feet. They forced them over to the far wall and started to place blindfolds to cover their eyes.

It was an execution!

Joseph gave a loud panicked gobble. Suddenly, there were dozens of responses from all around him. Lakota warriors in full battle dress and war paint appeared from behind nearly every tree. Instantly, Joseph felt a renewed confidence.

He stepped out from behind the tree and cupped his hands yelling: *HOKA HEY!*

The air was suddenly fill with a chorus of blood curdling screams, repeating the ancient battle cry. Wolves howled like a furious Cat Five Hurricane.

Joseph ran full speed down to the compound, heart pounding, his grandfather's large Buck knife grasped firmly in his right hand, his senses hyperaware. His blood boiled hot to save his friends and Alice.

Lakota Braves on white, brown and black paint horses galloped ahead of him carrying eagle feathered lances in one hand, a tomahawk in the other. The horses ran without saddle or reins and glided silently across the ground. These were spirits of long dead warriors and their ponies that had been summoned to fight these Destroyers. Joseph felt empowered and ran faster than he ever had in his life.

The Cubans and guards saw the apparition army attacking and heard the war cries. They quickly formed a ring of protection around Mendoza and Schmitt. James and the guards cowardly scrambled to leave through the back gate wanting no part of this supernatural attack. The mercenaries fired their automatic weapons but the high velocity fully jacketed slugs could not kill the already dead. They then focused their fire on Joseph but he had an ancient ring of protection around him and the projectiles whizzed by, missing an easy target. The warriors ran down the Cubans and pierced their souls with their lances and on their second pass, split their skulls with an expert tomahawk swing. The men fell dead without an external wound save for a tiny ribbon of blood just below their scalp line. The Braves circled back as a ferocious roar shook the air. A pair of Andes Pumas leapt from the top of the enclosure's wall onto a screaming Mendoza and Schmitt. Two of the largest predators in the Los Arrayanes Forest were crushing limbs, ripping entrails with to razor-like claws and in the end severing the Nazi's trachea while breaking his cervical spine.

Mendoza's pristine white uniform was now bright crimson and his visage colorless. The cats stood over the dead men for a few moments and then passively walked out the gate like nothing had ever happened, followed by the white buffalo calf.

Alice ran to Joseph and leap into his arms as the Peacock called out his approval. They kissed and became one at last.

The carnage was complete, the enemies of life once again defeated.

The Destroyer was dead.

EPILOGUE

Fort Peck Indian Reservation

Thanksgiving afternoon

Alice had chosen Joseph's home for their wedding ceremony. They stood near a slight rise of land that was the gravesite of over two hundred cattle that had been murdered there nearly three years before. It was where Joseph met Tom, Kate and Brad and where his great grandfather had commissioned them to find the first Destroyer Berhetzel.

The wind always seemed to blow cool and fresh on this rise. In the spring, the prairie grasses and wildflowers were greener and more beautiful than anywhere else on the prairie. The Tanaka and herds of grazing cattle refused to forage here and there was a twelve foot high volunteer Burr Oak that was growing at an incredible rate, promising this ground would one day be an oasis.

A traditional meal of Thanksgiving was offered before the wedding, what Brad called a reverse reception. Everyone savored the special meal on Alice and Joseph's special day.

The wedding party was small. Brad was best man, Kate, the matron of honor.

Jules and Jean had traveled from Paris and Jules had brought Simone for a long avoided trip to see the United States. He had recommitted himself once again to his beautiful wife.

The three French soldiers had recovered from their injuries and made the trip to stand with the young man who had saved their lives. They were wearing elaborate traditional dress uniforms from their unit, complete with medals, sash and heavy red epaulets. Each man carried a gleaming battle saber.

Sullivan was seated with Alice's father. The retired FBI agent had decided that retirement was boring and had been put in charge by the group to recover the fortune buried under that hill in the Los Arrayanes Forest. All the gold was to be returned to the Holocaust survivors families and museums, which Jean would oversee, but for the Conquistador treasure, they would receive a twenty-five percent finder's fee from the Argentinian government after three appraisals. The current estimated value of that treasure of silver, gold and jeweled artifacts was over two hundred million USD. Once the appraisals and museum bidding started, that value could triple. They all were set for life. Jules, who already was very wealthy planned on using his share for the families of the attack on Le Pasteur. The Creator again had generously rewarded His crusaders.

Kate had suggested a Thanksgiving wedding because they all had survived life-threatening events from bullets to bombs or pathogens. The fact they were all still alive was a testament to the love the Creator held for them.

The day was unusually warm, Brad called it Indian Summer. The sun was bright, a gentle breeze moved the tall grasses. The songbirds flittered in the golden tall seed laden stalks, singing sweetly as they dined on tiny morsels.

The elders of the tribe stood behind the Justice of the Peace, solemnly resolute as the ceremony proceeded. Simple questions were asked and simple two word answers given.

Their commitment final, Joseph kissed his bride.

The guests stood and clapped and cheered as the two walked past their family of friends.

Billy Eagles held the reins of two ponies, Wakinyan and the mare Billy had given the couple as a wedding gift. Her name was Wihinape or Sunrise. Alice was to be the light in Joseph's life.

They mounted the two horses and started their life journey. Wakinyan knew the way home, he had traveled it for years. As the couple left their friends, a white buffalo calf appeared into view of the couple and the assembled wedding party. It was a true blessing from the ancestors, a good omen for their future. They all watched as the calf turned and slowly walked to the west and then vaporized.

Kate smiled at her true love Tom with tears in her eyes and she kissed him. She had realized something profound.

Her life was perfect.

ABOUT THE AUTHOR

Pierce Roberts is a practicing companion animal veterinarian who combines real science with fictional science to weave together thrillers that span continents and generations. When he is not writing or working he enjoys, family time, grandkid time, fishing, reading and the outdoors.

Made in United States
North Haven, CT
28 April 2022

18666569R10312